THE PETULANT PRINCESS

M. A. FRICK

Also by M.A. Frick

The Fate Unraveled Trilogy
Forcing Fate
Following Fate
Fulfilling Fate

To all the girls who never wanted to be the princess.

PROLOGUE

In my mind, Sainte Nytestorm stood out among everyone else. In the midst of my world's darkness, he shone like the brightest star. His constant proximity, his mere presence, was a soothing balm to my childhood wounds. It was he who saved me, rescued me from a sure death at the hands of my mad brother, Prince Regent of Wynterborne.

That night, the chill in the air had nothing to do with the foul weather and everything to do with my brother's resentment. At six years old, I was bereft of my mother, who died giving birth to me, and my father, who succumbed to Winter's Bite not two days prior.

I recalled the chilling sensation of pressing myself into the corner, seeking solace against the unyielding, icy stone wall. All I had for warmth and concealment was a thin tapestry, barely enough to shield me from the passing soldiers. Shouts rang out for me, harsh and demanding, chased by my brother's hysterical laughter, echoing down the frigid corridors. Confused and scared, hopeless and cold, I hid, not knowing where to go or who to run to.

My brother was so much bigger, and my father was no longer there to protect me from his unpredictable bouts of violence and rage. Throughout my youth, Adastrus incessantly boasted of his impending kingship, and our father deflected his claims by reminding him of my potential to ascend the throne. However, with his demise, this only painted a target on my back. So I huddled behind the thick brocade, relying on its meager protection from my brother and the soldiers under his command.

Then Sainte found me.

Compared to my slight frame, he was a giant. He towered over, lifting the tapestry while I gripped the fabric with my tiny fists, as if it was my sole anchor to safety. He didn't smile, didn't offer words of comfort. In fact, I couldn't recall a single moment he held my hand or coddled me as a child. It wasn't in his nature.

I could still taste that surge of terror as he stooped low, then hoisted me over his broad, mail-plated shoulder. His pauldron dug into my abdomen with every jarring step as he rushed us out of the castle. Despite the pain, I was too terrified to emit anything more than a whimper.

The outside air of Wynterborne was no more friendly than inside. Bitter wind whipped and slashed, blowing up great gusts of snow. The blizzard was in full force, and few dared to brave the Howls of winter. This contributed to Sainte's success of wrapping me in a blanket and placing me on his horse unseen. The discomfort of sharing a saddle seeped through every tense muscle in my body with each jolt and turn. A frigid sting scraped against my throat as winter threatened to inflict its bite upon me, as it had my late father. I stifled my cries, and Sainte did his best to care for a child on the cold, lonely road.

Together, a young girl and a soldier, we survived. He led us south toward the warmer nation of Gladier. Then, with greater determination, pushed through to the warm coastal nation of Tilamuik, and into the Meeds, where I found my home.

He left me with a household of seven children, making me the tenth member of their family. I don't remember his departure, only waking to find he was no longer there.

On my eleventh birthday, I fought with Kelsie, the mother who took me in. If memory serves, it was an argument concerning whether or not I would eat the boiled squid—which, to this day, I still refuse. I stormed out of the house in tears, not only because she shouted at me, but because the rest of the children laughed at my refusal. To them, it was as normal as porridge, but to me it was as foreign as... well, squid.

The rickety shack bore no yard. It was crammed with multiple homes along a narrow, dirty alley. I sought solace beneath the decrepit branches of a stunted tree and sobbed. I cried for the familiar foods of my homeland, for the loss and abandonment that wreaked havoc on my heart. Alone. Truly alone.

"*Ghehent*, Elspeth."

Even if he spoke in the native tongue of Muik, I would have still recognized that voice. I blinked away my tears and swiped at my wet cheeks as I squinted into the southern coast's perpetually bright sky.

"Sainte?"

In answer, a shadow blocked out the sun, shielding my small stature. His broad frame loomed overhead, sword at his hip, battle ax strapped to his back. Still, I knew in my bones I had nothing to fear from this man.

"Why are you here? Alone?" He spoke in High Wynter, the language used in Wynterborne Castle, yet not a soul that shuffled through the alley paused to take note.

The passing years softened the edge of his gruff, curt voice. It wasn't unusual for him to check in on Kelsie and I. Though now he took time to speak with me, ask after me with a gentleness I was unaccustomed to. I shrugged and stood, dusting off my torn, tattered dress that frayed at the seams. My stare focused on the dirty cobblestones beneath my feet, unable to meet his cool blue gaze as I formed my lie.

"It's dinner time," I said in Common Muik. "I'm not hungry."

It felt like a betrayal to lie to him, as if I let him down by refusing to eat what the family provided while so many others went hungry.

"Some sweets then?" His voice caught on the last syllable as he still used High Wynter.

With a strange blend of shyness and joy, I smiled up at him, reveling in the fact that he hadn't forgotten me or my birthday.

At the markets, we splurged on treats, spending far too much coin. When we settled on the soft, hot sand at the beach to dig in, the little girl and big soldier didn't draw a second glance from the bustling crowd.

That was the first day I realized I had a crush on my savior.

It worsened every year he visited.

And so did I.

I rebelled against the household, shirking my duties, refusing to help where I was needed. My temperament grew loud and obnoxious, disrespectful and entitled. Heated disputes led to raised voices and harsh insults until I stormed off to the beach to cool down. Every passing day strengthened my awareness—I didn't belong here. Sainte paid the family handsomely for my care, so much that they refused to abandon me regardless of how poorly I treated them, and I tested this theory often.

On my sixteenth birthday, my world came crashing down.

Over the last three years, he pinpointed me no matter my whereabouts in the city. It became a game of sorts, to have him seek me out. I ventured into the slums, where—considering the vileness of the upscale parts of Landing's End—the worst of creation found themselves. With my hood up, hands shoved into the pockets of my torn trousers, and knives secured in my boots and tucked up against my navel, I shuffled through the riffraff, waiting for a familiar voice to surprise me in my native tongue.

I wandered there for the better part of the day, and as the sun crept toward the sea, the stone in my gut grew heavier. My heart longed for Sainte's comforting presence, his silent solidarity of my identity. He *knew* who I was. Irritability tiptoed in, and sour thoughts darkened my mind. Did he care? Was he worried?

Had he forgotten about me? Had he spent all those years feeding a child's dream, only to bring it all down with a laugh at the expense of a trusting young girl?

I ripped through the slums, heading to the beach with a rush of curses under my breath. I, the princess without a castle, dreamt that my knight cared enough to visit me once a year. Wynterborne required weeks of travel. Apparently, I wasn't worth the effort.

"Oi, wench!"

I grumbled and ignored the comment, thinking it was aimed at someone else. Clad in my 'sibling's' trousers, I could pass for a boy at a glance, but closer inspection would reveal my budding femininity.

A hand landed on my shoulder and jerked me around. I slapped it off as my heart took off racing. I'd been in street fights before, but none with—I raced to count—eight boys behind the leader.

The one who touched me sneered. "Ha! Told you it was a girl!"

He bore the classic slum traits: clothes too big for his frame and teeth that seemed as if a bright new apple might rip half of them out. His disheveled, matted hair hadn't been attended to in years, and a thick layer of sweat and dirt smudged the smelly scumbag's skin from head to toe.

"What of it?" I lifted my chin with a taunting leer. A quick glance behind showed at least three more figures blocked any escape.

He retrieved a rusty knife with jagged chips along its blade and pretended to pick dirt out from under his fingernails. "If you're down here, sweets, you must be looking for a good time."

"Looking for the exit," I grumbled, and shifted my feet to put my back against the brick wall.

"Well, I'm sure we could help with that, for a modest fee, of course."

He cocked his head to admire his dirt-caked nails, then peered up with hooded eyes. The whites were yellow from malnutrition or the spirits he drank. Either way, dread slid down my spine. I shrugged, then pulled my coin purse out of my trousers and tossed it.

He caught it with quick, nimble hands—at odds with his sickly thin frame. "Oh, that will help too." He waved the crusty knife back and forth in a mocking manner, as if daring me to challenge him. "Sweet lass, I won't need this, right?"

My teeth ground together as he bent to secure his blade in his threadbare boot.

As soon as he lowered, a cascade of black armor plummeted from the rooftop and crashed onto his back. His frail figure crumpled under the weight of the newcomer, and my heart took off like a startled rabbit. A giddy smile lifted my cheeks as the men beyond shuffled with frantic nerves, drawing their feeble weapons.

Sainte straightened and adjusted his grip on his battle ax. "*Killip Gheten.*"

Happy Birthday.

I beamed like a fool, lounging against the wall as he made quick work of those who dared try his talent with a blade. After he dispatched two thugs with ease, the rest stampeded away.

"I knew you would find me," I said.

My cheeks ached from the strength of my grin as he knelt to wipe his ax on a dirty cloak. The gore and loss of life were hardly worth considering. It came with existing in Landing's End. I crossed my arms and propped against the grimy wall, trying to appear more confident than I was.

Sainte grunted as he rose to study me. "Always."

My face warmed and tingled as his gaze tracked every inch, from my worn boots up to my orange hair. The strange hue came from attempting to lighten my sable locks with a potion I bought from a port witch. She warned me my heritage would not be hidden so easily. My head resembled a botched painting, an unnatural clash of bluish-black roots and carrot-colored strands that made it hard to look at without cringing.

"You've grown." Always High Wynter—it never faltered. He understood Common Muik, but never used it. He was far too proper for that.

"I have." I shoved off the wall and closed the gap between us in two swift strides.

As I gazed up at him, he pulled back to keep a distance between our faces, confusion swirling in his sky-colored eyes. With a sly grin and wink, I spun on my heel and started for the beach. I tried my best to saunter as I'd seen women in the lewd district do and heard him cough and clear his throat behind me. I held in my giggle and headed toward my favorite hideout.

He arrived a moment after I settled my bare toes in the tidepool. I stared out over the ocean, hood down, soaking up the sun's hot rays. It was a secluded area, framed in by coarse gray rock, facing the sea. I came here to listen to the waves as I worked out my anger and hurt. The little creatures in the pool didn't mind my curses as much as Kelsie did.

My eyes fluttered shut as my head fell back, embracing the heat warming my face. With no need to look, I heard him nudge my boots aside, then settle next to me. When he didn't speak, I cracked open one eye. A scowl weighed his rugged features, his dark brows scrunched together in thought as he peered over the green-blue water. It was suspiciously calm today. I took in his broad crooked nose, his long, thick lashes that could make any tavern wench jealous, and his thin lips set above a cleft chin.

Something in me liked this perplexed version of my soldier—confused and uneasy. I held a fair amount of confidence that I was the only soul that could make him so unsure of himself. When his frown settled on me, I grinned, holding his gaze as it danced across my face.

"Must be hot in all that armor," I teased.

Aside from the night he rescued me, he donned that same hard-boiled leather armor. I assumed it was lighter for the trek through nations to see me.

I received a grunt in response.

"Did you bring me a present?" I straightened, scooting close enough that my knee brushed against his thigh.

He stared at the contact as if I would spread a disease through our trousers.

"*Yen*," he murmured in the affirmative and reached into a large pouch at his side. He used the movement as an excuse to create space, and when he angled toward the sea again, he resettled with a gap between us.

He held a delicate wooden snowflake adorned with the whitest yarn I'd ever encountered. In the sunlight, its brilliance was almost blinding, forcing me to squint as I examined its intricate design. As I accepted it from his palm, I marveled at its unmatched softness, unlike anything I'd touched before. There wasn't much about Landing's End that was soft. This was a treasure.

"It's beautiful," I breathed, rubbing the threads.

"Perhaps you have outgrown the toys I bring." He winced, as if mentally berating himself.

I laughed, spinning the snowflake at the center of my palm. "Never."

"Remember your homeland." His words quieted as he gave my orange hair a gentle tug.

I recognized his good intentions, but I didn't want to think about that. His potential disapproval of my hair and my rejection of my heritage was a topic I'd rather avoid. Gods above knew I endured enough criticism from the witch when I bought the potion.

"I remember *you*," I said, a bit more forcefully than I should have. "You're the one who cares. I don't see anyone else remembering my birthdays or bringing me tiny treasures."

A muscle in his jaw feathered as his attention returned to the ocean. "No one?" he asked. "No boy?"

A rough edge tinged his words with an emotion I didn't understand. I threw my head back and laughed up at the sun. I mentally praised every god that I knew, reveling in this feeling. He was asking if I had a crush. I could pretend to interpret his tone as jealousy, rather than concern for a princess separated from her kingdom, but it didn't matter to me either way.

With an open smile, I shook my head and let my gaze linger on his lips. "No one, Sainte. No one but you."

My response seemed to scare him more than the prospect of another boy doting on me. I basked in the warmth of his genuine care and concern.

When we headed home to Kelsie, we stopped by a street vendor to grab hot food and sweets. I found every excuse I could to touch him—playful shoves, bumping my hip into his as we walked. A wrinkle of confusion embedded between his brows, and I loved it. I didn't know which was more intoxicating, being free with a man I liked, or his glances of pure bewilderment, as if I was a strange creature he'd never crossed paths with before.

When we reached the small house crammed in amongst the others, the sun bedded the ocean for the night. Hues of orange and pink painted the sky, and the street was quiet as the good folk tucked in with the fading light.

Sainte stopped at the door and rapped twice, as he always did. I took a deep breath and climbed to the step above him so I matched his height, then pressed my palm to his soft, warm cheek. His eyes narrowed and his jaw flexed as my touch wandered. Nerves tightened my throat as my thumb traced the corner of his lip, fingers brushing against the unseen stubble on his jawline.

"Bit of sugar there," I whispered.

His unwavering gaze locked with mine, revealing a determination I couldn't ignore, pulling me closer.

The door flew open, and I jerked my hand away as if it were on fire. I spun, facing Kelsie, and my joy faded into irritable rebellion.

"Beth!" she hissed. "I told you I needed you to–"

"The pigs can feed themselves for one day," I growled, crossing my arms over my chest.

She turned her plea to Sainte, who frowned at me with a flood of disappointment in his gaze.

"My dear sir," she said, "you must know–"

With a jingle of coins, he placed a small bag into Kelsie's upturned hands.

"Goodnight, Princess Elspeth." He rasped out a gruff farewell, punctuated by a brisk nod, then headed down the stairs.

"But, good sir!" she called.

"No doubt for the pigs," I muttered under my breath and pushed past her large frame to get inside.

Children sprawled on thin blankets along the floor, squabbling and wrangling for space. We were lucky to have the raised wooden flooring. It kept us above the tide during the annual floods. At least Kelsie and Juar's little ones stayed dry and well-fed.

The door slammed shut behind me as I picked my way across the mat of wriggling children. I could hardly hear my own thoughts over their bickering.

"Beth! Where were you today?!" she demanded. "And what were you doing with the good sir?!"

I ignored her and continued navigating to the back of the house.

"Acting like a dog in heat if I saw anything," Kadar jeered. He leaned against a bookshelf, his feet free of wriggling limbs. Even his siblings knew to keep clear of him.

With my jaw clenched tight, I leveled my glower at him and his brother, both of which were much larger than I, and therefore believed they had the right to bully me. They weren't the eldest of Kelsie's brood, but they were the oldest still living in the house. Adar and Kadar—twins and monsters. Their older siblings moved in with Juar, who worked as a diver, hauling crystals from the caves that littered the coast.

"You saw nothing, pisspot," I spat.

"Elspeth, the pigs need fed!" Kelsie shouted over the chaos.

I stepped on a stray hand and I swear little Harry bit my leg in return. I kicked his head and hopped a step.

"Soon enough she'll have her own pigs, now that she's bleeding." Adar's eyes glinted with mischief in the weak light.

"Shut your–"

"Did you see them? Two more seconds and they would have been rutting on the–"

I flung myself at Adar, aiming to slam my fist into his perfectly tan, chiseled jaw. Unfortunately, this was a common enough affair that he saw my swing coming and ducked, throwing his own at my belly. I choked on my breath as his blow drove the air from my lungs. Neither moved to catch me from my fall. I wrapped my arms around Adar's legs and bit his thigh straight through his trousers.

His elbow slammed into my temple, causing everything to go black as I collapsed. The children were like carnivorous fish that sensed blood in the water. Within the span of a breath, it was an all out fight, complete with Kelsie screaming for peace.

I grabbed Kadar's belt, using it as leverage to land a kick to his stomach. A strong hand snared my hair and jerked my head back. My eyes watered as my nails raked across skin, hoping I drew blood. A knee struck my hip, and I lurched. My forehead smacked against the splintered wood floor. I swung my leg out, knocking someone off their feet, then tried to stand. Adar hoisted me up by the collar of my shirt, chuckling as he pinned my arms to my sides. Meanwhile, Kadar shoved a kid aside to position himself in front of me.

"Call it, whore," Adar sneered.

His hot, wet breath against my skin made me want to retch.

Kadar pulled up his beefy fists, and I tried to get my legs up to kick him away, but some child or another hugged my right foot. Stars flickered before my eyes as his fist slammed into my cheek. My whole body jerked with the force, and I struggled to rally myself, feeling the burn and trickle of blood down my face.

"Call it." Adar practically giggled as Kadar readied for another punch.

I clenched my jaw and fought against Adar's hold as best I could.

The second strike never came.

The door flew open with a crash, slamming against the wall. Every child turned toward the disturbance with a blade or some other crude weapon in hand. Guilt and shame burned my cheeks as the faint light illuminated Sainte's frame. I knew it was him–I felt it in my bones.

"*Triu. Degeh. Miun.*"

Let. Her. Go.

No one moved a muscle.

I cursed a torrent of expletives as I translated his curt, unfaltering demand, and slowly, Adar released me. I shook off his hold, brushing at my sleeves as I scoured the frozen group. Sainte was cast in shadow, tension rolling off him in waves. With an irritable sigh, I shoved and kicked my way across the room.

Kelsie stood near the threshold, gripping the coin purse tight as if he might take it back. I pushed past her and stepped out onto the stairs, collapsing as the door clicked shut behind me.

"I could've handled it." Frustrated and embarrassed, I wiped at my tender cheek with my dirty sleeve.

He lowered himself beside me, and the black leather of his glove was warm and soft as he turned my face to his. His touch slid under the cut I was sure bled profusely.

"No doubt," he said.

"Sainte–"

I choked on his name, and his eyes darted to mine. Filled with hopelessness, weakness, and a sense of inadequacy, I realized I didn't fit in here, nor did I belong back in my homeland. Incapable of fending off the men in the slums or Adar and Kadar, I felt lost and adrift, with only him as my anchor.

"Don't abandon me," I pleaded, then pinned his warm hand to the curve of my cheek, holding it in place. An overwhelming surge of pain welled within my chest, sharp and acrid. I slid closer, seeking relief from the ache inside. My thigh pressed against his.

His steady gaze searched mine. "I always come back."

"Take me with you," I whispered, glancing at his lips. Heat and security bloomed from his warmth. Sainte was safe.

He was my home.

I leaned close enough to feel the caress of his sweet breath tease my skin.

"I can't."

He launched to his feet, breaking our contact, shattering our moment. My cheek ached from the loss of his touch, and my face burned with the shame of his rejection.

"Your brother is still regent. You cannot come with me." He cleared his throat, staring down the alley with his back to me.

"Then don't leave." I hated the note of desperation drenching my voice. "Don't leave me here, Sainte. Don't leave me alone."

He turned to face me then, and I slid to my knees before him. I had pride, but it was long gone. All I had was anguish.

"Please don't." I pressed my lips tight to keep them from trembling. I would have given anything to keep him there, to stay with him.

He heaved a heavy sigh and dropped to a knee before me. He lifted my chin with one gloved hand and met my tearful gaze. I pleaded in silence, hoping against hope that I could reveal the depth of pain and loneliness that consumed my heart. If he could only see how much I hurt, he wouldn't leave me.

His eyes snapped shut with a painful wince, and he stood in one fluid movement.

A sob tore from my throat.

Silent and resolute, he turned his back on me and strode down the alley. Abandoning me amidst the dirt and muck of the city streets, he left me to cry alone without saying a word.

He didn't have to.

CHAPTER 1

A groan rolled from my throat as the bells clanged their morning call. Beside me, a moan echoed within the brief pauses of each peal.

"I regret *everything!*" Lyana moaned.

She buried her face in my back while I grimaced and grabbed a pillow, pinning it against our ears. We waited until the bells went silent, each of us tense and stiff on our mattress, heads throbbing.

"I told you," a heaving retch from across the room interrupted my complaint, "Degor messed up his spirits!"

Lyana whimpered and wrapped her arms around me, pulling me closer. "I only wanted to have fun," she whined.

I gagged and rolled off the mattress. When I collided with the floor, I pushed myself upright. "Your breath reeks worse than rotting fish!"

Her eyes widened with pure betrayal. "Just because you didn't drink doesn't mean yours smells of roses, El!"

"Bet it smells better than yours!"

I snorted, then watched Ethyan vomit off the bell tower's edge. More often than not, he deferred to his younger sister's lead, proving age wasn't the sole measure of leadership. Lyana possessed a natural talent for it, while he took on the role of protector, always accompanying her.

I befriended these two street rats when I left Landing's End five years ago. Now, a few weeks shy of my twenty-first birthday, the seasons spent with them felt more like family than Kelsie's brood ever had.

Ethyan collapsed in a heap, then threaded his tan fingers through his sweat-streaked sandy hair, giving it a tug. "Never again, Lyana. Never."

"You say that every time," she sighed.

She curled up under the flimsy blanket and burrowed as deep as she could into the thin mattress. Stuffed with dried grass, it wasn't the most comfortable thing, but it beat sleeping on the floor.

I reclined against the stones, knitting my fingers behind my head as I gazed at the brass bell suspended several feet above. It swayed in a steady, slow rhythm, still easing from its morning call. Its rope extended down through the hole in the center of the floor. We made this place our home, a refuge where the incessant noise deterred other street rats. Up here, only the outer flooring remained from the tower's construction. It lacked weatherproofing. It was deteriorating and noisy—but it was safe.

That much-needed sense of safety was one of the many reasons I'd yet to try spirits. Too often, I watched strangers, kind people, turn into monsters. I witnessed the exploitation of dozens due to their altered states of mind, leading to regrets and lifelong consequences. Booze wrecked too many lives for me to consider drinking for pleasure.

Ethyan coughed and rested his head against the sun-warmed stone. "If only El loosened up and had some fun."

I scoffed, shrugging off the jab. "Someone has to watch out for you two."

"Thank the gods you did! Did you see Degor? He was as mad as a dock cat, spitting and hissing like that!" He laughed, then pressed the heels of his palms to his temples, most likely an attempt to ward off a winning headache.

"Which gods would you be thanking?" Lyana mused. "Niena of Luck? We're not close enough to El's birthday for that. Perhaps Fiera of Greed?"

"Rumen of Fun."

He snapped a glare at his sister, who cackled in response.

"Careful with that one," I said. "He takes what he wants at the end of the story."

"But his patrons have the best time!"

"Until the end."

After a half-hearted sigh, I pushed myself off the floor and adjusted my trousers. They were far too short and my shirt wasn't much better—tied together with a rope I salvaged from the docks. It wasn't fancy, but it kept me covered. I found my boots and pulled them on, wiggling my toes past the holes.

"Well, thank you for saving our hides, El," Lyana said as she wormed her way to the side of the mattress.

I straightened, lifting a single brow. "You were too far gone to notice." Despite my abstinence from spirits, I found it amusing to watch these two partake, even if their drunken antics might eventually land us all in the slammer. "I'm off to relieve myself and perhaps relieve a few traders of their coin. I'll meet you–"

"*Ghehent*, Elspeth."

I froze.

That *voice*—it pulled me a million miles away. Dizzy and lightheaded, a strange, conflicting sensation of ice and fire surged through my veins. Ethyan cursed, his movements frantic as he scurried into the rafters. His sister shouted something, yet it all seemed distant, like an ocean's murmur against the shore.

Slowly, I faced my mattress, where Lyana scrambled back on her hands and arse, brandishing a blade. Beyond our mat, a muscular figure clothed in darkness crouched on the wall's ledge, one leg dangling toward the uneven wood planks.

When I met his calm blue gaze, my heart leapt into my throat. "It's not my birthday."

Smooth, Elspeth. Real smooth.

His mouth curved in a subtle smile, reigniting all my long-buried teenage emotions. He was as fit as ever. The only way up required scaling the tower or climbing the rope. He discarded parts of his dark leather armor, presumably for the climb, yet it didn't diminish his bulk. He hadn't aged a day since I last saw him.

Whereas I had changed quite a bit.

"You know him?!" Lyana's disbelief and shock were evident in her strangled tone.

She edged against my shins, holding her blade at the ready. I had no doubt she could, and would, use it if necessary.

"Sainte." His name was a breathy whisper on my lips.

He made no effort to move. Our gazes locked, assessing one another after years of absence. The world around me faded, like distant hills shrouded in mist.

"Scumbag!" Lyana shrieked, struggling to her feet. "You shriveled chunk of gutter dung! You're worse than the entrails of a crab! The pox on your–"

"She knows of me?" Sainte asked, one dark brow rising in amusement.

Lyana aimed the blade at his crotch, ready to throw. "What did that heap of sea scum say?!"

My heart raced. Each frantic, stuttering beat sent pins and needles down my fingers. "Only good things," I choked out, registering the fact that she didn't understand High Wynter.

"Good things? *Him?*" She whirled, her sun-colored hair whipping my face. Her features narrowed on me with rage-induced skepticism. "Girl, just say the word, and I'll kill him. I swear."

She spun back, positioning herself between us. Though shorter, her fierce demeanor was akin to a cornered wildcat. I glanced up at Sainte, his figure framed against the golden frizz of her hair.

He tipped his head, as if fascinated. "She has a low opinion of me."

I drew in a deep breath, lifted my chin, then spoke in Common Muik to spite him. "She's not the only one."

I was no longer the poor little girl he left five years ago. Well, 'poor' was an accurate description, but that broken, fragile person he once knew, was gone.

"Curse it all, El! What's he saying?!" Lyana stomped her foot like some spoiled child.

I sniffed. "He refuses to speak the common tongue. It's below him."

Amusement dropped from his handsome face, and his brow pinched in thought.

I turned my back on him. He left me. And I outgrew that version of myself. "Meet me at the usual place," I said to my friends.

Lyana's tone was both perplexed and repulsed. "What about him?"

As I strode toward the opposite wall, I peered over my shoulder. "He'll disappear. He always does."

Sainte slid both legs to the wood planking and straightened, flashing a furious glare my way. No matter his agility, he couldn't clear the gap at the tower's center.

Ethyan cursed from his position up in the rafters, bowstring drawn and arrow nocked. "Don't move, pretty boy. I'll have you pegged like a hare on a spit before you can say, 'Squash El's heart.'"

I tipped my chin, giving him a small smile.

"Elspeth–"

Gods. No matter how long I fought to forget that voice, it resounded in my dreams every night. I ignored him and swung my legs over the aged wall. "She's dead."

Gravity embraced me. Wind snapped at my clothes and hair as I surrendered to the descent.

The fabric canopy caved with the impact of my weight, and I tumbled head over heels, grunting as my neck and back contorted in ways they weren't designed for. The shopkeeper blurted a slew of curses as I scrambled to the overhang. I hit the ground at a run, but he still managed to pelt me with some rotten fruit—a sun-baked tomato by the sound of its withered splatter.

I sped toward the beach, pumping my legs as fast as I could. On nimble feet, I maneuvered through the crowd, spinning and dodging. I leapt over a cart, snatching a starfruit along the way. A wave of insults and slurs nipped at my heels, but I ignored them as my teeth sank into the sweet fruit.

He was here *before* my birthday?

As much as I'd like to believe he never found me after I ran away, I couldn't lie to myself. Lyana and Ethyan quickly grasped that we had become nearly invisible on the day of my birth. We could pilfer or raid as we pleased, wander the slums 'til dawn, or slip into a noble's estate for the night. Regardless of the scheme's audacity, it always worked out, and with a laugh to spare.

That mysterious luck had nothing to do with the goddess Niena, and every-thing to do with Sainte. He never showed himself, but I sensed him watching over me. Every year, I found it increasingly difficult to push the limits of his protection. It was a sick, twisted punishment. He would suffer by cleaning up my mess, or his precious *princess* would be harmed. Either way, it would hurt him, and that's what I wanted.

My petty thoughts had me scoffing at myself. I was an adult. I should act like one. My steps slowed, and I came to a halt. The crowded market swarmed around me, but the path to the beach was clear. The warm golden sand beck-oned me... but Sainte knew that was my safe space. I muttered a curse under my breath and turned on my heel. I would pick a few pockets, or perhaps venture into the slums, where I blended in better. Though, if Sainte had coin to spare, I'd be ratted out soon enough.

My gaze danced over the busy stalls. Vendors hawked their wares, shouting above one another. They kept a careful eye on potential customers and any riffraff that lurked about. I ducked into a small alcove between the stalls of a crystal merchant and fishmonger. We were close enough to the port that the catch was fresh, but still carried the pungent scent of the sea.

Where would Sainte not think to look for me? He never showed up early. Despite all the years I wished he'd stay longer, he arrived the morning of my birthday and left before nightfall. If anything, he was predictable.

"Oi, lass! Git!"

The fishmonger clearly had enough of my loitering and yanked a handful of my short hair, while hitting me with a bloody carcass. I yelped, freeing myself of his hold and wiped the slime from my shirt the best I could. With a vulgar gesture, I backed into the crowd and let its flow carry me.

I cut my hair right after I ran away. The orange was terrible, and I didn't have the funds to keep up with the potions. So, I gave up coloring it and hacked it off, instead. I left enough length to manage a small braid on one side. The short plait was thick and messy, but was better than the two-toned disaster I had before.

The crowd carried me past the lewd district, and I hesitated in thought. It was early, yet women already exposed their goods to potential customers. Exhausted patrons stumbled out of makeshift huts pressed against the port walls. The streets bustled, though far less than the main market.

A safe place? No, but Sainte wouldn't think to look for me here. I pulled myself out of the throng and stumbled into the lovers' lane.

The fine hairs on the nape of my neck raised as if someone watched me, but surely Ethyan held that draw long enough to give me a head start.

That or he could have shot him in the leg.

Or arm.

Or crotch.

I wouldn't be mad about any of those outcomes.

"Well hello there, girly." A prostitute lifted a thin brow, appraising me as if I were her next meal.

I glanced her way and grimaced. Was it possible to catch a disease by just looking at someone? Her lips were bruised and swollen but painted red, as though that made them more attractive. She was plump, but her hand-me-down corset was so tight it creased her bust, as if it couldn't support the sagging things any longer. Her hair was an unnatural purple shade, littered with mats that hadn't been brushed out in gods knew how long.

I coughed, keeping hold of my coin purse. "A copper."

"Oh honey, you're not gonna have much fun with that." Her leer lingered over my frame.

"I only need a few hours."

"At a copper?!" She threw her head back and cackled.

I was desperate, not stupid. I would not throw all my coin at a whorehouse and not have any to bribe my way out of a guard's hands later.

"Off to the hag district, sweets. Even the inexperienced cost more than that!"

So be it. "Where would that be?"

"You sure? You'll catch more than just a bit of fun, if you catch my meaning," she crooned, shuffling closer.

I gritted my teeth and held my ground as a musty-sweet scent rolled over me—cloying incense and cheap perfume hung about her like a cloud.

"Where?" My tone sharpened with my impatience.

"At the end, to the left."

Her burst of laughter sprayed my face with spittle. Stuck between a scowl and a gag, I rushed off, hoping it didn't appear as if I fled. With any luck, an old hag would gladly accept a coin and let me be, allowing me to wait out Sainte undisturbed. I doubted a hag would be up to any... promiscuous activities, anyway.

I kept my head down and pace quick. Neither patrons nor workers spared me a glance. Albeit the lewd district was a deadend, it was the best place to hide from good folk. Sainte probably fell under that description. He rescued a tiny, helpless child after all. Never mind that he crushed my heart and abandoned me. I couldn't picture him walking through here, let alone taking advantage of the services offered.

Men had their needs, didn't they? Ethyan often dallied with tavern wenches. I didn't share in those desires, but weren't all men alike? I'm sure a good handful were loyal to their wives.

That thought pulled at my frown. Sainte never spoke of a family. A wife. Babes. Surely, he didn't have any.

I don't know why I seemed to need convincing of that.

At the deadend, I turned left where a pair of suboptimal guards sat at a table smoking some suspicious herb, though the rank concoction in their drinks was far more unpleasant. They eyed me in passing and went back to their game of chance, happy to ignore me as much as I ignored them.

Old women slumped on stools and crates along the grime-covered street, backs propped against their little huts made of driftwood and scraps. As I strolled by, they barely stirred, their eyes mere slivers of interest. A handful appeared as still as statues, prompting me to question if they drew breath or had silently slipped into oblivion, and no one cared to move them. The smell certainly didn't seem to belong to anything living.

A rasped word to my right pulled my notice. She was old—far older than I expected to find here. Her thin, wispy hair was grimy and peppered with lint. Her eyes were cloudy, and she lacked a good amount of teeth. Age spots flecked her face and scalp. Her hut was small, but large enough for two people to sit in... or do other things.

"A copper?" I murmured, stepping closer.

"Bless you."

Her voice was as dry as the skin on her hands as she took the coin from my palm. Covered in a blanket from head to toe, she shuffled into her hut. I followed close on her heels, turning around to drop the cloth door into place.

"I simply want–"

Her sigh of relief cut my words short. When I turned, she lay sprawled on the bed. With a happy moan, she let the blanket fall aside, revealing every inch of her worn, withered, very naked body. A gag choked my throat, and I scrunched my eyes shut, knowing that image would haunt me for all my days.

"That's not–" I hissed, clamping a hand over my face for good measure. "I simply want a seat!"

"I can," she sucked in a slow, wheezing breath, "sleep through anything."

"Fantastic," I drawled.

After I cracked my eyes open, I grimaced, then pulled the blankets over her body. She was already snoring. I heaved a sigh and nudged her aside to make room. Before I sat, I eyed her makeshift mattress with a scrunched nose. It probably had things living in it I'd rather not see. Part of me was thankful for the weak lighting. Considering the stench, the sludge-slicked ground didn't seem a safe bet either.

With a plethora of muttered profanities aimed at Sainte and the problems he caused, I perched on the bed's edge. Hopefully, whatever diseases infested this place couldn't travel through fabric. I'd need a soak in the ocean after this. Salt residue be damned. At least I'd be clean.

CHAPTER 2

I frowned as raised voices snared my attention. The hag didn't stir, but I straightened, tense. I couldn't make out what was being said, but it was obvious one voice among the others was angrier than the rest. I slipped off the bed and crept to the cloth door, pulling it aside to peek through. It was only midday, and I needed another hour or two of hiding until I could meet up with Lyana and Ethyan. It seemed like this side of the lewd district would be quiet any time of day, but the ruckus had me second guessing that theory.

I dropped the greasy fabric as the voices came closer. They were looking for someone... which didn't bode well for me.

"What's this girl of yours look like? She a mirror image of the hag that birthed you?"

Several men burst into raucous laughter at the remark, their amusement mingling with the shuffling steps and the clap of slapping backs in good humor.

"There was a young one."

Panic threatened to close my throat at the rasped words. So much for confidentiality.

"Fine lady, where–"

Curse that voice. I tore out, rushing past the group. A hand snagged my shirt, tearing it open. I cursed, holding it shut as I sped down the lane.

Just because Sainte never used Common Muik with me, obviously didn't mean he couldn't speak it.

Shouts and jeers broke out behind, but I distanced myself quickly. A heavy jingle echoing my every step told me he was on the move, tight on my heels. I scoffed at the idea of being outpaced by anyone, let alone a man in armor, and I pushed myself harder, clutching my shirt together. Not that anyone in this district would bat an eye at some bare skin.

Around the corner, I sidestepped and whirled behind a couple navigating the busy street. Despite a slip on some grime, I maintained balance and lunged ahead. I was born for this. These were my streets, and I cursed the day some outsider caught me.

I was close to the main road. From there, I could make my way anywhere in the city. When I rounded the next bend, I pulled short so fast that my feet slipped from under me, and my arse collided with the hard ground. At the lane's entrance, a squad of soldiers fixed their gaze on me, unlike any I encountered before. Clad in dark armor that bespoke neither mercenary nor local, they stood out with a striking presence.

"Pig dung and fish guts!" I cursed.

Their heavy jogging steps closed in, and I scrambled to my feet. I dashed between two huts, causing the residents to scatter. Gripping the stone wall, I searched for footholds, only to find the surface slick with grime and soot, denying me any purchase.

"Elspeth."

"Sainte," I sneered, drawing out his name as I faced him.

His eyes darted to my shirt, then back to my face as I lifted my chin and crossed my arms, emboldened with defiance. His breaths heaved, though not as heavily as I preferred after the run I just gave him.

"Come with me."

"No."

His features flashed with irritation, revealing a side of him I'd never seen before. Perhaps, like me, he had undergone his own growth during our time apart.

"I am not asking."

"And I'm not negotiating." I snarled.

He moved fast, catching me off guard as I backed into the wall, my blade forgotten. The notion of needing it against Sainte hadn't crossed my mind. He cornered me, hands by my head, his large frame blocking my path. His proximity allowed me to notice a few silver hairs near his temple. Just a few, but enough to challenge me to surpass him.

"We can do this the easy way, or the hard way. You choose." His High Wynter was crisp and cold, like everything from the North.

My breath quickened, and my ears perked to the sounds above. I reached out, fingers tracing the contours of his chest before cupping his face. His eyes transformed from anger and irritation to that familiar scowl of confusion and perplexity, an expression I dreamt of often.

I held his glare, my own narrowed with repulsion. "I don't choose you."

My knee snapped up, landing a blow between his legs. He doubled over with a wheezing grunt. Ethyan took that moment to loose an arrow, straight through the arm boxing me in. Sainte growled, dropping to one knee as a rope fell onto my shoulder. I spun and climbed it with the agility of a jungle monkey, hauling the rope's tail along with me. Sainte was as stubborn as I remembered. He would've attempted to follow.

Lyana gathered the rope from me when I reached the top.

"Go!" I shouted, breaking into a sprint.

Ethyan kept pace beside us, his bow slung over his shoulder. "I thought he was a good guy?!" he yelled over the cacophony of birds and sailors' calls as we neared the bustling docks.

"Good guy?!" Lyana hissed, arms pumping at her sides. "Crushing El's heart, leaving her in the dirt?! Good guy?!"

I ignored them as we rushed into the port, edging around shipmen and, in all probability, pirates as well. We slipped into an alley under the cover of men loading barrels into a wagon.

"He's—normally–" I gasped for air, propped against the wall as my limbs trembled from exertion.

"Gods and goddesses!" Lyana stood before me, her stance defiant and eyes ignited with determination. "I will kill him. I will cut past those abs of steel and rip out his heart," she snarled as she tugged the scraps of my shirt closed.

With a breathless laugh, I straightened to tie the scraps with the rope—it was gone.

"Curse it. I lost my rope." I fumbled about my body for something else to use.

"Here." Ethyan removed his belt and offered it to me. It was a beat up strip of leather barely hanging together, but belts were hard to come by.

I gave a remorseful smile in thanks, then gestured to the tear. "He didn't do this. I think it was a guard as I ran past."

His sister sighed, her anger hardly diminished. "Hiding in Hag Lane was a good bet, though." She collapsed beside me and let her head fall back to peer into the cloudless sky.

We took a moment to catch our breaths, then made our way out. Neither sailors nor guards would take kindly to street rats hanging about the port. Too many high-end goods came in and out for it to go unguarded.

"What does he want?" Ethyan murmured as we kept our heads down, walking aimlessly.

Lyana snorted with a roll of her eyes. "To kiss and make up?"

I limped along feeling a pebble work its way in through a hole in my boot. "He's never come early before. And he's always been alone."

"Those were Wynterian soldiers?" she asked.

"I'm not sure."

Most of my memories were a blurred haze at this point. I was only six when he rescued me. I shivered at the reminder and shoved it aside.

"They seemed to be with him," she offered.

"But not hired help," her brother mused. "Their armor was too fine."

"Why would he need backup for a visit? Oh, don't tell me he switched sides!"

"Traitor," he muttered.

"I don't think so," I said. "He wouldn't stoop that low."

"Then why the show of force?" she asked. "If he came to apologize, why would he need others?"

"He wanted me to go with him."

Ethyan wiggled his eyebrows. "To Wynterborne or an inn?"

Lyana and I shrieked in unison as I gave him a playful shove.

"You never know, he could just want to 'kiss and make up.'"

I scanned the crowd as the two bickered. Sainte was stalking toward me, his eyes locked on mine. He led the small group of soldiers in our direction, bystanders ducking out of their way.

"Guys?" I groaned.

Lyana grabbed the crook of my arm. "Oh, son of a sailor."

"Are we running?" Ethyan asked, gripping his bow.

I stood my ground, clenching my jaw, staring Sainte down. I hoped for a limp in his gait, but found none. Instead, I noticed a white cloth wrapped around his right forearm, soaked in fresh crimson.

For some reason that didn't bring me any joy.

Ethyan bounced on his heels, ready to dart. "Perhaps the caves?"

"El can't swim," Lyana grumbled.

"What about the temple? Would they offer harbor?"

She ignored him, tugging on my elbow. "Shouldn't we be running?"

My confidence faltered and I sighed. "He always finds me."

Sainte and his group came to a stop ten paces away. His mouth set into a firm line, disapproval heavy on his brow.

"*Eneyet.*"

Always.

The escort made us feel like criminals—which we were—though I didn't appreciate feeling that way. His soldiers surrounded us. Their silent, brooding gazes openly sized me up while ignoring my friends. One dared a smile and winked, as if this were all a game. Perhaps he was the friendliest of the lot.

Sainte guided us away from the port, eastward, toward the more reputable part of town. We rarely wandered here, simply because we had morals too, and the people who worked and lived here were generally good folk. We stuck to the undercity, where survival meant taking—a gritty realm of constant exchanges and murky intentions.

We entered an inn far more respectable than the ones I frequented, though I never slept in one, only tasted their fare. I narrowed my eyes at the abundance of flickering candles scattered around the room, noting the pristine condition of the tables.

Ethyan let out a low whistle.

"No layer of grime," Lyana murmured, crowding so close she bumped into me. "You didn't tell me he came from money."

"He's from Wynterborne." I shrugged, watching as Sainte turned his head a fraction so he could hear us more clearly.

"Got his hand in the royal coffers, eh?" Ethyan jeered. "Talk about a traitor."

"Elspeth, come with me," he called in High Wynter.

My feet slowed to a stubborn halt, trying to appear braver than I was. "Where I go, so do my friends."

"Where you go," he said, stepping into my space, "your friends cannot."

"Then I'll stay."

A soldier to my side snorted, and I glanced at him, raising an eyebrow. He was tall and lanky, with light-brown hair that hung over his forehead in a boyish way. His amber gaze twinkled with mischief as he offered a grin in response to my study.

Lyana put her back to her brother, eyes dancing between me and Sainte. "What's he saying, El?"

He glanced up at the ceiling as if sending a prayer to the gods for patience. "I would have a word," he tried. "Your friends can stay here."

I rocked on my heels, kicking out my hip with a brow raised high. "And what will stop your friends from getting a little excited and lopping off heads?"

"Whoa, what?" Ethyan choked.

"Please..." Sainte's jaw tightened as he spoke, muscles twitching.

"Aren't these the good guys?" Lyana's voice pitched higher. "That was established... wasn't it?"

"Us? Good?" The friendly one tilted his head back, releasing a hearty laugh that reverberated throughout the room. The remaining servers departed in a hurry. "Sweets, we're not the good guys."

At least he wasn't afraid to use the common tongue.

"Comforting," Lyana replied with a dry scowl.

"Urien, enough," Sainte snapped.

He grabbed hold of me with his uninjured arm, and the soldiers encircled us. They fidgeted with nerves, each resting their hand on the hilt of their weapons.

"When she acts like a princess, feel free to treat her as one," he bit out, then hauled me across the room.

I yelped and fought, wrenching at his strong grip, while my friends created a commotion nearby. Unfazed, he continued, dragging me up a flight of stairs and down the hall. I fired curses, stumbling behind and jerking my arm for good measure. He kicked open a door and practically threw me inside, then stormed in after me, slamming it shut. When he faced me, I propped my hands on my hips and arched a daring brow.

"Honestly?" He exhaled, motioning toward his injury. The haphazard bandage was damp with fresh blood. It was obvious he dressed it in a rush before intercepting us at the port.

"Well, are you the good guy?" My tongue tripped over the High Wynterian. After all this time, it felt more foreign than Muik.

"Do you know who the bad guy is, Elspeth?" His tone dropped to a tired drone as he pulled a chair in front of the door and settled in.

"According to you, it's my brother." I glanced toward the window on the opposite wall. I had jumped from greater heights. "What do you want with me, Sainte? You left me alone for years. Why now?"

He squinted at me, lips pressed in a firm line as if working some mystery out. "You're almost twenty-one."

I blinked, waiting for him to elaborate, but he stared, as if expecting a response.

"And that's different from my twentieth birthday... how?" I asked. "Don't act like I'm supposed to know anything, Sainte. You took me from Wynterborne when I was six. It's not as if I was an endless fountain of knowledge at that age."

He groaned and dropped his head. His left hand dragged down his face, pulling at his distraught features.

My heart twinged at the sight, and I rolled my eyes at my stupidity. I would not argue with him about this. It was pointless to even ask about it. I dipped into a crouch in front of him, waiting until his bright gaze met mine before I spoke. "Twenty-one or no, I'm not going back."

That got him to sit up.

He straightened as if someone shoved a rod up his arse, his glare piercing, cool eyes ablaze with fury. "You are Princess Elspeth, second in line to the Kingdom of Wynterborne."

I waited a moment, then pushed myself to stand. "What, no more titles to add?"

"You've been missing for fifteen years. You've earned no titles beyond the Lost Princess. People assume you ran, succumbed to Winter's Bite."

"See? Lovely place. I'm sure everyone wants to go where winter gnaws off fingers and limbs, where cold steals away your breath and turns your lungs to ice. Sounds grand, but I'll pass."

"You have a responsibility to your people."

"My people?!" I scoffed. "Let them think I'm dead. I owe them nothing. When were they there for me? When did they rise to protect me when my brother cackled down the halls of my home, singing about my head on a pike?"

"The affairs of court are not for the common man to interfere."

Frustration edged in, furious that he attempted to burden me with the weight of an entire kingdom. "And you're not a common man? What makes you so special? Why did you save me, Sainte?!"

"To save our people!" he roared and launched to his feet.

I scrambled backward, my heart pounding, and flinched as he stormed toward me with swift, purposeful strides.

"You criticize their lack of protection, but are you not equally to blame, allowing a madman to rule in your stead?! You're not doing them justice!"

My back thumped against the wall. But he kept coming, sparks flying from his eyes.

"I rescued you, believing you might one day be our people's salvation! Not to watch you roam the streets like some common thief. I didn't risk my life for a petty brat!" He threw his right fist at the wall, wincing at the pain, his glare intense as he loomed over me.

Hot, angry tears blurred my vision, and I gritted my teeth, trying to blink them away. They spilled down my cheeks regardless of my efforts, scouring slick trails through the sweat and grime. "Sorry to be such a waste."

If I could turn back time, I'd have thanked him for leaving me. His words cut deeper than his absence ever could.

"Elspeth." My name sounded as if it was being torn from his throat. He groaned and dropped his head to my shoulder with a sigh. "You said you owe no one. That's a lie."

I clenched my jaw, unwilling to accept the next words I knew were coming. "Don't," I whispered.

He pulled away, leveling his gaze with mine. "You owe me."

"Don't ask this of me," I strained. "Sainte, I would have given you anything if you had stayed—my heart, my crown, my life. All of it was yours." My voice broke, and I choked back sobs.

He was right. He was the only person I owed anything to—the one I owed everything to. I shook my head, ducking under his outstretched limb to distance us. He let me pass, resting his forehead against his injured arm.

"Elspeth, stay with me."

Those words crushed my heart all over again. A sob tore through me as I flung the chair aside and yanked the door open. Without a word, I walked away, leaving him as he once left me.

CHAPTER 3

In the hallway, I paused to compose myself. I wiped away tear streaks with the heels of my palms, then used my sleeve to dab at my nose. The stench of fish guts and musk from the lewd district clung to my clothes, making me grimace. A dip in the ocean was definitely in order. Seaweed would smell like a rose compared to this.

Sainte remained in his room, silent as a tomb. Hopefully he was reflecting on the time when he left me in such a manner. Some pain on his part would be fitting. It would only be a fraction of what I endured over the past five years.

I descended the lone flight of stairs, anticipating the need to intervene on behalf of my friends. However, upon entering the dining room, I halted, taking in the unexpected scene. Lyana sat at a table across from a large man with tattoos decorating his arms, playing a game of knucklebones. Ethyan stood in the corner with two men, enthralled in a round of darts.

Lyana glanced up as I approached, a smile on her face as she shook the bones in a cup. She shrugged in response to the disgust souring my features.

"They're not that awful, this lot," she said.

"I thought we concluded these were the bad guys?" Amusement lightened my tone.

"Well, definitely not the good guys, I'd wager."

I faced the man with the boyish charm from earlier, Urien, as Sainte called him. He sat at a table near the bend in the stairs, giving me a small smirk. He kicked the chair out across from him with his foot.

"Princess."

The sarcasm in his tone wasn't lost on me.

With one hand, he gestured for me to sit. With the other, he raised a mug of ale. He wouldn't get sick from the spirits served here...

Probably.

I sighed with a glance about the room. Lyana tossed the bones onto the table, immersed in her match. She almost slammed heads with the giant sitting across from her as they peered down at the runes together. Ethyan still hadn't noticed me—caught up in some drinking game. He chugged his spirits before throwing a dart. It landed smack in the middle with such force the target swiveled.

"Nothing better to do, I suppose," I muttered, taking the seat he offered. I angled my back against the wall to keep a clear view of the room and door.

"To you, the Lost Princess, and your safe return home," Urien said, then lifted his mug for a drink. His eyes studied me over the rim.

He might have boyish charms, but this was the type of man others took for granted, easily underestimated. I knew his kind well from picking pockets in the noblemen district.

"I'm not returning."

"Staying lost, then?" he asked, setting his mug aside.

"I simply don't need finding." Gods, how I wished my friends would wrap up their games.

"More than a few people might argue that."

My eyes rolled. "Sainte being one of them?"

"Aye," he chuckled, "he would be the first to say it, and I don't suppose he would be the last. Many would welcome your return."

"Would you?" I asked, watching him carefully.

He leaned back and threw an arm over the chair beside him. "Do you think I would be here if I didn't want you in Wynterborne?"

"I don't know anything about you. You could be loyal to King Adrastus, sent to–"

"Prince Regent Adrastus. Please do not exaggerate his title." His nose lifted in the slightest distaste for my brother's name.

I shifted in my seat. "Not king? Was he not crowned after my father passed?"

Urien cocked his head, casting me a sidelong glance. His features narrowed with suspicion. "No. He is named regent. Did you not know?"

"I left when I was six," I spat, arms crossed tight.

"He cannot ascend the throne as king—perhaps in name only for now. The official claim to that title hinges on those Borne of Wynter relinquishing their rights. And the whereabouts of a particular princess remain unknown, her body never recovered."

My lips pressed into a tight frown. "Not that I'm interested, but what exactly is expected of me?"

"Challenges, sweets. You cannot slip in and take the crown from Adastrus, but you can confront him. He would falter in the face of the gods' trials, and that's what we're counting on."

"So you expect me to undergo some challenge, *survive*, then rule a kingdom I know nothing about?"

"You think you know nothing? It's in your blood," he said. "We were in the dark. We had no hope—until two months ago. Sainte claimed he knew the whereabouts of the Lost Princess, the one capable of challenging Adastrus. Few believed him, and even fewer followed his lead."

"Why now? If my safety was a concern before, why the sudden change?"

"You're nearing your twenty-first birthday," he said, shaking his head at my ignorance. "Adastrus cannot rise to the throne until all siblings come of age and forfeit their rights. If your survival is known, you can challenge him."

"Then tell them I'm alive and leave it at that. Let him be regent. Surely he grasps the intricacies of ruling better than I do."

The room stilled, and I bit my cheek to refrain from glancing at my friends for support.

"Choose your words carefully." Urien's voice lost all semblance of friendliness. "Prince Adastrus has no allies here, and you would be wise to remember that."

"Sorry," I huffed, staring at the tabletop.

"You're our last hope, sweets. We only ask that you ride to challenge him. The gods will sort him out, but without your intervention, he will assume the throne on your birthday."

"I don't think you understand," I murmured. "I was never meant to rule. I have no allegiance to Wynterborne. Most of my life was lived away from it. Do I strike you as leadership material?" I scoffed, throwing my arms out.

Covered in fish guts, blood, sweat, and grime, emitting an odor that rivaled a pigsty, I managed a rueful grin. My shirt hung in tatters, fluttering with each movement. My trousers barely reached mid-calf. One boot was held together with twine after the laces snapped.

His gaze tracked my body, as if taking in every flaw. "Appearances are not everything," he said. "It's what is inside that makes the difference."

"I'm a street rat. I steal and pilfer to survive. That's the sort of moral compass people need." I rolled my eyes, dropping my hands into my lap.

"You carry blades, yet you didn't draw on the captain."

I glanced down at my trousers and boots, checking that my blades were safely concealed out of sight where they belonged. A frown creased my brow as I wondered how he knew I carried them.

"Ethyan's a good shot."

Truthfully, I had no idea they were up there until the last moment. I hadn't drawn my blade on Sainte because I trusted him.

Trusted him.

Ugh.

"I understand your hesitation," he said, examining his oddly clean nails. "Sometimes we have to do things we don't want to do."

"Right. I'm done here." I lurched to my feet. "Lyana, Ethyan, I'm headed out. I'll meet up later."

"Wait, El–"

Ignoring Lyana's call, I stalked toward the door. I wouldn't hear anymore of this responsibility dung. I owed them nothing, not these soldiers, and not Wynterborne.

"Captain."

I glanced back to see Sainte step into the dining hall. His cool eyes caught mine, laced with anger and hurt.

It served him right.

My shoulder rammed into the door, shoving it open with all my might. As I stepped into the early evening, a string of curses flew past my lips to soften the pressure building in my chest.

There was still plenty of time to relieve some scum of their coin. Whistling, I strolled through the cooling air, determined not to dwell on someone else's problems.

I grunted as I hauled myself up the bell tower. Ethyan could do it without breaking a sweat, but my strength didn't compare. I considered myself more delicate and nimble, more suited for picking pockets rather than scaling towers.

I had a good meal too, courtesy of a lovely chap sleeping on the roadside. When he woke, he'd find a stone where his coin had been. Such was the way of life when one slept on the street in a drunken stupor.

The meat pie sitting in my stomach probably added to my difficulties climbing the tower.

With a huff, I hoisted myself over the ledge, grateful for the sight of a flickering candle casting shadows across our hideout. Lyana sat near it, threading beads onto a strand of her hair. Ethyan lay on his mat, his breathing steady and quiet with sleep, though, knowing him, that peaceful silence wouldn't last long.

"A good night?" she asked without looking up. She stuck her tongue out in concentration as she secured another bead, tying it off.

"Not too bad. Enough for a meat pie," I said, tossing her two coins.

"Oh, we ate with the soldiers."

My positive spirit sank like an anchor.

"Make some new friends?" I snatched my coins back and settled next to her on our mattress.

"Oh, my gods and goddesses! And you complained about my stink this morn!" She pinched her nose and glared at my tattered shirt.

I chuckled as she shoved me off the bed, then rolled onto my belly. My ribs pressed against the wooden planks as I rested my chin on my hands, watching her work.

"Honestly, they're not *that* bad," she said. "There were a few reserved ones. I didn't catch their names. But Ethyan had a grand time drinking with Linus and Otto. The two play a fair game of darts, though perhaps not as good as my brother. And Grimm was a joy to play."

"Did you take all his coin?"

"He earned half it back."

"Playing you?" I gasped in feigned shock.

"Aye, surprising, isn't it?" She smirked, squinting to thread a small green bead. "I might've let him win a bit."

"No..." I whispered, horrified. Lyana only allowed men she favored to best her.

"He's a good chap. Wish we could have gotten on a little more."

"They're leaving?"

"Aye, first thing in the morn."

I held my breath, wondering why that made me so anxious. I should've been happy to be rid of them. Sainte's departure was a relief. After all this time, I was only a tool to him, a means to an end. I should have let it go when he abandoned me on the street that night, but no. I had to get my hopes up, believing he actually cared about me, only to have him crush me again.

Nothing would remain of my heart when he left.

At least it felt that way.

"Oi, El." Lyana's words pulled my attention from the floorboards. "Come here, stinky."

I sniffed, then attempted a smile as I climbed into bed beside her.

She blew out the candle and wrapped her arms around me. "Did you two fight?" she whispered.

"Aye." A tear slipped from the corner of my eye. Here, hidden from view, my tears went unnoticed. No one would judge my vulnerability.

"Tell me."

We lay there, deep into the night as I relayed, yet again, how Sainte had been both my savior and my downfall. My rescue and my end. She murmured and agreed at all the right moments, brushing my hair from my face without a word of complaint about my stench.

Which I sincerely appreciated.

CHAPTER 4

My rest was fitful, drifting in and out. Murmured voices tugged me to awareness just as a horrible stench tainted my senses, and I sank into darkness.

When I finally came to, my face banged against something warm and firm. Thoughts blurred and foggy, I groaned, willing my sluggish body to move, though it didn't respond. As I lifted my head, my neck gave out, slamming me into that thing again, bloodying my lip.

"Hold!"

Curse it all. I knew that voice.

The swaying motion halted. A horse? It stamped its foreleg, jarring me. A bit of horsehair worked its way inside my mouth, and I struggled to spit it out. I attempted to pull my arm down–

My hands wouldn't move.

I thrashed, wriggling to regain control of my body as Sainte dismounted. The beast snorted, shifting with a nervous whicker, and my heart stuttered with panic.

Sainte pulled me headfirst off the horse, catching me in strong arms. My head lolled back, and I was sure dried drool crusted my face as I peered into his eyes.

"Mmm ghill voo!" Funny how drugs could muddle death threats.

His lips pressed into a firm line, and he ignored my slur. He held me snug against his disgustingly muscular chest, carrying me to the road's edge. I caught a glimpse of his men on horseback, waiting patiently in the warm sun.

"Can you move your legs?" he asked.

A sparse forest lined the path. The thin foliage blocked the sunlight as we passed the treeline. My glare intensified as a tingling sensation coursed through my limbs, promising a slow return of my control. With a valiant attempt at kicking a boot toward his head, my leg lifted in a pathetic, limp swing.

"Good. Take the time you need to relieve yourself, then we'll be on our way."

He spoke as if this was a common everyday occurrence. As if he expected me to be accustomed to waking up sprawled across a horse like a sack of potatoes, unable to move or speak.

He set me down at the base of a tree, straining a bit with the effort.

"Mmmans," I grunted.

"Hmm?"

"*Mmmans!*"

I attempted to shift enough to wag my fingers at him. Unfortunately, I hadn't regained complete control over my core. When I turned, my weight pulled me over into a fern. I slurred a plethora of curses, spitting at the plant.

"Hands. Right."

The rope around my wrists fell away, and my arms dropped to my sides. I took a moment, flopping like a fish out of water before I got them under me to push myself upright.

I struggled, limbs shaking as I propped against the tree. "You'll ay fr'tha," I snarled.

"I'm sure I will, just not now." He shrugged, angling his small blade at the ground. "I'm going to be on the other side." He patted the oak I leaned against, loosening some of the bark. "Don't try anything."

"Me?"

I massaged the sore skin on my wrists, giving him my most innocent smile. My lashes fluttered to top it off. Though, in my current state, it probably looked as if the drug he used affected my brain.

He stood with a grunt and rubbed at the bloody bandage on his arm. With another stern look, he stepped around the tree, out of my line of sight.

Slander and insults spilled from my mouth as I struggled to stand. I had to have been out for quite some time—my bladder was screaming. My plan to kill Sainte would have to wait.

"You snathd me away!" I stumbled a step, catching myself on the tree before I toppled. "You idnappd me lie a 'ommon fief!"

I worked on my trousers, confident he would at least give me privacy.

"I understand your reservation—"

No, I don't think he did.

"—but this has to be done. It's not about what you or I want. There's a bigger picture, Elspeth."

I screeched as I tumbled over in my crouch, landing in my piss. I threw my head back, ensuring he stayed put, and cursed loud enough to wake the dead. Furious, I thrashed, pulling my trousers over my hips. They were soaked in a vile mix of urine and mud, adding to my already questionable decorum and lovely scent.

My cursing paused only to take a breath as I rolled to the side, grappling to stand. Sainte gripped my arm and hauled me to my feet, supporting my precarious balance.

"And here I thought you couldn't reek any worse."

I dropped my weight, and he grunted, struggling to brace me at the odd angle. He glanced at me and I matched his glare.

"Stand."

"No."

"Petty brat," he growled, then drove his shoulder into my stomach.

My breath huffed out in a gust as he lifted me off the ground, but I took pleasure knowing I got piss-mud all over the front of his armor. Every step back to the road sent a jolt of pain through my middle, and it was almost worth it until I heard the soldiers' muffled snickers.

"You ride with me, or I'll carry you as the burden you are," Sainte hissed.

I managed to wriggle enough to ram my knee into his chest, eliciting a satisfying grunt. In return, he dumped me onto the ground near his horse. I peered up at the white beast towering overhead. One misstep from those massive hooves, and I'd live with it for the rest of my life.

Before I realized what was happening, Sainte pressed a cloth over my face, gripping the back of my head. I gagged on the putrid stench, jerking and clawing at his hands. In seconds, my limbs fell like limp noodles, and my mind slipped away in a foggy breeze. The last thing I saw was Sainte's conflicted frown.

I drifted awake, finding myself in a much more agreeable position despite the throbbing pulse in my skull. I lay on a blanket spread on the ground, my head propped up on a saddle. Bile surged up my throat, and I threw myself onto my side, retching all over the tack.

Someone gripped my shoulders as I panted, rolling me to puke on the green grass instead. I moaned as my stomach settled, but my headache thrummed as it did in the bell tower during the midday prayers.

"Water," Sainte murmured.

I spit to the side and let his strong hands resettle me against the saddle—hopefully not in the puke. When the waterskin pressed to my lips, my eyes fluttered open. Sainte crouched beside me with Urien standing close behind, features drawn into a frown. Dusk's golden sheen dimmed the daylight, and small tents littered the clearing.

I gulped the cool water, letting it wash the sting of bile from my mouth and throat. My brain was slow to register my surroundings as he pulled the waterskin away with a wince.

"I told you she'd come to," Urien sighed, shaking his head.

I peered at him through heavy eyelids. It was hard work to wake up only to eject the contents of one's stomach.

Sainte grunted and stood, keeping his injured arm tucked against his chest, stiff and unmoving. Urien glanced at him before some silent order sent him off to the others huddled together eating a cold meal.

"Grimm will take you to relieve yourself," Sainte said.

I groaned and closed my eyes. Would the torture never end?

"You've been out for three days, Elspeth."

I squinted at the back of his armor. Was that guilt I heard? With a sigh, he left me, joining the others. He settled on a log, speaking to his men in hushed tones.

Every part of me ached—arms, neck, legs, even my toes were sore. Stiffness and fatigue enveloped me. My wrists were raw, pinned behind me with tight ropes. A throbbing headache accompanied my growling stomach. Gods, I was hungry, but the mere thought of food reignited the nausea in my gut.

And I had to piss.

Three days was a long time to go without relieving oneself.

Grimm stomped over and picked me up as if I was nothing more than a babe. I sighed in resignation, refusing to take my anger out on this man. He chose to follow Sainte's lead, driven by a desire to see his country thrive. I couldn't fault him for that.

"Do you often steal women out of their beds?" I rasped as he carried me away from the small camp.

He chuckled, the deep tenor rumbling through his chest. "This'd be a first, I'd say."

"It's not a great habit," I muttered.

He set me down, out of the camp's view. "I shan't make it a common occurrence then."

His teeth gleamed with a bright smile, and I huffed, stumbling a step away. He spoke with an odd cadence, as if High Wynter was not his first language. Perhaps he was not from the palace. The nobles in Tilamuik communicated differently than the Common Muik in Meeds. Still, I understood him enough to make sense of his words.

"Need help?"

"Gods, no," I shot back, prompting an amused smirk.

I turned, waving my fingers, hoping he would be so kind as to remove the rope. He obliged, untying it rather than cutting it. A sigh of relief escaped me as the cool air brushed against the open wounds on my wrists. I shook them out, and the motion shifted my balance. With palms pressed to a nearby tree, I steadied myself to avoid collapsing. After a moment, I braved a few steps, tripping on a twig.

"Don't go far, not so many friendlies in these parts," Grimm warned.

I waved over my shoulder in acknowledgement.

Once I managed a safe distance, I took care of my needs, then settled against a tree, glad to not have ended up in my piss this time.

Had I truly been out for three days? Headed north, I assumed. Depending on our route, we might be near Landing's End. That road was populated with travelers. Surely there would be plenty of inns to rest in along the way instead of setting up camp.

I wasn't stupid. I was well aware I couldn't manage the trek back on foot. Even if I slipped off into the dark, Sainte had horses and a handful of soldiers. I was one woman—one tired, hungry woman that wouldn't make it far.

If we were a three days ride in, that meant at least six of walking, if not closer to nine. I couldn't set traps or scavenge for food in the wild—I was a city girl. I'd have to rely on relieving travelers of their goods to survive.

Those odds were less than appealing.

Yet, what was my alternative? Return to Wynterborne to be used as a pawn? Wear fancy dresses and pretend to be royalty?

My options were miserable either way.

I needed more time, perhaps an opportunity to lodge at an inn where I could secure a horse and some coin. Surely, we wouldn't be camping along the road for the entire journey. They'd have to restock their stores or re-shoe their horses eventually. I decided to wait for that opportunity and seize it when it came. Traveling in this state would be too risky.

"Oi, Princess?"

Ugh.

I pushed myself to my feet and wandered back to Grimm, stumbling only because I couldn't see in the dark. The moon cast his silhouette, but little else. As he moved, I squinted, realizing he had offered his arm. At least he knew how to treat a woman.

My hand found the crook of his elbow, and I let him lead me back. I picked my feet up high as I walked to avoid ending up on my face. At the camp, I grimaced as he returned me to the spot that reeked of vomit.

I settled in and crossed my legs, watching as Sainte rinsed puke off the saddle. The moonlight was feeble, casting uncertain shadows. He'd likely miss a few spots.

Good.

"Eat." He jerked his head toward the corner of the blanket, where a small portion of food waited for me.

I prodded at it, uncertain. "Could be poisoned."

"No point in killing you now."

I pressed my lips and nodded. He had me there. I palmed the dried meat and hard biscuit. The bread felt more like a rock than anything edible. How appetizing.

I ate, or rather gnawed, until my jaw ached, then swallowed. My stomach settled with every bite I forced down.

Sainte spread out the horse blanket and glanced between what I presumed was his bedroll, where I sat, and the blanket. I shifted my weight, smearing in whatever stink I could as I grinned, hoping my teeth were visible in the dark.

Choose your smelly options, Captain.

With a sigh, he reclined on the horse blanket, his lower half draped along the cold grass. He bent one leg at the knee, running his fingers through his hair. I stared, feeling a twinge low in my belly.

No. There would be no thoughts on his good looks. No resurrections of any childhood crushes. I was beyond that.

"So, to Wynterborne?" I asked.

He closed his eyes and dropped his hand over his belly, keeping his right arm stiff against his chest. "Yes."

"Where are we now?"

"Thinking of running?"

I scoffed, then rested my head on the clean part of the saddle, gazing up at the starry sky. "Even I know I wouldn't make it back."

There was a grunt of agreement, then he went quiet.

Don't do it.

Don't, El.

"Will your arm be all right?"

His amused snort sent a wave of self-disgust rolling over me. I wasn't worried. He deserved what he got. Right, I'd just keep telling myself that.

"I've suffered worse."

"Ethyan is a decent shot."

"I can vouch for that."

I chuckled, a small smile pulling at my lips.

"You know how we met?" I didn't wait for his reply. "Not long after I arrived in Port Siren, I stumbled into trouble with a bad lot at a tavern. They bested me of my coin, and I was about to lose the shirt off my back when Ethyan intervened, winning a game of knife toss. He and Lyana managed to win enough to keep me from going hungry, and I've been with them ever since."

Sainte was silent, either waiting for me to go on or he had fallen asleep.

"I guess when you want a family, you'll build it with anyone you find," I breathed, studying the night.

Stars twinkled, blue and purple streaks above, illuminated by the moon. I had a vague recollection of the night in Wynterborne being more vibrant. In my memories, the northern sky swarmed with bright auroras, dancing streams of green and blue.

"I left you with a family."

Apparently, he hadn't fallen asleep.

"You dumped me in a house as a burden and inconvenience, Sainte. Sure, I had food and a roof overhead, but that was all. I was surviving, not thriving."

"I suppose running the streets and thieving is where you thrived."

Annoyed, I rolled onto my side and squinted at his shadowy figure. "You don't get it. I didn't fit in—wasn't welcome. There was no kindness in Landing's End, aside from you—then you left."

"Strange, I remember you being the one to leave."

"You walked away first."

Heavy silence lapsed, and I flopped onto my back. Now was not the time to hash this out. I wanted to lash out, to make him feel the same pain he caused me.

"I had to."

"So you've said," I spat. I didn't want to talk to him anymore.

"I had to secure my position at the palace. Without that, your return would've been impossible."

"Just a tool," I muttered. How had I ever found this man charming?

I scrunched my face to keep from getting sappy. He did not deserve my tears. I could hold myself together. He saw me as a pawn, using gifts to sway my loyalty. Butter me up so I'd blindly follow his lead.

His voice dropped to a low rumble. "Do you know what I did when I returned on your seventeenth birthday?"

I didn't grace him with a reply.

But, *gods*, how I wanted to know.

"I tore Landing's End apart. Didn't rest, didn't sleep. I scoured whorehouses and slums, searched the common man's graves. I hunted for three weeks, Elspeth."

"Because your pawn was gone."

"Because the girl I... cared for was gone."

Pig guts.

My heart twitched in response to his words, the fragmented shards trying to fuse together. I didn't care about him. Not one bit. Nothing he could say would ever take away the hurt he caused.

"Why didn't you stay?" I whispered, half-hoping he wouldn't hear me.

There was a pregnant pause before he spoke again.

"I faced a flogging if I arrived late. As a recruitment officer, I had three months of leave before my scheduled return. With four weeks of relentless riding to reach Landing's End, and the need to gather soldiers, I had no evenings to spare."

"Not one?" I pressed.

"Not one."

My heart twisted, and I curled into myself. For once in my life, I wasn't sure he was telling me the truth.

CHAPTER 5

The soldiers had all horses saddled and ready before dawn. How exactly, I wasn't sure. Perhaps whoever stood watch roused them.

"Who's riding the chestnut mare?" I gestured toward the horse being led by Grimm.

"Princess Elspeth," Sainte said as he held his white gelding for me.

I checked over his men, then my boots, which were still firmly planted on the ground. "Do you have another Princess Elspeth in your pocket there, Captain?" I asked, batting my lashes.

"When you act like a princess, you may ride alone."

"What, you don't trust me?" I slapped a hand over my heart in mock betrayal.

"No."

His expression was empty of all playfulness as he knelt, interlacing his fingers. I heaved a dramatic sigh and stepped into his hands, allowing him to lift me. The horse snorted under my weight, waiting as Sainte slid his boot into the stirrup to mount.

"I've ridden two to a saddle before," I whined, dreading what came next.

"You were smaller then."

He pushed me forward and found his seat. I huffed and shoved my hips back, fighting for space. It was painful enough, and gods knew how long this man intended to travel today. He shifted his weight as the horse danced beneath us, and I tried to settle in. Luckily, the man wasn't armored at his crotch, sparing me that challenge. Dealing with his sheer size was plenty to contend with.

After much jostling and cursing on my part, we settled into a somewhat comfortable but shared position in the saddle, each lacking a full seat. My arse nestled against his hips, which sent my stomach fluttering—and annoyed me to no end.

He was in a foul mood as we started out, and it did not improve as time passed. We followed the road for the better part of the day, leaving it around midday. Now and then, his soldiers drifted off, either to scout ahead or to relieve themselves. Sainte and his men had some silent communication. While he sported no badge or indication of rank, it was clear he was the captain of this little troupe.

Soon after we left the path in favor of a game trail, the rush of water rumbled in the distance. It wasn't a light gurgle, nor was it as loud as the pipes spilling into the ocean in Port Siren. It was a quiet, gentle cadence, and it dawned on me why we veered off the main road.

"We'll break here."

"Camp?" I asked.

Though the sun was still high in the sky, the ache in my thighs and lower back had me sincerely hoping this place marked our halt for the night.

"Break," he repeated. After dismounting, he adjusted his trousers and shook out his legs.

I frowned at his wounded arm, which he held close to his chest. He utilized it, like when he gave me a leg-up, but it clearly caused him considerable discomfort. I would not feel bad about it.

I simply wouldn't.

Ready to be off the thrice-cursed saddle, I swung over the horse's rump and lowered myself. My feet flailed, searching for solid ground. Warm hands found my waist as Sainte eased me down.

"I had it."

"Clearly."

I disregarded his remark and scanned the small clearing while he tended to his horse. Beyond the lush meadow, the sun's glint danced on the river's surface, drawing me closer. The men paid no heed as I navigated through the long, swaying grass and brush.

The river was extensive, so wide I would be hard pressed to throw a stone to the opposite shore, but its water ran clear. Algae-covered stones and waterweeds littered the bottom, swaying in the current, and fish darted away at my shadow.

We were hopefully only here to get a drink.

"This way."

I turned to see Sainte with a bundle under his arm, headed upriver. He glanced behind and waited for me to catch up.

"I hope you don't have *expectations* of me," I huffed, slipping on a rock as I stumbled after him.

"Only the bare minimum."

"Good. I'd hate to disappoint," I called, then focused on my footing across the smooth round stones.

Ahead, a massive rock jutted from the riverbank, where the water curled around it like a giant snake. Sainte guided me up the hillside, then crossed to the boulder. The terrain sloped down to the river, preventing a gradual descent.

"The current is calmest here," he said, setting his bundle on the boulder's surface. He crouched, digging through the pack, and retrieved a bar of soap. "It will be as private as can be."

"No." I backed toward the hillside, ready to scramble up the incline. "No, no. That's a hard pass from me."

He peered over his shoulder with a bored blink. "The men are gagging around you."

"Then tell them to toughen up their stomachs. I'm not getting in there."

"Enough, Elspeth." He straightened to his full height. "I'm tired of fighting you."

"Then just accept it. I smell. Move on."

"Don't make me throw you in."

I froze, horrified. "You wouldn't dare."

He held my gaze, glare unwavering, lips pressed into an unamused frown. Neither of us moved a muscle—then we lurched at once. I turned and ran, managing two steps closer to the soft, grassy hillside before he snared my arm and spun me toward the boulder's ridge.

"No, no! No! *I'll die!!*"

"Not likely."

I latched onto him, fingers digging into his leather armor. Panic set in full force, and I thrashed as he shoved me near the ledge. A scream tore from my throat as the earth disappeared from under my boots, and I dropped like a stone.

Water flooded my mouth. The cold shock silenced my screams as I plunged below. On instinct, I snapped my eyes shut upon impact, the frigid embrace disorienting me. My limbs flailed, seeking direction in the murky depths. Which way was up? Was this down? I forced myself to look, instantly regretting it as the sting blurred my vision. My lungs demanded air. I kicked and clawed, desperate to reach solid ground.

My head broke the surface, and I sucked in a breath, with only a bit of water. I sputtered and coughed, staring at the boulder wide-eyed in a silent plea for help, hoping Sainte would grasp that I couldn't swim.

He was shedding his armor fast, fingers yanking at the buckles as I sank. I kicked and splashed. Coughing, my body acted of its own accord, aching to breathe. I tried to suck in a breath and the river poured down my throat.

Everything burned, and water filled my lungs—where it had no place being.

A violent surge of choking racked my frame, liquid expelled from me in gasping heaves. The sensation of drowning lingered despite the solid ground beneath my hands and knees. Air rasped through my stinging throat like acid with each strained gasp. When I collapsed onto my back, panting like a dying fish, I fisted handfuls of sand and pebbles. Fluid rattled in my lungs with every breath as I stared wide-eyed at the sky. A shadow blocked it out.

"I told you I would *die!*"

Relief flooded Sainte's features. Droplets splattered onto my cheeks from his wet hair as he lowered his forehead to mine.

"You can be a touch dramatic," he said, breathing hard.

I growled, shoving him until he sat up. When he shuffled off me, I lunged, pinning him to the ground. I sat on his chest, hands hovering above his neck. My fingers wiggled, straining with the urge to choke the life out of him.

"I could kill you! You didn't even ask *why* I refused to bathe! *No,* you just tossed me in, assuming I'd be fine! Did you listen to me, or pause to think it through? No! You *threw* me like a—like a–"

"You were raised in a coastal city. I assumed you knew how to swim."

He gently pulled my hands from his neck and placed them on the ground beside his head. I bowed myself low, so my nose touched his and snarled into those blue depths.

"Well I don't."

In one fluid movement, he knocked my leg from under me and rolled me onto my back. He braced himself above me. A wince marked his features as he relaxed his weight off his injured arm, leaning left. He dipped low to press his forehead against mine.

"I apologize," he bit out.

I drew in a deep, rattling breath that ended in a cough, then shoved him aside. He let me sit up, and I breathed hard, eyeing him. His armor was gone, his dark garments drenched. With an exasperated sigh, he pushed his hair off his face, glaring at the river. We were further downstream. Far enough that I couldn't spot the boulder anymore. Had the current carried me far?

"Your clothes are clean, at least," I mumbled.

He grunted, pushing to stand. "Too bad. I planned to give you my dry set."

"Ha!"

"I'll be back with soap. Stay in the shallows."

"Oi, I'm not stepping foot in that water." I shook my head and sent droplets flying.

The glower he gave me in return told me I'd end up in that river one way or another.

I pulled off my boots, shaking out the sand and stones, then searched my shirt to make sense of what remained of the scraps. At this point, a sleeve was attached to the tattered neckline while the other was torn, draping over my shoulder and down around my belly. The belt held true, though it wasn't managing a lot.

Sainte came back a few moments later, the bundle of clothes and what I assumed was soap and a comb under his left arm. He tipped his face to the sky and took a deep, calming breath when he saw I hadn't gotten into the river.

"A single swim wouldn't scratch the surface of that grime," he called, picking his way over.

"Well, it will have to do."

"Take pity on the men," Sainte set the bundle on a cluster of dry rocks, "and me."

He tossed the bar, and I caught it, giving it a sniff. Mint and pine. Fresh. I snickered and shuffled to the water's edge, settling on my knees. After cupping some water, I lathered the soap.

"Off with those things you call clothes."

"And trust *you?*" I called over my shoulder.

"I'm not above tossing you in a second time."

"You said you were sorry!" I snapped a glare, checking to see if he started toward me.

"I'd apologize again." He shrugged, then turned his back on me, perching on a chunk of driftwood.

"Your word, Sainte." I set the soap aside, rising to my feet.

"What would you like me to pledge, Princess?"

"You'll not look."

"Yet, if you manage to get swept away in two paces of water, I daresay I'll have to break that vow. I cannot."

I snatched a pebble and threw it at him—then reminded myself I was an adult as his shoulders shook with his light laughter.

"Swear you'll not look unless I call for you."

"Or I hear flailing, with no response."

"Fine."

"I so swear."

I undressed quickly, glancing at the tree line. Despite my disdain, I believed he wouldn't intentionally endanger me. He stripped me of my freewill, forcing me on this journey. But he saved me when I had no one else, cared for me, doted on me, and ensured I had something to look forward to throughout the years. He was nothing if not loyal, and I couldn't recall a single instance of him deceiving me—aside from drugging me and stealing me from my bed.

My foolish heart trusted him.

I cursed myself under my breath and waded out. Water lapped at my waist, and I lowered, keeping my chest below the surface as I scoured the dirt and grime from my skin. To be honest, it felt amazing, not that I would admit it. I scrubbed at my hair, grimacing at the cloudy haze that floated away. Surely I just kicked up the sediment. That much scum couldn't come from one person.

Movement along the shore made me glance up from my washing. I watched as Sainte walked backward toward the water. "Oi, you were supposed to stay where you were!" I called out, hugging my arms over my chest below the surface.

"I never swore that." He collected the fragments of my tunic, holding them up, turning them this way and that.

"Put my shirt down, Sainte!"

"This is a shirt?"

I slapped the water. "Stop!"

"Tell me, is this the shirt?" He held up one piece. "Or this?" He held up the other and peered at them as if he were trying to figure out a puzzle.

"Put it down."

"Your wish is my command."

I stared, horrified, as he balled them up and threw them into the river. They hit with a wet splash, bobbed once, then the current swept them away. I spewed every curse imaginable as he set his dry shirt onto the shore and reached for my trousers.

"No!"

I stood up and marched over, challenging his word as I approached in naught but my skin. He snorted and returned to his driftwood to sit with his back to me. With a slew of grumbled curses, I tossed the soap aside and struggled into my soaked trousers, then pulled his shirt overhead. I used Ethyan's belt to keep it from catching the wind and blowing off with me. The tunic reached mid-hip, and I batted it out of the way as I stepped into my soggy boots. It was a relief to have full coverage without needing to piece scraps together, but... it smelled like him.

And that did funny things to my heart.

"Decent?"

"Couldn't say the same of you," I shot back.

The slap of his wet pants against his legs signaled his approach, and I sincerely hoped he was uncomfortable.

"Dare I ask the same vow of you?" he asked, passing me as he started for the water.

"Oh, no. If you call my name or I hear flailing, I assure you, I will gladly watch as you float downstream."

His chuckle faded into a hiss as he ducked his head and tugged his tunic over his left shoulder. As he revealed his back, my jaw fell open, eyes widened in horror. I must have made a choked sound of distress, because he glanced over at me. I snapped my mouth shut, clenching my jaw as I quickened my steps to get a better view. He remained still and silent as I took the sight in, dread filling my soul.

"This was the price for traveling to Landing's End?" I whispered, unable to keep myself from tracing the raised scars that marred the entirety of his back.

The price for visiting a 'petty brat?'

Layers upon layers of long, thin lines crisscrossed his taut skin from the top of his shoulders to his hips. There was no way to count them as they blurred into one mangled mess in the center. He was lucky not to have his spine damaged and that he could still move freely.

Sainte was silent as I traced the newest marks. The red welts were healed, but obviously fresher than the rest. He shivered as my fingertip trailed to the center of his back, and I pressed my palm where the indent of his spine should be.

"A month isn't long to gather recruits."

I frowned, stepping aside to search his face. He held my stare with an un-readable expression. Not angry or hurt, simply resigned to his punishment. He didn't drop his gaze. Instead, he studied me, watching for my reaction.

My stomach churned as shame sank like a stone in my gut. "Why? Why did you keep coming?" I whispered, my features contorted with guilt.

"I couldn't let a little girl down."

His lips pressed tight and attempted to shift the sleeve off his injured arm with a grimace. I reached out to help, removing the wet fabric.

I dropped his tunic and pulled him toward me to inspect the wound. "You were the only one who didn't."

The arrow had pierced his bicep, leaving an angry red wound free of streaks, reassuring me it wasn't infected. Carefully, I rotated the limb to check the exit, relieved to find it clean and healing. Both marks were scabbed over with slight cracks oozing fresh blood.

"You'll live." I cleared my throat, stooping to retrieve his wet tunic.

"I'm relieved."

With a haughty sneer, I left to hang it on a branchy section of driftwood before finding a seat facing the woods. Birdsong and wind rustling through the foliage entwined with the soft brush of fabric as he undressed, followed by the splashes of his washing.

As a child, I believed he cared, missed me even, and that was why he visited. As I grew, I didn't care why he came, just that he did. He was the highlight of my year, the one who put up with my rebellion without a judgmental word to say about it. After my sixteenth birthday, I mentally accused him of stringing me along for the fun of it. With recent developments, I still felt used—but that was a lot to endure for a person.

How many times had he been flogged?

I'd seen my fair share of flogging scars in the slums, yet none amounted to that mass of marred skin. He suffered that much to use me? Couldn't he have sent someone else to keep an eye out, to send word that I was alive and well? Why risk such pain to spend one day with me?

Unless...

Unless he really did care about me.

I curled over my knees, pressing my fingers over my eyes. Out of everyone I knew, I trusted him the most. Despite his departure and the sense of abandonment it brought, even after he kidnapped me, it was hard to erase years of loyalty. Sainte was embedded into my soul as deep as my own heart. He showed up regardless of weather or circumstance. He was the single person I could count on who never failed me.

If only I could convince him I wasn't cut out to be a princess.

After blowing out a shaky breath, I glared up at the sky. Religion was not rampant on the streets, nor in Kelsie's home. My faith in the gods was faulty at best. But I would've prayed to one if I knew which would hear me.

The slosh of water signaled him getting out, and I waited patiently while he dressed.

There was an extra horse—a potential means of escape. Though the thought of returning to my friends sent a pang of regret through my chest. The more I learned about Sainte and Wynterborne, the worse I felt for planning my escape.

That, and he would always find me.

A strip of white linen dangled beside my face, pulling me from my spiraling thoughts. Twisting, I squinted up at him, doing my best not to gawk at his bare chest. I was a grown woman. I knew better than to ogle my kidnapper.

He dipped his chin, gesturing to his right arm, then wiggled the linen again. I threw my legs over the log and took the bandage. My heart settled with a sense of rightness, like it was happy I saw to his wounds.

"Stupid," I muttered, securing the bandage a little tighter than necessary.

Sainte grunted as I finished tying it in a bow with a flourish. The red that already seeped through pulled at my frown. Slowly, he raised his arm and flexed his biceps with a wince, revealing the strain of his injury.

Fish guts, he was built, though.

I cleared my throat, then strode over to his drenched tunic. With a swift turn, I made to throw it without realizing he followed close behind. The fabric slapped against his chest, and I glared, frustration evident in my expression.

"We're headed out after this."

"Right," I grumbled. "Have to take the princess to her prison. Ahem, I mean castle."

Stupid heart. Stupid, stupid heart.

CHAPTER 6

I clung to Sainte, my arms tight around him, resting my forehead between his shoulders. My body shook with a wet cough, rattling my lungs. As it faded, I rested more of my weight against him, seeking support.

"She'd do better in an inn," a soldier suggested. Otto?

I hadn't a clue what half their names were, and my exhaustion made it so I couldn't care less.

"Dare we risk it?" another said. "We're too far from a city for my liking."

"That, or risk her in the open air with water in her lungs."

Oi, I got most of it out.

"It's not Winter's Bite. She looks strong enough to handle it."

"She'd be more suited to handle the Bite. I say we push on to an inn. Captain?"

Sainte remained silent, and the gentle sway of the horse nearly lulled me into sleep before he spoke.

"No—the next hut we see."

A chorus of disappointed groans rolled through the group.

As I cracked my eyes open, the fading sun painted the overgrown road in hues of gold and shadow. I wasn't too concerned about finding a roof over my head—exhaustion lured me into its embrace, and all I craved was rest.

Our little crew pressed on, slowing as the moons rose. The night's chill bit at my fingers, and at one point, Sainte cupped his hand over mine, pinning them to his abdomen. I grabbed fistfuls of his tunic, trying to stay coherent enough to keep my seat.

He jerked on the reins. "Hold."

Startled, I broke into a fit of coughs, my throat sore and raw.

"Urien–"

"Aye."

Quiet creaks of leather and the snap of small twigs disturbed the night's silence. I straightened, examining the crowded road. Twin moons mirrored each other above, both full, lending ample light despite the shroud of trees. A dim, flickering candle cast a soft glow through the carved window of a shack nestled along the path ahead. The structure, akin to a horse stall at a typical inn, offered enough space to shield from the cold, but lacked the roominess to be comfortable during warmer seasons.

I rested my temple against Sainte's shoulder as Urien approached the small door hanging precariously on a single hinge.

"Hail." His call was soft, yet carried through the night, barely audible above the nocturnal creatures.

A muffled response came from inside, and at Sainte's nod, Urien approached, gently pushing the door open. He paused, surveying the shack's interior before returning to the group.

"It's a witch, but she's alone."

"Do you trust it?" Sainte asked quietly.

The moonlight illuminated a figure in a long dress with a shawl over her head, standing at the threshold.

"'Tis my principle never to trust a witch," Urien scoffed, then shrugged. "I don't think we'll be wandering upon any better tonight, though."

"Bring her in," her dry voice rasped from her hovel.

The ambient sounds around us dwindled into silence. Crickets ceased chirping, owls silenced their hooting, rodents halted their scurrying—everything fell quiet.

Sainte grunted, shifting in his seat. "Where there's a witch, there's a town."

Witches were familiar territory. They spoke in riddles and claimed to have visions within their dreams. Still, their usefulness usually ended with potions, and even then, few concoctions actually worked for me.

And they all had something to prophesy about my 'heritage.'

Sainte clicked his tongue, urging his horse to walk. "Move on."

Urien mounted, and we rode past the witch's shack. Her skin resembled an aged grape, wrinkled, dry, and sagging. A long, crooked nose adorned her face, while her jowls hung low, revealing the redness of her eye sockets. Her dark, mysterious leer followed me, glittering in the dim light.

"Peace, *Princess*," she hissed.

I huddled into Sainte's back, a shiver of fear shooting down my spine.

The witches I'd encountered before were unsettling with their potions and cryptic words, but this one exuded raw power. Her dark gaze held a knowing, haunting intensity.

"Steady." Sainte spoke low and placed his hand over mine, holding me against him.

Maybe it was the eerie glow of the twin moons that heightened my unease, but encountering a witch lurking in wait as we passed didn't bode well for my nerves.

Sainte's earlier assessment proved true when, moments later, the dense forest gave way to a village nestled among the trees. The cozy homes, clustered together, appeared inviting yet secluded. We approached the first house. Its quaint fenced-in yard and small stable added to the rustic charm. As we neared, Urien dismounted and started for the door.

A man draped in a fur cloak answered. He eyed our group warily, speaking in low tones. Coin exchanged hands, and we secured refuge for the night. A bed—even a simple mattress on the floor would be welcome. It wasn't like I was accustomed to much, princess or not.

I stumbled behind Sainte as he walked inside. A candle cast flickering light across the modest room, its warm glow dancing on the walls. I coughed, the air heavy with the scent of woodsmoke and dried herbs. My eyes roamed the shadows, wondering where everyone would sleep.

The stranger folded his beefy arms across his chest, lifting his chin. "If ye'r carryin' the plague–"

"A tumble in the river," Sainte interrupted, speaking Muik. "A single night under a roof is all we ask."

The man grabbed the candle, lifting it to peer at me. He was in his middle years, eyes weary, dark hair mussed with sleep. Satisfied with what he saw, he huffed and walked to a corner where a blanket was nailed to the ceiling. He pushed it aside to reveal a small mat stuffed with straw.

"'Tis the best ye'll find 'round these parts."

I blinked, waiting. When Sainte gave his nod of approval, I needed no further encouragement. I flopped ungracefully, pulling the worn blanket to my chin. My heavy eyes fluttered shut, and exhaustion dragged me into a glorious sleep.

We traveled hard the next few days, resulting in sore legs and nether regions, but the ache in my heart worried me the most.

When I stirred from my slumber, unease weighed heavy on my chest. The men bustled about the campsite. Their hushed conversations and movements held their focus elsewhere, oblivious to my presence. I frowned, burrowing deeper into the blanket, then slid my fingers between my legs. At the feel of dampness, my jaw clenched, and I brought my hand into the sunlight—a sheen of crimson.

"You're hurt?" Sainte's voice was rough with sleep.

I yelped, shoving my arm beneath the fabric, then scrunched my eyes shut. Maybe I could ignore him. Perhaps this was simply a terrible dream.

One could wish.

I grimaced as Sainte crouched beside me, his hand gently tugging at the blanket.

"No," I grumbled, holding it tight.

"Are you hurt?" he repeated.

"No," I snapped again, burying my head as if I could hide from all my problems.

After a moment of silence, the sound of his retreating footsteps signaled his departure.

I sighed with relief and scowled at the morning sky. This was miserable. At least I had Kelsie when I first started bleeding. When I fled, Lyana taught me how to care for it on the streets. Now, I had to figure out how to cope surrounded by a group of men who wouldn't understand. Chances were, my trousers needed a good wash, as well as the blanket. Though my pants weren't high on my priority list, they were already being stained beyond repair.

Ethyan avoided Lyana and me when we bled, treating us as if we had some contagious disease. We used that time to enjoy each other's company, free of his incessant nagging.

Funny how he would exhale in relief upon learning he hadn't fathered a babe, yet was repelled by the physical signs of a woman's body showing it was without child.

Men were so double-minded.

As footsteps approached, I twisted to see Sainte. With a swift tug, he stretched a tunic to its limits before it tore. Each rip drew a wince for the wasted cloth. He moved closer, gaze fixed on his task, and I frowned, curiosity piqued. When he dropped into a crouch beside me, holding out the strips and a waterskin, I froze.

"Go, clean up," he said.

I stared at his offering with narrowed eyes. He didn't appear disgusted or appalled, and spoke as if this were a common occurrence. It certainly was for *me*, but I wasn't accustomed to men treating it so casually.

"You don't happen to have a spare pair of trousers?" I shoved myself upright, accepted the items, then sipped from the waterskin.

"None that would fit."

"That doesn't matter," I muttered. "I'll be riding a horse, Sainte. I want clean pants."

He pulled his lips to the side thoughtfully, watching as Urien finished saddling his stallion. He eyed our scrutiny with a raised brow, then headed our way.

"Good morn, Princess," he called with a cheerful cadence, though his smile wavered as I shifted with discomfort under his gaze.

Sainte pushed himself to stand. "Your trousers, Urien."

"Eh?" He peered at his pants, then up at Sainte with a confused wrinkle on his brow. "What about them?"

"I need your spare—"

Urien blinked, looking between us.

"—Now."

The soldier turned on his heel, rubbing the nape of his neck as he trudged back to his horse.

Men lingered near their mounts, now watching our exchange.

"Is it safe to assume your soldiers won't shy away from a bit of blood?" I asked, mortified that a group of strangers would witness this.

His blue eyes darted over his group, and he pressed his lips. "I'll saddle your horse."

My face brightened as I gazed up at him. The situation wasn't nearly as bad if it meant I'd finally ride on my own. My poor muscles were exhausted from riding double with Sainte, balancing behind him. And my crotch ached from pressing against the lip of the saddle, a discomfort I was sure he was aware of.

Also... that chestnut mare had long legs—perfect for outpacing the men's sturdier drafts.

Urien retrieved a pair of trousers and headed back our way with a frown. When he handed it to Sainte, who then passed it to me, recognition lit his features.

"Ah, she bleeds!" he said, dipping his chin.

I glared, though it wasn't like I'd be able to hide it. Still, his blunt voice was far more uncomfortable than Sainte's subtle nature of addressing it.

He waggled his brow with a jeering smirk. "At least there's not a bastard on the way."

There it was. The relief that a woman wasn't with child.

"Not that it's your business, Urien, but I could have told you that," I grumbled.

Sainte jerked his head toward the others. "Clear the men out, but leave the chestnut. Wait for us on the road."

I scowled, waiting for him to turn his lanky arse around. He shot me an obliging grin, then nodded. On his way back, he barked orders to mount up. The men shared a few confused glances and half-hearted shrugs, and soon, they disappeared beyond the treeline.

"Clean up." Sainte stalked over to the mare to finish readying her tack.

After a deep breath, I detached myself from the blanket and stood. Bright red blood stained the inside of my thighs, but the bedroll was a dark brown, proving my pants saw the worst of it. After I gathered the fabric strips and waterskin, I hurried into the trees opposite of the men.

I washed up, folding my torn, withered pants. I wasn't one to waste and planned to clean them at the next water source. Urien's trousers were too big, hanging loose around my waist. I rolled the hems, then secured the waistline with Ethyan's belt, cinching it tight.

When I returned, Sainte watched as I approached, holding his hand out for my trousers and waterskin.

"Thank you," I said sincerely, surprised by his reaction and assistance.

I expected to be treated as a burden as I always had by men. When I looked at the mare, thinking of how fast she might outpace the others, my heart felt heavy.

Curse this guilt.

Without a word, Sainte packed the items away, then knelt near the chestnut, knitting his fingers. No time to dwell on the fact that I'd never ridden a horse by myself.

It couldn't be too hard, could it?

I cleared my throat, stepped into his hands, and pulled myself into the saddle. As the mare shifted beneath me, I grabbed her red mane and reached down to Sainte, who stood holding the reins.

He arched a single brow. "I'm not that stupid."

While I cursed under my breath, he mounted, and we rode to meet the others. Most avoided eye contact, behaving as I anticipated. It was as if I carried some dark curse, and they feared that by staring too long, I might cast it upon them with a mere flick of my fingers.

The group paused often, allowing me to wash and bury the bloody rags. Riding was uncomfortable, but it was a far cry from having to share horseback with Sainte. We maintained a steady pace despite the frequent breaks.

A few days and ripped tunics later, my bleeding stopped, and I was permitted to continue riding alone. Of course, I was ponied along, never allowed to have the reins.

Regret burdened me as time passed. Did Lyana and Ethyan miss me? Were they convinced I'd seize any chance to return? My heart ached for them, but unlike the people of Landing's End, Sainte extended a rare courtesy. He took care of me, treating me as his equal.

He was such a polite abductor.

The next city we rode into was small compared to those along the coast. The dirt-packed streets housed a few shops, homes, and a well-established inn with a large tavern and clean stable. A rickety sign on the post near the entrance read, 'Wandering Wolf.' A fitting name considering the nightly howls.

We enjoyed our first warm meal in weeks, and I devoured it. With Urien seated on my left, and Sainte on my right, my eyes scanned every exit and hiding place, even as guilt ate me inside out. The plan was to wait until nightfall, sneak out to my horse, then push south. There were busier roads than the one we traveled, allowing more opportunity to profit off passing travelers.

"There's nothing like hot food to warm the bones after a long journey!" Grimm bellowed with a bright smile as he patted his belly.

Urien laughed, then smirked at my plate. "Better than most fare you ate, I'd wager."

"Aye, though I always had fresh fruit," I said, poking at the dried apples in my pork pie.

"Stolen, no doubt."

"But just as sweet."

He rested his elbows on the table, clasping his fingers below his chin. "Stolen goods leave a sour taste."

"Perhaps in the vendor's mouth," I shrugged, "but not in mine."

Once I finished my meal, I stretched my hands overhead, forcing out a yawn, then stood. "Well, I should probably head to bed."

Sainte watched me out of the corner of his eye, nudging his empty bowl away. "Watch Grimm," he said to Urien as he pushed to his feet.

The man in question had migrated to a game table where he slowly edged his great frame onto a bench. The others in our troupe gathered around as he palmed a hand of cards.

"Might win some coin tonight," Urien mused.

"Don't let him make a scene."

I gave Sainte a sidelong glance. Surely he would let me have my own room. He respected my privacy thus far. I just needed one more night, one more lapse in his judgment.

With an outstretched arm, he herded me between the crowded tables to the small staircase tucked between the dining hall and bustling kitchen. As he led the way, ascending the stairs, I tried my hardest not to watch his strong legs move beneath his trousers as a sense of disappointment nipped at my resolve.

No.

I would not feel bad about leaving him.

He drugged me, *kidnapped* me. If I thought too long about it, I could still taste that vile potion on my lips. And, to top it off, he nearly killed me by tossing me into the river. Not to mention he threw away *my* shirt.

I glanced down at his tunic that I wore.

Curse it all, he'd stick in my memory for weeks unless I ditched it for another.

Down the hall, he held open the door like a proper nobleman, allowing me to pass through first. I stepped inside the cramped space, noticing a bed so small I doubted I'd fit on it. He started to follow me in, but I pivoted, halting his entry.

"Oh, no," I said, placing a hand on the doorframe. "Not tonight. I want privacy."

He stopped short with a furrowed brow. His mouth was pressed in a firm line, and I tore my gaze away from his lips. Something low in my belly fluttered at his proximity, and I cleared my throat, trying to hide the blush that crept to my cheeks.

"Why?" he asked, eyes narrowed.

I heaved a dramatic sigh and braced my weight against the door. "I've been plastered to your side for weeks, sleeping among your men under the moons. My only privacy has been a blanket between us and trips to relieve myself. Please, just this once, give me space."

My stomach clenched as I erased all sign of nervousness from my face and lifted my eyebrows in a pleading gaze.

I hoped it worked.

He took a deep breath, and I grinned, knowing I had won.

"I'll be right outside your door. Urien will be at the window."

I swallowed past the lump in my throat and lunged, grabbing him in an embrace. He grunted as I squeezed my arms around his middle, pressing my cheek against his chest. It would be the first and last time I held him—I would allow myself this moment.

Sainte didn't move, his muscles clenched and tense. When I backed away, his eyes were wide and somewhat horrified. My heart twisted, and I ignored the stab of betrayal.

"Thank you."

"Elspeth—"

I backed into the room.

"—don't run."

"I won't."

I shut the door on my lie, chewing my lip. I hated this. Why did he have to make this so hard? Why couldn't he just leave me alone? Or at the least *act* like a bad guy so that I could actually be mad at him?

Rubbing my chest to ease the deep ache, I approached the window—a mere hole covered with thin fabric to keep bugs out. The road below was empty, save for a few patrons meandering about. Urien wouldn't be down there yet, likely engrossed in watching Grimm.

With another glance at the door, I sucked in a steadying breath. This was it. I was done playing his game. It was time to make my move, not follow his lead.

I turned back to the window and slowly ripped the edge of the fabric.

CHAPTER 7

The chestnut mare went lame after my second day on my own. I didn't know enough about horses to determine if it was due to a stone in her shoe or something more serious. Perhaps she was simply fed up with my rambling conversation and inexperienced riding. I removed her tack, keeping the bridle for trade and the blanket for warmth, then sent her west, hoping to confuse Sainte and his men.

By my fourth day, I had traded the bridle for a hunk of musty cheese and hard bread. It was a poor exchange, but I didn't have many options. Most folk just eyed me warily and crossed the street. I ended up taking another road east, hoping if I followed it, I might get close enough to Landing's End to know my location.

My current predicament found me with a gnawing ache in my belly, a stark reminder of my unmet hunger, running from the man I tried to rob in the dead of night. I sprinted through the darkness—a tiptoeing, prancing gait, but running nonetheless. It was the best I could manage in the utter black. The sky was veiled in dark clouds, obscuring even the faintest glimmer of moonlight that tried to filter through the dense canopy overhead.

As I sped through the forest, my foot caught on an exposed root, sending me sprawling. My palms slammed against the damp earth, and I shoved myself up, leaves rustling under my frantic movements. I knew my pursuer couldn't see me, but my clumsy escape was a symphony of noise, betraying my position.

Low-hanging branches and thorn-covered brambles slashed at my arms and legs as I fled. If I'd only triple-checked the man was asleep, I wouldn't be in this situation. I had hoped to secure *something* to fill my belly, but instead, my efforts led to stumbling through the woods in a hunger-induced haze.

Footsteps crashed behind me, closing in fast, and I mustered energy from somewhere, forcing myself to move faster.

Ahead in the darkness, it looked as if the trees thinned into a clearing. Were my chances better in the open? I might outpace him on even terrain. Mind made up, I propelled forward. I burst through that treeline, taking a glorious bush-free step–

Right into a ditch.

I fell flat on my face, nose smarting as my head smacked into the dirt.

"Got you!"

I rolled onto my back as his tall shadow detached from the woods, looming over me.

"See now, I didn't mean any harm." I scrambled backward. "I only–"

"El?"

I froze, then flopped to my belly, squinting down the road. Two figures sat atop bedrolls not fifteen paces off.

One with a bow drawn.

"Ethyan? Lyana?"

"Off with you then, you big oaf!" Lyana cried, pushing to stand. She stalked over with all the confidence of a port guard, swagger in her step and all.

"She's a thief!" The man jabbed an accusing finger my way. "Tried to rob me in my sleep!"

I pulled myself onto the road, limbs shaking from exertion, though he made no effort to retrieve me.

"We'll deal with her," Ethyan called, his aim steady.

"I expect you will," he hissed, "or you'll be missing bits when you wake."

"'Tis our risk to take."

Lyana rushed to my side, offering a hand. I gladly took it, and she grunted as she helped me up. The traveler grumbled a few curses, spat in our direction, then disappeared among the trees.

"Fancy seeing you here."

I wrapped my arms around her and squeezed so tight she fought to get a breath. Tears pricked my eyes as a surge of relief washed over me like a warm tide. These were my people, allies who had my back. No longer would I have to scheme for escape or flee.

They were the family I chose.

"Robbing a man in the dead of night? Alone?" Ethyan asked. "You must be hungry."

I loosened my grip and peered through the darkness as he rummaged through his things.

"There's only a few scraps left from our hare," he said, "but it's better than nothing."

I ran to their blankets and plopped beside him, picking at the thin carcass. "I can't believe you followed."

Lyana dropped next to me, a lopsided smile on her cheeks. "Well, we didn't really follow. Gods above—we don't know anything about tracking across miles of countryside. But we had a general idea of direction."

"But look at you, girl! You got away on your own," Ethyan mused, rubbing at his arm. It had to be sore from the length of the draw he held on the man. He lacked the strength to sustain a draw for long, but he was a fantastic shot when he loosed arrows in quick succession.

I smirked, shaking my head at how easy my escape was. Sainte either trusted me to stay put or Grimm played a furious game, keeping Urien distracted. Now I only had to evade them until my twenty-first birthday, which was closing in fast.

We conversed well into the night as I recounted the experience of my near-drowning and the witch with her ominous knowledge of me. Lyana narrowed her eyes at the mention of Sainte, and I averted my gaze, worried she might notice my guilt.

When all was said, we curled up together on the side of the road, and I slept peacefully for the first time in weeks.

I chuckled as Lyana danced atop the table, her feet prancing along with the bard's tune. Patrons cheered and moved their mugs to make room as she twirled. Meanwhile, Ethyan lingered in the corner, engaged in a game of knife-throwing with some locals, winning us each a savory hand pie and a refreshing mug of water.

After three days of traveling, I found myself cherishing their company more than ever. Our time apart gave me a newfound appreciation for their presence. Lyana was the friend I never had growing up, ready to listen whenever I needed to talk. And Ethyan embodied the protective brother figure I always wished I had. His caring nature often masked his playful, sometimes obnoxious, demeanor.

I hummed along with the bard as he worked his fiddle, patrons drumming against the tables in time. Lyana, breaths heaving, danced with increased vigor, leaping from table to table as cheers erupted around us. Her energy was infectious, filling the tavern with a sense of celebration. Amidst the laughter and music, I couldn't help but smile, knowing that despite the chilly night ahead, our bellies would be full and our spirits high.

A sour thought wormed into my mind about a certain man searching for me out in the cold. I frowned, squashing the image before it consumed me with guilt.

I hadn't told Lyana how I felt about anything yet, but by the looks she gave me whenever Sainte came up, she knew.

Swirling the water in my mug, I peered into it, contemplating my situation. I didn't regret running for my freedom. Everyone should have the right to choose their path in life, free from coercion. I considered myself lucky to have escaped a royal upbringing that would have forced me into a role I despised. Instead, I was instilled with the belief that I belonged among the common folk, regardless of my bloodline, and I was fine with that.

My childhood dreams were a far cry from the typical fantasies of little girls. They imagined themselves as forgotten princesses from distant realms that would someday be summoned back to a life of luxury and adoration.

All while I suffered nightmares of my brother killing me if I ever returned.

For that, I was quite content with my commoner's status. However, my rebellious spirit prevented me from pursuing a conventional trade. In cities like Port Siren, opportunities for women were limited—mainly regulated to the paths of a whore or a wife.

Still, I was happy with my friends and our bell tower. Sainte's distant presence brought a sense of security, knowing he was out there, but far enough away that I could harbor my bitterness.

Why did he have to stir all this up?

"El!" Lyana struggled over, shoving through the crowded tavern.

I sucked in a startled breath, my gaze snapping toward the open door. There, the setting sun cast a silhouette against several familiar figures.

Urien, with Grimm and the others a pace behind.

"Gorseth's blue balls!" I cursed.

My chair toppled as I leapt from my seat, darting for the rear of the tavern. I shoved people aside, and a maid's tray toppled, splattering my back with hot soup. The sting had me biting my tongue, but I didn't slow. I squeezed between two burly figures, a clamor of crashing objects echoing in my wake.

The innkeeper cupped his mouth, pointing toward the exit. "That way, girl!"

With a nod of thanks, I rushed in the direction he gestured. Before I sped through the kitchens, I glanced over my shoulder to see Lyana jumping onto Urien's back, while Ethyan charged, blade in hand.

I practically fell down the few slick steps outside, then took off down the alley at a run. When I found the main road, it was eerily quiet, which should have been my first warning... but I ignored it.

I rushed for the shops, hoping to slip into a barn or shed until the men moved on. Hoofbeats pounded against the hard-packed earth, closing in fast. I urged my legs to move faster, then turned, darting down the nearest alley. Breath heaving, I whirled, spotting a familiar white stallion, Sainte hauling back on the reins.

"No, no, no!" I ran, blood rushing to my ears.

Hooves slammed against the cobblestones. Curse the beast's agility!

I burst from the end of the shops, frustration gnawing at me as I faced the woods, legs still pumping. With nowhere to hide—even in the forest, I couldn't outpace him. Shifting tactics, I pivoted on my heel and staggered back, raising my hands in surrender.

"Look, I'm sure we can talk about this—oof!"

Sainte didn't stop. Gods, I don't think he slowed as he snared my wrist, pulling me through the air. The momentum jerked me off my feet. I screamed, clawing for purchase to pull myself away from the horse's pounding hooves. He grunted and yanked the reins left, hauling me up at the same time.

Then he threw me over the front of the saddle as if I were a sack of grain.

I cursed with each stride, the hard leather digging into my ribs. I twisted, ready to demand he let me up, but the words died on my lips.

Rage seeped through his glare and I didn't think there was a curse strong enough to express the anger in his eyes. As the stallion galloped out of town, I could only try to keep myself still, and pray I didn't break a rib in this position.

Gods knew Sainte didn't seem to care.

We rode in silence throughout the night. Horse sweat drenched my tunic and trousers. I winced with each step of its trotting gait, but was fairly confident I hadn't broken anything. My feet and hands felt as if a thousand bees were stinging them, and no amount of wiggling or shaking relieved it. My head throbbed, a relentless pulse behind my eyes. Every muscle ached, protesting each jostle and bump of the journey. Despite the discomfort, I didn't dare ask for a break or a chance to sit upright. Even my bladder's urgent demands went ignored.

Sainte's current state was unlike anything I'd witnessed before. He'd been angry or disappointed with me in the past, but this level of ire was unprecedented. Normally, he took my well-being into account, albeit in a bull-headed manner. This new carelessness cut deeper than his anger ever could.

We stopped once in the early morning, when he dismounted to relieve himself. I attempted to shift and straighten to share the saddle, but an icy glare over his shoulder killed my effort. After fixing his trousers, he pivoted toward the horse and mounted.

"Care to allow me the same relief?" I asked with a nervous grin.

He ignored me without so much as a glance as he shoved me forward, almost on the horse's neck. It snorted and stamped its foot as Sainte gathered the reins, then urged the beast back into motion.

We rode through the day with no breaks, and as the sun began its descent, nausea set in. The swaying gait combined with my awkward position, the meager food in my belly, and the day's thirst, resulted in me spewing all contents from my stomach. The horse shied to the side, snorting as I wiped my mouth.

At least I didn't puke on anything valuable.

Sainte pulled to a halt and dismounted without a word. At my feet, he shoved one of my legs upward. I obliged him, moaning as I shifted my body to sit in the saddle and lean against the horse's neck. He refused to look at me, his jaw clenched tight as he strode forward guiding the horse with a firm grip on the reins. I was too ill to find any sense of accomplishment or pleasure in my small victory.

He walked through the night, pressing on until morning. When the stallion faltered beneath my weight, he stopped, assessing the animal's weary legs. With a sigh, he guided the beast to a nearby tree, securing it before slipping the bit from its mouth. Without a word, he reached below to loosen the saddle's girth. I scrambled to dismount before he stranded me up there. My attempt resulted in a less-than-graceful fall on my arse, leaving me to gaze up at Sainte beneath the horse's white belly. The muscle in his jaw flicked as he looked away, continuing his task.

I tried to stand, struggling with my balance on legs that felt as if they weren't my own. After a few curses, I got myself upright with the help of a low branch, then limped from tree to tree, deeper into the woods. I swear I heard the first curse grace Sainte's lips before he stomped after me.

With a hand on my hip, I spun, giving him the deadliest glare I could muster. "Look, I've been holding my piss for over a day, Sainte! If you can't leave me in peace, prepare for a show!"

He stopped five paces from me and crossed his arms over his armor, returning my glower, though his was far more frightening. Muttering every curse I knew about stubborn men, I stepped behind a tree that I hoped was big enough for decency's sake and relieved myself. He at least stayed on the other side, allowing me a semblance of privacy.

Once I finished, I returned to him, arms spread wide in good humor. "Look, I didn't run!"

He snatched my arm, leading me back to the horse.

"Sainte, really?" I stumbled, struggling to keep pace. "Stop—please."

"Stop?!"

Throw me in a pigsty—that was apparently the wrong thing to say.

"*Stop*, Elspeth?!"

I flinched at his tone and attempted to pull away as he yanked me closer to his chest. Blue sparks flew from his glare, and a vein pulsed at his temple.

"We have seven days to make it to Wynterborne, and you want me to *stop*–"

"Yes!" I jerked my arm, but his grip held. "I don't want to go! Just–"

"You've made that clear," he spat. "Yet, here we are. You're going regardless."

"Gods above, Sainte! What happens when we get there and I say, 'No, actually I don't mind at all if you are crowned, brother.' and slip away?"

"Slip away? He'll kill you."

"And that will be your fault for dragging me there!"

"Guilting me over your death before you even arrive? Try harder," he snarled, shoving me off.

"You're petty and selfish," he growled, removing the saddle.

"What can I say? It's how I was raised."

"You were raised better than that."

"How would you know? You were barely ever there!"

"Thrice-curse it all, Elspeth! Do you not remember when we talked about Wynterborne? When I told you the horrors your people lived through?"

"Of course not. I was a *child*. Nothing sticks."

He tore a brush from his pack and set to brushing the horse with harsh strokes. "I was preparing you for your return, as the salvation–"

"How exactly do you expect a child to process horror stories of her homeland? Stories of people starving, locked away in isolation?"

"You do remember." He ducked under the horse's neck to tilt his head in an 'I told you so' fashion.

"No, actually, I don't! I tuned out all those awful things, choosing to focus on the fact that the *one* person I believed truly cared about me was there!" I shouted. The horse nickered, pushing Sainte with its shoulder. "Come to find out, he didn't care! I was just a tool, a pawn he could slip into place for his own agenda. Someone he could control!"

"You were never a tool to me." The brush strokes faded as he stilled. "You were only ever Elspeth."

The remorse in his tone sapped the anger from my bones, if not the rebellion. "Sainte–"

I sighed and walked around the stallion to face him. He refused to meet my gaze, staring at the sweat-soaked horsehair.

"If I was not a tool then, why am I now?"

My heart twisted and ached in my chest as he took a deep shuddering breath, then braced himself against the horse, studying me.

"Who am I?"

"What?" I shook my head, confused.

He closed his eyes, forcing his patience, and repeated his question. "Who am I?"

"Sainte...?"

"Aye, now *what* am I?"

"A soldier?"

"A Wynterborne soldier," he corrected. The dark circles under his pained, tired gaze conveyed just how hard he pushed himself on this journey. "A Wynterborne citizen sworn to uphold and honor the people. I serve the crowned, and uncrowned—the protector of both. Does that make me only a tool?"

A scowl scrunched my features. "Well, I guess you're a pawn too, then," I huffed. "Is that supposed to make me feel better?"

He pushed off the horse and held his arms out in supplication. "Am I not still Sainte? The man who rode hard for weeks to greet a girl once a year? Tell me, Elspeth, am I just a tool for your birthday mischief?"

I dropped my gaze and scuffed the dirt with the toe of my boot. He couldn't fathom his significance in my life. To express the depth of my feelings, the extent of how deeply I cared, seemed impossible. He wasn't a tool or a pawn—not to me. I considered him a friend, a loyal companion, even if only for one day.

I sniffed and ignored his question, choosing to go sit by the saddle. He let me sulk as he tended his horse. His only words were soft murmurings as he felt the beast's legs. As the sun sank near the horizon, I curled into myself. Exhaustion weighed heavily on me, both physical and mental. Inner conflict ran rampant—a desire to please Sainte, to do as he asked, clashed against the urge to flee.

I was scared.

I wasn't afraid to voice my thoughts—I was terrified. Not because of my brother. I hadn't seen Adastrus in years. He was nothing more than a terrible story, a bad dream. With Sainte at my side, I feared no man.

I was afraid of letting people down.

I was a street rat. A commoner. I was Elspeth of Landing's End, not a princess. I didn't know the first thing about high court or politics. What about the dances and proper etiquette? Not only would I make a fool of myself, but I would embarrass all those who hoped I was something more. I stuck out like a sore thumb in Port Siren's noble district. How much worse would I fare when thrown into a palace and paraded about as royalty?

Sainte's groan echoed in the dimming light as he settled beside me. The sudden widening of my eyes betrayed my surprise as he took hold of my hands, winding a rope around my wrists. A sharp sting of betrayal cut deeper as each knot tightened. Tension sparked, palpable and all-consuming, as he looped the rope about his waist, securing our bond.

"You are Princess Elspeth of Wynterborne, a tool to be used *wisely*, by yourself and others." He pushed out an exasperated sigh, leaning against the saddle. "But you are also a person. You won't lose yourself."

I deflated, and the emotion clogging my throat seeped through my chest, straight to my heart.

The rough rope dug into the soft skin on my wrists as I fought to hold the flood of hopeless tears at bay.

"I wouldn't let you," he muttered.

CHAPTER 8

Days blurred by in a rush. And while the animosity and tension between us dissipated, we only spoke as much as necessary. I struggled to maintain my anger at the man who, no matter what I threw at him, still cared about me. No matter how often I ran away, or spit in the face of his efforts, he always found me.

He was nothing if not loyal... even if only to his own cause.

I curbed my tongue, resigned to the fact that there was no escape this time. When we weren't riding his tired horse, we were walking at a brisk pace. His attention and focus no longer wavered between me and his men. We met others on the road, but only managed a nod or glance in acknowledgment. No one cared who we were or where we came from.

The further north we ventured, the colder the air grew, its chill pierced like tiny needles. Sainte offered his cloak, which warded off the worst of the bite, but it still seeped through, nipping at my skin. The extra layer concealed the soup stain on my back, masking the scent that inevitably blended with my unwashed state. Even Sainte carried an odor, one that was far from pleasant.

The wind howled across the vast plains, stirring the weathered grass as a city's silhouette emerged in the distance. Encased in towering walls, it stood as a fortress against the outside world. Two wagons halted at the gate, the guards mere specs from my vantage point. I squinted, trying to make out their movements as they inspected the cargo.

A gust tore my hood back, and my short black hair danced about. I grumbled, pulling it over my head. With aching fingers, I clutched the fabric, holding it in place against the frigid breeze.

"Tell me we're stopping," I groaned.

"No."

Our relentless hunger worsened with each passing mile, for which I was probably to blame. Sainte shared his meager rations, though they amounted to little more than crumbs at this point. The horse trembled beneath our weight, its gaunt frame a testament to our journey's hardship. Exhaustion slackened our shoulders and slowed our progress, and we probably looked as bad as we felt.

"I would kill for a hot bowl of soup."

Sainte pulled off the road, into the sparse woodland. "There will be time for food later."

"That doesn't help my belly *now*."

When he dismounted, I sighed, assuming he meant to relieve himself before we made the trek across the plains. Instead, he rummaged through his pack, retrieving his rope.

"What's that for?" I asked, eyeing it with disdain.

I understood his need for it at night, but we shared the saddle now. Escape seemed impossible with his chest against my back, and his strong arms around me.

Not that I took special note of how strong they were.

Without a word, he pulled my left hand down, motioning for my right.

"Really, Sainte? I won't run, I swear."

"You've said that before," he sighed. "These men can't perceive you as a threat to the throne."

My heart thudded hard with anxiety. How many days had we traveled again? Was there still a chance to get out of this?

"Are we that close to Wynterborne?" I glanced at the city, extending my right hand without thought.

He tied the rope loosely about my wrists. I looked down at him and frowned, wiggling my fingers.

"Two day's hard ride," he said. "We'll make it in one."

The weight of it all crashed into me, as if the air grew heavy. A shudder snaked down my spine, coiling in my gut.

"I can't do it," I whispered to myself.

"You can." He mounted behind me, urging the stallion back toward the road. "You will."

The shiver rattling in my bones had nothing to do with the cold as I yanked the hood lower over my face. There was no shirking this now. No escaping. I was doomed to whatever fate had in store for me.

"Easy."

It might have been my imagination, but I swore his arms squeezed me tighter. Not caring if that was the case, I burrowed against his chest and tugged at the rope securing my wrists.

"Make those look tighter than they are. And keep your head down."

"Else someone might murder me on the street?" I muttered.

"It's a possibility."

I hoped to detect a hint of humor... but there was none.

At a brisk trot, we arrived at the city gates quickly, Sainte shifting uncomfortably in the saddle.

"Halt!"

He pulled back on the reins, and I immediately hated having the hood so low that I couldn't see the guards' faces. How would I know if one wanted to remove my head from my shoulders?

"Hail, gatekeeper."

"Ah, 'Sainte the Great,'" someone mocked. "How are your bastards in the south?"

"Passing through to Wynterborne," he replied, ignoring the comment.

Is that what men thought? That he had a mistress and bastards? I resisted the urge to rub my sweaty palms on my trousers.

"Always, always."

The mocking tone grew curious, and I squirmed as footsteps against the cobblestones signaled his approach.

"Thief tried to rob me in the dead of night," Sainte said. "Managed to throw some dirt in their eyes. Ended up cutting them to bits—"

I frowned, squinting at my hands. Why was that important to our ruse?

"—can't see a thing now," he added.

I can't? I immediately obeyed his silent order and scrunched my eyes shut.

"Ah, serves them right, then," the guard commented.

My head snapped back as something hard struck me. A whimper escaped my lips, and I clutched the horse's mane as my hood tore away.

"Take care, gatekeeper," Sainte warned. "I've saved this one for the dungeons. I'd hate for them to meet their end this close to Wynterborne."

"Such a shame it would be. Looks like they'll still make for a decent plaything if anyone wants a round with them." The footsteps receded. "Go on, then."

"Good day."

Sainte tensed, nudging his mount onward. I held my breath, loathing my inner turmoil. While I hoped for safe passage, I dreaded the idea that every step drew us closer to Wynterborne's grasp.

"Breathe," he whispered, pressing his mouth close to my head.

"Can I look?"

"Wait till we dismount."

Bound and unable to survey our surroundings, my frustration welled. I trusted him, but that was a lot of vulnerability to ask of any street rat. Every muscle tensed, wary of potentially being recognized. Who would recognize me, though? It had been fifteen years since Sainte tore through this city with me curled to his chest.

His solid warmth at my back served as a steady assurance that everything would be fine. I might have known Landing's End and Port Siren, but in a sense, this was *his* world.

After an eternity, we came to a halt. Panic thrummed through me as he dismounted, taking the security of his presence with him. He yanked me from the saddle in a show of force.

"Stable him, feed him well. Ready another horse within the hour, then send mine to Wynterborne in three days."

Sainte spoke with curt precision to who, I assumed, was a stableboy. His fingers dug into my shoulders as he spun me toward him. When he reached past my cheeks to pull my hood up, I opened my eyes, catching his reassuring gaze for a split moment before he gave the slightest nod, then tugged it in place.

At the inn, he paid for an hour-long stay, eliciting a disturbing chuckle from the innkeeper. He led me up the stairs with a firm grip on my arm, strong but not bruising, then shut the door behind us.

I raised my tied hands, letting the hood fall back to take in the space. It was simple, small and sparse, exactly what a weary traveler needed. A place to rest, a basin, a polished brass square on the wall for reflection, and a window covered by a thin tanned hide.

"Wash up," Sainte grunted, shoving the bed in front of the door. He collapsed onto it, muddy boots and all, groaning as his body slowly relaxed.

He went still for so long, I thought he had fallen asleep.

"Time's wasting," he said, voice raspy with fatigue. "This is your only chance to bathe before tomorrow."

Tomorrow—when he presented me at the palace, to my brother, to the high court.

At the brass mirror, I worked my hands free of the rope. Growing up in the slums left little opportunity to study my reflection.

Despite the lack of familiarity, I couldn't help feeling sorry for the person staring back at me. Deep circles hung over sunken cheeks, a sharp contrast to the dark lashes framing my peridot-green irises. Short black hair, matted and oily, stuck out at odd angles. My features, though plain, were a bit more striking than others I'd seen on the road. Aside from my eyes, I resembled nothing close to a princess.

Heaving a sigh, I shed the cloak and dipped my hands in the basin, grimacing when the crisp water immediately darkened. I washed up as best I could, submerging my hair and swishing it around to rid it of grime. With a nearby rag, I scrubbed the sweat and dirt from my skin, mindful of the male presence in the room.

As soon as I finished, Sainte took a deep breath, drawing my attention. His features scrunched into a grimace before he threw his legs over the bedside. Without glancing my way, he traded places with me.

I cringed as he reached for that nasty, used rag. "Oh—that water is vile."

He paused, peering into the basin where dirt and particles of who knows what floated within. "Aye, it is."

As he dunked the rag and dragged it over his face and neck, my nose wrinkled. That water would make a decent fertilizer.

He patted dry with the front of his tunic, then faced me. "Ready?"

"Not at all."

I pushed to my feet as he shoved at the bed, moving it back into place.

"You would've had more time…" The accusation fell away with a one-armed shrug, then he reached for my wrist, rope in hand.

"If only I hadn't tried for my freedom." Sarcasm drenched my tone.

He snorted, shaking his head as if he found it somewhat amusing. "If only."

He tied my wrists gently, his calloused fingers brushing along my skin in a way that made my heart pump too fast.

Curse the blasted organ.

He kept the rope loose, granting me just enough slack to slip it off if necessary. I watched his blue eyes, hoping for a hint, a fraction of reprieve. I hoped against hope that he'd change his mind, take back everything he said thus far and tell me I was free to go.

When his gaze caught mine, he hesitated. His lips pressed into a thin line and his jaw worked, his silent remorse evident.

Please, don't make me do this.

He jerked my hood up, pulling the brim low enough to cut off our contact. Brushing past, he grabbed my arm and hauled me out–

To the fresh gray horse.

To Wynterborne.

He pushed the sturdy gelding at a horrible speed. We leaned over the horse's sweat-soaked neck, Sainte pressed against my back. Everything ached because of the position. My arse felt as if it was one enormous bruise and my stomach rumbled, but there was no rest for either of us.

As morning broke, the horse stumbled, barely catching itself as it panted and snorted. Sainte blew out a hiss of impatience, then pulled into an alley. The beast trembled as he dismounted and helped me down. I bit out a curse as my knees gave out, and he grunted, holding me up. I clutched onto the front of his armor, forcing my legs to take my weight.

"When we mount again, we will not stop until we reach the castle."

"You'll kill the horse." There was no accusation in my tone, just a flat statement.

"What is a single horse for a kingdom's future?" he asked. His voice was rough with lack of sleep and several days of fast travel. His lips were pressed together in a frown as his blue eyes danced over my face.

Even though I found my balance, he still held me against his chest. My teeth ground together, dreading what was to come. I closed my eyes, hoping he wouldn't see the fear there. He knew I didn't want to go. He didn't need to know I was terrified.

"Do not speak until we breach the throne room, when we–"

"The throne room? Right away?!" I cut in, pulling back. "I'll have no time to prepare myself? To bathe?"

"You sacrificed that when you ran. Again." His gloved hand pushed my dark hair from my face. "You will say, 'I, Elspeth, Second Born of Veiled King Vardis, challenge Prince Regent Adastrus to the Rites of the Gods.' You must speak those words exactly."

"Sainte, I don't even know what that means! No one's told–"

"Repeat it."

"No! Tell me what I'm agreeing to first!" It was too late to turn back. I was too close to the castle to get away. But I *needed* to understand what I was walking into.

"Say it."

"I, Elspeth, challenge–"

"Say it *right*."

"Sainte!"

I slammed my forehead against his armor. He remained obstinate, failing to grasp my plea for gentleness. I craved his protection, his assurance of safety and guidance.

I was scared.

And I needed him.

His warm hand cradled the nape of my neck, letting me have a moment as I fought my panic. My breaths came in quick gasps. I was an adult, a princess, for gods' sake. I could do this. Right?

I had to.

"I, Elspeth, Second Born of Veiled King Vardis, challenge Prince Regent Adastrus to the Rites of the Gods," I whispered, voice catching.

Sainte lifted my chin to force my gaze to his. Fear, iced and acrid, shivered through my being. We were about to get back on that horse and not stop until I was truly and utterly snared as a Princess of Wynterborne.

"*Killip Gheten*, Elspeth."

Happy Birthday.

CHAPTER 9

I f I thought we rode hard before, it was nothing compared to the speed that we flew down the streets as dawn broke. The gray horse wheezed, stumbling to obey the harsh demands. Its mane whipped across my face as I pressed against its neck, moving with the rise and fall of each rapid stride. Sainte's chest pressed against my back, his arms locking me in place as he maintained control of the reins.

Wynterborne's changes over the years were hard to gauge, considering there wasn't much to recall. There was little chance to absorb the sights amidst the chaos we stirred. Shouts and yells trailed us, resounding through the streets as we raced uphill toward the castle.

I dared a glance upward, coarse hair stinging my cheeks. A large common bridge and several narrower ones connected the city to the royal grounds. They resembled massive ropes, tethering the grounds to the mainland. I lowered my face and shut my eyes, trying to dredge up my memories of the terrain.

Ahead, a clamor erupted, and Sainte pressed on without hesitation.

"Clear the way!" His voice sliced through the chaos, raw and harsh.

Shouts erupted around us, punctuated by Sainte's curses. He veered left, forcing me to hunch down as our horse lurched in response. It swerved, but Sainte spurred it onward, charging past the two men stationed at the bridge's entrance.

The thunderous gallop reverberated across the stone, hooves striking a rhythmic beat that echoed through the snowy abyss below. Behind us, voices rose in shouts, summoning more guards to arms.

"Captain Nytestorm!" a loud baritone voice rang out.

I dared to peer up as he slowed the horse to a quick trot, nearing the bridge's end. Once we crossed, we would be on royal ground. The man addressing us had dark hair and a clean, open face. A giant black stallion clad in a white and green blanket stood at his side.

"General Jorgeson?"

"Hail, Captain. Counselor Dyre sent me to wait for you."

"Where is he?" Sainte called, his tone guarded.

"At the coronation. He told me you might need help getting there." The man tipped his head, then mounted.

Sainte's relief at his words was evident, still he wrapped around my waist, pulling me close against his chest. "Aye, aid would be welcome," he said.

"Is it truly her?" Jorgeson asked as he turned his horse toward the castle, urging it into a quick trot.

Sainte didn't answer. Instead, he pulled my hood back just enough to show my eyes.

The general's expression slackened with shock, then a slow grin crept over his face. "I daresay we're late then."

With that, he spurred his horse into a gallop, prompting our gray to match his pace. We tore past guards engaged in conversation, yet none dared to impede us. It seemed General Jorgeson's presence was the key to our safe passage.

The horses raced through the courtyard and gardens, scattering the light snow that settled on the trees and hedges. The gray stumbled and let out a sharp neigh as it regained its balance, struggling to match the relentless pace. Our rush disrupted the people going about their day, each absorbed in their tasks. At the stairs, the horses snorted and balked, but the general and Sainte dug their heels into the beasts' flanks, urging them on.

Guards spilled out of every passageway, like termites from rotten wood. They brandished their weapons, but at the sight of their superior, they kept their arms lowered.

We neared two immense oak doors, guarded by four footmen who exchanged confused, horrified glances.

"Clear the way!" Jorgeson bellowed.

I ducked my head, hoping we wouldn't collide with the doors in a heap of sweaty horseflesh.

After a series of shouts and a resounding crash, we burst into a brightly lit corridor.

Lanterns flickered from decorative sconces. Sheer fabric covered the windows, allowing in light while tempering the chill of the outside world. Tapestries adorned the walls, displaying elaborate coats of arms that hinted at the noble lineage of this place, though I struggled to recognize them.

I had no time to process as we pivoted left and cantered down the wide corridor. Shouts and screams filled the air as staff dodged our path, prompting me to pull my hood further down, shielding my face from their shocked glares.

With the black horse ahead of us, we ascended through the castle, navigating more stairs and crowded halls. The walls narrowed, and the ceiling descended, raising concerns that further progress might force us to dismount.

For some reason, that unnerved me.

Perhaps because I would not feel Sainte's strength against my back.

As we skidded to a stop, I straightened my shoulders, trying to rally myself. Panic hummed through my veins, and Sainte tensed as the gray staggered a step.

Jorgeson shouted at the eight men who barred the door ahead. "Make way, you fools! I'll have you flogged for this!"

"We're not to let—"

"I am your general! By the gods, you will permit me!"

"The orders were given—"

The soldier did his best to appear confident, but his voice pitched higher as Jorgeson dismounted and stormed over. He towered above him, backing the man against the wall. The others stayed true to their purpose, blocking the door, but watched with wary expressions.

"Orders from *who*, whelp?!"

"The king, sir!"

"You have no king!"

With a sharp *crack*, Jorgeson slapped him across the face. The soldier jerked aside, taken aback by the betrayal. The general wasted no time. In one swift motion, he pulled the oak latch loose from its stay before his soldiers turned on him.

Sainte wasn't one to waste an opportunity, and before they replaced the latch, the gray horse was upon them. It screamed as it crashed through the door, stumbling to its knees.

When I laid eyes on the scene before me, my stomach clenched as if someone landed a punch to my gut. The throne room, fit for a king—or king-to-be—was a spectacle of opulence. Hundreds adorned in fine, shimmering attire filled the space, their gold and gemstones sparkling in the cold light streaming through the grand windows behind the dais.

The horse's shrill neigh echoed through the room as it struggled to rise. My gaze shifted upward, discovering another crowd nestled on a balcony along the back wall. Returning my focus to the throne, silhouetted against the cold white snow and pale sky, I locked eyes with my brother.

Fifteen years had passed, yet no amount of time could erase the fear that surged anew as his piercing green irises fixed on mine.

His hair was short, almost clean shaven on the sides, with the top long and hanging in his face. It gave him a roguish appearance, and the madness that twinkled in his gaze, even at this distance, turned my stomach.

There were people whose eyes betrayed a deeper complexity, as if they were not quite like everyone else. Some carried a sense of innocence, forever locked in a childlike state, unable to fully embrace adulthood. Others appeared constantly on edge, their attention and focus darting with nerves, avoiding any prolonged contact.

And then there were those like my brother, whose eyes spoke of darker intentions, a desire to inflict pain on people.

Or creatures.

I shivered as memories stirred—him hurting animals, killing pets for sport. Unbidden, those harrowing images flooded my mind, casting a darker shadow over the present moment.

Almost as if he sensed the fear swirling within, Adastrus' smile widened, sending a chill down my spine. Beside him, a man dressed in vibrant green and white attire held a forest-colored pillow. Atop it lay a silver crown adorned with delicate emeralds.

My brother reached for it, his movements commanding the shocked crowd's attention. Gasps and exclamations rippled through the throng.

That terrible smile, tinged with malice, turned my way. Even from across the grand hall, his peridot eyes gleamed with cruel delight, feeding off my palpable fear.

At that pivotal moment, I contemplated staying as a passive observer of my brother's ascent to the throne. The safety of my position, nestled against Sainte's reassuring warmth, tempted me to stay put. However, it seemed as if the gods were, perhaps, not happy with that choice.

Our horse rebelled, letting out a wild scream as it reared, its forelegs flailing. Sainte's powerful arm encircled me, anchoring me amidst the chaos. I clung to the mane, fighting to keep my seat.

That shattered the spell.

"Hold!" Sainte roared over the crowd which broke into horrified cries.

When the horse steadied, I acted swiftly, fearing if I hesitated, I might lose my courage to follow through with this. With Sainte's steady grip around my waist, I swung my leg over the horse's sweaty neck, and he lowered me with the utmost care. My body slid against the gelding's damp hide, and I stumbled when my feet hit the ground. After a tentative step, I stopped. The crowd blocked my view of the dais.

The horse bit my shoulder, and I hissed, jerking away. It snorted and thrust its nose between my shoulders, pushing me forward.

This beast was in on the whole conspiracy. I knew it.

"I am Elspeth! Second Born to Veiled King Vardis!" I called out with all the strength I could muster, my voice cracking.

The crowd pivoted, turning their backs on my brother. Shock painted the faces of some, hands flying to cover gaping mouths, while others murmured and exchanged skeptical looks, their expressions a mix of disbelief and curiosity. I strode forward, my posture rigid and determined, each step purposeful. Bystanders, sensing the importance of the moment, parted like a sea, creating a clear path down the aisle leading to the dais.

My brother's sneer faltered, his fingers twitching just above the crown.

Taking a quick breath, I marched toward him, pasting a cocky smile on my face. "I challenge Prince Regent Adastrus to the Rites of the Gods."

Gasps and chatter echoed through the chamber, hardly masking the crowd's shock. Suddenly, curiosity and wonder stirred among the people, and the tense moment was lost.

Stepping up to the prince regent, I threw back my hood and met the simmering hatred in his glare.

"Hello, big brother."

CHAPTER 10

A dastrus kept his eerie eyes on me, unblinking. There was no warmth, compassion, or even shock in that gaze, as if he predicted I'd show up and pluck the throne from his grasp.

I sincerely hoped he hadn't been expecting it.

"Princess Elspeth," a clear voice called from the crowd.

With a final glare at my brother, my attention shifted to the approaching older man. His dark green robes, edged in black, billowed gracefully with each step. The crowds parted for him, easing his approach.

A steady presence crowded my back. Without looking, I knew it was Sainte. With him behind me, I noticed a surge of strength, as though I truly were a princess capable of handling whatever challenges this man threw at me.

"I am confident I speak for our entire kingdom when I say that I am pleased to find you're alive, and... as well as could be expected." The man's light-brown eyes, the color of warm honey, darted to my sweat and grime-covered clothes.

"We were in quite the rush to get here," I said, stumbling over my words in High Wynter.

"Not a day late," Adastrus spoke up, lifting his chin and arching a brow at Sainte behind me, "to issue the challenge, that is." His voice was lilting and lovely, if not for his haughty tone.

I shrugged, not knowing what to say.

As if sensing I needed help, the man watched me with wary eyes before turning to his sovereign. "Prince Regent—"

My brother's sneer turned to utter annoyance as he leveled his glare at him.

"—Princess Elspeth has had quite the journey. Might I suggest she retire to her rooms? The whole of Wynterborne would celebrate her return, with you, as her brother, leading the festivities." His voice flowed as smooth as oil, eyes fixed on Adastrus with a deferential tilt of his head.

He didn't trust my brother, but I doubted I could trust him, either. Politicians were never anyone's genuine friend.

"I think that would be best. She does appear as though she's been dragged through a dungheap, no?"

"At the very least, Prince Regent."

The crowd's laughter was hesitant, tinged with uncertainty. I could hardly blame them. I just upended their political world, and now they didn't know what to expect.

"Princess Elspeth, Anderz Dyre of the House of Meledis, at your service." The older man dipped into a bow, then joined my side, offering his arm.

I glanced at Sainte, looking for assurance or a warning. He would identify who to trust, not I. His cool blue eyes flicked to meet mine, then to Adastrus.

No help there.

Anderz's sharp gaze studied my face as if it held all my secrets. Swallowing past the nervous lump in my throat, I forced a smile before glancing at Sainte. It dawned on me that he wouldn't join me if I didn't speak up. With a hand on Anderz's arm, I allowed him to lead me to the side.

A recruiter had no place with a princess.

I opened my mouth to say something—anything—to allow Sainte to accompany me, when Anderz spoke.

"Your Highness, I respectfully request that Captain Nytestorm join us. His firsthand knowledge of her journey would assist the healers in understanding her needs more effectively."

"Like an erring bastard?"

I flinched as if I had been struck, and my lip curled in a snarl as I turned toward my brother.

A slender yet firm hand gripped mine in a bruising hold. I whipped my glare to meet Anderz's eyes, but didn't find shock or urgency there.

He was deathly calm.

"We simply must be sure she is in perfect health and able to present the challenge to our prince." Those cunning honey irises studied my brother. "If Captain Nytestorm were to offer any information concerning her injuries on the journey, they would all be taken into consideration."

"Go then," Adastrus huffed in disgust, shifting his attention to the crowd with hungry anticipation. "But, Captain," he glanced back at Sainte with a sneer, his expression filled with disdain, "I see you've brought no recruits. 'Tis a pity."

Panic rose in my chest and squeezed my throat as my brother grinned. His eyes were wide in a horrific kind of way.

He was evil.

There was nothing more to it, Adastrus was evil.

Another squeeze around my hand warned me not to interfere, and I bared my teeth in a hiss, spinning to Anderz. His unblinking gaze held mine, a silent warning.

"I shall be at the stake at first light," Sainte replied in crisp High Wynter.

"I look forward to it."

Without a thought, I whirled, yanking my hand from Anderz's grip. Sainte stepped between me and my brother—a wall of protection. Rage trembled through me as I glared. His gaze remained cool, unmoved by my silent command for him to move his arse before I handed it to him.

"This way, Princess."

I clenched my fists so tightly my fingernails bit into my palms. Sainte held my stare, urging me to regain composure and act with dignity.

Curse that.

I spun and grabbed Anderz's arm, glaring at the man. "Please hurry, I'm quite tired," I growled.

I needed out—away from the stares, the brightness, the gaudiness. It was all too much. And I wanted to hurt someone.

Preferably my vile brother.

Anderz seemed to understand my urgency and led me through the sea of people. Gowns of silk and satin, woven with gold and silver threads, bodies adorned in jewels that made the room gleam. Every one of them parted, clearing a path.

Whispers and hushed voices followed as we hurried through the crowded doorway. Sainte stayed close to my heels, his presence a soothing balm to my rage. Anderz guided us deeper into the belly of the castle, and as we passed, servants paused their duties to steal glances at me. Their expressions shifted from curiosity to horror when they saw my disheveled state, then bustled off to resume their tasks.

The castle was a maze of passages I should've known like the back of my hand, but instead I relied on some old man to guide me. I kept pace with his surprisingly quick gait, only shaking my boot once when a pebble rolled under my foot. He moved through a towering corridor, its vaulted ceilings lending an air of grandeur. Though spotless, the space exuded a chilly darkness, illuminated by sparse lanterns along the walls. Portraits adorned rich tapestries, predominantly of royalty, their features reminiscent of my heritage—dark hair and piercing peridot eyes.

"This is your wing, Princess."

My brow furrowed as I surveyed the space, empty save for the flurry of servants darting about. Their hurried movements and wary glances our way spoke of their unease.

"It has been empty since your disappearance," Anderz said, slowing our pace a margin. "Please forgive the maids as they freshen your rooms."

"Anything is more welcome than a saddle on horseback," I muttered.

The women chatted in hushed whispers, darting in and out of the room at the end of the hall. More carrying armfuls of blankets appeared through a thin door tucked away behind a massive tapestry—a servant's passage. I remember them magically appearing as a child, not knowing where they came from or where they went.

Anderz cleared his throat. "I imagine a bath is in order."

I shrugged, watching an older woman with silver hair and a stern face glide down the corridor. She moved with her back straight, and chin raised high, as if she were royalty herself.

"Your Highness," she greeted. She sank into a deep bow before rising to peer down her nose at me. At Sainte, her eyes narrowed into a squint, as if we somehow disappointed her.

"Princess Elspeth, this is Master Servant Bernita. She will see to it that every need and desire you have are met," Anderz said, coming to a stop in front of the woman.

I lifted my chin and matched her stare.

"The hearth has just been lit, my lady. It will take time to warm the rooms. We readied them as quickly as we were able. If, perchance, a messenger had been sent, we would have been ready to receive you."

Clearly, she wasn't among those who were pleased to see I was alive. I bristled and opened my mouth to speak, but Anderz beat me to it yet again.

"They were traveling with all haste, Bernita. You will prepare a hot bath and send for a healer to tend your princess."

I noted the care he used with his words, rebuking her but, at the same time, being gentle. Her sharp gaze settled on me once more and, sniffing in distaste, she turned, disappearing into the room. We waited while she chased all the maids out, each trying their best not to ogle me, their long-lost princess, and each failing miserably.

When we had her nod of approval, Anderz stepped forward and held out his arm in a gallant gesture toward the door. I took a steadying breath and rounded the corner to look into the rooms that would now be my home.

I stopped in my tracks, both horrified and awestruck.

The room gleamed in hues of gold and green, adorned with intricate tapestries depicting vibrant spring scenes—a golden sun casting its warm rays over blooming trees and dancing girls. Thick doeskin hides covered the stone floor, offering warmth and comfort underfoot. Lanterns, brighter than any I had seen in Landing's End, lined the walls with an inviting glow reminiscent of a sunny day, a full contrast to the snowy scene outside.

This had to be the receiving area, featuring an ornate table and six carved chairs placed opposite the roaring fire in the hearth. Beyond, I noticed a doorway leading to another brightly lit space. A bed, larger than most fishing vessels, caught my eye from within.

"Does it suit you, Your Highness?" Bernita asked.

"I can't go in there like this!" I choked out. "You don't even want to know what I've stepped in with these boots–"

"Princess, please. A bath and fresh clothes will be readied," Anderz cut in, and I swear Sainte stifled a laugh with a cough.

Bernita's stare fell to my shoes, and her lips pressed into a thin line.

After a moment, I swallowed past the nervous lump in my throat and took a step forward—then stopped, causing Sainte to plow into my back. I dropped to the ground in the middle of the corridor and sat on my rear, yanking my boots off.

It wasn't as if my feet were any cleaner due to the number of holes in my boots, but at least I felt like I was making an effort to keep the furs clean. I shook out the few pebbles that had worked their way in and looked up as Sainte offered his hand. His eyes twinkled with mischief, even if his face was still and serious. I gave him a shy grin and allowed him to pull me up.

"If you will…" Anderz prompted again, gesturing to the doorway.

With an apologetic wince, I stepped inside, then cleared my throat against the groan that threatened to come out when my feet hit the furs. I had never felt something so soft against my bare toes—aside from warm sand.

That would have been welcome in this chilly climate.

I drifted further, taking in the sparse decorations that lent the room a cozy yet impersonal air. There weren't many trinkets of my own to personalize the space. It felt like someone else's home, not mine.

"I'll not be long with the water and healer," Bernita said, before she excused herself, pulling the door shut behind her.

After a moment, Anderz turned to Sainte, all formalities forgotten. "Cutting it a bit close, weren't you, Captain?"

"We ran into a few minor issues along the way." Sainte gave me a flat look.

"A few more breaths and we would have welcomed you in an entirely different manner." Anderz walked to the fire and used the iron rod to adjust the burning logs. "The regent is seething. I hope you're prepared for tomorrow."

"I will do my duty."

"Your duty will see you pass through the Veil if you're not careful," he hissed. "Princess Elspeth has very few supporters. Don't waste your talent."

"She is here, is she not?" Sainte asked, tone weary.

"I am," I snapped. "And I have quite a few questions, so if you both could stop talking about me as if I'm not standing right beside you, that would be splendid."

Anderz turned, his movement slow and meticulous as he scrutinized my face. "You hid her in Tilamuik? Among the Meeds?" he murmured.

"Gladier didn't seem safe."

"As it wouldn't have been. Adastrus never thought to search southern ports. I'm surprised she wasn't sold into slavery."

"I know my way about the slums," I shot back, angry that he was still not addressing me. Perhaps the two had a lot to catch up on, but I was standing right here, could they not talk *to* me instead of *about* me?

Anderz appeared taken aback for the first time, and he turned his frown on Sainte. "You didn't put her in a noble's house?"

"They would have betrayed her."

"That would have been a risk, but now we have to deal with her Common Muik."

"It slips out," I grumbled, then crossed my arms over my chest, my boots dangling from my hand.

"And her High Wynter is horrendous."

I was an adult—but at that moment, I did not act like it.

I jerked, throwing my boot. It struck true, bouncing off of Anderz's shoulder.

He froze, not moving a muscle, and I wondered if I misjudged his loyalty. If Sainte trusted him, then I would too... but perhaps Sainte was the only one that could deal with my level of rebellion.

"I'm right here," I said again, suddenly unsure of myself. This was a counselor to the high court. I didn't know how much power he had, and if I acted rashly, I had no idea how he would respond in turn.

"You threw a boot at me."

His unblinking gaze met mine, and I ground my teeth to hold it.

"I did."

"A boot you would not dare step on a fur with, yet you deemed it acceptable to throw it at me."

"Yes, because I'm–"

"I now understand the issues you ran into along the way." Anderz's face broke into a smile. He walked to the table and pulled a chair out, motioning for me to sit. "If you would, my petulant princess, have a seat?"

My lips pressed into a thin line as I stole a glance at Sainte. Despite the sweat and grime from the road, a hint of amusement tugged at the corner of his mouth.

Surely that meant it was safe.

I sat, dropping my other boot to the floor and leaned forward on the table, eager to participate in the conversation as an equal.

"Sit up straight, Princess." Anderz settled across from me.

I cleared my throat, obliging him, then placed my hands demurely in my lap.

"Let me be blunt, the Wynterians have long mourned your death. Today you rode in looking like someone that the regent aptly described as 'dragged through a dungheap.' Besides Captain Nytestorm and myself, only General Jorgeson knew you might be alive. The band of men that joined our captain were the most trusted of our warriors. The court will follow the crown, whoever's head it lands on.

"You are stirring up the emotions people have both feared and hoped for over fifteen years," he murmured, leaning closer. "Few friends remain by your side in this endeavor. You have set down a challenge that many have not seen in their lifetimes. Remember, you stand at the mercy of both gods and priests, and the priests, my dear, are firmly aligned with Adastrus."

Deep unease flitted through my chest—I was out of my depth. I had avoided anything Wynterian in Landing's End and the ports. And now, confronted with this venture, I couldn't shake my inadequacy.

"Can I trust you?" I blurted.

He lifted a single peppered brow, then a sly smile split his face. "Perhaps."

"Counselor Dyre is the only one who would keep Adastrus from outright killing you," Sainte said as he sank into a chair. He groaned, lowering his weight with care.

"What's in it for you?" I asked.

Surely if he was a politician, there was a motive behind his desire to see my brother removed and me put in his place.

"I'm a simple man. I have no agenda," he said, watching me with hooded eyes.

"Doubtful." With a scoff, I flicked my wrist in a show of dismissal. "I haven't met a noble that doesn't have an agenda."

"Met many nobles, have you?"

I snorted. "Pilfered their treasuries enough."

When Anderz deadpanned, I couldn't help but grin. Even if I didn't get a rise out of him, watching his face shut down told me I hit some kind of nerve.

A knock sounded, and Sainte shot to his feet, his speed belying his weariness. He managed to push the chair in and take a few steps back before the door was thrust open and a woman wearing white and gold strode in.

She was tall and thin, a wisp of a woman. Her long black hair was as dark as my own, but lacked the blue sheen mine had... when it was clean. Her light eyes widened when she saw me, but her mouth lifted in a small smile.

"So it is true," she murmured, walking over. "My name is Gilead, Your Highness. I am to tend to you."

"I need no tending," I stood with a wince, muscles sore and stiff from so many days of riding, "though a bath would be welcome."

"The prince regent asked that we care for you, see to any wounds you might have," she pressed.

Her face was kind and her eyes shone with honesty, but I didn't trust her.

"She's one of the best healers," Anderz said, standing as well. He offered her a nod as two servants followed her in hauling a tub between them.

A strange sense of longing bore into my chest. I hadn't experienced a proper bath in years. I relied on streams, rainwater, and tidepools full of curious sea life. More often than not, I went without. The idea of having a warm soak with no danger of floating down a stream and drowning... I glanced at Sainte, who studied the servants hauling buckets of steaming water.

"It is my sole purpose to verify that you're well," Gilead said. "You will have the Rites of the Gods to get through soon. We must ensure you are fit to compete in them."

"You mean, make sure I'm not carrying a bastard?" I accused.

A servant stumbled in shock, and harsh whispers berated her for reacting.

The healer only folded her hands in front of her. "If you were with child, you would be in no condition to complete the challenges, that is true."

I sighed, peering at Anderz and Sainte, then at the tub being filled with steaming water. "A look-over, just to see I'm as fit as a fiddle, then a bath?" I was ashamed at how my voice came out as a whine.

"Well, perhaps bathing should be our first order, then I'll examine you."

I conceded to Gilead as a seamstress entered with Bernita. She took measurements while Sainte and Anderz retreated to the far corner, muttering to one another. I couldn't help but wonder what plans they were plotting behind my back.

Moments later, the men left with Anderz promising to stay close by if I called. As soon as they departed, I shed my clothes and eased into the steaming tub, wincing at the heat. Halfway in, I froze, my gaze fixed on the two maids and Gilead lingering in the room, faces drawn with shock.

"Is this not how it is done?" I asked.

"Oh, it's just—they haven't seen so much dirt on a living soul in quite some time," the healer offered with a reassuring smile.

She tucked her sleeves up and selected a jar from the many set out along the table. The maids nodded emphatically at her excuse for their stares and I shrugged, slipping further in, hissing as the heat pricked at my skin.

"This is... actually pretty clean," I squeaked, forcing myself lower into the scalding tub. This wasn't as great as I remember it being.

I scrubbed, oblivious of the water which was now a murky brown. It was so saturated with debris and grime that bubbles barely formed in it. Gilead came over to help, which I objected to until she rubbed some sweet-scented oil onto my shoulders. My protests died out as she worked loose, tense muscles that had been tight and nervous my whole life.

"Tell me, where have you been all this time?" she asked, pulling me out of my lull.

"Somewhere safe." I ducked beneath the surface, coming up only when my lungs demanded air.

"I meant no offense, Your Highness."

Gilead stood at the ready with a towel warmed by the fire. I stepped out of the bath and took the warm sheet gratefully, wrapping it around myself.

"You'll also be pleased to hear I've begotten no bastards, nor am I with child now." I stepped over to the hearth, which crackled and popped with comforting heat. "I bled on the way here."

"As a healer, it is my duty to care for you," she said, comb in hand, then motioned to my hair. "May I?"

I scoffed with a shrug. "Not much to work with."

"Why did you cut it?" A note of sadness lingered in the question.

Behind me, the maids began emptying the tub, and I took a slow breath. What could I tell these people? Without Sainte, I had no idea what I was doing. I didn't know what to say, or if I should say anything at all. Perhaps I ought to act as the proud, conceited nobility I witnessed in Port Siren, and simply ignore the healer.

"It was easier," I hedged. "Not everyone can keep long hair clean."

I stretched my fingers toward the crackling fire while she brushed out the mats and tangles. The sensation of someone combing through my hair was strangely comforting, a rare luxury. Memories sifted through my thoughts of nannies combing, braiding and primping. The bluish-black hue, along with our vibrant green eyes, served as a potent symbol of our royal lineage. From a young age, I was taught that it was a divine blessing, a mark bestowed by the gods to identify Wynterborne rulers. Places like Landing's End didn't follow such beliefs. The populace had the liberty to select their leaders.

Not that it benefited them.

The witch who concocted the potion to lighten my hair always warned me about angering the gods by concealing their gift. I never bought into her warnings, as I'd never encountered a god, nor had one ever spoken to me.

The priests and temples only exerted control over the population, dictating orders and laws. And not just in the religious sect, but the government as well. They stripped away the people's freedoms. It didn't sit right with me. Too many individuals sacrificed everything to worship in a temple, only to endure a lifetime in the slums.

It wasn't worth it.

"You should grow it out," she urged, voice soft. "Let it be your sign of your right to challenge. You have the means to care for it now." With a gentle touch, she shifted to the side, weaving the small section of length.

"How long do I have to prepare for this *challenge?*" I asked.

She glanced over her shoulder at the maids, who struggled out with two buckets of murky water. "There are three rites, not one. Prince Regent Adastrus would have you start today." She finished the braid, then stepped before me, mouth dipping in a slight frown. "Yet, I would not let him."

"You?" I asked, arching a brow in disbelief. "You can step in his way?"

"I am a Priestess of Togamar. The prince does not dictate what the gods say."

I drew back, regarding her with fresh insight. Anderz mentioned the priests being on Adastrus' side. I was uncertain of her intentions. Perhaps she harbored a noxious potion or magical spell to use against me. Sainte's absence skittered down my spine, and I glanced toward the door. The maids were gone now, leaving me alone with her.

"You follow his lead."

"I follow Togamar, and if there were a king or queen on the throne, I would follow them. I am not bought, as you accuse," she spoke with a certain calmness, despite the bite in her words.

She set the comb on the table, then began organizing her things. I watched her with a frown, tucking the sheet more firmly around myself. More maids knocked and entered, each carrying buckets. One paused by the tub, her eyes widening in surprise as she glanced at me. I managed a faint grin before the other servant nudged her, a silent reminder of her station.

It wasn't long before the seamstress returned with Bernita, trailed by a maid who carried bolts of fabric and a case full of dresses.

Annoyance crawled beneath my skin, and I wondered if I shouted for Anderz, if he would save me from the torture about to ensue.

I was proud of myself. I conducted myself with maturity, allowing them to drape cloths and gowns around my body. Years in the slums had stripped away any sense of modesty or privacy, leaving me unfazed by the exposure. The seamstress took care, avoiding my bruised ribs and thighs, and Gilead applied salves to my battered skin where she saw fit.

After a time they allowed me to dress in a thick cotton gown adorned with lace and flat opals.

I peered at it in distaste, picking at the teardrop stone near my neckline. "You want me to go to a ball, or can I sleep?"

"Sleep. Tomorrow you will have a good meal and feel better for it," Gilead said as the others filed out.

"Where's Sainte?" I asked, gravitating toward the bed. Every single muscle in my body got heavier just looking at it. Was it safe without him? What if someone tried to kill me?

"He is resting as well. It took quite a toll on him, retrieving you."

She drew the heavy blankets aside, revealing a stupidly soft mattress stuffed with—I reached out to pat it—feathers?!

"Shouldn't I stay up to wait for him?" I asked, sliding onto the bed. My body had a mind of its own—it knew what I needed.

"He needs his sleep as you need yours. Rest, Princess."

She pulled the blankets over me. I moaned as I sank into the mattress and my eyes drifted closed at the heavy warmth.

"But–" I mumbled, unable to form more words.

"You're safe here."

Safe? In a castle with my mad brother who tried to murder me at the age of six?

My mind struggled, fighting to stay awake, but I fell into a dreamless abyss to the faint hush of Gilead dousing the lamps.

CHAPTER 11

"Hush now, you'll wake her!"

"I am hushed!"

I drifted awake, feeling as though I floated through the clouds. Everything ached, but I was so warm and comfortable that I couldn't make myself move.

"She doesn't look much like I expected."

"What did you expect? I thought she was a corpse. Help me with these ashes."

"Ma says she really is the Lost Princess, and she would be better than—"

"Bite your tongue!" the harsh whisper cut off the other girl. "If anyone hears you say such a thing, you'll be food for the pigs!"

"I'm only saying what Ma said."

"Well, she's a fool. Look at her, she couldn't take the regent if she had an army behind her. She's just a helpless—"

"Actually," I moaned, eliciting two quick gasps, "I am quite capable of taking care of myself."

I chased my words with a contented yawn and stretched beneath the blankets. The pleasure ended abruptly when my muscles spasmed and cramped. I yelped, curling in on myself as I rubbed my thighs.

"Your Highness! Should I send for the healer?" A girl's panicked voice called from across the room.

I opened my eyes and squinted against the weak light that filtered through the heavy curtains. Two girls stood by the fire, buckets of ash and piles of wood at their feet.

With a grim smile, I tucked the blanket to my chin. "No. I've suffered worse, unfortunately."

I surveyed the room anew, absorbing its beauty. Warm golds and inviting greens adorned every surface, complemented by potted plants scattered throughout. A grin crept across my face, appreciating the effort to infuse verdant life into the frigid castle. The plants must have been moved overnight or early this morning. They couldn't have survived in a vacant, fireless space.

Heavy curtains, the color of dark ivy, draped over a giant window. The glass must have shielded against the cold, as I would have felt a chill if it were just a hide. As I observed, a slip of a girl in a plain brown apron dress scampered over, quick and nimble.

"Would you like me to open the curtains?" she asked.

Despite the wear, her clothes were cared for. Her brown hair was plaited and piled atop her head, keeping it out of her way. She offered a shy smile, awaiting instructions.

"Yes, please," I said, offering a small nod.

She drew the curtains aside, and I clamped my eyes shut. Rich, bright sunlight flooded in, nearly blinding me as it reflected off the fresh snowfall.

"Gods, does this window face north?" I asked, wincing at the intense morning light. I wasn't sure I wanted to be greeted by a blinding northern sunrise each day.

"Nay, Your Highness, it faces east, toward the Great Iceland."

Comforting. My room faced the land of giant ice bears and snow wolves.

"Wait," I shot upright, cursing myself as my head pounded in response to the sudden move, "what time is it?!"

"Almost high noon, Your High–"

"Quick! Where are my clothes?!"

I leapt from the bed as if it were on fire. The servant near the hearth ran from the bedroom, and the girl at the window stood with her mouth open in shock.

"I swear by the gods, if you don't tell me where my clothes are I will storm out of here wearing this!" I said, plucking at the heavy sleeping gown.

To be fair, it was far thicker and modest than what I normally wore, but it seemed to strike a sense of urgency.

"Here!" the other called.

I raced into the receiving space, through another doorway, then skidded to a halt.

Racks displayed an array of dresses, boots, belts, hats, cloaks, and scarves in every imaginable shade, along with colors I had never seen. A large silver mirror, rather than brass, leaned against the far wall. Padded chairs encircled a platform raised at the center.

"I will help you dress, Your–"

"It doesn't matter! Grab the fastest thing I can get into!" I growled, pulling the nightgown off, my muscles screaming in agony.

"What color–"

"I don't care!" I shrieked, throwing the gown to the floor.

My frantic gaze scanned the space, and the girl rushed over with a light blue dress. It was long, but would stop at my ankles, perfect for running—just as I intended. I snatched it, then jerked it over my head. The material was soft, a tanned hide of some kind, with fur inlays.

As I adjusted it, I accepted a black belt adorned with shining blue beads. I looped it on, not for fashion, but practicality. Women girded their loins this way, and if I needed to hike up the skirt, I could.

"Boots!" I spun, facing the ridiculous amount lining the far wall. "Make haste!"

She fetched a pair made of soft doeskin lined with thick white fur. I grabbed them and collapsed into a chair, struggling to pull them on. They likely used my old, ill-fitting ones as a size reference.

"Cloak!"

"For inside the castle or–"

"Outside!" I cried, shoving my foot into the second boot.

I ran over as she pulled a heavy blue garment off the stand. She held it open as I slipped my arms inside, letting her fasten it around my neck.

"I need you to take me wherever they flog soldiers."

Her eyes widened in horror, and her fingers fumbled on the clasp. "Your Highness, it's not... I wouldn't–"

"I'm not asking," I said, giving her my sternest glare. If acting like a princess got me what I wanted, I would act like a pissing princess.

"It's just—you see, we're not allowed–"

With a heated curse, I stormed past her and ran for the door to my rooms. I flung it open, heaving the heavy wood with all my might.

Anderz stood with his fist raised to knock on the door that was no longer there.

"Take me to the flogging stake," I demanded.

He lowered his hand, watching me with guarded eyes. "Princess," he started, his tone careful.

I interrupted him with a curse and stormed past. He caught my arm and pulled me to a stop with a strength beyond his years. I spun to face him, baring my teeth in rage, a slur of curses burning the tip of my tongue.

"I will take you," he said, "but I ask that you remember who you are." His warm features were full of meaning as he held my angry gaze.

"I know who I am, *Counselor,*" I spat. "You would do well to remember who you are."

Panic clawed at my throat, and I let it fuel my rage. I directed most of it at myself for oversleeping, but I would take it out on anyone who got in my way.

"Come along."

Anderz was a portrait of calm as he placed my hand on the crook of his arm. He led me down the hall in a subtle manner, as if he weren't hauling me with him. I tightened my grip, keeping pace. All the while cursing this man for his perfect decorum, his stupid strength and speed despite his age.

"I participate in physical activity daily," he said in response to my muttered curses, nodding at a guard as we turned down a corridor. "Keeps the mind sharp and the body limber."

My lip curled in a scowl. "If you don't bring me to Sainte–"

"I'm taking you where you asked to go, my petulant princess, though I do not believe you truly *want* to go there."

"I won't let him be–"

"Oh, but he already has, dear. You slept through most of it."

I snarled like a wild animal, tearing my hand from his grasp. He stood, unperturbed, as I retreated, breaths ragged. If only I had a weapon—a blade, a vase—anything to break this man's perfectly calm serenity.

"He is doing his duty, and you would be wise to let him."

"He's being flogged for bringing me, your thrice-cursed *Lost Princess*, back to you! Shouldn't you be throwing a feast in his honor? Celebrating his finding me?!" I shrieked, past caring who heard me.

"He has failed to do his job." Anderz stepped up to me and bravely took my hand, placing it on his arm. "He is protecting you. Let him do that."

"How? How is this *protecting* me?!"

"He is suffering the prince regent's wrath. It will buy you time, though if you put yourself in the prince's sights, it will be in vain."

"Is he still being flogged?" I asked, cursing myself that my voice cracked with the question.

"The regent... he likes to draw it out. As he chose to see to the flogging personally, yes, I imagine he is."

"Then take me to him."

"As you wish."

I wasn't so foolish to miss the note of resignation in his words, as if he was appeasing a child. We hurried through the corridors and down the stone staircases. Anderz nodded and greeted everyone we passed without halting, as if sensing somehow that stopping would trigger my flight.

Mentally, I chastised myself for my stupidity. Sainte had ridden just as hard and eaten less, yet there I was sleeping the day away while he suffered my brother's wrath. I was a princess, for gods' sake. My jaw clenched as I recalled the mass of scars on his back. This time, I could protect him, at least.

"Elspeth, do not forget yourself," Anderz whispered as we turned a corner and headed into the crisp sunshine.

My heart dropped, and my blood ran as cold as the dusting of fresh-fallen snow. A hundred yards out, a tall, thick pole jutted from the ground with a chain threaded through a hole. Shackles clung to the chain, encircling Sainte's wrists. A small crowd lounged on wooden benches, chatting and chuckling over steaming mugs. They were bundled against the elements, a sharp contrast to the bare-chested man shivering against the pole.

My gaze fell to the vivid red splatters staining the snow, remnants of the whip tearing flesh. Nausea surged as I lifted my eyes to Sainte's back, where a piece of skin the size of my finger dangled.

"Curse you!" I spat, wrenching my hand from Anderz.

The crowd fell silent, faces turning toward me, expressions filled with intrigue. Adastrus swung the short whip like a pendulum, keeping his back to me. He stood there, having shed his cloak, donned in an embroidered dark tunic and tight-fitting trousers. Black boots hugged his legs, ending at his thighs. He turned, watching me from the corner of his eye with a smile. A sick slash of joy marred his handsome face.

"Curse you all!" I called out louder, stepping away from Anderz.

Sainte leaned his head against the stake, panting. He made no move to look at me, even if he could have managed the movement. My brother stood still, swinging the black whip with its many tails, back and forth, sending fresh droplets of crimson to stain the white snow.

"I am Princess Elspeth, lost to the Kingdom of Wynterborne."

I halted within the half-circle of onlookers, their eyes trained on me, a few stealing glances at my brother. Panic raced through my chest, screaming for me to act.

"You should rejoice at my return," I demanded, voice tinged with bitterness. "Your *Lost Princess* has returned. The gods chose Captain Nytestorm to bring me back, and this is how you repay him? This is how you repay the gods?" Disgust curled my lip. I could play on their fear of divine retribution. If they were religious, they would feel the sting of that accusation.

"Gods, dear sister?"

Dread hit me like a stone in my gut.

Adastrus turned, the motion slow and meticulous. His hair, damp with sweat, clung to his forehead. Madness glittered in the depths of his green eyes, and I stifled a shudder. I was a princess. I could do this. We were equals.

"The throne and gods dictate the laws," he murmured, as if enlightening a child. "Have you been removed so long that you've forgotten the punishment for a soldier's falsehoods?"

"Falsehoods? He never lied," I said, proud that my voice remained steady.

Adastrus didn't even blink, but held my glare with an unnerving ease. "Oh, but he did. A recruiter makes a vow of thirty recruits a year, in exchange for a full belly and roof overhead."

He dropped his gaze and gave an innocent shrug, swinging the whip and splattering blood on my boots. I shook with caged rage, and clenched my jaw so tightly it popped.

"See, I've kept my vow. I fed him, sheltered him, paid him handsomely... and do you know how he repaid me—?"

By bringing your challenger to you.

"—With not a single soldier."

"I am worth thirty recruits," I shot back. "Am I not?"

Murmurs rippled through the crowd, accompanied by subtle headshakes and shrugs.

"Some might contest that notion." Adastrus laughed darkly. "Regardless, a vow remains binding, does it not, dear sister? A ruler should exemplify honesty, setting a standard not just for themselves but for their subjects. Or do you envision a realm built on deceit?"

I took a calming breath, steadying myself. He was pinning me in a corner. I had to be smarter than this. "He believed bringing me here was the honest thing to do, rather than waste time gathering men."

Adastrus sighed, a tinge of sadness in the sound. "He will be held to his vow. A man's worth is measured by his word. If that fails..."

I drew a sharp breath, my heart pounding as he inched closer. His unblinking green eyes bore a disturbing fascination as he loosened a dagger from his belt. I recoiled, jerking back from him.

Sinister laughter rippled through the crowd and my brother shook his head, yet his gaze betrayed a deadly intent. He would kill me if given the chance.

"If his words fail," he added, "so should his heart. A liar does no one good."

No, no, no. He would not kill Sainte.

"I offer my pardon," I said, lifting my chin.

His face changed from malice to confusion so quickly that I second-guessed myself. I cast a quick questioning glance at Anderz, but he watched on with his hands tucked in his robes, as silent and calm as ever.

"You pardon him?"

I cleared my throat and returned my attention to my brother. "Aye."

He threw his head back, roaring his laughter. His body shook with the force of his vile mirth, and the crowd echoed it.

At that moment, I would have killed them all if I could.

A flush of anger heated my cheeks despite the chilled breeze, and my lips pressed tight. As a princess, surely I could grant pardons.

"Ah, my sweet, naïve sister—"

I flinched as his arm draped over my shoulders, pulling me close.

"—you cannot pardon anyone. Only the regent holds that authority."

I shivered in disgust as his hot breath brushed my cheek.

"I'll teach you a lesson, little sister." His tone sweetened with false comfort, as though he were a caring brother ready to offer genuine guidance.

I doubted that completely.

"Serve him his last five," he commanded, thrusting the short whip against my ribs.

Blood smeared my dress, and my ribs smarted.

"It would have ended, if not for you," he hissed, pressing his lips against my ear. "Thank you for that."

Revulsion surged through me as I shrugged him off, hurling the weapon to the ground with a thud. I stood a few paces away, panting in my rage. His grin only fueled my anger, his demeanor akin to a brother teasing his sister.

"Then I'll deliver his true punishment," he said, shrugging a shoulder. With a swift motion, he tossed the dagger into the air, flipping it skillfully to secure a better grip.

"No!"

"Crimes deserve discipline. You'll have to learn this sooner or later."

Terror seized me as he strode over to Sainte, gripping his hair, wrenching his head back—then braced his blade against his throat.

"Mercy!" I cried out. "A true king would know when to show mercy!"

Adastrus froze, his gaze fixed on the dagger pressing against Sainte's neck. "A true king?"

Sainte swallowed, the knot in his throat moving with the action. His eyes remained shut, a sense of resignation. I despised that look, the acceptance of his demise. Why wasn't Anderz intervening? Why wasn't *anyone* stepping in to support my plea?

Angry, helpless tears welled, burning with frustration. I had no weapon. My only tool was my voice. Sainte's life hung by the thread of my words.

Adastrus shifted, his damp hair falling across his face. "You would recognize me as true king? After you challenged me?" His tone carried a dangerous, quiet edge.

I had to tread carefully. One misstep and Sainte would be lost to me forever. "I would have you mentor me," I replied, my hands clenched into tight fists at my sides. "Teach me to rule as a king would their heir."

His green eyes gleamed with fatal intensity.

I waited in tense silence, my breath held as I realized I had no more words left. There were no other pleas to make, no arguments that could sway him or the crowd.

"Of course, sister."

As he released Sainte's hair, he allowed the dagger to trace a gentle path along his throat. A choked cry escaped me as Sainte gasped, his head dropping forward to the ground. His back heaved as he struggled to breathe.

With indifference, Adastrus approached me, sheathing his blade without bothering to wipe the blood off. He picked up the whip as he passed by.

"Come."

No.

Yet, my feet moved as if I were a puppet, bringing myself closer. Bile rose in my throat, burning as it came.

"Hold it like so."

He snaked behind me, his grip firm as he pressed my back against his chest. Terror and horror flooded my senses. I sent a desperate glance at Anderz, a silent plea for his intervention to end this nightmare. Adastrus placed the weapon in my hand, enclosing my fingers around it.

"Watch."

Silence enveloped the crowd as my brother urged my head forward, compelling me to witness the horror of Sainte's mutilated back.

"Like this."

In a blur, the whip descended, and I gasped as it struck. I struggled to break free from his grip, but his hold remained unyielding. His frame was solid and unforgiving against mine, towering and overpowering in contrast to my smaller form.

"Again."

He wasn't laughing.

He didn't jest or act malicious.

The whip raised, and Adastrus moved me, bringing it down on Sainte's back, spraying the red snow with fresh blood.

"No..." I pleaded, tears stinging my eyes.

I racked my mind for an escape. This was a nightmare. I had to wake up. Wake up. *Wake up!*

"Only three more." My brother's voice was calm and reassuring as he guided my hand to raise the whip once more.

"No!" I choked as it came down.

Sainte collapsed forward against the stake, his silence broken only by the ragged movement of his back as he struggled for air. Crimson formed rivulets from his wounds. He wouldn't survive such massive blood loss. The realization hit me hard—I was still going to lose him.

"Two more, little sister."

It felt surreal, like an out-of-body experience, as my brother guided my hand once more. I sensed the flex of his chest against my back, the arc of his arm as the whip descended. Blood sprayed across my face and dress.

"One more, then it is all over," he murmured, his tone deceptively sweet and calm.

I flinched as if his words were venomous whispers in my ear. The weapon cracked down, rippling loose the skin that dangled from Sainte's back. Adastrus released me, and I crashed to the blood-soaked snow, retching as the full horror of the moment washed over me.

Through a haze of tears, I gazed up at my brother, who retreated, each step slow and deliberate. His expression was devoid of emotion as he walked, the whip in his hand swinging with each step he took. Blood dripped from the strands, splattering the snow.

It was then that I fully grasped what I was up against.

A monster.

CHAPTER 12

S ainte received a tonic to numb the pain and lull him to sleep while we tended his wounds. Gilead, understanding my silence and my need to help, handed me another strip of gauze. I pressed it against his raw, torn flesh, focusing on the task. Anderz's watchful gaze burned into me, a silent accusation that I couldn't ignore, as if questioning whether I learned my lesson.

I bit my cheek and withdrew my hand as Gilead finished dressing his wounds. My mind raced—would he ever regain his former agility, or would he suffer for the rest of his life, for my sake?

I wished he had never come back for me.

Tears streaked down my face, leaving hot, angry trails.

"Counselor Dyre, please fetch something to eat," Gilead said, her voice hushed and calm.

"As you wish."

I ignored Anderz's departure, wiping my cheeks as I glanced around. The room was pristine, with white sheets adorning every bed. A few patients lay resting, each with various injuries, but all were in a state of peaceful slumber. The air felt sterile, almost too clean against the backdrop of suffering.

"He will heal," Gilead murmured as she knelt before me. "You're hurt as well."

My once-elegant blue dress, now smeared with blood, clung uncomfortably to my skin. "No, it's not mine." My voice cracked with emotion as I wiped my face.

Her eyes studied my features, her smile tinged with sadness. "You hurt here," she said, placing her hand on my chest.

Tears pooled and spilled over, blurring my vision. "I can't do this." The confession tumbled out, choking my tight throat. "I couldn't even help him. I didn't know what to do or what to say."

My actions were driven by impulse, by a desperate need to save him, only to have delivered the final blow.

I would never forgive myself for that.

"Anderz was right to let you go."

I blinked away the haze to stare at her in disbelief. "What?"

"He allowed Prince Regent Adastrus to teach you a valuable lesson."

"That my brother can do what he wants? Sure, I learned that. Crystal clear."

Her hand rested on my knee, in an attempt to soothe my rising anger. "You learned not to act in haste. If you aren't prepared, you will fail every time."

"Don't you believe in the gods?" I scoffed. "Why prepare if they'll help you through?"

"They won't do for you what you can do yourself." She smiled, glancing at Sainte. "Don't shy from asking Anderz for guidance. The man is wise beyond his years."

"That's shocking, considering he looks like an old fart."

A throat cleared behind me. When I turned, I spotted the counselor giving me a droll stare.

"I sent for your midday meal," he said.

I sighed, returning my gaze to Sainte. He slept soundly, his face relaxed in a way I'd never seen. On the road, he'd always been guarded, even in sleep. Now he seemed at peace.

"He has suffered this before," Anderz added.

Not by my hand—the girl he saved and cared for.

"He will heal," Gilead said again, rising to stand. "I must tend to others. Stay here for the day. It would be expected."

I frowned, staring at my hands as she left. I would gladly hide away here for several days until Sainte recovered. He lay prone on the cot, his fresh bandages already spotted with crimson. With his boots removed, his wool-wrapped feet dangled off the edge. I stood, grabbed a blanket from a nearby cot, and draped it over his legs.

"Could you have stopped it?"

"Princess, no one could have prevented it." Anderz scratched his jaw as he let out a heavy sigh. "I would've had you wait until it ended, rather than see him in that condition."

Was that supposed to make me feel better?

"This is my fault," I whispered.

"In a sense, it is."

Usually, people offered consolation or comfort, insisting the blame was elsewhere. But I was a princess, and he, a counselor, was telling me that yes, I was responsible for Sainte getting beat within an inch of his life.

"This is the price he paid to bring you back." Anderz held my stare in that unnerving way of his, as if he could read my thoughts and intentions. "There will be far greater prices paid before this is over, Princess."

If these people truly wanted to remove my brother from power, one would think they would've devised a more effective plan.

"What am I supposed to do now?" If my mistake before was not seeking his advice, I wouldn't make it again. "Where do I go from here?"

He observed me for a moment, scrutinizing my expression. "You would do well to lie low, Your Highness. Gilead will inform the regent that you require time before the first rite, and we will use that time to prepare."

"What is it, the first rite?" I asked, wiping my wet cheeks on my sleeve.

"Trial by Nellium."

Days later, the significance of naming the rite after the Goddess of Frost and Chill became painfully clear. Isolated in a courtyard encircled by a tiny audience, I sat huddled on the frigid stone. Within a circle crafted from ice, courtesy of the Priests of Nellium, I was told if I left the boundary or called for warmth, I would fail the trial.

A cold breeze teased my brother's hair, seated a few paces away, his eyes locked on me with unwavering intensity. His posture remained composed, legs crossed beneath him, palms resting on his knees, his breath visible in the frosty air.

Clad in white linen, both of us endured the hostile elements with bare feet and hands. The garments were devoid of gems, stones, or any form of embroidery. They embraced simplicity.

With nerves wreaking havoc, I rubbed my palms together, hoping to generate some heat, all while cursing Sainte for having me raised in a tropical climate. I longed for the familiar clammy warmth of the ports, not this bone-chilling wasteland. Only moments passed, yet I trembled and shivered uncontrollably, my skin prickling with gooseflesh, desperate for respite from the numbing chill.

For the first time, I regretted chopping my hair short—its warmth would've been a solace against this freeze. Though, knowing my brother, he would have insisted it be cut to match his.

As if being raised in this bitter climate wasn't already an advantage.

My face scrunched when I peered over to find his relentless, emotionless stare. To distract myself, I surveyed the small gathering assembled. I appreciated the privacy of the event, limited to priests, healers, and select nobles who sought attendance. They sat with focused expressions, gloved hands wrapped around steaming mugs.

Sainte's absence stirred conflicting emotions within—sadness, but also gratitude. His role as a recruiter limited his access to many aspects of my new life, leaving me uneasy. He was the sole person in this gods forsaken place I trusted.

Anderz sat near the rear of the meager crowd, draped in a thick fur cloak. The last few days, his demeanor exuded reliability, and I did my best to lean on his counsel. He had been invaluable in helping me avoid my brother while providing insight into what was expected of me. In uncomfortable situations, when I struggled with words or actions, he covered for me. With him, the facade was easier to maintain.

And Sainte trusted him, so that had to count for something.

His handsome face came to mind, free of the stubble that grew during our long journey. Gilead worked wonders, cleaning him up until he resembled the man I remembered.

When I had voiced my pitiful wish that he could be at this trial, he simply replied, "Likewise, Princess. Likewise."

My shoulders dropped as I wiggled my fingers in my lap. He was still healing in the clinic. He sat up with more ease now, and thankfully there were no signs of infection. Though his movements were stiff, Gilead insisted on gentle exercises, and massaged oils into his back to aid his recovery.

I offered to do it once. Their reaction, the glances exchanged, clarified that my bid to assist was deemed inappropriate for a princess.

I only wanted to help.

It had nothing to do with the fact that a knot twisted my gut every time I witnessed her gentle hands on his skin.

Gods, I wished he were here. His presence brought a sense of reassurance, a semblance of safety that I craved. It wasn't about lingering emotions or romantic interest—it was purely about feeling secure. That's all.

"Ugh," I muttered, rising to stand. I had to get my mind off him.

The priests leaned forward in their seats, stares fixed, assessing if I'd step beyond the circle.

"Cold, little sister?"

I forced a haughty grin. "Not at all."

Anderz explained earlier that movements were permitted, as long as I stayed within the boundaries, though he cautioned me against sweating as it would chill me faster. The priests would supply cold water, a bowl shared between me and Adastrus. If I could exercise without worrying about dehydration, what better way to warm up than to move?

I jumped into a star shape, extending my limbs outward. Bystanders gasped and checked that my feet were within the circle—which they were. Returning to a straight position, I clapped my hands on my thighs, then with a grunt, repeated the star jump. After a few more sets, my quick pulse warmed my blood, and I settled onto the ground.

Adastrus observed me with a narrowed glare, his handsome face etched with a deep frown. He really did get the good looks of the family. High cheekbones, full lips, powerful green eyes, and blue-black hair cascading over his forehead. He was quite attractive.

I hoped the women he bedded knew the glitter in his eye was not from charm, but madness.

I pulled my knees to my chest and tugged the thin dress closer to shield against the bite, though the chill seeped past the fabric. With each breath, a puff of frosty air escaped in a halo of gray.

Either Adastrus would die or I would bow out. I doubted this would end any other way, but I would give it my best.

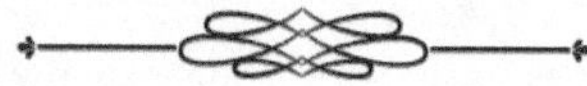

Night descended and the first layer of frost nipped at my blue skin. The nobles retreated to the castle's warmth, but the Priests of Nellium and Counselor Dyre lingered, bundled in furs.

Adastrus and I were given nothing, left exposed.

My exhaustion discouraged further exercise. The chill seeped too deep into my bones, making it unbearable to rise. The water given only intensified the cold—and now I had to piss.

But I was pretty sure I was frozen to the ground.

A shiver jerked my entire body as I struggled to open my eyes. My teeth chattered, rattling my head where a steady, pulsing headache throbbed beneath my skull.

With no lanterns or torches casting a warm glow, the twin moons hung full and luminous, their silver light bathing the scene like a celestial spotlight.

Adastrus shivered as well, his eyes shut against the frigid air. His fingers developed a dark blue tint, a testament to the bitter cold. He maintained the same dignified composure, sitting motionless, as if carved from stone.

I whimpered, trying to curl into a tighter ball. The thin dress offered little protection, and I cursed myself when my movement shifted the fabric, letting loose a pocket of marginal warmth.

I lay that way for what felt like ages, each second stretching into an eternity of shivers and chattering teeth. Everything ached. My heart thudded, slow and heavy. Every breath was a struggle, as though my ribcage was frozen solid, resisting my attempt to draw in air.

In that frigid darkness, I wondered if I had the strength to crawl out of the circle, to escape this icy prison. But exhaustion weighed me down, pulling me into a numbing haze as I closed my eyes.

A giggle jolted me awake, a tinkling rich cadence, like ice crystals clinking together. The sound pried me from the cold, dark abyss of sleep. I took a gasping breath as waves of pain washed over me, but I lacked the strength to cry out.

Forcing my eyes to flutter open, a ripple of panic quickened my pulse. Anderz and the priests were gone. Adastrus remained in his circle, his expression contorted in agony, his fingers a deep, bruised blue, as if crushed by a hammer.

"Oh, good morn!"

A little girl's face dropped before mine, tilting as if to get a better look. Brown waves cascaded, obscuring part of her features, yet her golden eyes gleamed with mischief. Icy flecks danced within her gaze as she giggled again, then straightened. I tracked the motion, mesmerized as she twirled, her fluffy pale blue dress swirling around her. Frost cascaded from her like a gentle snowfall, scattering in all directions.

I was dreaming.

Or dead.

That was a definite a possibility.

"It's... it's still... dark," I mumbled, gaze fixed on the starless sky.

The twin moons vanished too, leaving nothing but a void above. Yet I could see everything with clarity as if they were both full and vivid.

"Oh, but it's morning!"

She laughed, her cheeks rosy with warmth while I shivered blue with cold. She crouched in front of me, her eyes sparkling.

"I always run away when Loth comes out. She's too bright and scary." She scrunched up her face as if recalling something distasteful. "But once night ends and morning arrives, Papa says I can do as I wish!"

"Papa?"

The cold didn't seem to touch her. She twirled and leaped around the courtyard, her movements light and joyous.

"Nothar! Don't you know anything?"

The girl laughed again, but it faded when she noticed Adastrus. She approached him, her curiosity piqued, and circled him like a cat inspecting a new toy.

Nothar was a god... wasn't he? The one that Gilead served? None of this made sense. I'd never seen this girl before, yet she acted as though she owned the castle. Her confidence and ease felt out of place in this cold, desolate courtyard.

She stopped behind Adastrus, peering at me with bright, curious eyes. "Oh! You really don't know?" After another giggle, she skipped over and dipped into a curtsy. "I'm Nellie!"

With a spin, she kicked her leg out above me. Her hair splayed, giving her an ethereal, fairy-like appearance.

"Goddess, actually. I told you, silly. My papa is Nothar. You know, God of Snow and Cold?"

If I could feel any colder, I would have.

I was definitely dead—gone beyond the Veil.

"You're not dead, chicken." Nellie clamped her hand over her mouth to stifle her mirth. "I found you two! You've got my papa in you, otherwise you wouldn't see me."

Was she saying Nothar was my father? None of this made sense.

"You're royalty, chicken." She settled outside my circle, staring at her feet. Her bare toes, warm and toasty, wiggled as if she were on a sunny beach in Landing's End. "You're part of my papa's line. That's why we can see and talk to each other!"

If only I could get my mouth to move.

"Oh, let me help you!"

Nellie tapped a single finger against the ice ring encircling me. Frost flared out, spreading like delicate tendrils on a windowpane. An unfamiliar sensation crept through my body—uncomfortable yet oddly soothing. The biting chill dissipated from my skin and limbs. While warmth didn't replace it, and my bones still ached, I wiggled my fingers, marveling at the sudden ease of movement, free of pain.

Cautiously, and under the watchful gaze of Nellie's twinkling eyes, I sat upright. Apparently, I was not frozen to the ground, and my skin was pale blue, not blackened or broken.

"See? Now I won't have to look into your soul."

That wasn't disturbing at all.

"My name is Elspeth." I spoke slowly, testing out the movement of my lips. They were numb and dry, but no longer painful or splitting.

"Oh! Ellie! Like my name!"

I tried out a smile as I tucked my stiff legs underneath myself. "My friends call me El."

Her mouth formed a hard line, and she tilted her head, studying me. "Ellie's better."

Probably wise not to piss off an imaginary goddess.

"Ellie is great. I like that, too."

"Good! What are you doing out here tonight? Waiting for me? Oh, we could have a party! I could ask Papa if—"

A broken growl interrupted her excited words, and Nellie yelped as she whirled to face Adastrus.

Great. Now I not only had a tiny imaginary goddess to keep me company in the afterlife, I had my brother as well.

"I didn't wake you!" she shrieked, bumping into my circle as if it were a wall.

His teeth gritted in pain. Blood dripped freely from his cracked lips, staining his chin. His fingers, frozen to his knees, looked as stiff as his entire body.

"Nellium... free... me..." The words tore from his throat, spraying flecks of red.

"Only Papa can call me that." The girl pouted, crossing her thin arms over her chest. "It's *Nellie*."

"You... are... a goddess!" Adastrus spit. "Free... me." His eyes darted my way, spewing hatred.

"That's right, I am! So ask *nicely!*" she huffed, turning enough to watch him from the corner of her eye.

At that moment, I noticed something beyond her childishness. Her countenance flickered with otherworldly power and fury. No doubt, my mind had conjured an impressive goddess.

"Nell...ium..."

"I told you, only Papa calls me—"

A terrible sound erupted from Adastrus, blood gushing from his lips as he raised a stiff arm and thrust it over the circle of ice. He pointed at Nellie, who shrieked. A cloud of white materialized out of nowhere, flying at my brother with incredible speed. It enveloped his hand and collided with an invisible barrier at the ice's edge, dissipating against it.

His mouth gaped wide with his raw scream. Blackness crept from his fingertips to his knuckles, toward his palm. He yanked his hand into the safety of his circle, cradling it in his lap. He rocked back and forth, his head bowed, moaning in agony.

I pulled my limbs closer, scooting to the center of my circle.

"You scared me!" Nellie cried, backing away from Adastrus. "I'm a goddess, as you said. You should know better than to frighten me. I might only have the frost that answers my call—but it's enough to take a few fingers!"

I stared, horrified.

Now I had to serve eternity with an imaginary goddess, and my brother minus a few fingers?

When Adastrus looked up, a monstrous fury coiled in his eyes. He fixed her with a gaze of raw pain and unfiltered hatred, his expression twisted and fierce.

"Nellie… maybe you should go," I said, torn by my concern for this imaginary girl's well-being.

Despite my confusion, I didn't trust the ire on my brother's face. When animals hurt, they lashed out, but this was different. His glare blazed with a desire to inflict genuine pain.

"Fine," she huffed, smoothing out her dress. "Promise to come play again? I'm sure Papa would let me have a party with you."

I lifted my chin with a bright smile. "Aye, I'd be happy to. Will there be tea?" I hoped with all my heart for warm tea in the next dream.

"Gods, no. You sound like Loth!" Her crystal laughter clinked and chimed. "Bring some syrup, and I'll ask Papa for some snow and we'll mix them!"

"All right."

"Well then, I'll leave you two to it." She cast another wary glance my brother's way, brows lowered with a warning. "Be good. Or I will tell Papa you tried to catch me."

Please, no dreams of an enraged father.

Adastrus remained silent, prompting me to glance back at him. His expression sent an unsettling shiver down my spine, one that had nothing to do with the cold.

"Till next time!" Nellie said with a wave.

She skipped through the courtyard, humming and laughing as she went. Frost glittered where her bare feet touched the stone, spreading in a delicate lacework of ice across the ground. As she disappeared over a low wall into the gardens, her tinkling laughter faded with her.

The bitter cold surged, and I cried out in agony, every muscle tense against the assault. My body collapsed like a sack of rocks as frosty tendrils gnawed at my exposed skin and cheeks. A heavy weight settled on my mind, dragging me back into the abyss of darkness.

CHAPTER 13

I hurt.

Everywhere.

A profound, relentless ache gnawed at me, tearing me apart. I writhed as invisible hands pulled each bone from its joint, placing them aside in a neat, torturous pile.

An agonized wail pierced the air, echoing my silent torment.

But it wasn't me. I didn't have the energy to make a sound like that.

My eyes fluttered open, frost clinging to my lashes. My brother convulsed on the ground, encircled by priests. He clutched his wrist close to his chest.

The same hand Nellie, from my dreams, blasted with a cloud of icy magic.

He slammed his head against the frozen stone, arching his back in excruciating pain. When he rolled onto his side, his blackened bare feet flailed outside the line of ice. His skin was a terrible blue, smothered in bright angry blisters.

Priests surged forward, lifting his screaming form to carry him into the castle, out of my sight. I tried to shout for them to stop, to take me too, but only a moan escaped my lips. Tears threatened, but I held them back, fearing the icy trails they would leave on my cheeks.

Gentle hands gripped my shoulders, lifting me upright. "Nellium told me you would make it."

Agony flooded my senses, and I choked on a breath, straining to crane my head to see the stranger who spoke. My frozen bones refused to twist, and a wheezing, airy scream slipped past my cracked, split lips. They placed me on a cot, but it felt like being thrown down a cliffside, and four Priests of Nellium carried me inside.

My head lulled to the side where I found Anderz following behind, conversing in hushed tones with a priest.

They brought me to my chambers, where Gilead waited. I couldn't contain my screams as they tended to me. The room's warmth intensified the dull ache into a searing, stabbing torment.

The ordeal that followed plunged me into a haze of consciousness and piercing screams of agony. Blades sliced through my limbs, the sensation like a thousand shards cutting through my nerves. Powerful hands pinned me down, and I struggled against their grip, each movement a battle against overwhelming force. Chants rose, prayers invoking Nellium's name. I didn't have the strength to tell them she went by 'Nellie.'

When Gilead forced a scalding liquid down my throat, it seared a fiery path to my belly, leaving a burning taste in my mouth before I succumbed to sleep.

I awoke enveloped in a snug embrace, cocooned in warmth that seeped into my bones. Nestled against a sturdy chest, I inhaled the comforting scent of woodsmoke mingled with the faint aroma of pine. The crackling fire cast a gentle glow, its flickering dance painting warm hues on the walls. As I burrowed deeper into the plush furs, the crackle of flames whispered a lullaby, soothing my groggy senses as I slipped into consciousness.

"Easy."

My body tensed, startled by Sainte's hushed words. My heart stuttered, racing as blood throbbed in my ears. I clutched the heavy fur to my chest, fingers curling tight, while my other hand slid beneath, meeting the warmth of my skin.

My skin.

"Sainte!" I choked out, cursing myself as my lips split.

"Hmm?"

"Where are my clothes?"

In panic, I reached back, fumbling amid our closeness. A sigh of relief escaped when I found the fabric separating us. He chuckled, the sound followed by a subtle shift as he pulled his hips out of my reach.

"They were taken away."

Gilead's response made me wince, prompting me to crane my head back for a better view. She lounged in a nearby chair by the fire. The steam from her mug curled upward as she observed me, an amused arch to her brow.

"The priests believe they have been touched by Nellium. They claimed your dress as their relic."

"Nellie," I muttered.

"Pardon, Your Highness?"

I sniffed. "Nothing."

It was a dream, a fleeting hallucination, like the aftermath of eating tainted mushrooms. Certainly not a goddess in the guise of a giddy child, visiting me amidst a trial.

With a groan, I rolled onto my back, keeping the furs tucked close to my chin. "Why—how are you here?"

Sainte propped his head up on his hand, his other on top of the blankets for all to see.

Probably safer that way.

My cheeks stung with embarrassment.

"It's common practice to use body heat to warm someone who has the Crown of Frost," Gilead explained.

Sainte's blue eyes reflected the fire's glow as he studied my face, a faint smile tugging at his features. "Anderz declined," he said.

The healer scoffed with a mirthful shake of her head. "Sainte offered."

I smiled, though I regretted it when the tender skin split further. Wincing, I licked at it, and Sainte's gaze flicked to my lips. A frown creased his brow.

Not the reaction I hoped for.

"Help her up," Gilead said, moving to the kettle near the fire.

I squeaked a protest as he pushed himself upright, lifting the blanket with his movements. I hissed with pain, but quickly tucked the furs around my body.

It struck me as amusing how I didn't mind when a seamstress and crew of maids saw me without a stitch on, but with Sainte thrown in the mix, I became as prudish as a priest.

I glared at the smile that threatened to lift his lips. He cleared his throat, then climbed behind me to lift me against his chest. I clung to the blanket for all I was worth.

Gilead extended a mug of steaming liquid. The rich aroma of cinnamon and cloves teased my senses, promising comfort.

"Drink," she ordered.

"I can't," I said, eyes pleading.

My stinging fingers clutched the fur close. Nestled between Sainte's legs and thankfully shielded by his trousers, I refused to let go.

Sainte chuckled, a deep rumbling sound, and I tried not to think about the funny things it did to my stomach. The weight of his presence pressed against my back, the heat of his breath brushing my ear. I sat frozen, my pulse pounding, feeling both foolish and exposed.

He stretched around me, securing the blanket tight to my chest. I attempted to turn enough to give him a skeptical glare, but my stiff body wouldn't allow it. He leaned over the rest of the way so that I could see his eyes.

He winked.

I felt like someone had just shot my heart with an arrow, sitting there like a fool as he straightened behind me.

"Drink, Princess."

I cleared my throat and reached for the mug. When I saw the state of my hands, I froze, turning them over, horrified. Swollen and red, my fingers glistened with oil. Gauze wrapped several spots, and small, angry blisters swelled with fluid.

"It's not too bad," Gilead said. "We had to lance the largest abscesses. Better to relieve the pressure and keep the wound clean than risk it bursting on its own and getting infected."

"My feet?" A similar stinging sensation and dull ache pulsated there as well.

"The same, I'm afraid."

Her frown deepened as she held the mug out. I fumbled for it, gripping it as steadily as I could as I brought it to my lips. Hot and sweet, the spiced tea warmed my mouth and throat, its comforting heat spreading to my belly.

"Adastrus?" I asked.

"Suffered far worse."

"Not only are you the victor," Sainte cut in, "Nellium marked you as chosen."

Nellie. The imaginary girl in my head likes to be called Nellie.

"His left hand..." I hedged.

"It can be saved." The healer shrugged, a line creasing her brow. "His fingers cannot, not without Togamar's intervention."

"Who?"

"Goddess of Healing," Sainte supplied.

"He'd be hard-pressed to receive aid from her." Gilead shook her head. "Regardless, you are the victor, and Nellium marked you. This bodes well."

After I drained my drink, she retrieved the mug, and Sainte lowered his hold, allowing me to support the blanket over my chest. He made no effort to move, providing a comforting anchor for me to lean against.

I had completed one trial, with two more ahead. Each step brought me closer to leading a kingdom of strangers. Passing that first rite felt like chance, not skill. And why was I marked? I knew nothing of leadership. I'd be at the mercy of people like Anderz who would use me as a puppet.

Gilead gave me a knowing look, as if she sensed the direction my thoughts wandered. She headed for the door, then paused at the threshold. "Stay with her, Captain Nytestorm. Send word if she catches a fever."

As her footsteps faded and a door creaked open and closed, I gazed into the flames. Sainte's sigh brushed against my back, and his forehead rested heavily on my shoulder.

"Tired?" I asked. All this moving about had to be wearing on him. His injuries were nowhere near fully healed.

"Elspeth, you could push a man to an early grave."

I grinned to myself, staring at my bandaged, swollen fingers. "It wasn't that bad."

A blatant lie.

His head lifted from my shoulder, his warm breath brushing against my bare skin. "I believed in you."

This wasn't safe. Nothing about this was safe.

I sniffed and slid down his chest to burrow into the mass of furs and blankets on the floor near the hearth. Gaze fixed on the dancing flames, I forced myself to ignore his presence. My feelings for him faded long ago, and I was no longer the type to be swept off my feet by the first man to pay me attention.

He cleared his throat. "Are you warm enough?"

"Yes," I said with a bit more bite than intended.

I pulled the furs snug to my chin. It wasn't my fault I couldn't reciprocate his affection. He had my heart at sixteen and crushed it. I wouldn't give him another chance.

I didn't care—not anymore.

He settled in behind me. Even without touching, his presence brought more comfort than the amber flames. In the quiet, a thousand words sat unspoken until sleep claimed me once more.

"The Rite of Hearth and Home," Anderz said again. "You will have to practice, as you have no faith in the gods."

"Yet, you have enough faith for all of us," I grumbled, refusing to look his way.

Sainte sparred with another soldier in the courtyard below. Today's swordplay demanded agility over the brute strength his ax required. From my balcony vantage point, I could see the crimson stains seeping through the back of his shirt.

"Not I, Princess," Anderz grumbled. "Chosen of the Gods or no, I don't hold much stock in them heeding mortal matters."

I slouched against the stone railing, resting my chin on my palm. "Too busy doing their godly duties?"

"Regardless of your disbelief, you must prepare—"

His thin hand settled beside mine, urging me to meet his eye.

"—if you do not pass this second trial, it could kill you."

"The first almost killed me," I stated, examining the closed wounds along my skin.

They had healed remarkably well. Most of the small blisters had faded. Those that burst and were lanced remained free of infection.

Adastrus was not so lucky.

Despite the impossibility, his blackened, dead fingers clung to his hand, immobile at the knuckles yet able to move as a unit. His preferred method of unsettling dinner guests became drumming the table with the lifeless limbs. The dreadful sound stirred unease among the guests, much to his amusement.

"I suggest you go with…"

Anderz's words faded into the background as my attention sharpened on the figure entering the courtyard.

Urien?

Men trickled in behind him, their faces rugged from the trail yet not as worn as Sainte's had been. Practice halted, replaced by enthusiastic greetings and rough embraces. Sainte enveloped each in a one-armed hug, and they handled him with care, mindful of his back, as if this were routine.

"Don't tell me they're all going to be flogged."

I didn't recognize half of them, and the other half I resented for their involvement in my kidnapping. Despite this, I couldn't bear the thought of them being harmed.

A frizzy halo of sand-colored hair among the men caught my notice. Lyana? I leaned over the railing and my breath caught in my throat.

Anderz followed my gaze. "Everything all right?"

Her ocean eyes found mine, and she lifted her hand to shield out the midday sun.

"Lyana!" I shrieked.

Her smile brightened, consuming the whole of her face as she smacked the chest of the big warrior beside her. "Grimm, my man! Which way to that balcony?!"

He gawked at her, then blinked up at me. When he met my eyes, he dipped into a modest bow. Sainte's words from Landing's End echoed in my mind, as though spoken ages ago. 'When she acts like a princess, feel free to treat her as one.' I grabbed the sides of my lush green dress and curtsied.

"Scale it!" I called.

Amidst the small crowd, I spotted Ethyan giving me a salute. I squealed, throwing him a cheerful wave. I could hardly believe they were here.

Was 'here' even safe for them?

"I'll put up ten coppers!"

"A silver!"

Wagers went up among the men as she headed my way with a swagger and a grin. We scaled the bell tower regularly. What was a cold icy wall but another test of our skills?

I leaned forward as she reached the wall, peering over the edge. The stone's chill bit against my palms. Beside me, Anderz made a thoughtful noise as Lyana threw her cloak aside and searched for handholds along the rough, weathered surface.

"I'm coming for you, girl!" Her voice echoed across the courtyard as she began her ascent.

I grinned, captivated by her progress. This was nothing like climbing in Port Siren. The longer one's fingers gripped the stone, the colder and stiffer they became, weakening the grip. The height wasn't daunting, though a fall would shatter a few bones.

"Ha!" She slapped a hand on the railing.

I laughed, grabbing hold of her to help haul her over. She landed with a bounce in her step. Her eyes flicked to Anderz before settling on me, then dropped to my dress. Without waiting for her comment, I enveloped her in a fierce hug. She wheezed in complaint, but wrapped her arms around me just the same.

"What are you doing here? I didn't think you'd come!"

I held her at arm's length, taking her in. She wore ratty trousers and a tattered shirt, with what seemed like an overskirt tied about her waist, the fabric worn and frayed.

"Such little faith," she chided, picking at my fur-lined cloak. "Look at this! Such finery!"

"There's a whole room of dresses!"

Her eyes widened, lit with excitement. "No!"

I never kept my true identity a secret from Lyana and Ethyan, and they never gave a flying turd about it. She, ever the supportive soul, never wavered whenever I mentioned Wynterborne, even though my heart never harbored a desire to return. Her acceptance of that truth solidified our bond. Ethyan, bound by sibling loyalty, followed his sister's lead without question.

I turned my beaming smile to the counselor. "Anderz, I would like to retire to my quarters."

His sharp eyes darted to Lyana and back to me with a slight dip of his head. "Of course, Princess. Would you like a room made up in your wing for... Lyana, was it?"

"Lyana of Port Cara, at your service." She gave a playful attempt at a curtsy and peeked up at him from beneath her lashes, a sly smirk dancing on her cheek.

His smile mirrored hers. "A door with a lock, no doubt."

"A lock? How horrible!" She clapped a hand over her heart, feigning distress. "I should fear for my life!"

"We should fear for our valuables."

We followed Anderz, laughter bubbling between us. His grasp of Common Muik shouldn't have surprised me—he seemed to know everything. Yet, the warmth that filled me when he understood her words was undeniable.

Lyana recounted the dreadful journey, painting vivid pictures of Grimm's thunderous snoring and Urien's awful jokes. As we strolled to my quarters, Anderz departed to make preparations, leaving us to converse freely.

We talked until the sun dipped below the horizon. For the first time, I found contentment without Sainte by my side. Lyana, smelling of horse and sweat, brought a sense of familiarity that this frigid castle lacked since my arrival.

With Lyana, Ethyan, and Sainte here, Wynterborne almost felt like home.

CHAPTER 14

I kept a careful eye on Adastrus, positioning myself between Lyana and his intent gaze. She evaded his presence for three days, claiming fatigue from her journey. But now, she had no excuse to refuse his royal summons to dine with him.

Clack, clack, clack.

His lifeless fingers drummed against the table, each tap echoing through the tense silence.

My worried glance found Anderz, who conversed with another noble across the way. He gave a slight nod, lowered his goblet to respond to their remark, then turned his attention back to them.

Clearly, he was no help.

I still hadn't gained any new allies at the high court's evening table. A nobleman to my left griped about western trade, lamenting that our borders were too tight, stifling the flow of goods.

What was I supposed to say to that?

"You weren't kidding," Lyana whispered, stealing a glance around me to peer at Adastrus. "The way he taps those... *things,* it's unnerving."

Clack, clack, clack.

I shifted in my seat, once again putting myself between their gazes. My brother was usually cool and aloof, content to let me sit in peace at the opposite end with the lower nobles. Even Anderz sat closer to Adastrus than I did. I settled in, placing my napkin in my lap, ready for the final course. After poking around the last dish, we could retire to the safety of our rooms.

Ethyan escaped Adastrus' interest, as far as I could tell. He had a room in the common wing as my guest, but Anderz warned it would be grounds for hanging if he was found unescorted in my quarters. As a *virtuous princess*, strange men who weren't staff or nobles were forbidden without an escort.

Something about keeping my virtue intact.

A servant approached from behind, replacing my dish with a pastry drowned in glistening fruit preserves and dusted with fine, white sugar. The sweet aroma mingled with the rich scent of roasted meats. Lyana moaned as her plate was swapped, her eyes lighting up before she attacked the dessert like a wild boar.

I smiled to myself, nudging my serving toward her. The thought of eating felt impossible with my nerves twisted in knots.

Clack, clack, clack.

I frowned, glancing up the table. My brother leaned back in his chair, openly staring at us, his black fingers tapping the oak. His features set in a flat line, brows furrowed, eyes narrowed in contemplation.

I cleared my throat, waited a few moments, then excused myself to the minor noble on my left, whose name I still didn't know, and stood. A servant hurried to pull my chair back.

Lyana glanced up at me, sorrow clouding her eyes, purple preserves smudging the corner of her lips. "Now?"

"Aye."

Curious heads turned our way whenever we used Common Muik. Few in Wynterborne understood it, and even fewer spoke it. As far as I knew, Sainte, Anderz, Grimm, and Urien possessed both comprehension and fluency of Muik. Among the soldiers Lyana traveled with, only a few grasped its nuances, but she did her best to teach them every curse she could.

With a whine, she stood. A servant rushed to pull her chair back while she stared at her dessert.

"Don't–" I interjected, though not fast enough.

She seized the plate with the half-eaten pastry and twirled away, the scent of warm berries trailing behind her. With a confident swagger, she sauntered out of the dining hall, humming to herself.

I glanced back at Adastrus.

Clack, clack, clack.

After a deep breath, I rolled onto my side, bumping into Lyana's prone form. As I attempted to turn again, I teetered close to the edge. She was such a bed hog. With a gentle kick, I nudged her to make space.

A faint murmur escaped her lips, and she kicked me back.

I huffed, then shoved myself upright. I threw my leg over her, crawling to her side–

Crack!

I froze, then whipped toward the window, wondering if the icy chill might shatter it. Thick curtains shut out any moonlight, and I squinted in the dark.

"El?" Lyana moaned underneath me.

"Shh!" I hissed, eyes wide, searching the darkness for any movements in the shadows.

Glass exploded with a sharp crash. I didn't wait for a shout or war cry. I tumbled off the bed, pulling Lyana with me. The thud of us hitting the floor muffled her startled yelp, the impact jarring my shoulder. With my back plastered to the bedframe, I strained to hear over the blood rushing in my ears. The rapid pounding of footsteps echoed across my room, drowning out everything else.

I nudged Lyana, adrenaline heightening every sense. "Go! Get out of here!"

I seized a decorative book from my side table and hurled it toward the window. Whoever lurked would soon face a barrage of objects. Lyana darted as I grabbed everything within reach and launched it in a frenzy—candles, books, a vase. An audible 'oof' sounded as an object struck true. Out of hard things to grab, I yanked the blanket off the bed. As I held it out, ready to gather it to throw, something slammed into my stomach.

The impact forced a guttural sound from my lungs. I collapsed with a visceral scream, writhing like an eel out of water, as the weight of my attacker pinned me, the blanket between us.

A slew of High Wynter curses pierced the air, and I lurched to the side just as a heavy blow landed beside me with a resounding thud. By the searing sting in my hip, I could only assume it was a knife.

With renewed vigor, I unleashed a flurry of kicks, bucks, and frenzied thrusts. I managed to tangle their hands within the blanket's folds, attempting to grasp their wrists beneath the fabric.

The sudden crash of the door slamming open accompanied the resounding thuds of heavy footfalls. Startled, my attacker retreated, their oppressive weight lifting off me. Fueled by determination, I lunged, seizing whatever I could—be it a boot, a pillow, anything—to ensure they wouldn't get away.

"Hold!"

I struggled on the floor, legs twisted in the fabric.

"Shoot, you dirty piles of worm dung!" I shrieked as I kicked the blanket off and leapt to my feet.

Four armored guards positioned themselves within my chamber, two brandishing drawn swords while the other pair aimed crossbows toward my window. Startled, I spun around to face the source of disturbance, only to discover Lyana perched amidst the shattered glass, her figure silhouetted by a lantern's glow. She peered upward with a mixture of frustration and anger evident in her cursing.

"Your Highness! Are you all right?!" one guard asked, lowering his sword.

Another, with a bow, darted for the chamber's entrance, bellowing something down the hall. Lyana approached, the warm glow of her lantern casting eerie shadows along the walls. My gaze shifted downwards, fixating on the crimson stain seeping across my white nightgown.

"I guess not."

"We knew it would happen sooner or later."

"I hoped for later."

My breath hissed past gritted teeth as Gilead worked. The promised numbness from the ointment she applied did nothing for the sting of someone threading a needle through flesh.

In the dim confines of the windowless chamber, I lay on my side, the sterile scent of medicinal supplies pricking at my nausea. Across from me, Lyana watched Gilead's meticulous work with a mix of fascination and concern etched into her features. Sainte perched on a stool nearby, his piercing blue gaze fixed on me, carrying an unspoken accusation, as if I was to blame for the entire situation.

Anderz maintained a composed stance at the foot of the bed, hands clasped together in a quiet display of resolve. Meanwhile, Urien lounged against the doorframe, picking his nails with a wicked-looking dagger.

"Something sent him over the edge," he said.

Anderz gave him a bored leer. "Prince Regent Adastrus is not her only enemy within the castle."

"The only one so bold," Sainte added.

Lyana leaned closer to the wound along my side. "Do you tie it off like a regular stitch?"

"Watch," Gilead murmured.

Sainte winced, straightening his posture, eyes locked on me. "She needs a Valahant."

"A what?" I asked.

"Careful, Captain," Urien warned. His hands went still as he stared at the back of Sainte's head.

"What is that?" I never heard the word before, but it was familiar, as if it had roots in Wynterborne.

"Done," Gilead sighed, gathering her supplies.

Anderz tapped his lip as if contemplating. "A Valahant is..."

"An extension of yourself," Sainte finished, cool gaze still fixed on mine.

The counselor nodded. "Many countries refer to them as champions or protectors."

"A personal guard?" I offered. "I've seen them in the ports."

"It's more than that, Princess," Anderz said. "They are, as the captain put it, an extension of yourself. They would be bound to you in life and death."

"Never free to pursue their own will," Urien added, deathly still.

Lyana scoffed. "Well, that's awful."

"It is," he agreed. "Post her own guard. The prince can't deny her request for protection."

Anderz lifted a gray brow. "And you would trust those picked by our dear regent to protect her?"

With Lyana's help, I sat upright, adjusting my gown. "Do I get a say in this?"

"No." Every man in the room answered in unison.

Lyana snickered, and I turned my glare on her. With a huff, I folded my arms, the movement slow to avoid tugging at my stitches.

Sainte dipped his chin. "I will do it."

My glower narrowed. "I choose Urien," I said, just to spite the men and their plans.

"You can't." Urien pushed off the doorframe, straightening. "If you did, the prince would claim Sainte and pit him against us."

"Then what's stopping Adastrus from claiming you? Wouldn't the result be the same?"

"He would never pick me." A dangerous glint sparked in Urien's gaze, dark and menacing. "He learned that lesson before."

"How ominous," Lyana muttered.

"He poisoned him once," Sainte ground out.

Urien scoffed, waving him off with a flippant gesture. "Rumors, rumors."

Anderz cleared his throat, directing the conversation back to the topic at hand. "The Vahalant has to be willing. They would forfeit the possibility of familial ties and any titles or land they may have. They would offer their entire life."

My mouth parted. "No."

He had no family, and gods knew deep down I was jealous of that possibility. Yet, in all the desolate expanse of the Great Iceland, I would never shackle him with such an agreement.

"I am willing."

"And I said no!" I shot back, looking to Anderz for help.

He watched me with that annoying calmness of his. "What is your reasoning, my petulant princess?"

"Deeply held religious beliefs." I sniffed, lifting my chin.

Lyana cackled, and I'm pretty sure I heard Gilead choke on a laugh.

"As a Valahant, he would go where you go, sleep where you sleep—"

My gut twisted with nerves.

"—eat what you eat and drink what you drink. It was common practice for generations."

"Back when we were all barbarians?" My voice pitched unnervingly high.

"Would you consider the prince regent anything less?"

"Ugh!" I spun, finding Lyana with a silent plea for help.

Her eyes opened wide in understanding, and she cleared her throat. Propping her chin on her folded hands, she batted her eyelashes at Anderz. "What if she happened to have romantic feelings for the Valahant?"

"Lyana!"

"In the past of course!"

Heat stung my cheeks as I hurled a pillow at her. Pain flared from the stitches in my side. I thanked the numbing cream for dulling the ache.

"Though I wouldn't advise it, pleasure would not be a question of morality."

"Gods, no." I buried my face in my palms, positive the tips of my ears were on fire.

"Children, however, could be a problem," Anderz continued, "especially if you take a spouse."

"Gods and goddesses above and beneath, Lyana. I'm going to kill you," I growled.

"I would have a moment with Princess Elspeth," Sainte murmured.

Oh, if given a moment with Sainte, I'd murder him out of sheer embarrassment.

"Well enough," Anderz replied.

The small group shuffled out, Lyana's fingers brushing my shoulder in passing. The door clicked shut, sealing in the awkward silence.

"Elspeth–"

"No, Sainte. No."

"Look at me."

"If I do, I'll slap you."

"Then slap me!"

I yanked my face out of my hands and stared at his livid features.

"Do you know how close that was tonight? How close I was to–" He took a sharp breath and exhaled through his nose, keeping his eyes on mine. "I have a blanket to thank."

My pulse slammed in my chest. "It was a lovely blanket."

"A cursed shred of fabric is all that saved you. That and the sheer luck of Lyana in your bed."

"Better her than you."

He flinched as if I had slapped him, recoiling with an expression of confused shock.

"Sainte, if you were my Valahant, you'd sleep where I sleep?!" I spat, shaking my head in disbelief.

"I've no care who you take to your bed."

For some reason, that hurt more than I expected.

"You don't get it," I shot back, rising to poke him in the chest. "You would give up your life—that part I understood as clear as day. I'm free to do what I want, apparently, but your future vanishes with one lousy vow. No wife, no children, no cottage in the woods—you'd lose it all!"

He lunged forward, causing me to drop onto the bed. He advanced with a menacing glare, slamming his hands on the mattress. I scrambled backward as he loomed over me, his breath hot on my face.

"No. You don't get it, *Princess*." His eyes, cold and angry, bore into mine. "I swore my allegiance to the kingdom years ago. My life is forfeit, my–" He broke off, shaking his head and looking away, wrestling with something deep inside. When his gaze returned, it was softer, calmer. "I made a vow, Elspeth. I vowed to serve the throne, and I cannot serve this regent."

Understanding dawned as I realized his urgent need to bring me to Wynterborne. This wasn't just about the kingdom or my duty. It was about his honor. He embodied loyalty and integrity. My Sainte couldn't uphold his pledge to the throne with my brother on it.

"But what about your desires? If you could choose freely, without your vow?" I bit my lip, exhaling slowly. "What would you do? Where would you go?"

"Nowhere."

"Your dreams, Sainte. What do you envision for your future? I don't want to rob you of a family, of the freedom to choose."

He drew in a deep breath and held it, locking eyes with me. Silence stretched, and my heart raced as I studied his cool blue irises, flecked with silver under the lantern's glow.

"I would choose you, Ellie. Every time, I would choose you."

Anderz warned me. Sainte assured me. Yet nothing prepared me for my brother's reaction.

"What?!" Adastrus abandoned all decorum, his hair brushing across his furrowed brow.

"I demand a Valahant of my choosing," I reiterated, chin lifted in defiance.

As Counselor Dyre instructed, I approached him in the Hall of Receiving, prepared to confront him. He told me I could seek him out privately, yet facing him in front of nobles would compel him to honor the request. Surrounded by onlookers, my breath seemed to reverberate against the lofty ceilings. Sainte stood behind me, a silent support. Meanwhile, Anderz mingled with the crowd, whispering to a nearby noble.

Adastrus lounged in the gem-encrusted chair atop the dais. It resembled a throne more than a seat for common pleas, but who was I to judge?

"That's an ancient custom you invoke, sister," he remarked, his posture relaxed yet his eyes sharp and calculating as they fixed on Sainte.

"Tradition is tradition. Law is law. I'm not asking, brother." I quoted the words Anderz told me to say. He said it would move the nobles, and as I spoke, murmurs rippled through the crowd.

"Ah, so there it is. You survive one rite unscathed and believe you're destined for the throne."

My lips pressed tight. I needed to choose my words with care. I was ill-equipped for this conversation.

"Less than a month you've been here and already you try to remove me." His dead fingers drummed on the hard wood of the chair.

Clack, clack, clack.

"I would name Sainte Nytestorm as my Valahant."

"Predictable."

Adastrus pushed to his feet. Angry sparks flew from his eyes, a sharp contrast to his easy smile as he descended the steps, reaching me on level ground. It must have irked him that I was nearly as tall as he was—he couldn't look down on me anymore. I struggled to stay composed as he drew closer, his gaze flicking to Sainte.

"Do you know the old customs, Captain?"

I turned, keeping Adastrus in my sight as he circled Sainte, who stood unwavering under the scrutiny, his head held high.

"Do you realize you'll be a mere puppet—"

I fought a thrum of panic as he moved behind Sainte and whispered in his ear.

"—just as they wish her to be?"

As my lips parted to speak, movement from the crowd caught my eye. Anderz shifted in his seat, pressing his fingers to his mouth. His golden eyes bore a silent warning.

"I am willing," Sainte declared, gaze fixed ahead.

"Willing, but not eager? Yes, I can't imagine any man would be eager to provide for her needs."

A tic worked in Sainte's jaw, but he remained still.

"Him?" Adastrus' hand settled on his left shoulder, resting his chin on the other. His dead-black fingers dug in as he smirked behind Sainte. "You would demand him?"

"Yes. I demand Sainte Nyte–"

My teeth slammed together as my brother rammed his fist into the small of Sainte's back. He grunted, staggering with the blow, but remained upright. His eyes fluttered shut, as if he were pulling himself to another time or place.

"The first lesson, dear sister, is that your Valahant must take a beating," Adastrus declared, dragging his lifeless fingers across his back, eliciting a wince, before circling to his front. "We wouldn't want," he threw a fist into his stomach, causing him to stumble and gasp, "you to be protected by someone weak."

My whole body trembled with rage, my vision blurring with red as I witnessed my brother pummel Sainte.

And he took it.

He stood firm, absorbing each blow.

"You see, little sister. Your Valahant is a part of you, almost as if they were you." When Adastrus' fist collided with Sainte's face, blood spurted from his nose, an angry welt forming on his cheek.

This wasn't about Sainte or any bones he might have with him.

It was about me.

"Truly brother, if you want to strike me, I'm right here." My voice shook with anger. It was reckless, but I couldn't care less.

Adastrus turned and Sainte's heaving breaths filled the silence. His sickly green eyes locked on to mine as he raised his hand, licking the blood from it like a cat would clean its paw. Disgust surged through me, and I couldn't hide my grimace.

"Oh no, sweet sister. I would not hit you." The malice in his words hinted at other forms of torment. "I'm merely teaching you a lesson. Remember our last? You were such a good student."

I struggled to maintain composure, forcing myself to stay calm. I couldn't lash out. Impulsivity was not an option. It would endanger both my life and Sainte's.

But if I was ever given the chance...

I would kill him.

"I remember it well. Will you provide me a velebond, or must I seek out a common smithy?"

Adastrus made a sound of contemplation as he tapped his jaw, turning back to Sainte.

No, no, no.

My brother gestured for a servant to leave, and they scurried off. He then circled behind once more, resting his head on Sainte's shoulder, casting a sidelong glance my way. Despite his bleeding nose, swelling eye, and ragged breath, Captain Nytestorm stood resolute.

"Have you bedded him?"

My cheeks flushed with fresh anger as my hands balled into tighter fists, nails biting into my skin.

He smirked. "Not yet then, I see."

"Whom I bed is none of your concern, nor anyone else's," I spat, thrusting my chin up.

"So long as you take the blood tea, perhaps not. But remember–" He snapped his fingers, as if recalling something, then returned to Sainte's front. "When you rut like dogs in heat, do be silent. Not everyone wants to hear a howling bi—" he snapped his knee up but Sainte's powerful thighs caught the strike before it hit true. Adastrus stumbled, bracing himself on Sainte's shoulders. A calm, deadly storm swirled over his features.

"Careful, Captain." He leaned close, resting his forehead against his. "Treason is but a breath away."

A sickening feeling churned in my stomach as Sainte relaxed, letting him go. My brother grinned and patted his shoulder, as if this entire scene were a jest.

Fury boiled within, fueled by the helplessness of the moment. Adastrus planted a hatred in me I'd never felt before. I would claim the throne, not for power, but to shield Sainte from such malice. This growing contempt only strengthened my resolve. He would never be king—he'd be a tyrant, seizing whatever he desired, whenever he pleased.

There was no place for Adastrus on the throne of Wynterborne.

Quick footsteps approached, echoing through the chamber's silence. The servant bowed low before the regent, presenting an ornate box.

"Ah, the velebond. I trust you chose only the best for my little sister." He snatched the box, his grip rough as he peered inside. "A kitten, quite suitable."

When he tossed it to me, I caught it, fumbling in my rage.

He turned away, striding back up the stairs to the dais, gesturing dismissively. "Be sure to collar your kitten tightly." He spun and collapsed into his seat, bringing his bloody knuckles to his lips. "Wouldn't want him to stray."

CHAPTER 15

"Now, when I hand this to you, you will touch it to the band. Don't exert force or push too hard." The jewelry smith demonstrated by pressing the thin rod to the gap. "Make haste, as you do. It's quite hot."

Sainte sat with a chain wrapped around his neck. Two fingers fit between his throat and the metal links, but it was tight enough that removal would be impossible. A matching set of lynx heads adorned the ends, their mouths frozen in a silent hiss. Between their teeth lay a single silver loop with a gap in the center. Once it was filled, the chain would be sealed forever.

A thick leather strip shielded his neck and chest from the molten silver I prepared to apply.

I took a deep breath as the jeweler heated the metal in a small kiln, its end burning with a heated orange glow. Sainte's battered face remained emotionless—the left side was a swollen, bruised mess. A sickening tightness churned in my gut as I examined his injuries, imagining the countless gashes and fresh wounds from the flogging.

Its power felt terrible, like a dark beast born from fear. It started small, with Adastrus' cold gaze—the dread he instilled gave it breath. His abuse, forcing *me* to punish Sainte, fed the creature. The worst of it, the act that turned it into a monster, was my brother beating Sainte to torment me.

Now, that monstrous feeling coiled inside, angry and helpless and bitter.

"Are you ready?" the jeweler asked.

I chewed my lip, peering at Sainte below my lashes. "Are you sure?" I whispered.

He held my gaze and gave the smallest of nods. I tried to smile, but my nerves made it impossible. It wavered, then fell away. I stood on the brink of taking a man's life, future, and freedom.

"Make haste."

My movements were careful as I grasped the small rod, its end glowing with molten metal. Sainte sat straighter, and I hesitated.

Could I do this to him?

He already gave so much to me. I never asked for this. As a child, he offered hope and a glimmer of happiness in an otherwise dull world. Sainte was always there, my star in the night sky, constant despite clouds or circumstances.

"Princess—"

I took a sharp breath as he pushed his chest to me.

"—this is my choice."

My teeth sank deeper into my lip at those words. Hand trembling, I eased it forward and dabbed the glowing metal to the band.

"Here now," the jeweler said.

I handed over the small rod, watching as the silver cooled before my eyes, turning a sooty black.

"Once it cools, you are free to go to Togamar's temple," he added, cleaning his workstation.

"Togamar? Goddess of Healing?"

"Yes, Your Highness."

Sainte pulled the leather away from his neck. The chain clinked against his collarbone, firmly in place. I admired it—a small thing to bear for such a heavy weight of loyalty.

"Can't we use Gilead?" I asked, assuming the jeweler mentioned the temple for Sainte's sake.

"When we return, we can see her," Sainte grunted, standing stiffly, "if you would like."

"For your sake, I would," I replied, skimming the empty shop. "But why do we need to go to the temple?"

"To finish the velebond."

"Oh." My voice carried a hint of surprise, though my expression remained neutral.

I assumed the bond was complete. No one told me there were additional steps. Anderz instructed me on how to ask for the Valahant, and demand the velebond, which I recognized as a type of necklace.

Apparently, crucial details were omitted.

We walked in silence through Wynterborne's quiet streets. I matched his gait as he endeavored to mask a visible limp. People observed us with unabashed interest, acknowledging my presence with nods or graceful curtsies. No one approached, and most maintained a respectful distance as we passed by.

He flinched at a wrong movement and sucked in a hissing breath.

"I'm sorry," I whispered.

"Anderz warned you–"

"You said it would be harsh. I thought you were speaking metaphorically, not literally," I grumbled.

"Would that have swayed your decision?" he asked, scrutinizing my expression.

I returned his gaze with a furrowed brow. "Perhaps."

"Hmm," he grunted, limping forward.

"I'm sure that wasn't easy for you, Sainte. It wasn't easy for me either," I confessed, anxiously twisting the folds of my dress. "I didn't know what to do, or how to make it stop. And I hate it. I wish I could've–"

"Elspeth." He stopped me, flinching when he tried to press his lips together. "Princess, you did what needed to be done. I knew what would happen. I was ready for it."

With a scoff, I turned on my heel, continuing without him. His readiness to endure abuse didn't mean I was fine with standing by and letting it happen. "You could've worn a steel plate beneath your tunic or something," I muttered. "Prepare better next time."

"Yes, Princess," he replied, tone light.

I side-eyed him and scoffed, a small smile gracing my face for the first time since I approached Adastrus that morning.

He guided me through the streets, creating the illusion that we walked side by side rather than him leading the way. The slush underfoot squelched with every stride.

Our path took us down a broad street, spacious enough for several wagons. The road had been cleared of snow, unveiling the intricate patterns etched into the wet cobblestones. Few travelers ventured down its length, lending an essence of solitude to the scene. Large temples flanked our path, the ancient architecture casting long shadows in the fading light. The faint, rich scent of incense drifted along the breeze, blending with the crisp winter air. Ahead, a statue snared my notice. A girl with flowing hair, frozen in a spin within a shallow pool of ice.

Nellie.

"Suiting that you take note of that temple," Sainte commented.

My gaze wandered over the structures, each adorned in intricate designs, possessing an ornate, distinct style. "You said she marked me as chosen. What does that mean?" I asked, pulling my cloak tighter to ward off the chill.

"The priests fashioned those circles using melted frost. They chanted their incantations over it and waited," he explained. "It's been observed in past rites that one combatant might endure longer than the other," he broke off with a hiss, clutching his side for a moment before resuming his stride as if unaffected, "but only a few instances are documented with Nellium's design within the ring. To her followers, her touch upon your ring signified you were chosen by the gods."

"Or Nellie simply thought it was pretty."

Sainte turned to study me, prompting me to clear my throat and glance down at the damp pavers. As if sensing my hesitation, he refrained from probing further.

As we neared, our pace slowed, bringing us to a temple hosting a statue of a woman in its courtyard. The statue portrayed a tall figure, clad in a flowing apron dress with pockets brimming with flowers and herbs. Atop her head sat a scarf, caught in an invisible breeze. Her gaze was fixed upwards, her expression filled with wonder and curiosity. One hand held the scarf in place against the wind, while the other gripped a sickle and a handful of freshly harvested herbs.

"The Temple of Togamar." Sainte unlatched the clasp on the small iron gate. The metal squeaked as he eased the way open.

"She seems nice," I said, stepping into the courtyard.

I ascended the steps alongside Sainte. Priests and priestesses wearing thick green wool nodded in acknowledgment as they moved about. This place seemed more active than the others I had visited, with a larger number of clergy present.

"Our Lost Princess!" a raspy voice greeted.

I offered a warm smile to the elderly woman, her gray hair peeking from beneath a vibrant green scarf. Despite her cloudy blue eyes, she observed me with a keen gaze that seemed to take in every detail. I curtsied to her, as I felt I should, and she laughed, delighted.

"She, who would rule, bows to me!"

A priest with dark hair approached her and gently quieted her. "Hush, Edne," he murmured, placing a comforting hand on her shoulders. His irises, a striking emerald hue, sparkled with warmth as he smiled. "Not everyone holds the same sentiment," he explained.

As I glanced around, I noticed a mix of reactions among those present. Some greeted us with warm smiles, their eyes crinkling at the corners in genuine welcome. On the other hand, a few wore furrowed brows, their disapproval evident in their tense expressions and clipped movements.

"Are you here for your wounds?" the man asked, reaching out to examine Sainte's cheek.

Sainte pulled away before his touch could land and looked at me expectantly.

"I've taken him as my Valahant," I said, swallowing around the lump in my throat. "We just sealed the velebond."

"Dead chain isn't the velebond, my dear," the old woman, Edne, remarked with a grin, her wrinkles deepening with the gesture. Despite missing several teeth, her smile remained radiant and welcoming.

I stole a glance at Sainte for help. He inclined his head to Edne, ignoring me.

"We have not had a royal take a Valahant in generations," the priest said softly.

"Even I've never seen a velebond!" She spoke around her cackling laughter. "What a blessing! Togamar foretold that I would live to see this day."

"Edne will show you to the chamber. She's the oldest that has been schooled in the ritual," he said with a nod, then hurried off, calling out to another priestess.

"Ritual?" I asked.

Sainte didn't meet my eyes—definitely ignoring me.

"This way, Princess," Edne beckoned, her voice echoing in the temple's vastness.

With a turn, she hobbled through the ancient corridors, her weathered walking stick tapping against the mosaic floor. We trailed behind, drawn to the warmth emanating from the open doors ahead, leading us deeper into the temple's heart.

My questions caught in my throat as she struggled down the worn stone steps. The staircase descended into a dimly lit cavern, bathed in a mystical blue glow that danced across the rough-hewn walls.

"Need a hand?" I offered, wincing as she faltered, her fingers clinging to the railing for support.

"Oh, if I fall down these stairs, I will gladly meet my death."

I froze, horrified.

"Togamar has blessed my life indeed by bringing you to see me in my last days," she continued.

"I should help you." I stepped in front of Sainte and placed her hand on the crook of my elbow, our steps measured and deliberate as we descended the ancient staircase.

"She told me you would be fire and honey," she remarked, joy lightening her tone. "Fire to purify the wound. Honey to soothe it."

"How... how does she talk to you?" I asked, forming my words with an air of caution.

"I dream of her," Edne stated, nodding along.

My shoulders sagged in relief. "Oh, a dream," I murmured.

Her thin hand tightened to a bruising grip, and I yelped. Her cloudy blue eyes were deathly serious as she pulled me down to her hunched height. "Some dreams," she said, her voice eerily calm, "are not merely dreams, but messages from the gods."

I searched her gaze, unsure how to respond. Then she released me and descended the last of the stairs without my support. She hummed as she went, as if she hadn't just pulled me down with a strength beyond her years to warn me. At least it seemed like a warning.

"Couldn't have helped there?" I hissed, leaning close to Sainte. "You're supposed to be my protector now."

"Protect you from the little old priestess?" he asked, lifting a single eyebrow.

At the base of the stairs, the room opened into a vast natural cave beneath the temple. Dark yet warm, it featured a few lanterns along the rough stone walls. The air smelled faintly of damp earth, and the soft sound of dripping water echoed through the cavern.

At the center, a pool radiated an unearthly blue light. Its surface shimmered, casting delicate reflections, creating an ethereal atmosphere. I had seen clear shores before, but this was unique. Its glow was self-sustained, needing no sunlight to reveal its mesmerizing color.

I doubted it was safe.

Edne made her way to the shallow end of the pool, leaning on her cane as we trailed behind, her figure silhouetted against the radiance. I crouched beside her, peering into the depths. This close, it was clear the water itself wasn't emitting the light, but something along the bottom—a strange, luminescent plant or... *creature.*

My nose wrinkled with dread. "Don't tell me we have to drink it."

"Oh, no dear!" Her mouth spread into a mirthful grin. "You two must bathe in it!"

I lost my balance and fell on my rear, gawking at the woman. She peered down at me, a twinkle in her eye. I glanced at Sainte, who promptly averted his gaze.

"You knew!"

"Here come the apprentices with the gowns," Edne said.

I stood, brushing off my cloak. Several young people descended the stairs, led by an older priestess holding a lantern. They came with a hum of excitement, but a seriousness that indicated the gravity of the moment.

I cringed when a girl approached me, extending her arms.

"May I hold your garments, Princess?" she asked.

Her little face was so hopeful, and I dreaded disappointing her. Sainte was removing his tunic while a boy waited on him, features etched with awe.

"Sainte," I hissed between my teeth.

It was one thing to get undressed in front of women, to lie naked in a bed, concealed by blankets and furs. But disrobing before an audience? That was too much.

His eyes found mine as he struggled out of his tunic, wincing from the pain of his bruises. He paused, studying me for a moment, trying to discern what could be wrong. Then realization dawned. "A robe," he said.

A little girl ran up to him, offering a swath of thin white cloth. He accepted it with a nod and stepped closer to me. Spreading it wide, he held it out, a feeble wall of privacy.

"They study the body. Nudity is simply baring their canvas to heal," he said, as if that was his reasoning for stripping before a meager crowd.

"Feel free to bare your goods," I mumbled, unclasping my cloak behind the relative safety he provided. "But I'll keep mine covered, if you don't mind."

When I held the garment out, a small hand grabbed it with a giggle. I hurried to undress. After the last of my things passed the fabric, the young priestess offered a silken white shift.

I stared at it, shook it out, then examined it again. "I'm bathing in this?"

"You'll be covered," Sainte said.

A slight strain edged his words, and I realized it must be taking a toll on him to hold the robe up for so long.

"This doesn't cover any more than a bride's veil!" I growled, pulling on the simple gown. The fabric sent a chill through me as it touched my skin. I crossed my arms over my chest and cursed in four languages.

Slowly, Sainte lowered the cover. His gaze traveled from my hair, down my frame, to my toes peeking out from beneath the hem. A faint smile flickered on his lips before he cleared his throat and turned, passing the robe to a small boy.

As Sainte openly disrobed, I wandered over to Edne, who watched us with a knowing grin.

"Have you led a velebond ritual before?" I asked, crouching to test the pool. It was surprisingly warm, and I jerked my hand away before dipping my fingertips back in.

"Never."

"You've seen it done then?" I swirled my fingers in the liquid. It felt like water, but thicker. The trail I left along the surface lingered longer than it would in a drinking well.

"Nay."

I looked up at her with a frown. "Have your teachers ever completed it?"

"No."

Was this tradition so ancient that no living person witnessed it? My father never had a Valahant, but I assumed it wasn't so far removed from history for Anderz to recommend it.

I pushed to stand, glaring at her mirthful countenance. "I assume, then, that you have records of this that you'll be following?"

"The velebond is not documented, because there are no established rules. The Valahant creates them."

"Can I say I don't want to get in?"

She chuckled and wagged her finger at me. "Dear princess, you will follow your Valahant until he chooses to let you lead."

I scrunched up my face in a grimace. What was that supposed to mean?

Splashing sounds made me turn, and I choked on a breath. Sainte stepped into the pool wearing naught but thin silken trousers. The water's glow illuminated the dark, angry wounds on his back and chest. My jaw clenched, memorizing every painful mark on his skin.

That monster within coiled tighter.

Sainte extended his hand to me, and I regarded the liquid with caution. The glowing things at the bottom swayed, moved by an unseen current. He seemed unfazed as he strode over them. In fact, they flared brighter beneath his feet.

Perhaps that was their self-defense.

Squashed by something? Glow brighter.

"Princess."

I blinked, then, with a dramatic sigh, took his hand and eased into the pool.

I should have taken a piss before all this.

Shoving that thought aside, I pushed at my gown as it threatened to balloon around me. Sainte was patient, waiting with a stoic expression, and I glared at him in return.

He guided me to the center, where the warm water enveloped us, its gentle ripples lapping at my chest. I clung to him as my body threatened to float in a way I couldn't control.

"I can't swim." My nails dug into his skin like tiny anchors.

He spun me to face away from him. "I remember."

"Well, don't let me drown this time," I hissed.

The priests and priestesses encircled the shimmering pool, interlocked as a barrier of unity. Even Edne, usually reliant on her cane, clasped the hands of two young girls, forming an unbroken chain.

"Trust me," Sainte whispered in my ear.

"I do–"

He dropped his weight, drawing me under the water with him. Panic surged through me, my heart pounding as I struggled against his hold. My limbs flailed, though he didn't keep me submerged for long. We rose, and I gasped for air as his arms wrapped around my middle, holding me to his chest.

"Trust me, Elspeth."

"Trust you?! You just–"

Once more, he dragged me beneath the surface, and a string of curses spewed, muffled by the water. I thrashed my legs, aiming for a solid strike to his nether regions.

He resurfaced, bringing me with him, and I sucked in greedy lungfuls of air.

"Sainte, please!" I begged, my voice tinged with desperation.

At that moment, the crowd's presence faded to insignificance. My heart thudded in my chest, a relentless drumbeat of terror. I didn't want to drown. The water closed in around me, each passing second a cruel reminder of my vulnerability.

"Deep breath."

I listened, sucking in a huge mouthful just before he submerged us. His weight pressed against my back, his arms encircling my chest, securing me in a tight embrace. My fingers dug into his skin as I trembled, panic coiling. Right as I was about to flail and demand release, he pushed upward. We broke the surface, and I gasped for air, blinking to clear the water from my eyes.

His touch glided along my arms, intertwining his fingers with mine. A shiver of warmth slid across my skin. The gentle hum of a melody reached my ears, drawing my gaze to the priests. Their features relaxed in serene concentration as they swayed in unison, their clasped hands creating a tangible bond of unity and peace.

"Elspeth—"

"What?"

Sainte stepped, pulling me with him, and I stumbled, gripping his fingers awkwardly.

"Move with me."

His warm breath grazed my skin, sending a tingle down my spine. The closeness of his body became overpowering. His chest pressed close, our arms entwined. Our hips nestled against each other, and his leg hooked around mine, drawing me closer.

Stepping again, I mirrored the movement. A low rumble of approval escaped him, eliciting a delightful tightness low in my belly. His arm moved in a gentle motion, and I followed his lead, in sync with him.

I wondered if this was what those fancy ballroom dances were like. Sensing his subtle cues, I flowed with his movements rather than being directed or coerced. We spun together in a fluid dance, synchronized to the haunting melody crafted by the priests.

As time stretched, I began to grasp the ritual and the importance of moving as one. He was mine now, but more than that, I was his—in ways beyond his comprehension. I was his to safeguard, his to embrace and cherish. He served as my guardian, a shield and sword at my side.

We moved together, a seamless melding that blurred the lines of who led and who followed. As we glided through the water, the plants on the pool's floor radiated a vibrant spectacle, glowing brighter with each graceful step.

As the song crescendoed, our pace quickened. Sainte's movements became swifter, and I anticipated each step, moving in harmony. He mirrored me, without constraint or hindrance or confinement.

We were one.

He propelled me away, and a gasp escaped as our connection broke. The intensity of the moment dissipated with the priests' final note, and Sainte drew me back into his embrace, tucking me against his chest. His breaths were ragged, as though he just finished a race, and I found myself mirroring his rapid inhales and exhales. My gaze drifted down to his water-dampened lips before returning to meet his hungry eyes.

The priests raised their voices as one. "*Vele Valahant!*"

CHAPTER 16

That night, I lay awake in my bed, motionless, silent, lest I disturb the man sleeping nearby.

Planks of wood covered the window until a glass smith could repair it, and staff brought a cot for Sainte's use. His proximity unsettled me. Yes, we slept together on the road, but this was different, more intimate. This closeness wasn't forced by a rushed journey. He was a part of me now.

My Valahant.

Our moment in the pool repeated in my mind in an endless loop. The memory replayed in vivid detail—his hands enveloping mine, how good his hard body felt pressed against mine.

Frustration quickened my pulse, and I shoved myself upright. Silently, I threw my legs over the bedside and took three soft steps. Sainte rested on the cot with one arm shielding his head, his gaze meeting mine in the lantern's dim glow from the adjacent room.

Without a word or question, he drew in a slow breath, then rose. His blankets dropped to his waist.

The exposed skin clashed with my emotions, warming my cheeks.

I ignored him, then headed for the receiving area. After I grabbed the lantern, I wandered into my dressing room. I donned thin slippers and a light cloak before spinning on my heel to leave-

Only to collide with Sainte.

Dressed in a thin tunic and dark trousers, he adorned his belt with two daggers. His gaze fixed on me while securing his leather chest piece. Swelling and bruises marked his face, unexpectedly stirring a maternal instinct—as though I were responsible for his well-being.

As I squeezed through the doorway, my chest brushed against his arm. I crossed the room with his silent steps trailing mine. When I opened the door, I was grateful for the oiled hinges, a small mercy during late-night wanderings.

Down the hall, I dimmed the lantern to a flickering flame, then entered Lyana's room without bothering to knock. After I placed it on a small wooden dresser, I glanced over the royal decor. Golden threads in the curtains and tapestries shimmered in the lantern's light, adding a touch of elegance to the cozy space.

I kicked off my slippers, then draped my cloak over a chair as Sainte eased the door shut. At the bedside, I lifted the blankets and slid underneath. Lyana let out a sigh, swatting at me, accidentally striking my face. I grunted as I settled onto the bed and tucked the furs to my chin.

"El?" she whispered, groggy with slumber.

I rubbed my cheek. "Shh, sleep."

"El?"

"Ethyan?!" I jerked upright, hissing as my stitches pulled.

His silhouette straightened in the chair near the window.

"I was scared," Lyana murmured, pulling me close.

Ethyan yawned, relaxing into the cushioned seat. "Gotta have her big brother to protect her."

I rolled onto my side, facing the door, and Lyana wrapped her arms around me, snuggling into my back. Sainte shook his head, a soft smile playing on his lips as he leaned against the doorframe, hand resting on his dagger.

If only I could trust my brother like that.

"Your Highness, Prince Regent Adastrus requests your presence."

My laughter at Lyana's joke faltered as a servant interrupted our midday meal.

"Now?" I asked, dipping my bread into the bowl of warm stew.

"Yes, Your Highness. He requests Lady Lyana as well."

Dread hit me like a punch to the gut. The savory stew lost all flavor in my mouth as I chewed, nodding to her. "Wait in the hall, please."

She obeyed, pulling the door shut behind her.

"Anderz–" I started, my heart in my throat.

"Lyana is of Tilamuik. She is here as your guest and his reach to her is limited," he said, brushing out his dark robes.

"Then why does he want her there?" I asked.

Lyana shrugged and stood. Her wide blue-green eyes showed just how nervous she was, though.

"I would assume we will find out, Princess."

The counselor walked toward the door, and we trailed behind, Sainte bringing up the rear.

"Should I run?" Lyana whispered.

"There's no place to go. A Howl is brewing," Anderz remarked without glancing back.

She swallowed audibly as we followed him through the corridors. I recognized the route. He was leading us to the Hall of Receiving. Adastrus either wanted to assert dominance or bind me by the noble crowd, as I had done when I named Sainte my Valahant.

I rubbed my thumbs against my palms as we walked. My grasp of High Wynterian was lacking, and with Lyana present, I found myself using Common Muik more often than not. In front of nobles, I was vastly ill-prepared. I rehearsed the curses I would spew at my brother given the chance, but there was a political game to be played, and Adastrus had outmatched me too many times.

A knot twisted in my gut as I anticipated what manner of torture I'd have to endure. My gaze drifted to Lyana, I couldn't stand by if he hurt her. If he found some way to abuse her, I would attack him with all the ferocity of a dock cat.

The doors to the receiving hall opened at our approach, and Anderz slowed his pace ahead of us.

"What did he do?!" Lyana whispered, horrified.

Grimm stood with his thick legs spread apart, hand braced on the sword at his hip. My gaze traveled upward along his large frame, snagging on the velebond chain wrapped around his neck. My lips parted in silent terror—the link joining the chain was seared into his flesh, the wound red and angry. As we advanced, his bloodshot eyes locked onto ours.

A single tear tracked down his bloodied and dirt-covered cheek.

Lyana lunged. "No! You can't–"

I snatched her hand, pulling her against me as Anderz turned, issuing a silent warning. I wrapped my arms around her, ignoring the murmurs rippling through the crowd.

"He can't!" She shook with rage, eyes locked on Grimm.

"Lady Lyana, might I introduce you to my Valahant?" Adastrus said, standing in a smooth motion, grinning as he descended the stairs. "Oh, it appears as though you already know him."

"What did you do?!"

She tried to pull away, but I held her firmly, seeking guidance from Anderz. He remained motionless, his golden eyes taking everything in.

"I bound him to me, dear lady. Watch, it's a lovely trick!" He spun on the heel of his boot and snapped his fingers at the big man. "Come doggie, come!"

Bile rose in my throat.

Grimm's jaw was clenched so tight I expected to hear it crack. He took quick steps to Adastrus' side, where he glared down at his regent.

"Sit!"

Lyana seethed. "I'll kill–"

"Surely, brother," I interrupted, halting her treasonous words, "you did not summon me just to flaunt your own Valahant."

Grimm lowered himself to the ground, wincing in pain while Adastrus's features lit up with glee.

"You're right, little sister," he said, his mad eyes locking onto mine. With a predatory smile, he clasped his hands in front of his belt. "I wanted to inform you that a Howl is imminent, and I propose we embark on the second rite."

His posture remained relaxed and calm as Grimm sat at his feet, staring blankly into the distance, a stark contrast to his usually cheerful demeanor.

"When?" I spat.

"Tonight."

I glanced at Anderz. We hadn't even practiced or gone over the fine details of the Rite of Hearth and Home. All I knew was it involved a lot of walking in the snow.

"Well enough," I replied, gently pulling Lyana with me as I took a step back. She trembled with rage and I had to get her out of there.

"Oh, and *Princess?*"

I paused, every intention to kill the bastard clear in my eyes.

He tilted his head with a smile, his black hair falling across his forehead. "Did you know you can duel with your Valahant?"

"Pardon?" I asked, squinting as I struggled to grasp his meaning.

"As your Valahant is an extension of you, you may use them as a stand-in for a duel." He sidestepped, his sickly gaze locking onto Sainte with a dangerous grin. "Would you wager mine against yours?"

My blood turned to ice, and I fought the urge to look back at Sainte. Grimm stood among his handpicked men, one he trusted to cross borders to fetch me.

I would not have him fight his friend.

"I will prepare for the rite," I growled, turning away.

With a glance at Sainte, my resolve hardened. A muscle twitched in his jaw as he looked at Grimm once more before leaving with me. I pressed my lips together, holding Lyana's arm, practically dragging her along. Anderz followed, his steps measured and calm.

"Pack warm, sister!"

Adastrus' laughter echoed throughout the room, haunting us as we departed.

I was going to die.

That fate was certain.

At least Sainte accompanied me, not that he was allowed to hold me in death's cold embrace. He watched me from beneath his cloak's deep, fur-lined hood. Flakes swirled, covering him in a dense layer.

It wasn't even pretty snow that glittered in the sun, but a thick haze of white under a dark gray sky. It settled on my lap and Sainte's hood with unnerving speed. The accumulation rose higher than my crossed legs, and I brushed it off in a vain attempt to stay dry.

Blindfolded, I endured a wagon ride lasting over a day. The rough, jarring journey left me sore and frustrated. Eating with my eyes covered was an unpleasant experience.

They dumped us somewhere... Whether we stood on a mountain, in a valley, or on a plain eluded me. Flat ground stretched beneath my feet, but it could change at any moment. I had no idea how Sainte and the priest would get home when I died.

"You may begin."

I squinted up at the Priest of Nothar, wrapped in a fur cloak.

"Is it too much to ask for a pointer?!" I shouted over the gale.

He offered no direction, only stared at me with disturbing gray eyes, his stark-white hair snapping in the gust. I couldn't fathom how he discerned the time of day, or how he knew when the rite should begin. He was there to enforce the rite's law, nothing more.

I cursed, knowing he wouldn't hear over the torrent, then pushed upright, shaking off the snow that piled on my lap. The bitter wind whistled and shrieked, shoving me until I staggered.

Sainte stood as well, keeping his distance. Anderz informed me Valahants were permitted to attend the trials, but any assistance would result in my forfeit.

I shielded my eyes from the glare and scanned my surroundings. Beyond a few paces, nothing popped out—no trees, rocks, not even the sky. I lifted the hem of my skirt as it snagged on the drifts. The fur trousers provided comfort, and the dress added warmth, but with it dragging, it wouldn't be long before it froze solid.

I stopped, pulling the front of my dress to my thighs, then reached between my legs to yank the hem forward, tucking it into the thick belt at my waist. I'd seen women girding their loins like this as they walked the shore, searching for clams.

What I would have given to be back at the coast. To feel the salty breeze cooling my cheeks, reddened by the sun's warmth. Gritty sand between my toes, with cool foamy water lapping at my ankles.

Grunting, I trudged forward into knee-deep snow, the priest and Sainte trailing behind. With each heavy step, the frigid stuff threatened to swallow me. At this rate, I would be buried in a few hours. I pushed onward, hoping I was headed in the right direction.

Anderz warned me to stay dry. Logic said to find a cave and wait out the storm, but this was the Rite of Hearth and Home. I needed to brave the Howl and make my way back to the castle.

Hopefully, they hadn't dropped Adastrus off any closer.

I wouldn't put it past him to cheat or abandon Grimm in a snowdrift.

Lyana was devastated over Grimm's condition. She bonded with the big man during their journey, growing close to him. She spoke of him often, and I guessed she planned to make her move soon.

Then Adastrus snatched him from her grasp.

The vilest of people inflicted pain by targeting their victim's friends, and that was exactly what my brother did. He didn't choose Grimm because he was the best candidate, but because it would cause the most harm.

Anderz reassured me that Adastrus could only claim one Valahant. The Priests of Togamar were furious with him for not fulfilling the velebond in their temple. His actions not only offended the goddess, but also tarnished his reputation among the people. The inhabitants of Wynterborne would hesitate to follow a leader who disregarded the old traditions.

I couldn't envision them ever completing the ritual. The thought of Grimm submerging Adastrus under the water, working out who was the leader, brought a sad smile to my lips. Their bond lacked trust, and while I didn't view it as magical, their neglect of the pretense felt like a poor decision.

A gust of wind roared over a snowdrift, knocking me to the ground. I landed flat on my back, gazing at the swirling gray mass above before closing my eyes. I needed to stay on my feet and keep moving.

Struggling, I fought to stand. Only moments into the trial, I was already weary and frozen.

I was going to die very slowly.

Darkness enveloped me like a heavy cloak, muffling the world around me. With each step, my boots crunched on the snow, the sound echoing eerily in the silent night. I trusted that Sainte was following, but I couldn't be certain about the priest—he might have been lost in a snowdrift.

My arms and legs grew numb, the icy chill seeping through layers of clothing. My wool scarf covering my face was dampened from breath condensation and frozen to my skin, each exhale creating a frosty barrier. My clothes, soaked through with snow and sweat, had turned to solid ice, weighing me down and hindering my movements. Hunger gnawed at me—I hadn't eaten since the wagon ride, unable to carry rations.

I stumbled and fell face-first. The icy sting assaulted my cheeks, almost burning my skin. I tried to move my hands, but they barely twitched. The chill numbed my fingers, sapping strength from my bones with every passing second. Each deep breath turned into a choked gasp as the wet snow filled my mouth and nostrils, suffocating me. It felt like drowning, and I fought to free my face, to roll over, to sit up—anything to escape the oppressive cold that seeped into my very soul.

I moaned and struggled, slowly fading into darkness.

Something shifted me, rolling me onto my back. Ice forced my eyelids shut, frozen in place.

Warm hands, almost scorching, pressed against my cheeks, thawing the frost. I moaned, attempting to turn away from the intense heat, but they held me firm, forcing me to thaw. After a moment, the touch moved to my eyes, melting the freeze, and I coaxed them open. I blinked and squinted against the brightness, struggling to discern the figure that shielded me from the snow.

Golden hair cascaded from the woman's head, wind teasing it into a wild dance. She wore a wool scarf, shielding the worst of the torrent. Unnaturally bright green eyes glowed with light as she smiled down at me. Her skin bore a warm bronze hue, reminiscent of those from coastal regions. Her mouth moved as she lowered her hands to my shoulders, but her words were lost in the roaring gale.

I gawked at her, wondering who she was and why she was helping me. Gratitude welled within, and I would've thanked her for saving me, but my frozen lips wouldn't allow it.

A bone-aching warmth expanded through me from her touch. Heat radiated from her in a way that shouldn't be possible.

I lifted my hand and examined it, relieved to have movement. Each tiny sensation brought a sense of hope. It was a slow, painful process. The gradual thawing accompanied by a faint tingle of pins and needles. Despite the chaos of the roaring wind and the threat of her scarf being snatched away, she smiled down at me as if everything were perfectly ordinary.

As warmth spread to my toes, I sat up, cradling my side where it felt like my stitches had torn. She tilted her head, and the soft brush of her hand covered mine. An odd sensation followed. The nerves beneath my skin twitched and wiggled, as if worms crawled across my flesh. I scratched at my wound—or tried to—but she held me firm. When she loosened her grip, the twitching stopped, and so did the pain.

"Who are you?!" I screamed over the gale.

In response, she simply smiled and patted my hand. When she looked up, eyes locked on something behind me, her mouth moved, but no sound came out. I attempted to read her lips, but whatever language she used was neither High Wynterian nor Muik.

I twisted, trying to see whatever she spoke to. Sleet swirled and howled, wrapping around itself, then scattering. There was nothing.

Yet, as I watched, a shape solidified in the distance, enough for me to discern the outline. A white stag, as pure as the swirling snow that enveloped it, stood calmly in the storm. Its antlers stretched toward the sky, framing a tall figure astride its back. The figure, uncloaked, displayed only a crown upon its head, crafted from ice. Its crystalline facets glinted in the faint light.

A warm hand gripped mine, and my attention returned to the woman. She stood, pulling me with her as her mouth formed a silent shout. It wasn't the wind that whisked away her voice—there was no sound. She pointed at the stag, then nudged me toward it. I stumbled a step, peering around her in search of Sainte and the priest.

"My friend!"

She hesitated, scanning the Howl as if she could see through it. Her lips moved, and I focused on her mouth, struggling to decipher the word.

Valahant.

"Yes! Yes!" I shouted, nodding in case she couldn't hear me. "Valahant!"

She smiled, her expression tender, as if I were a child professing love for their mother. She cupped my cheek, her touch warm and comforting, and I gawked at her, confused. Her mouth opened in a silent laugh before she gestured to the side.

At her command, the haze of snow parted, revealing the priest and Sainte huddled together among the drifts.

"Sainte!"

He didn't move.

Again, she pointed toward the distant stag, its powerful silhouette turning its rump on us, blending into the snowy landscape. Urgency flashed in her eyes as she released my hand, a silent plea in her gaze. She made a shooing motion, the movement sharp and insistent. As she stepped back, the wind swirled in a vortex, carrying the scent of pine and frost.

"No! No, don't leave me!" I shouted, stumbling after her. "Please!"

Frantic and unsure, I glanced between her, the stag, and Sainte. Confusion and fear churned inside. Following her seemed the safest bet, but she was clearly leaving me. The stag began walking away, its rider twisting to peer at me with glowing green eyes.

I cursed under my breath. The woman, radiating warmth like summer sunshine, stood there with a sad smile. I turned back to Sainte, uncertainty gnawing at my resolve.

"Sainte! Sainte!" I screamed, voice swallowed by the howling wind.

I stumbled toward his huddled shape, snow crunching beneath my boots. When I collapsed beside him, as if breaking a spell, he looked up. His blue eyes squinted against the swirling flakes before they widened and he pressed his lips in determination.

My vision strained, the biting wind stinging my cheeks, trying to make out the rump of the white stag in the blizzard's haze. Its faint outline was barely discernible. I trudged toward it, stumbling as the woman's touch began to fade. When I glanced over my shoulder, Sainte was helping the priest to his feet, pulling the man's arm over his shoulder as they stumbled after me.

I staggered through the snow, my gaze fixed on the stag's rump, determined not to lose sight of it. There were fleeting moments of doubt, wondering if I was hallucinating or indeed following a man atop a stag. Logic didn't intervene to question the absurdity of the situation; instead, I blindly followed the figure the woman had indicated, placing my trust in the warmth I had seen in her eyes.

It was the only hope I had.

CHAPTER 17

I panted and stumbled to my knees. The snow, bleak and dense, rose to my chest. I doubted I could stand.

The stag halted, its fur shimmered in the pale light as it faced me. The snowfall lightened, revealing the figures more clearly. A man crowned with ice—his glowing green eyes marked him as more than a mere mortal. Was this another dream? A hallucination brought on by fatigue?

I panted for air, my lungs ablaze and my chest throbbing. The blizzard's fury lessened, but the wind still whipped around me, stinging my face. Snowflakes clung to my eyelashes, and the cold numbed my fingers.

"I can't!" I shouted with as much force as I could.

He watched me in silent disinterest.

My lips trembled. "I can't," I whispered.

The man shook his head, disappointed, and the stag turned, changing direction. Had he given up on me? Did he realize I couldn't go any further and decide to abandon me here?

Deflated, all fight left me, my shoulders drooping with exhaustion. They vanished into the blowing snow as Sainte staggered behind me, gasping for breath while supporting the priest's weight. He stopped, noticing my expression, and I shook my head, sorrow etched on my face. Tears threatened, but would have frozen on my cheeks. Too exhausted to cry, I knelt there, numb.

"Elspeth."

I stared at my gloved hands, unable to feel them, as if they weren't my own. I'd come this far, and now blame wreaked havoc inside for entangling Sainte in this mess. Grimm was suffering because of me.

Why did anyone think I could lead?

I lived my life in a coastal city, only to be thrown into a frigid wasteland. They believed me to be chosen by the gods, destined to rule Wynterborne. In reality, I was a street rat. It was nonsensical. Following a man on a deer through a storm was absurd. Little girls who laughed and danced, leaving frozen circles around people, defied logic.

None of this made sense.

"Elspeth—look."

It dawned on me that he spoke instead of shouted, the storm's fury having subsided. Frowning, I observed his gaze shift upward, prompting me to turn and discover what had caught his attention.

Wynterborne.

The castle stood before us, its towering walls casting a shadow over the landscape. Its cold banners snapped in the dying gusts of the storm.

"She's been touched by the gods!"

"Her face!"

"She passed the rite! This is her home, her hearth is here!"

On a white horse, gripping the mane tightly, I navigated through the bustling streets of Wynterborne. The crowd's collective awe murmured around us, blending into a low, continuous roar.

Beside me, Sainte rode astride another horse. We exchanged weary glances, and I managed a smile. He responded with a faint grin, shaking his head in wonder. I threaded my fingers through the coarse mane, bracing myself as we crossed the narrow bridge to the castle.

Staff whisked me away to my rooms, the shattered window replaced. Sainte collapsed on the cot as priests of Togamar fussed over him. Gilead approached me as I fell onto the bed, two healers trailing behind her.

"That is no mark of Nothar," she murmured in awe. Her eyes lit with curiosity as she brushed her fingers against my cheek.

"There was a woman," I sighed, weariness tugging at my mind.

Gilead drew her touch away. "What was she like?"

"Like... summer sunshine."

"Togamar!" a girl gasped.

"There was a man, too," I said, trying to sit up.

The healer clicked her tongue. "Easy, Princess. Lie still."

Hands tugged at my sodden clothes, their urgency palpable as they worked to strip them off and warm my frozen body.

"He rode a stag..." I murmured.

"What was his name?"

Exhaustion tugged at my senses, dulling my thoughts.

"His name, Your Highness?"

"I don't know," I moaned, fighting a yawn. "He had a crown of ice. Green eyes... the color of emeralds..."

Someone gasped. "Nothar!"

"My dear princess, the God of Snow and Cold guided you," Gilead whispered, voice tinged with awe. "Rest now. You're home."

Those words wormed their way into my heart, warming me from the inside out. I didn't know why they meant so much to me, but hearing them sparked a tiny flame in my soul. My eyelids drifted shut as I sank into serene oblivion—the dark abyss a welcomed embrace.

"Therefore, the high court will be calling you to meet on occasion."

Anderz droned on while I studied my reflection in the polished silver mirror. I traced the fading pink handprints framing my face. The impressions were elegant, marked by long, delicate fingers, thumbs pressed against my nose, and palms cradling my cheeks, with fingertips stretched toward my temples.

Riders set out to retrieve Adastrus, Grimm, and the accompanying priest. They found them a few hours from Wynterborne, heading eastward, away from the castle.

I hadn't laid eyes on him since his return, but the servants' hushed tones and nervous demeanor spoke volumes about his mood.

"I wager my brother is thrilled," I muttered.

"Beyond measure," Anderz replied dryly. "The council has requested a formal gathering to celebrate your victory over the second rite."

"I haven't passed the third. Isn't it a little early to celebrate?" As I wandered over to the table, I caught Sainte's gaze, his intense stare leveled on me. Butterflies fluttered low in my belly.

Anderz leaned on his elbows, his golden eyes roaming my face. "The third rite involves a test of the gods' choosing. We will summon Nain and Yail to call upon the deities for their response. However, it's evident you already have their favor."

Sainte strode over, pulling out my chair for me. I offered a small smile and settled into the seat, amused by the unnecessary gesture.

As if I couldn't have pulled the thing out myself.

"Are there any rumors that the priest or my Valahant touched me during the trial?" I asked.

Anderz rubbed his jaw with a glint of mirth. "A man's hands couldn't have made those marks, let alone those of a mortal."

I sighed, knitting my fingers on the table. Emotions swirled within me, a mix of confusion and reluctance. Winning the rite felt hollow, and leading a kingdom seemed meaningless. Despite my hatred for my brother, I couldn't bring myself to embrace the idea of ruling. The evil he embodied made it impossible to give up, yet I hesitated to move forward.

Survival was the only thing driving me.

"Tell me about Nain and Yail," I said, lifting my gaze to Anderz. "What are they?"

"The names given to the God Stones. They're remnants from an ancient era when rulers sought guidance from Nothar, their father."

I pressed my lips into a flat line, remembering how Nellie alluded to there being divine blood in mine and Adastrus' lineage.

"They illuminate when a descendant of Nothar seeks counsel," Anderz continued. "Nain for no, and Yail for yes. Quite straightforward."

"And if the answer's complicated?" I asked.

"Then there will be no answer. Such questions are for the high court to address."

"Comforting."

In Tilamuik, citizens practiced a laid-back approach to religion, invoking their favorite deities when it served their needs. In Wynterborne, residents were devout. Even minor events were seen as divine responses. With that logic, it seemed anyone could shape their own 'favor' with the gods.

"The question should be simple: 'Am I favored by our great father and god, Nothar, to lead his people?' The council will finalize the wording to prevent any misinterpretation."

"And you're sure these stones will glow? You've seen it?"

"Princess," Anderz started, with a solemn shake of his head, "for generations, the gods have been little more than a formality. You have sparked something profound in the people, a quiet yet fervent belief in an essence more powerful than themselves. The gods' judgment has been neglected and elusive within my lifetime. If legend holds true, Nothar will answer."

Legend? That's what all this boiled down to? Sheer luck and lore.

And hallucinations of a wild man atop a deer, and a woman whose aura exuded summer and sunlight.

"So, if Yain glows—"

"Yail," Anderz corrected.

"If *Yail* lights up when I ask, I will pass the rite? What if it answers Adastrus as well?"

"Have more faith in the gods, Princess." A small smile lifted the corner of his mouth. "You bear the mark of the chosen. Nothar will answer you, not your brother."

"But if it does?"

He sighed, shook his head, and leaned forward, resting his forearms on the table, his deep black robes draping around them. "In that very unlikely circumstance, your victories outnumber the prince regent's, two to one. However, a response on his behalf would allow him to invoke the Rite of Combat."

"Gods! I assume Adastrus is skilled with a blade? It would be a fair fight?"

"Aye, Princess."

"I'd lose," I stated flatly, shooting him an exasperated leer. "Anderz, I grew up in the slums. I might stand a chance in a gritty brawl, where I could use my surroundings to my advantage, but not in a duel!"

"He would use Grimm," he said.

My heart twisted as I peered Sainte's way, though his gaze was fixed on the counselor with intense scrutiny. Tension crackled, as if he searched for hidden truths beneath Anderz's words, his expression a blend of curiosity and suspicion.

My throat tightened. "I would have to fight Grimm?!"

"No. I would." Sainte's voice carried a low, dangerous edge.

An unspoken exchange passed between their locked gazes, and I stared, desperate to gain some clarity.

"I won't allow it." My chin dipped, conveying my assertion.

Sainte had suffered enough. I wouldn't let him fight his friend for my sake.

"You'd have no choice," Anderz said with a small shake of his head, bringing his unblinking gaze back to me. A heavy frown rode his thin lips as he thought on it. "You would have no chance against Grimm, and it would be expected that a Valahant fight another, not the royal themselves."

"You said they are forbidden to interfere in the rites." Skepticism laced my tone.

"A Valahant is bound in life and death. If it comes to your demise, Sainte would intervene."

That would have been nice to know in the middle of the Howl.

"We need to find a way to release Grimm," I huffed, my frustration evident.

Knowing my brother, if there was an opportunity for him to invoke the Rite of Combat, he would. I lacked trust in gods who only manifested in dreams and hallucinations to depend on their response.

"Do you believe the regent wouldn't try to strip you of your Valahant if it were possible?" the counselor asked.

"There has to be a way."

Sainte's stare bore into mine. "I am bound to you in life and death."

"Why would Grimm agree to that?!" I cursed, bringing my palms up to my face.

"Princess, the velebond between you and dear Sainte is unique." Anderz's tone softened. "It's rare for a Valahant to choose their bonded. Traditionally, it is requested by a royal, and such a request given by Adastrus would only be a veiled command. Grimm of Strongstone had no choice."

I was out of my depth. Every aspect of politics was a foreign concept to me. Anderz did the best he could. His wisdom was a lifeline, valuable beyond measure. Without him, I was a fish floundering out of water. If he had no solution, I could only trust that there was no way out of the bond.

"Take heart, Princess. The God Stones will rule in your favor," Anderz said, his voice carrying a touch of optimism. "We face an incredibly daunting task ahead."

I peeked at him from between my fingers, dreading what came next.

"I must prepare you for your presentation... before the masses."

My head dropped to the table with a groan.

I squeezed my eyes shut, feeling a sharp pang of mental anguish. The maid's hands brushed against the hem of my dress, rustling the fabric as she arranged it around the stool beneath me. The soft swish of the material filled the room, contrasting with the tightness in my chest. Each adjustment she made sent a shiver down my spine, the cool touch of the wooden stool grounding me in the moment.

The seamstress's fingers, deft and cool, hemmed the sleeves tightly against my wrists. I stood stiff as a statue, each breath shallow. The scent of fresh fabric and sewing thread filled the air, churning my anxious stomach. The dress needed minor adjustments, yet the urgency from the council added a hurried tension. They wanted me presented with the handprints still vivid on my face.

The material, a rich green, shimmered with gold as I shifted. Inside the skirt and bodice, a thin fleece layer added unexpected warmth to the sheer fabric. The seamstress had explained its origin—a wild sheep from the Great Iceland, whose wool lined most of the elegant winter dresses I would wear throughout the season.

"I'll never be able to run in this." My voice trembled with frustration.

"A princess would not run, Your Highness. You would simply walk with considerable speed."

I scoffed, my eyes darting to Anderz seated nearby. He lounged, exuding a relaxed calmness as he watched the seamstress embroider gold thread into the fabric at my wrists.

My gaze shifted to Sainte. He leaned forward in his chair, elbows on his knees, hands pressed together with fingertips touching his lips. He studied me intently, and a thrill coursed through me when his eyes traveled down my figure.

"Be still now, Your Highness!" the seamstress pleaded.

I turned back to the polished silver mirror propped before us. The dress's high collar wrapped snugly around my throat, its fabric cascading in heavy swaths that covered me from neck to toes. I cringed at the excess, imagining how many garments could be made from the wasted material.

Not that there was anything to be spared from neck to hip.

The dress clung to me—a second skin. It was uncomfortable to see my feminine curves on display after endless years spent hiding them. I took shallow breaths, anxiety twisting in my chest, fearful that breathing deep might tear the seam.

"I look like a fool," I muttered.

"You look like a princess," Anderz cut in. "Thank you for your time and effort, *Master Seamstress* Floria."

Panic surged as I glanced down at her, the sharp needle poised near my wrist. Her frown deepened, reflecting her offense.

"My apologies," I blurted out before she could stab me. "I'm just used to loose tunics and trousers."

Her fierce gaze met mine and a smile bloomed on her rosy lips. "Then it is time you learn how a proper lady dresses. Beg your pardon, Princess, but tonight you will catch the eye of every soul this side of the Veil. You've brought hope to the people. Now, it's my turn to bring their eyes to you."

"Thank you," I sighed, checking my reflection.

"Hope in the gods, Your Highness—"

I caught her worried expression in the mirror as she tied off the thread.

"—that they still care for us mere mortals."

Adastrus' dark mood had quite the reach when staff in my own chambers were careful with their words.

The hairdressers had combed and styled my hair, transforming the short strands into soft waves adorned with peridots and opals. Despite their pleas to cut the long braid, I refused. I couldn't lose my identity. After much discussion and negotiation involving Anderz, we compromised. They pinned the braid underneath, keeping it hidden but intact.

"There," Floria stepped back to admire her work, "I've done my best, Your Highness."

"Many thanks."

I shifted slightly to get a better view. The lantern light danced across the fabric, turning it into a shimmering tapestry of gold against green.

"Allow me a few moments to ready the nobles," Anderz said to Sainte, rising from his seat with a sigh.

He remained in his dark robes, and I couldn't help but wonder if he ever changed his attire for different occasions.

As he and Floria took their leave, I admired the gown—a stunning creation that didn't quite feel like me. It was a masterpiece, and I felt inadequate for its beauty.

"Well?" I asked.

Sainte grunted, still perched on the edge of his seat.

"What do you think?"

"Of?"

"The dress, Sainte," I groaned, rolling my eyes. I swayed my body, testing the fabric's movement.

"It's a dress."

I shuffled my feet in a circle to face him, hands propped on my hips. His blue gaze twinkled, and a small crooked smile lifted his lips.

"I'm a man." He stood with a quick wince that he tried to conceal, and gestured to his thin leather armor, the daggers at his sides, and his dark trousers. "I'm not well-versed in such things."

"Does it catch your eye?" I asked, easing my hands to my sides. Quick movements didn't seem wise in the tight-fitting garment.

He tilted his head, a predatory gleam in his stare as he prowled toward me. He stopped close enough that the warmth of his breath tickled my face.

"You catch my eye."

The butterflies that had taken residence low in my belly fluttered like mad as he wrapped his hands around my waist. I held his gaze, as a dizzying sensation prickled beneath my skin. Those eyes would be my undoing.

With surprising strength considering his recent injuries, he lifted me off the stool with ease. I gripped his forearms as he settled me on my feet again. I tracked the dark bruises marring his face. They'd faded some thanks to Gilead's care. Anderz had suggested covering them with a skin-colored paste. That way, the people of Wynterborne would see my Valahant as strong and unharmed, but Sainte refused. He argued that the citizens should see the cruelty of Adastrus' rule.

"You're a princess, Elspeth," he rumbled, smirking. "A rebellious one." He gave my hair a gentle tug before stepping away.

When his hand dropped from my waist, I fought the urge to close the distance he created. The warmth of his touch lingered on my skin as if I'd been seared by a hot iron. I sniffed, shaking my head to rid myself of the sensation, then shuffled past him.

"I didn't choose this."

"We don't always get to choose our fates," he called after me.

"So I'm supposed to trust the *gods* with my future?" I rolled my eyes, and guilt prickled as I mocked the deities who very well might be the reason I survived this long.

"Elspeth—"

I halted near the door to the corridor, then faced him. His face scrunched into a mirthful mix of a cringe and a smile.

"—stop walking like a seal."

My head jerked back, stunned, then glared at the fabric wrapped around my hips before directing my glower at him. "Ever worn a dress, dear Sainte?" I asked.

He grinned, then passed me to hold the way open. "Can't say I have," he said, dipping into a bow.

"Then do not presume to tell me how to walk in one," I snapped, lifting my chin.

As I brushed past him, I let my shoulder ram into his chest, ignoring his low chuckle as I strode down the corridor with my head held high, hoping for all I was worth, that I didn't look like a walking sea creature.

CHAPTER 18

I was an intruder, a counterfeit, a fake.

A girl from the streets wrapped in a pretty dress paraded around like a princess. My heart pounded—a frightened rabbit in my chest. Shame burned my cheeks. I stumbled over proper terms, curtsied to the wrong people, and botched my High Wynterian.

I clung to Anderz's side, using him as a shield against the nobles. His presence deflected their probing questions. He steered conversations toward familiar topics or those where my ignorance wouldn't raise eyebrows.

Sipping my glass of water, I tried to stay hidden in the sparse shadows. Flames flickered in decadent lanterns, their light glinting off hanging crystals, scattering warm glimmers in every direction—making it infinitely harder for me to hide.

The dress was suffocating. I despised being here. People either bombarded me with questions or mocked my upbringing.

As if being murdered by my brother at the age of six would have been better than my life on the streets.

No one acknowledged that detail, though. I wasn't sure if they were unaware of that night's horrors or if they chose to forget, preferring to ridicule my High Wynterian accent.

When I asked the server for water instead of wine or ale, she gawked at me as if I'd grown two heads. She fetched it, but explaining my abstinence from alcohol seemed pointless. To her, I was a royal, and royals should glut themselves during feasts and drink like common drunkards.

My brother was across the grand room, engaged in conversation with two older men. A sea of mingling guests almost drowned out the small group performing in the corner.

Musicians.

I got corrected more than once—they were trained musicians, not simple tavern bards. I frowned, glancing at the quartet playing their stringed instruments in a slow, calm song. The bards I knew could create better entertainment with just their voices and a hand slapped on a table.

"Tiring of the festivities so soon?" A man approached, tall and handsome, with pale blond hair hanging past his shoulders. His eyes warmed, giving the illusion of old friendship.

Sainte stood behind me, watching him with careful scrutiny.

"I needed a drink," I said with a casual shrug. "I've had more introductions tonight than I have my entire life."

The man laughed, sipped his wine, and nodded to Sainte before stepping closer, blocking him from view.

I frowned.

"It is tedious," he agreed. "Though many would give their firstborn to meet you."

I arched my brow, unamused. "That's a bit dramatic."

"But you, too, have a flair for the theatrical, do you not?" His eyes lingered on the fresh, rosy handprints on my face.

I sniffed, turning toward the crowd. "I don't know what you mean."

A chill ran through me as I noticed Adastrus staring, his expression blank. He ignored the younger noble speaking to him, focusing entirely on our exchange.

"Chosen of the Gods, the one to guide us to the old paths, the Favored Princess—that's what the commoners are calling you."

"And what would you call me?" I dared, watching him from the corner of my eye.

"Ah, Leihim Hinyte at your service," he dropped into a deep bow, "Your Highness, My Lost Princess."

I scoffed, shaking my head. "I'm not lost anymore."

"There are those who wish you were." He straightened and sipped his wine, watching me over the rim. "Those who wish you were more than lost."

"Careful," Sainte warned, hand resting on his dagger.

"I mean no harm." Leihim smirked, raising his palm in a show of submission. "I'm simply stating a fact you must already be aware of."

"Well aware."

He seemed friendly enough, his body language open and calm. He didn't appear unnerved by my presence or words.

"I've watched you with Counselor Dyre," he said, stepping closer. He scanned the crowd as he leaned in to whisper, "Cunning, that one."

Something in my shoulders relaxed when Adastrus returned to his conversation, evidently dismissing any thoughts about me and Leihim.

"He's proved to be a well of wisdom," I said.

"He observes the old paths. Tradition and honor, always."

"That's not a bad thing."

"Not at all," he agreed. "Not at all."

A comfortable silence lapsed as the crowd moved about, nobles circulating among their acquaintances. People greeted those they knew and sought introductions to those they didn't. Some conversations were brief, while others were drawn out, as if they were essential sustenance.

A shy smile played over Leihim's lips. "Care for a walk?"

A few paces away, Anderz engaged in conversation with a small group. A young woman listened intently, sporting an eager grin.

What would he advise?

Wasn't I brought here to mingle? To be presented to the nobles and masses? Leihim seemed friendly, and Sainte would come with me...

I set my glass on the nearby table. "That sounds lovely."

"Splendid."

He offered his arm, and I frowned, sensing something was off. Anderz cautioned me against causing a scene or bolting. Tonight, I had to play the game. I placed my hand on the crook of his elbow, and his features warmed, blue eyes twinkling with silent mirth as he led me out of the stuffy ballroom. The weight of every gaze settled on my back as we departed, Sainte following close behind.

As soon as we cleared the door and entered the halls, Leihim heaved a dramatic sigh. "I feel better already."

"I thought a proper noble would enjoy the... mingling," I remarked, amused, as we strolled toward the gardens.

"Ah, but perhaps I am not a 'proper noble' as you would think."

"No?"

"Not quite. You see, I wasn't born into nobility. I worked my way up the social ladder, making a name for myself as a businessman."

"You?" I stifled a laugh, then made a show of looking him over. "A merchant?"

He stood tall and lean, dressed in some of the finest attire of the night. His cheekbones were high and sharp, with the striking looks of nobility about him; I wouldn't have pegged him as anything less.

"Oh, not anymore. Though I once was." He patted my hand and nodded at the guards, who stood watch over the gardens. "Now I oversee the merchant guild. I'm simply a person of necessity, which grants me status without an official title."

"You keep the food on their tables."

He laughed. "Aye, and coin in my coffers."

The walkway, cleared of snow, felt cold and crisp underfoot. A faint crunch of icy patches added a rhythmic melody to our steps. The winter night enveloped us in its brisk embrace, a welcome relief from the stifling warmth of the crowded room. A hint of pine lingered on the breeze, mingling with the subtle aroma of wood smoke from distant hearths.

I chuckled softly, the sound echoing in the stillness of the night, and shook my head as I gazed upward at the clear, cloudless sky. The twin moons, usually radiant, were veiled tonight, their subdued light casting a gentle glow over the winter garden. The chill in the air kissed my cheeks, a refreshing contrast to the heat trapped in my elaborate dress.

"I admit, I did not seek your company without purpose," he said. "You see, I have a bit of a problem you might be able to assist with."

"I have little power," I scoffed, then sat on a stone bench.

As I settled, Sainte's gaze met mine, a silent warning flickering across his features as he took his place at my side.

"Yet, you have enough." Leihim sat in the space beside me. He crossed his legs, clasping his hands over his knees, and tipped his head to admire the starlit sky. His pale hair cascaded over the back of the bench. "I've brought my... problem to the prince regent on multiple occasions. He dismisses me each time. So, with your sudden arrival, I thought to myself, now here is an opportunity for the both of us."

"I'm not sure you've shaken off your merchant ways, Master Hinyte."

"Ah, but I am a businessman at heart." He winked at me before returning his attention skyward. "There is a bandit, perhaps a group—"

Intriguing.

"—He, or they, as it might be, go by the name of Dire Wolf. They've been a plague on my caravans, raiding and plundering without mercy."

"Why do you suspect there's more than one?"

"There may be a single head to the spider, but it has many arms," he said, voice hushed. "I have reason to believe the lower class protects them. Rumors hint the Wolf shares its spoils with the destitute."

Well, that wasn't so bad. "What aid do you seek from me?"

"You carry a unique influence among the commoners," he remarked, tilting his head to flash a smile. "They adore you, their 'Chosen of the Gods.' I only ask that you make discreet inquiries, using your status to glean insights. Nothing overly perilous, I assure you."

"Why should I?" I smirked. "I hail from the slums, Master Hinyte. I understand hardship and the value of a kind gesture, be it a bit of coin or loaf of bread."

"Consider this a service," he offered, gesturing to himself. "I'd owe you, and it's time you forged alliances in the high court, Princess."

I snickered at that. "But you claimed you're not a true noble."

"I also mentioned how every noble seeks my favor," he countered, arching a brow in challenge.

My eyes narrowed, a faint grin pulling at my lip. Oh, how I missed haggling with vendors in the ports!

When I wasn't stealing from them, of course.

"You would ask my help to catch a thief? If the common folk are protecting the Wolf, wouldn't I betray their trust by exposing him? I risk losing their support."

"Merchants are common folk too, you know. They are the backbone, the lifeblood of any realm. Can a kingdom thrive without commerce? You can't redistribute wealth entirely to the needy without reinvesting some to fuel the economy. Otherwise, you deplete resources without replenishment. It would be a kingdom's downfall."

This man was a bargainer.

He leaned closer and continued, "I'm not asking for military intervention, dear princess. Just keep me informed. My people are hard workers, toiling day and night to scrape by, only to have some rogue thief rob them blind to feed the idle, those too lazy to step up and earn an honest living."

With a shake of my head, I laughed and offered a half-hearted shrug. "I'm a bit chilled, Master Hinyte. I should return to the festivities."

"Of course. It would be my pleasure to escort you."

His hand settled on my thigh, eliciting a wary glance from me as Sainte shifted.

"Will you consider my proposal?" he asked.

"I hope you know I have a great many things to think about."

"I can only imagine."

He stood, offering his assistance. I accepted it eagerly, rising beside him. He placed my hand on the crook of his elbow, enveloping my cool fingers within his warm palm and sturdy arm.

Our exchange was amiable, as if we were old friends bantering for the fun of it. I appreciated his company and his straightforwardness—a rarity among the nobility who often relied on deceit and schemes to maintain their status.

We made our way back to the ballroom, our conversation intermittent. Sainte trailed behind, his presence silent and unwavering, much like it had been throughout the evening.

Anderz whisked me away as soon as I entered. His golden eyes exchanged a lingering glance with Leihim's before the latter nodded in acknowledgement.

I followed the counselor's lead as we traversed various circles through the crowd, nodding politely. I maintained a quiet demeanor, doing my best to avoid appearing rude.

Leihim had not commented on my accent or my somewhat broken High Wynterian. He seemed indifferent to such details. If he truly lacked noble birth, he would have grown up with a distinct Wynterian dialect, which should have been detectable in his speech.

My gaze wandered around the room, pondering what social circles he frequented. According to him, nobles were at his beck and call, eager to curry favor. One would expect him to be surrounded by aristocrats.

My stomach dropped when I found him.

Adastrus curled lifeless fingers around Leihim's shoulder, drawing him in for a rough embrace. When my brother peered my way, his lips spread into a sinister grin.

"Your leaving with Hinyte caught me by surprise," Counselor Dyre said as we entered my chambers.

Fatigue slowed my steps and my thoughts, and my cheeks ached from forced smiles. "He offered a walk in the garden. I needed some fresh air."

Anderz came to a stop near the table, gripping the back of a chair. "Be cautious with him, Princess."

"And to think he warned me about you," I replied just as a knock echoed at the door.

"Oh?" He arched his brow, then called out, "Enter."

A team of servants bustled in, carrying a tub for me to wash up after the night's festivities.

"He said you were cunning."

"High praise from him, I must say." Anderz studied the maids as they worked, a slight frown drawing his features. "He's not bound by nobility, only coin. A true entrepreneur at heart. A potential ally if our interests align, but he'll switch allegiances if another party offers more."

At least with a merchant, there was no need to decipher hidden agendas or sift through half-truths. They followed the money, nothing more.

"I will leave you to retire. Tomorrow, the high court will request your presence. I shall see you then."

"Anderz?"

He stopped at the threshold, his face a perfect image of patience. "Yes, Princess?"

"Why are you helping me?"

He studied me with a gentle smile and clasped hands, then dipped his chin. "There are some who have faith in the gods, and there are some who have faith in certain people and their resilience. I'm a man of faith, Princess." He nodded, then took his leave.

Faith in me, or the gods?

I sighed, then turned to Sainte. "That was terrible."

"His answer?"

"The whole night!"

"I agree."

He pulled up a chair as the maids filled the tub with buckets of steaming water. They filed in and out, seemingly unaware of our presence, yet attentive in case we needed anything. I held deep admiration for the castle staff. They were some of the most observant people I'd ever known.

A maid stepped forward as the others departed. They learned by now that I preferred solitude during my baths, although Gilead's soothing oils would have been a welcome addition after tonight's events.

"May I assist you in removing your gown, Your Highness?" she asked, head dipped with respect.

"No." Sainte gave her a flat stare.

"Oh, uh... yes, milord." She lowered into a quick curtsy, then scurried out the door.

Before I could question his swift dismissal of her, he stood up, his muscles flexing as he stretched with a soft groan. His leather armor creaked as he unclasped and removed each piece, placing them on the table. He focused on the belt that secured his daggers, fingers working to unfasten the clasp.

"Like what you see?"

My heart raced, and I jolted like a startled rabbit, meeting his amused gaze with wide eyes.

Yes. Yes, I did like what I saw.

I pushed to my feet, tugging at the back of my collar to find the seamstress's thread. My fingers fumbled until Sainte batted them away. His warm touch grazed the sensitive flesh at the nape of my neck, sending a delightful, dangerous shiver down my spine.

With a deft tug, he loosened the dress, and a rush of cool air caressed my skin as the seam relaxed. Heat flushed my cheeks, and I faced the hearth to hide my embarrassment. His touch lingered, fingertips tracing a path down my shoulders before he withdrew.

When I looked over, he had taken a seat with his back to me. He leaned on the table, fingers pressed to his lips, his gaze fixed on the door.

A smile crept across my face.

"What do you think of Leihim?" I asked, as I shed my dress and slid into the tub. The water's warmth drew a hiss—almost too hot. Still, I sank in, easing into its comforting embrace.

Sainte cleared his throat. "I don't know him well enough to make a judgment call."

"What about this Dire Wolf character?" I reached into the basket beside the tub, pulling out a bar of soap.

"Heard of them in passing."

"I think I should meet them."

Sainte shifted, glancing over his shoulder to observe me from the corner of his eye. "He's killed before."

I batted my lashes, feigning innocence as I sank lower. "So it's a 'he,' is it?"

"It's no place for you, Elspeth."

"So you know where he is."

"El," he pivoted fully, bracing his hands on his knees as his sharp gaze flashed a warning. "This is a dangerous game. If we make enemies of the common folk, we won't survive. And crossing Hinyte will have the nobles at our throats."

"I have to learn to play, eventually." I shrugged, then lathered some soap in my hair.

"Anderz can guide you. Ask him for advice."

I ducked under, scrubbing at my scalp before resurfacing. Gasping, I rubbed the wetness from my eyes. "Do you think he knows where to find him?" I asked, noticing he had once again turned his back to me.

"Dyre knows more than you can imagine."

I squinted at that. His tone carried a hint of mystery, suggesting more than his words revealed.

"Why won't Adastrus aid Leihim?"

"The prince regent can't be bothered with their issues."

"There's a bandit in the kingdom. Wouldn't he want the matter resolved?"

"Not if he doesn't care enough. To him, it's the caravan's problem. They should hire more security. He won't send soldiers to defend a common merchant."

My frown tightened, and I finished my washing.

It didn't add up. If Hinyte was as influential as he claimed, the regent would want to stay in his favor and, at the very least, pretend to address the issue. Something seemed off in this political web, and I hadn't been raised to navigate the nuances of such intrigue. I was a simple girl, masquerading as a princess.

At least I had Anderz.

Resigned to seek him out in the morning before being summoned to court, I glanced at Sainte's back before rising from the tub. I stepped out, quickly wrapping a robe around myself and plucked my dress off the floor. Approaching Sainte, I draped it over the chair beside him. His eyes tracked from my robe to my face. Something dark and dangerous heated in that cool gaze, and I responded with a sweet smile.

He grunted, standing abruptly, and pulled his tunic from his trousers. As he neared the tub, he set a dagger beside it before yanking his tunic over his head. A quiet hiss escaped his lips, drawing my attention to his injuries. The wounds from the flogging healed into long red welts, some still scabbed over, bright pink flesh exposed where scabs fell off. A faint bruise lingered on his lower back, a reminder of Adastrus' blow when I claimed him as my Valahant.

I stepped forward, compelled by an unseen force to touch those wounds. Sainte froze at the sound of my footsteps, glancing over his shoulder. My fingers traced along his skin, drawn tight over a layer of muscles. The thick, uneven ropes of scar tissue weren't ruggedly handsome in some dangerous way—they were ugly.

"Fifteen years' worth?" I murmured.

"I managed to recruit enough to save my hide a handful of times."

He turned to face me. I swallowed hard, the sound loud in the quiet room as my gaze roamed over his chest and abdomen. Sainte stood solid and powerful, his thick muscles defined beneath a dusting of dark hair, which almost concealed the bruises left by Adastrus' fists. I held my breath, finding his face. Bruises still stained the right side, and I reached up, my fingers brushing his discolored cheek. His eyes fluttered shut at my touch, and something twisted in my heart.

"I'm sorry."

When his stare met mine again, a strange emotion flickered across his face. Without warning, he nipped at my finger. I pulled my hand back, a surprised smile playing on my lips. He shook his head, then turned to the tub, unfastening his trousers.

I took that as a sign to leave and retreated to my dressing room to slip into a nightgown. My heart felt light, a rare happiness settling over me.

That night, my dreams were filled with thoughts of Sainte.

CHAPTER 19

I expected the high court to consist mostly of nobles, and therefore, after last night's festivities, anticipated them to be late in rising.

I was wrong.

Summoned before dawn, even Sainte groaned. I missed my opportunity to speak with Anderz, who sent word he would meet me there. My handmaids rushed to dress me and make me presentable, while Sainte donned his armor and combed his short, dark hair.

We hurried along the corridors, led by a servant until we reached a set of large wooden doors flanked by four soldiers.

"Her Highness, Princess Elspeth," he announced with a bow as he stepped through.

I followed and steeled my expression to mask my shock. Instead of a handful of high court members as I expected, nearly fifty people surrounded an enormous stone table. The size of it seemed impractical. I'd wager servants had to crawl across it to clean its center.

"Princess, we have been eagerly awaiting your arrival." Anderz stood, motioning to the empty seat beside him.

I inclined my head and walked with quick strides to my place, our footsteps echoing in the silent room. I sat next to a young woman with golden hair. Though petite, her posture exuded inner strength. She nodded and smiled, and I returned the gesture before I glanced around the many faces.

I didn't see Adastrus, but my gaze locked onto Leihim, whose sharp eyes watched me intently. He flashed a bright smile, which I returned with a tight-lipped nod. Anderz took his seat as a man far to my left spoke.

"Having passed two rites, we have requested your presence during our high court meetings. It is fitting that our *potential* future ruler makes informed decisions."

"And where is Prince Regent Adastrus?" Leihim inquired.

He asked what I wouldn't have been brave enough to. And by that bright, cheery grin plastered on his cheeks, it seemed he knew it.

"As you well know, Master Hinyte, he is far too busy managing the kingdom to honor us with his presence," the older man replied, resting his hands on his large belly.

"He trusts his advisors to inform him of any... areas of concern," a woman added.

Her skin, pale as snow, contrasted with her dark appearance. Hair the color of fresh ink framed her hooded brown eyes, giving them a deeper, mysterious shade. Black robes concealed her figure, and she wore her locks braided and piled high, which added an air of elegance.

The room buzzed as nobles and council members clustered in animated discussions about trade and law. Conversations flowed about the success of breeding wild sheep in captivity and the advantages of farming their wool instead of hunting them for pelts. Another group debated the poor yields from food plots in one district and negotiated trades with other districts to alleviate the shortage. I tuned out, catching snippets of a debate about changing the color scheme in the castle's main entryway and the expenses involved.

Adastrus' absence made sense now. The meeting dragged on, half the counselors dozing in their seats. Leihim, however, leaned back, his keen eyes observing everyone. He resembled Anderz in this way, always alert. His careful nature ensured everything stayed within his sight.

I felt fortunate to have Counselor Dyre on my side. Even though I hadn't pegged down his motives for helping me without promise of reward, he proved to be loyal to my cause. He studied the councilwoman speaking, golden eyes focused. Only his long fingers moved, tapping against his thigh under the table. Otherwise, he remained still, not a gray hair out of place.

"What of Ambassador Piers?" someone asked.

Anderz shifted, snaring my attention. His gaze narrowed on the noble who spoke, and I followed suit. The man, with a peppered gray beard, leaned back in his seat, exuding an air of relaxation as he surveyed the table.

"Dead."

A chair slammed onto all four legs, drawing my line of sight toward the youngest councilman—his face still bore traces of boyish charm.

"How do we know?" another pressed.

"His head arrived by messenger last night."

"A man can't live without a head," someone muttered.

How observant.

"One of our ambassadors?" I whispered to Anderz as comments ricocheted around the table.

"Yes, to the Glades," he murmured, eyes flitting as different discussions broke out.

Gladier, a nation we had traveled through, sprawled to the southwest. However, a narrow strip of its land separated Wynterborne and Tilamuik. Poor relations with that region meant we risked losing commerce with the deep south. And if I learned anything throughout this meeting, it was that trade was important.

"Does our prince regent have a replacement?"

"Who would go willingly? It would be a death sentence."

"Was there no cause?"

"No, a rumor of him bedding King Reid's daughter."

The room dissolved into murmurs, and I leaned toward Counselor Dyre again.

"How do we know it's a rumor? Wouldn't that be a crime?"

"Piers was... a man who did not enjoy women's company," Anderz said, studying a woman across the stone table. "To say that he lay with King Reid's daughter... He would sooner grow a pair of wings and fly to the gods than do such a thing."

I hummed in interest and leaned back in my seat.

"He was a citizen of our country," a councilwoman bit out. "There should have been negotiations."

Leihim shook his head and spoke up. "Our ambassador was killed without trial. My merchants would not dare to pass through Gladier." His light hair swayed around his shoulders as he scrutinized the paper before him, jotting notes with a quill and ink.

"We need those crops."

"If the southern trade route is severed, our people will starve."

"Does the prince regent know of this? He needs to send another ambassador."

"It is not his priority," the woman cloaked in darkness remarked.

I frowned, tilting my head at her.

Right, my brother's main focus was either eliminating me or expelling me from the kingdom. If he had the throne, he could do whatever he wanted. He only needed to kill me first.

"The rites are important, but this has greater urgency, Reuthland."

"Prince Adastrus attends to matters he deems fit, and he sees this as a situation for future consideration," she said.

Her dark stare flicked toward me, sending a cold shiver down my spine.

"Then perhaps we should send someone who thinks it is a priority." The room fell into a sudden hush at Leihim's suggestion.

I met his unblinking gaze as he focused on me, and the weight of everyone's stare pricked across my skin, all of them anticipating my response. Silence lapsed and no one offered a comment in my place.

I cleared my throat, forming my words with care. "I await the third rite."

"The God Stones are on their way, but with the Howls upon us, retrieval might take weeks." Leihim leaned forward, a smile forming. "If a member of the royal family were to visit, perhaps King Reid would be more open to another ambassador, and trade could resume."

"Sending Princess Elspeth into such a volatile kingdom is a grave request, Master Hinyte," a woman's voice cautioned.

I didn't dare break my gaze from Leihim—his intensity held me captive.

"A risk. A gamble," he mused, tapping his finger against the paper. "Perhaps a test."

"You go too far!" someone snapped. "It is not our place to test the royals. That's for the gods!" Hushed, murmured agreements followed that sentiment.

I deciphered his message through his silent gaze—he was daring me. It was a risky move. If Sainte couldn't shield me, my life hung in the balance. Yet, if I succeeded, I could rally support from the high court.

Wasn't this the dangerous game I'd been warned about?

"Will the rite be forfeit if I'm absent when the God Stones arrive?" I whispered to Anderz, maintaining eye contact with Leihim.

"As long as you are *alive*, the rite will wait for your return, Princess," he assured me.

"I believe," the table fell silent as I leaned in, addressing the court but fixated on Leihim's challenging stare, "an ambassador shouldn't travel where a royal wouldn't dare."

"The prince regent–"

"Has other priorities," I stated, cutting off Reuthland.

"To ask the princess to–"

"I volunteer," I stated calmly, silencing another council member. "I would like to meet King Reid. As you know, I grew up in Tilamuik. I understand their culture better than most who might go in my stead."

"And what if you do not return, *Princess?*" Counselor Reuthland sneered. "What about the hope you've kindled among the common people? The belief that the gods care for the souls of mere mortals?"

"I suppose one would have to have faith the gods will protect me," I replied, tone dry. "Or else they might have higher *priorities.*"

Lyana was in the single place I wished she weren't—the Hall of Receiving.

While Adastrus attended to matters he deemed paramount, oblivious to the ambassador's murder, I attempted to slip inside. A noble in luxurious furs pleaded his case nearby. My brother's gaze locked onto me instantly, though he remained still, his eyes sharp with sinister intent.

Ethyan lounged beside Lyana, his hands folded behind his head against the wall. He grinned when I joined them, while his sister focused on Grimm, as if she might convey a message through sheer willpower.

I composed my expression and observed my brother's Valahant at the foot of the dais. Once a jovial figure, his eyes lacked their usual sparkle. The velebond link embedded in his skin seeped red, with angry crimson lines extending from the wound, vanishing beneath his tunic.

It looked terrible—painful.

Urien's voice, hushed yet intense, reached my ears as he conversed with Sainte beside me. The man showed a newfound concern for my companions, a protective stance against Adastrus' threat.

"I'm going on a trip," I murmured, glancing at Lyana before returning my gaze to my brother, who slowly straightened in his chair to peer at me.

I wouldn't have long, lest he enact some cruel deed to assert his authority as regent over me, a point made with reckless disregard for consequence.

"Oh?" Lyana's voice carried a note of curiosity, her gaze fixed on Grimm.

A hint of redness tinged her ocean eyes, evidence of her recent tears. The dark circles beneath them betrayed her lack of sleep. If my trip weren't imminent, I'd have stolen a moment tonight to hold her.

"I'm bound for Gladier," I said, my tone light with anticipation. "Their winter games are underway, and I thought you might like to come."

Truthfully, I wanted to whisk her away from this place, far from Grimm. Her whispered confessions to me in the dead of night tugged at my heart, fueling a wish to move the sun and moons to free him. Yet Anderz made it clear there was no way. Even if Adastrus were to meet an untimely demise, his Valahant would follow through with the velefieor.

The passage of death.

I pleaded with him to continue his search for a solution, though his simple nods of understanding carried a weight of resignation. Hope seemed elusive, slipping through our fingers like grains of sand.

"I'll sit this one out, El," she said, hugging herself tight and leaned against her brother, who draped his arm around her, drawing her close. "I wouldn't enjoy any games right now."

A frown creased my brow. I didn't relish the idea of her staying here, worrying over Grimm. There was nothing I could do, nor she could do. Love, in my limited understanding, seemed too vast to bloom within a few fleeting weeks of travel.

My eyes slid over to Sainte.

A few years of moments, though... that might be–

"I have to go right away," I said, turning to her.

She nodded, as if she were a puppet controlled by unseen strings. "Safe travels."

Ethyan offered an apologetic smile with a shake of his head. He wouldn't leave his sister even if the sun itself tried to separate them.

"I'll be back as soon as I can," I whispered, stealing a glance at Adastrus. He sat upright, his attention fixed on us, heedless of the distraught noble at his feet who wailed and pleaded.

Something about sheep.

Lyana's response was a noncommittal hum, a clear indicator of her distressed state. I didn't want to risk her safety by lingering in this room. I stood and took my leave with Sainte close behind. As we rounded the corner, tears welled, blurring my vision.

"Urien will watch over them?"

"Aye." A slight wrinkle of a frown formed between his brows as he met my gaze. "He will keep them safe."

With a deep breath, I tried to compose myself. We faced far worse scrapes and pulled through.

But we always survived them *together*.

I drew strength from Sainte's nod of encouragement, then turned on my heel and strode down the corridor with renewed purpose. I knew my way around these halls now—almost as if it were home.

Unable to sleep, I tossed and turned.

It wasn't the bed. It was actually quite comfortable—a blend of feathers and straw—closer to what I slept on my whole life, unlike the plush pads in the castle. My mind just wouldn't be quiet.

Doubt crept in like tendrils of mist. Was I even capable of challenging King Reid over the death of an ambassador?

No member of Wynterborne's high court should ever fear for their lives. They were kin, part of our blood. They deserved our unwavering protection, and when that wasn't an option, then our vengeance.

"Do you know if Piers had a family?" I whispered into the darkness.

"His mother is still living," Sainte said.

"Is she cared for? Now that her son is gone, will she inherit his wages?" I asked, blinking at the dark ceiling.

The windowless room swallowed any hint of light. Despite the modest surroundings, the inn provided a welcome reprieve after two grueling days on the road.

"Piers came from the line of Gortyte, a noble family. She will manage well until the Veil calls to her."

I huffed and rolled onto my side, the rough blanket scratching against my skin.

It still didn't feel right.

"Sleep, Elspeth."

"I can't," I whispered.

My mind raced, tangled with questions. Why did King Reid blame Piers? If he needed a scapegoat for his daughter, surely his court offered better choices, ones that wouldn't offend a neighboring nation.

Sainte groaned from his place on the floor, followed by a scuffle.

"I'm sorry. I told you to ask for a cot. If you want—oof!"

A strong hand nudged me aside, and I yelped, wriggling to the edge of the mattress. The bed dipped under his weight, rolling my body toward his. He pulled me against his chest, and his warmth seeped through my nightgown. His scent—a mix of earth and leather—filled my senses.

"What are you doing?!" I hissed.

"When you can't sleep, you lay with Lyana." His deep voice rumbled, the vibrations tickling my back.

"You are *not* her," I mumbled, my voice a mix of frustration and exhaustion.

"I am your Valahant. Sleep."

I pressed my lips together, forcing myself into silence. With my eyes shut tight, I struggled to quiet my mind. Images of fish swimming upstream flickered through my thoughts. I counted them over and over, then when that didn't work, I repeated words in a futile attempt to exhaust myself.

Don't move. Sainte is holding me. Don't move.

"This isn't the same!" I hissed, trying to scoot away.

He tightened his grip, pulling me closer. "Tell me of Landing's End."

I frowned, stilling against him. "Pardon?"

"Talk. It will help to get your thoughts out."

"That's not what I'm thinking about."

"What are you thinking about?"

My heart pounded, cheeks burning in the darkness as I focused on the heat of his body against mine. Safe. Secure. In his embrace, I felt undeniably feminine, an unfamiliar yet welcome sensation.

No, I wasn't sharing those thoughts with him.

"How terribly uncomfortable this must be for you," I lied, clearing my throat. "I warn you, I kick in my sleep."

"Lyana seems to manage just fine."

"She kicks back."

"I'm sure I can handle it."

"Share a bed with many women, have you?"

I cringed, slapping a hand over my mouth. This wasn't the question to ask the man I had crushed on as a teenager, especially while he held me tight.

In a bed.

In the dark.

Alone.

Sainte stiffened, the silence stretching between us. I bit my finger, torn between hoping he would stay and wishing he would return to the floor.

His sigh tickled my neck, and he relaxed, settling deeper into the mattress. "Can't say that I have," he murmured.

"Really? A dashing man such as yourself?" I asked, thankful for the darkness that concealed my blushing cheeks.

"No."

Oh, don't do it. Elspeth! No–

"Surely, there was a maid in the past. Someone you swooned over."

Thrice-curse it and dunk me in a pit of pig dung.

"Swoon?" He chuckled, his chest rumbling against my back. "No, I can't say I've ever swooned."

"Never?" I pressed, surprised. How could any maid resist him? "You're a simple man, perhaps a tavern wench or two?"

He laughed, then pushed upright, propping himself on his elbow to look down at me. "Did you just call me simple, and accuse me of having my needs met by a tavern wench?" Amusement lightened his tone. "Tell me, Ellie, how many men have you slept with?"

I grimaced, sensing the tables turn. His use of my nickname didn't go unnoticed. This was a private conversation between friends. No harm would come of it.

I hoped.

"Did you keep score?" I asked the darkness. "Surely you counted–"

"I assure you, I take my *score* with all seriousness. I know my number well."

"Likewise," I huffed.

A pregnant silence followed, Sainte remaining still beside me. My heart pounded in the quiet, anticipation mingled with uncertainty. Would he return to the floor? Stay on the bed? Push for more?

"How many?" he asked.

Something changed in his tone. The playful mask slipped, and I suddenly didn't want him to think poorly of me.

"A few."

"A few?" His voice pitched higher, strained, as if he struggled to remain calm.

"There were a handful in the ports that I experimented with."

By experiment, I meant I tried to flirt, to find the same connection I had with Sainte. Each time, I fell short. I sought that blend of respect, adoration, and attraction, but it always eluded me.

At Lyana's suggestion, I even kissed one or two. Each encounter left me feeling dirty and used. The experiences were uncomfortable, to say the least.

None of them were Sainte.

"I'm not sure I want to know how you *experimented*." His words held an edge of curiosity that he wasn't willing to admit.

I huffed, desperate to take the heat off me and my past choices. "Well, what's your score?"

"Not a *few*," he mocked, settling against me.

He didn't hold me as tightly as before, and guilt pricked at my skin, as if I let him down somehow.

"So more? And you mock me for my few!"

"I'm not mocking you, Elspeth. People have different needs."

"No, no. You don't get to take the high road, Sainte." I jabbed my finger into the darkness, wagging it as if he could see. "How many women have you been with?"

"None."

My hand froze mid-air, and I went rigid. "What?" My voice squeaked on the word.

"None."

"You've never–" Horror crept into my tone.

"Never."

I jerked upright, taking this discussion far more seriously than I ever intended. "Fine, well let's be clear–"

"No, Elspeth, I've never bedded a woman—never rutted like a dog in heat." His words were dry, clipped, as if angry. "I choose to believe I'm above that kind of behavior."

"Are you like Piers? Do you prefer–"

"Sleep, Princess."

Gods above. He must see me as a whore, boasting about my experiences while he took the moral high ground.

"How old are you?"

"I don't think I'll answer that."

"Sainte, how–"

"I'm not a dog, Elspeth. Don't expect me to act like one."

Oh, that stung.

I frowned and flopped back down, sulking. This wasn't how I expected the conversation to go. I meant to tease and flirt, not belittle him or end up feeling guilty.

"It was just kisses," I mumbled into the pillow, curling away from him.

How could one man's words make me feel so small?

"What was that?"

I lifted my face. "It was just a few kisses!" I snapped, then dropped back down with a thud.

"Ah," Sainte sighed, shifting to embrace me from behind. "Did you enjoy them?"

I resisted his advance, kicking at him. "If you must know—no!" I spat.

His laughter filled the room before he ensnared me with his leg, anchoring me to the mattress. "I left you in one of the most vile cities, and all you have to show for it is a few kisses?"

"Are you doubting my seductive capabilities?!" I fought with renewed vigor, struggling to free myself from his hold.

"Not at all! In fact, I distinctly remember a certain sixteenth birthday–"

"Don't you dare!" I managed a kick to his thigh, shoving his hips from mine, creating valuable space.

"The tugs on my tunic... The press of your hips against my—oh probably my knees at that age–"

"My head was to your chest!"

"Ah, my thighs, then. Yes, I have every faith in your art of seduction."

Part of me was thrilled at his recollection, while the other seethed with irritation at his jest. I had meticulously planned that day for months, brimming with confidence in my allure, convinced he'd notice my blossoming curves. I believed he came because he cared, because he wanted my happiness...

And my happiness was intertwined with him.

"That's not funny," I snarled, driving my elbow into his chest.

He wheezed at the force, and I wrestled myself loose from his grasp. He chuckled, leaving me to simmer on the opposite side of the bed. I found a semblance of safety in the scant handspan that separated us.

"I didn't think it was," he said, a smile lingering in his tone as he shifted onto his back.

I sniffed. "You're poking fun at it. I assure you, I was quite serious at the time."

"As was I." A moment of silence settled before he continued, "I was serious when I told you I couldn't bring you with me."

The teenage girl inside me flinched at the memory. "That hurt."

"I know."

He reached out and drew me close. I released a contented sigh as I rested my head near his heart.

"I was…" He cleared his throat, "I was afraid."

"Of what?" I murmured, surprised that anything could scare him.

"I feared the consequences of you coming after me. And when I couldn't find you… I was terrified."

He took a deep breath, his chest rising beneath my cheek. "I was afraid of losing you."

CHAPTER 20

We rode with purpose, our horses moving at a fast trot. Ten soldiers clad in the distinctive black armor of Wynterborne flanked me, with Sainte on my right and a sturdy, compact man on my left.

Kaen accompanied us on the recommendation of Anderz. He was not only the sole volunteer to venture into Galadier but also versed in their customs—enough so to help me teach King Reid a lesson on respecting Wynterian ambassadors.

He was of modest stature, and his wispy brown hair formed a halo around his balding scalp. As he rode, the wind tugged at the strands, creating a tattered banner trailing behind him. His nose bore the marks of multiple breaks, now healed at a slight angle, while his bouncing cheeks displayed several scars. Despite his unconventional appearance, his brown eyes sparkled with wit and intelligence. He defied the typical noble image, yet he was worth his weight in gold for the wisdom and insight he provided thus far.

We had a plan. As long as King Reid didn't strike before we reached the city and Sainte's soldiers refrained from stabbing me in the back, I had a chance. Kaen stressed the importance of my status, insisting I embody my royal demeanor. I had to command respect. The Glades were like sharks sensing blood, they would attack without hesitation.

This was why Sainte brought so many soldiers when he first retrieved me from Landing's End. He assumed there would be complications sneaking me across the border. Thanks to my detour, we avoided the main cities, allowing us to travel faster than gossip could spread.

When we reached the gates, four guards formed an escort toward the palace. Castle Gladier towered above, its white walls reflecting the midday light onto the city. Larger than Wynterborne, it sat exposed on flat land, far more vulnerable than our fortress. Hooves pounded against cobblestones, melding with the clink of armor, each sound echoing my frantic heartbeat.

"Open! At the request of Princess Elspeth of Wynterborne!" Kaen bellowed.

We rode into a clearing before the palace, and guards scrambled to obey the order. For such a small man, his voice was large and commanding. The courtyard gates swung open amidst the commotion. Our horses stormed through without slowing. We bypassed the stableboys running to retrieve the reins and pivoted toward the white marble steps.

I slid off my horse, bringing it to a halt with a movement that looked braver than I felt. Sainte's boots hit the ground right after mine. The sound of his following footsteps bolstered my resolve as I hiked up my dress and stormed up the stairs.

The scribe near the entrance wrung his hands, dark eyes flitting over our group. "Your Highness, Princess, if we only knew–"

"If I wanted to inform you of my arrival, I would have," I snapped, then lifted my chin high to stare him down, or at least try to, given he was the same height. "I demand an audience with King Reid."

"I shall inform him you would like to–"

"He grants audiences now, does he not?" I replied, striding toward the castle doors. "Had an ambassador from Wynterborne made a request, your king would have seen him at this time. I will take his place."

Bluffing with Kaen's advised words, I relaxed a fraction when the scribe jogged to catch up, waving at the guards. They hesitated, but opened the way for me and my party at his insistent signal.

The heavy door creaked, echoing through the vast room. The musty scent of old stone mingled with the aroma of polished wood as we entered. Boots clinked against the marble floor as our Wynterian soldiers took their positions along the corridor as ordered. I prayed they would stay at their stations in case things went poorly and we needed to make a quick escape.

The scribe scurried to keep pace with my purposeful strides, struggling to lead the way. Sure, I risked going the wrong direction, but if I slowed, it would give them the opportunity for someone to send guards to prevent my audience with the king.

We approached an open doorway, and my nerves wavered as I glimpsed a dark figure on the throne in the distance.

I could do this. As a princess, I bore a responsibility to my people. They depended on me, and I couldn't let them live in fear.

I had to be brave for them.

I stormed into the hall, striding through aisles of gathered nobles with my head held high. Silence fell, broken only by the rhythm of our boots on the polished floor, the jangle of Sainte's armor, and the soft swish of the folds of my dress.

The noble before the dais edged aside with a horrified expression. My eyes locked on the king's dark gaze. As I approached, guards shifted around him, more rushing in from the doorway to join the ranks.

Clearly, they weren't taking any chances of an attack.

"Your Majesty," I said, tone dripping with disdain. I halted and dropped into a deep bow, keeping my stare fixed on him.

King Reid bore a robust figure, one that commanded respect and distance. His dark eyes remained unreadable, and his mouth formed a hard line, shadowed beneath a thick mustache. His tanned skin spoke of sun and heritage, while his black hair, slicked back with oil, added to his imposing presence. Clad in gold and crimson, his attire caught the light from stained glass windows that framed the room.

"You must be–"

"Princess Elspeth, Second Born of Veiled King Vardis of Wynterborne."

He studied me with a glint in his eye as he leaned on the arm of his throne, tapping a finger against his lips. "So it's true, then. You live."

"Unlike our ambassador, Piers of Gortyte," I shot back, hoping my gaze reflected my anger and not the insecurity of my station.

"Ah." He shifted, straightening his posture.

I followed his gaze toward the front of the crowd. There sat a woman with sharp cheekbones and perfect lips pursed tight. The only thing soft about her was the swell of her belly. Her kohl-lined eyes, an alarming blue, contrasted sharply with her dark complexion. A thin golden tiara marked her as royalty.

Bastard royalty.

There lay the reason for Piers' death.

"Have you come to apologize for his treasonous actions?" King Reid glanced over the crowd before his steady gaze settled on me again.

I recognized cold cruelty well enough from Adastrus to read the nervous edge to this king's actions.

"Rather, I would beg *your* apology."

Murmurs drifted through the mass as I continued, my voice carrying through the chamber, "Our ambassador was promised protection, shelter, and provisions in exchange for an alliance between our nations. Piers of Gortyte was a citizen of Wynterborne, not Gladier. He was ours, and you sent his head back to his mourning mother. You've committed an act of war against our people."

Shocked gasps reverberated through the room, tension spiking so high it was palpable in the air.

"You believe attacking my daughter—raping her and filling her belly with cursed Wynterborne seed was not an act of war against *my* people?!" His baritone voice roared over the crowd's rippling distress.

"I think you needed a scapegoat, dear king, and I believe you chose poorly."

"You call me a liar?" he seethed.

Beside me stood Sainte, a pillar of steadiness amidst my nervous trembles. My hands quivered, refusing to be stilled, yet I clenched them against the urge to adjust my dress.

"I call you a fool."

"Take them away!"

Guards sprang into action, and the room erupted into chaos as they scrambled toward us. Nobles shouted over one another while two of my soldiers drew their weapons.

Calmly, I extended my left palm.

Sainte placed a weighty gauntlet in it, the metal cool against my skin.

King Reid observed the exchange with suspicion, his eyes narrowing as he assessed the situation.

"*Ach neight duan tiel!*" I called above the din, then tossed the gauntlet at the king's feet.

Everyone froze at my words, and the cacophony fell into immediate and absolute silence. The guards' gazes shifted between the king and me. Kaen's warning flitted through my thoughts—this was the tricky part. I had to goad King Reid into action, rise to the bait. He was no fool, no matter how I accused him.

He scoffed, the sound dripping with disbelief. "You dare challenge me? Risk all-out war?"

"You've ventured into that realm already, Your Majesty. I'm simply offering you a scapegoat."

His eyes darkened, a dangerous glint flickering within as he leaned forward, holding my gaze. Kaen advised this plan for the same reason Anderz had me request a Valahant in the Hall of Receiving. With the crowd, the king would find himself cornered, compelled to respond to my challenge.

"My daughter's honor has been tarnished."

I highly doubted that. Based on her swollen belly, this was a misstep from months past, and Piers likely spoke out of turn, then suffered for her sake.

"Wynterborne's honor was tarnished by the untimely death of our ambassador, without negotiations for his return."

"And what happens when your challenge puts you in a grave? What will your brother say?"

I had to proceed with caution. Any hint of Adastrus' disregard for me could prove fatal, yet suggesting my death would trigger open conflict would land me in the dungeons.

"I came to discuss this breach of trust." My chin lifted, steadying myself. "I've spoken from my *own* convictions, and stand by them."

"Your life is in your hands, then."

"So be it."

He stared at me long and hard for a moment, before his fingers curled, tightening along the armchair. "Send for the Obelisk."

His champion.

"As for the duel, I choose to use my Valahant."

King Reid's gaze darted to Sainte, narrowing with scrutiny, as he looked him over. His lips pressed into a tight frown. "The velebond is an ancient custom among your kin," he remarked with caution.

"As is hiding behind a champion."

He recoiled as if struck, unable to conceal his offense.

In tense silence, our gazes clashed until a colossal figure entered. I observed the towering bronzed giant with interest, noting his long, dark, braided hair as he strode from a distant doorway. Clad in steel armor, he wielded two swords that, while hand-and-a-half for most, appeared as mere shortswords in his grip. His countenance was rugged and formidable, his eyes menacing.

He aptly bore the name Obelisk.

Sainte stepped forward, tightening a strap on his remaining gauntlet.

"You would battle here?" I asked, clenching my jaw as I noted the limited space and the civilians around us. "You would have bloodshed in your hall among your nobles?"

"All the more witnesses to your folly."

And all the more obstacles for Sainte to work around.

With a hard swallow, my gaze shifted between my Valahant and the giant. My role was fulfilled—I had done my part. He trusted me to get him this far. Now, I had to rely on his trust. I was asking a lot of him. The weight of my request mirrored the demands placed on me by the high court.

Bystanders shuffled aside without a word. The king's daughter approached the throne, a protective hand draped over her belly, fixing me with a spiteful glare.

Sainte stepped ahead, and for the first time, I sensed the unease he must have felt escorting me to Wynterborne. This was his job, his expertise—he was a warrior. As a princess, born for this, yet as I watched him draw his battle ax from its sheath on his back, fleeting doubt crept in.

Would he survive?

The Obelisk smirked as he cracked his neck from side to side, then rolled his shoulders. Sainte drew in a deep breath, settling into a wide stance that emphasized his strength, his fingers tightening around the ax's hilt.

I had to trust him.

He was my Valahant.

He was my champion.

The room fell into an eerie silence as the combatants assessed each other. When I turned, I found the king observing me with one dark brow arched in silent challenge.

A thunderous bellow erupted from the Obelisk, making me flinch. Kaen steadied me with a hand on my back before positioning himself beside me. As they sprang into action, there was little reassurance the advisor could offer. The giant advanced, swinging both swords in a sweeping arc that forced Sainte to duck and twist away.

The two spun as Sainte tried to get behind his adversary, deflecting blows with calculated precision. A moment of imbalance caused him to stumble, and I clutched my dress as the giant closed in. With a swift kick, the Obelisk raised his swords over his head.

"Poor choice," Kaen murmured.

His words drew my frown, and Sainte lunged forward like a striking viper, crouched low, slamming the butt of his ax onto the giant's foot just as the blades descended. With nimble agility, he rolled out of harm's way, evading the furious swing.

The Obelisk's relentless pursuit didn't falter as Sainte darted around. The clash of their weapons filled my throat with a foul, bitter taste. Locked in battle, I wished I could avert my eyes. My Valahant was deliberately trying to tire him out, and I knew that, but I couldn't help but cringe at each near miss.

I matched the king's stare, lifting my chin to level my glare his way. He offered me a sneer that told me he saw my reactions to the fight.

Have faith.

I ground my teeth, refusing to look at the men despite the grunts and growls. A sword clattered near me, making me flinch, but I kept my head high and my gaze steady. My Valahant had a job to do, and so did I.

A mighty scream shook me to my core. I broke contact with the king, bracing myself. The giant fell back, grimacing as his blood gushed onto the floor from where the ax had embedded in his stomach.

Sainte placed a foot on the Obelisk's chest and heaved his weapon free. Something wild and dangerous flickered in his eyes, sending shivers down my spine—shivers not born of fear.

"A life for a life," I called, my voice ringing clear as I held Sainte's gaze.

He prowled my way, like a lion after a kill. Red seeped from a gash on his temple, mingling with the Obelisk's blood splattered along his jaw, but the corner of his lip twitched up the tiniest bit.

He was ready.

He stood at my side and I turned a cruel smile on King Reid.

I held out my hand.

A gauntlet fell into it, and I hurled it at the foot of the throne. It skidded across the floor, colliding with its match.

I raised a brow. "Now, do you understand why you don't take things from Wynterborne?"

"Retract your challenge!"

I tipped my head in a show of innocence at his demand.

Kaen explained during a formal challenge, one could only offer a single champion in their stead. Sainte defeated the Obelisk, an imposing figure chosen to intimidate, and now the king stood vulnerable, forced to fight any subsequent challenges himself.

"No negotiation was given for Piers. And I have no desire to negotiate with you," I said.

Silence gripped the room as he stared me down.

"You kill me, and my heir will take the throne. Do you believe your life will be spared in his vengeance?"

"Do you have so little faith in yourself?" I gestured toward Sainte. "My Valahant is tired, weak. You are fresh and well-armed. I expected a king to stand tall and fight for his subjects."

"Hold your tongue–"

"Piers belonged to Wynterborne. He belonged to *me*, and you took his life."

"You don't know what you're doing," he scoffed. "You're nothing more than a little girl who–"

"Who knows the importance of her people!" I shouted, standing as tall as I could. "My ambassadors wear their nationality as a badge of honor, a shield of protection while abroad. They should never enter a nation that claims friendship, only to be murdered behind closed doors!"

I took a deep breath, hoping Kaen's guidance would hold true as I made my move. With slow, deliberate steps, I advanced towards the giant's cooling corpse. As I held the king's gaze, I set my palm in the sticky pool of crimson staining the polished floor. Blood dripped from my fingers as I approached the throne. His soldiers braced their weapons, but he lifted his fist, staying their defense. When I knelt at his feet, I dipped into a bow while holding his glare.

"I retract my challenge," I said, then extended my hand. Crimson splattered onto his golden boot.

His upper lip twitched in a silent snarl, but he placed his palm in mine, the blood slimy between our grip. I lifted his fingers to my lips and kissed his signet ring, seeking forgiveness.

"I warn you," I said, tightening my grip, "if ever a Wynterian comes to harm on Gladier soil, there will be far more blood on your hands."

He recoiled, releasing my hold. He tried to play off his disgust by leaning casually on his throne. With a smirk, I retrieved the gauntlets and faced the crowd, holding my head high.

Let them see a true Wynterian ruler, one who wasn't afraid to avenge her people.

I moved past the giant's corpse and between Sainte and Kaen. As I passed my soldiers, they sheathed their swords and fell in step with me. I strode with purpose, navigating the corridors with brisk strides. Placing guards at strategic points served two purposes: clearing our path for a swift escape and to guide me on the way out.

I resisted the urge to run as my soldiers hummed the Wynterian anthem, falling in line behind me. Shouts erupted from the hall, but the men's humming drowned out the chaos in our wake.

Clearly I had made an impression on King Reid, if his shouting was any indication.

We rode hard and fast. Kaen warned that lingering would risk King Reid's wrath—and our lives. He needed time to stew, and he assured me there would be plans to smooth over the incident.

Politics involve give and take. We needed to cause a scene to make them think twice about harming one of our people, especially our ambassadors. Yet, I insulted the king himself. If left unaddressed, his bitterness would strain relations between our nations.

Kaen hinted that an invitation to the coronation would be in order. He proved invaluable, and I realized I wouldn't be alone if I took the crown. People familiar with this political world were ready to help and guide me. I wouldn't have to rule alone or without advice.

By the time the sun kissed the horizon at dawn, we crossed Wynterborne's borders. Confident the God Stones hadn't arrived during our absence, we opted to rest in the relative safety of our own land before pressing on to the castle.

Entering my room at the inn, I glanced out the window. The bubbles along the glass surface distorted the view, but allowed the sun's first rays to filter in.

After the door shut behind me, I spun around, biting my lip as I awaited Sainte's reaction.

He turned toward me and halted. His expression shifted from relaxed and tired to confused and wary. Flecks of dried blood splattered his cheeks, and the crusted-over gash near his temple gave him a rugged appearance. The tear at the neck of his tunic revealed strong muscles beneath. Guarded blue eyes locked on me as he sidestepped, keeping his chest to me.

"Why are you walking like that?" I asked, a haughty smirk plastered on my cheeks.

"You look..." He trailed off, a frown pulling his brows together. He fumbled with the strap to his sheath crossed over his back.

My chin dipped with a playful tilt of my head. "I look like what?"

I wanted his approval—his validation. Despite winning two rites, *this* felt like a success. The prospect of claiming the crown seemed within reach. If the *gods* continued their elusive ways and offered their insight during the final rite, I just might handle the complexities of the political world.

His stare narrowed as he lowered his sheathed ax to the floor. "Different."

"What kind of different?" I swished my skirts and headed to the washbasin atop the end table. After I dunked the rag into the frigid water, I pivoted on my heel when he offered no response.

The expression on that man's face had me choking back my laughter. He took on giants, endured floggings and beatings, yet when faced with a woman's emotions, he appeared as bewildered as a newborn calf.

"Tell me what you're thinking," he said, eyes darting to the rag, then to me.

I started toward him, adding a little extra sway to my strides. "What's the fun in that?"

He fell silent, his form immobile as he collected his thoughts. I stopped close enough to feel the warmth of his breath on my cheek, then patted the damp rag along his wound, cleaning the dried blood. The gash, while not deep, had bled profusely, as head wounds do.

"Did I do well?" I finally asked, backing away.

Recognition and relief flashed across his features, and my heart swelled with warmth. Sainte embodied loyalty and resilience. His demeanor was unyielding and sharp, his physique robust and unwavering—yet even he had moments when he needed guidance.

He cleared his throat, unbuckling his belt. "You did. Kaen already told you. You were perfect."

"I wanted to hear it from you," I muttered, a satisfied grin spreading across my lips.

I rode a wave of confidence, exhilaration coursing through my veins. We hadn't died, and we evaded imprisonment. While the gravity of a man's demise should have been taken more seriously, I was far too elated to focus on that now.

He pulled his belt loose from his trousers, setting his daggers beside the bed. With slow strides, he closed in, pressing into my space. For a long moment, he peered into my eyes, then traced his fingers along my jaw while a faint smile played at the corner of his lips.

"You did well, Ellie."

My grin widened until my cheeks ached. Pride swelled within me. It was a simple statement, just a few words—yet, coming from him, they meant everything.

"You did pretty good yourself," I said, brushing my thumb near the gash on his temple. "Though, next time, do try not to damage my Valahant."

"I'll do my utmost," he pledged, his eyes tracing down my face until they settled on my lips.

Suddenly, the room felt stifling and cramped.

"Sainte?"

"Hmm?"

My hands grew clammy and butterflies fluttered through my belly with frenzied abandon. "Have you... ever kissed a woman?"

"Can't say I have."

Hunger swirled in those blue depths as he swallowed, his throat bobbing with the motion.

I licked my lips and mustered my courage. "Do you want to?"

What a stupid question, Elspeth.

"I would."

My heart stuttered before it took off like a rabbit, and my breathing drew shallow.

He met my gaze. "Yet, I would save that for my wife."

A rush of coldness swept over me, as if I had fallen into a pit of icy water, leaving me breathless. When he smirked and pulled away to kick off his boots, I choked on my gasp.

I froze, lips parted, grappling with what just transpired. Had I imagined the spell? Did he even want to kiss me—or was that a creation of my sleep-deprived mind?

He glanced my way with a low chuckle.

Curse men. The whole lot of them.

CHAPTER 21

We journeyed to Wynterborne Castle, savoring the exceptional weather. The sun beamed, casting a radiant glow on the glistening snow, illuminating our path as we headed north. Kaen suggested we ease our pace, immersing ourselves in the surroundings and allow the locals to see me as their princess.

I relished my moments with Sainte and the other men; even Kaen was surprisingly pleasant company. Laughter filled our conversations, often centering on the whimsical wool hat he wore, complete with flaps over his ears and a playful yarn tassel atop. Despite Kaen's maturity, the sight of him riding a horse in that hat added a touch of youthful comedy to his demeanor.

As the days passed, the soldiers relaxed, sharing stories of their families over steaming dinners at various inns. They confided their fears and aspirations, creating a bond of camaraderie. We learned about Sole, a young man with a deft hand for blades, who, after much probing and prying, revealed the name of his beloved—Millie. Amid laughter and jests, the men teased me for insights on how to win a lady's heart. In those moments, Sainte's gaze would shift to mine with a careful intensity.

Each night, he shared my bed. I made no comment, fearing to break the spell. He stayed silent in the face of my taunts, maintaining his aloof demeanor. Yet, a spark of hunger ignited in his eyes when his gaze lingered too long.

He was more intoxicating than any vat of spirits.

Laughter rang out at a joke about Valen's backside as we rode two abreast across a bridge to Wynterborne Castle. A smile tugged at my lips.

"You complain about the saddle, but forget about Dane's training," Sole jeered.

The men groaned, their chuckles trailing off. Dane, the rigorous training officer, kept the guards in top shape. His dedication bordered on legend.

"What of Jorgeson?" I asked, recalling the general who escorted Sainte and I when we first arrived.

Hanek barked a laugh. "Nah, he's all bark and no bite."

"He leads by example," Sainte cut in. "He doesn't ask his men to do something he wouldn't."

"Like you, Your Highness," Sole said. "The general would have done exactly as you did if he had the power to do so."

Pride warmed my heart. "I couldn't send another ambassador to Gladier without going myself. Their life would be forfeit."

A boy darted through the courtyard as we reached the castle grounds. "Princess!" he called, waving his arms. "Your Highness! Princess!"

My horse snorted, shifting its hooves as I pulled it to a halt.

Kaen slowed his stallion next to mine, his sharp gaze fixed on the boy. "Spit it out, lad."

He slid to a stop, panting, his eyes wide with fear. "I—Counselor Dyre told me to meet you!"

"What is it?" A knot tightened in my gut. Something was wrong.

"Now?" Kaen asked.

A wailing bugle pierced the air, halting everyone. Dogs and horses stood still, ears pricked. Heads turned westward, drawn to the echo. Its high, ominous note froze even the courtyard staff.

"A stag," Sole whispered.

"That is no stag." Kaen's voice, low and chilled, hinted at fear. "That is Nothar."

"A god that sounds like a stag?" I asked, ignoring the sinking feeling in my gut.

Kaen dismounted with an eerie stiffness, eyes locked to the west. "Don't make light of it, Princess. He is warning you."

I followed his lead, glancing at Sainte, whose deep frown mirrored my unease.

"Tell Counselor Dyre that Princess Elspeth will meet in her rooms–"

"Begging your pardon, but he said to meet in his chambers."

Kaen's nervous eyes flitted to me before giving the boy a quick nod. "You're off to fetch him?" he asked.

"Aye. Shall I see to your horses?"

"Go, lad." Kaen shooed him, and he took off running, kicking up snow with each stride. "Sole, Valen—take these horses to the stables."

The two wasted no time leading the travel-weary beasts away. The courtyard, filled with an uneasy silence, eased into motion as servants resumed their tasks. I cast a worried glance to the west, where the eerie call still seemed to hang in the air, casting a lingering spell over us all.

"Kaen told me about your visit to Gladier," Anderz said, entering his chambers. "I'm pleased to see you in one piece."

Perched on the edge of my seat at a small table, I felt Sainte's presence beside me, his back to the neatly made bed. Anderz's room surprised me with its simplicity, not what I expected from a member of the high court. Dark and sparsely decorated, it seemed more suited to someone of lower status, though the many books and maps crammed onto shelves hinted at his importance.

"King Reid wasn't happy," I said as Counselor Dyre closed the door, dismissing Kaen with a nod.

"I imagine not. We were equally displeased to hear of Piers' untimely death."

Anderz took the remaining chair and collapsed into it with a sigh. After a moment, he rested his forearms on the table, pinching the bridge of his nose. My anxiety spiked at the sight of his uncharacteristic demeanor. When I noticed the muscles in Sainte's jaw tense, I knew I wasn't alone in my worry.

"Why am I here, Anderz?" I asked, treading carefully.

"Sainte, I trust you to keep Elspeth detained in this room until I am finished."

My world spun as my heart dropped. What in all the nations could have happened?

"Until you give the word," he agreed, dipping his head in a show of respect.

Golden eyes bore into me as Anderz pressed his thin, steepled fingers to his lips. He studied me for a moment before speaking. "There has been an incident involving the prince regent—"

My mind raced. Was he killed? Was the blame placed on me? Would I ascend the throne without trial?

"—and the lady, Lyana."

I shook as a shudder ran through my body at those words.

"Where is she?" I whispered, pushing my chair back.

"Sit."

"*Where is she?!*" I screamed, causing Sainte to jump.

He grabbed me before I could run to the door. I couldn't fight him. Instead, I held myself, trembling with rage as he gripped my arm.

To his credit, Anderz didn't flinch or look surprised. His infuriating calmness somehow fueled my fury. If my brother harmed a hair on her head, I would kill him. I would rip out his heart and feed it to the pigs.

"She is safe in her rooms, as well as Sir Ethyan."

His words did nothing to calm the dark creature inside me thirsting for blood.

"What did he do to her?!" I hissed through clenched teeth, my mind racing with horrifying possibilities.

"Please sit."

"No!" I snapped, refusing to comply. "Tell me what he did to her. I will have his head! You don't get to–"

"Actually, my petulant princess, I do," he cut in, his tone dripping with condescension. "You forget you are not regent. Here, you are a pawn, like all the rest. Here, without us, you have no power."

A red haze clouded my vision. "I trusted you!"

I tried to wrench my arm from Sainte's grasp. He grunted as I swung a fist at his chest, but he took the hit with no complaint, pulling me close and wrapping himself around me.

"Yet," he growled in my ear, his grip tightening as I struggled against him. "You have no power *yet*."

I panted, more from restrained fury than exertion. Stilling in his arms, I glared at Anderz. "What did he do to her?"

"As a ruler, you will receive ill tidings," he said, gesturing to the chair. "Your heart will ache with news of war, famine, and destruction. You must learn to control your anger and use it to your advantage. To act out in wrath will lead to irreversible mistakes for you and all of Wynterborne. Now, sit."

I shrugged off Sainte's grasp, then seized the chair from the floor. After slamming it in place, a snarl lifted my lip as I sat, bracing my elbows on my knees.

"Tell me."

"Your brother did nothing she was not willing to suffer."

My face closed off in a frown, lip curling in repulsed confusion.

She bedded my brother?

Impossible. Lyana was no prude. She was quite free with her body, but touching Adastrus? Never.

"What are you talking about?!"

Anderz rubbed his jaw, as if his next words pained him. "Lady Lyana cares for your brother's Valahant."

"She loves Grimm," I said.

"Which makes this all the more tragic."

I slapped my hand on the table. "What happened?!"

"I will be blunt. There's no easy way to relay this. Sit back, close your mouth, and listen."

I bared my teeth, drawing a deep breath. With my nails biting into my crossed arms, I tilted my head, daring him to go on.

"Lady Lyana lingered in your brother's presence. Her purpose was to keep an eye on his Valahant, but she caught his eye. Urien and I warned her. Sir Ethyan swore he wouldn't let her out of his sight. Adastrus met with her, dined with her for two nights. I can safely assume she went because of her affection for Grimm, yet he spun a web of lies to trap her."

He paused, letting the details sink in a moment before continuing. "She drugged Sir Ethyan with a sleeping draft. Urien tried to intervene, but even he was helpless against the castle guard. Lady Lyana was escorted to the prince regent's chambers, seen of all, walking of her own accord."

He worked his jaw as though he tasted something bitter, then cleared his throat, picking at the table's wood grain to avoid my gaze. "She was abused."

I jerked my head aside, tears stinging my eyes. My breaths came in quick gasps at the thought of her suffering.

I wasn't there to stop it.

"Elspeth, there were witnesses."

"What?!" My voice cracked, shock and outrage flooding me. "Witnesses?!"

"As your Valahant sleeps in your rooms, so does your brother's."

No. Gods above, no.

"Beyond Grimm, Adastrus made sure others were involved. It's true that she appeared to welcome the abuse."

Anderz vanished from my sight. Tears streamed down my cheeks, a hollow ache spreading through my chest.

I wasn't here.

I was *enjoying* myself. Having fun. Laughing.

"Princess, do you understand?" Anderz's thin face and gray hair blurred through my watery haze. "She did not fight back. Your brother did not rape her."

I broke. My shoulders collapsed as I wrapped around myself. Sobs wracked my body, and a cold, nauseating wave of horror and guilt engulfed me.

She was here because of me.

She met Grimm because of me.

My brother singled her out because of me.

This was my fault.

"Do you understand?" Anderz's footsteps shuffled closer.

I gasped through my tears. "Why? Why would she–"

"We had our suspicions, but a witness confirmed it," he said calmly. "The prince regent promised her that if she lay with him, he would dismiss Grimm as his Valahant."

"He can't."

"As we told her—many times." A mournful note lingered in his tone. "Urien and I explained repeatedly—once the velebond is complete, they are bound in life and death. Adastrus could no more release Grimm than he could sever his grasp on this world and pass beyond the Veil. Lady Lyana would not listen. She insisted there was a way."

She would've listened to me. I should have warned her, but I feared it would crush her spirit even more.

I never should have left.

"Is she all right?" I asked, wiping my nose with my sleeve.

When he didn't answer right away, I froze, a sickening dread knotting my stomach.

"Anderz?"

"No." Regret seeped through his heavy sigh. "I will not lie. She is not well."

"Are you done?" I steadied myself, forcing myself to straighten as I fought to regain control.

"No. I need your word that you won't seek out your brother."

"I'm going to kill him."

"Save that for after your coronation, Princess."

Sainte wouldn't let me leave until Anderz secured my oath. He reassured me that once I ascended the throne, my actions would be my own. Until then, I was bound by law and his status as regent.

We walked through my silent corridors. The air felt thick, almost suffocating. A draft stirred the hall, but it couldn't dispel the lingering sense of evil that hung about like smoke.

At Lyana's door, Anderz stepped in front of me and knocked lightly. The room beyond remained quiet, nothing to rouse suspicion. When the way cracked open, and Urien peeked through, he took a long breath, his eyes darting over our group before he allowed us entrance.

As soon as I passed the threshold, my feet stopped working, shock freezing me in place.

Lyana lay on the bed, curled into a ball, a blanket pulled to her chin. She seemed so small—frail.

Ethyan sat on the floor, hunched against the bedframe. His dark, resentful eyes fixed on me over his knees. Bruises marred his face, his arm hanging at an unnatural angle at his side. Dried blood and scabbed wounds littered his body.

"Who did that to you?" I asked.

He raised his head and spat at me. "Your watchdog."

I spun on Urien with the fury of a thousand gods in my glare. He slumped against the door, wincing as he folded his arms across his chest, showing a fresh bandage beneath his tunic.

"That was *after* he stabbed me."

My fingers curled into fists as I turned on Anderz for an explanation.

"Would you rather him be dead," his gaze flicked to Lyana's unmoving form, "or worse?"

I ground my teeth together, biting down on my fury. If my brother was so vile as to abuse Lyana in such a way, he wouldn't have been above torturing Ethyan as well.

"Why didn't you send for a healer?!"

"We tried. He threatened them."

"If any of you Wynterian scum come near me, I'll kill you all." Ethyan's words hissed past bloody lips, glower locked on me.

My heart writhed as fresh tears burned my cheeks. I rubbed at them with my sleeve and headed for the bed, giving Ethyan a wide berth. My breath caught as I looked down at Lyana.

Her ocean eyes were dull, unseeing. Inflamed bruises stained the space beneath them. A gash near her temple seeped into her hair. Flecks of crimson shrouded her crooked nose and swollen split lips.

"Lyana?" I whispered, scared to breathe.

Her blanket concealed further carnage, and with trembling hands, I lifted the fabric, revealing the full extent of her injuries. A delicate white silk robe clung to her body, now a macabre canvas painted in crimson, filth, and unnamable fluids. The stench was overwhelming, a nauseating mix that threatened to choke me as I struggled to process the sight before me.

A surge of blistering fury welled within, a visceral response to the brutality inflicted upon her. The sensation battled with the raw ache of loss that tore at my core, a pain not for myself, but for her.

Her robe hung open, allowing a glimpse of the devastation beneath. Bruises mottled her skin, a cruel tapestry of violence. A jagged wound snaked from her ribs, disappearing into the fabric, its edges inflamed and oozing a sickly yellow discharge.

Hot tears streamed down my face, scorching trails of remorse. Guilt gnawed at my insides. Every ache and injury bore the weight of my mistake.

This was all my fault.

I slipped into the bed beside her, a futile attempt to absorb her pain with my presence alone. If only I could shoulder her suffering, I would do so in an instant, without reservation. I reached out to stroke her hair, studying the emptiness in her gaze.

"No!"

Her scream shattered the silence, and I reeled back as she thrashed. She yanked the blanket close, curling into herself. The wide-eyed terror in her glare pierced through me with unfamiliar intensity.

Hatred—anger. Hurt. Accusation.

"Lyana, it's me–"

I extended my hand towards her, a silent plea for recognition. If only my presence could bridge the chasm between us, if only it could convey the truth. I never meant for this to happen.

"Don't *touch* me!" Her scream sliced with startling force.

I darted from the bed, retreating until my back hit the wall. Her glare bore into me with unbridled loathing—a fierce manifestation of her contempt. I glanced towards Urien, whose expression spoke of sorrowful understanding. Anderz's eyes, golden and troubled, remained fixed on her, his frown etched with concern.

Sainte's stare locked with mine, unwavering even as tears cascaded down my cheeks, tracing the contours of my sorrow. A deep sob convulsed through me, my chest heaving with unrestrained emotion. His lips formed a firm line, a silent reassurance. His chin lifted slightly, a subtle gesture of confidence, as if to remind me of my strength.

But inside, I felt the fragility of my resolve. His belief in my resilience stood in stark contrast to the turmoil raging within, a tempest of doubt and vulnerability that threatened to consume me.

He believed I was strong enough for this.

He was wrong.

The room dimmed as evening descended. Not bothering to find a lantern, I lingered in the darkness as shadows stretched and deepened. Anderz and Urien departed hours ago. Counselor Dyre saw to the high court in my stead, while the latter sought respite, weary from his constant vigilance over my friends in my absence.

Ethyan, stubborn as ever, still refused to see a healer. His piercing gaze swept between Sainte and me, his animosity palpable. Each time his glare landed on my Valahant, it seemed to deepen, fueled by a simmering hatred that took root within him.

It was no comfort to know he harbored more contempt for him than for me.

We hadn't eaten or drank anything since our arrival. Endless tears stained my cheeks since Lyana's rejection, leaving me with a dry, empty ache in my heart.

"Sainte, can you leave us?" I asked, voice cracking.

"No."

When I met his gaze, his expression showed no anger or suspicion toward Ethyan. He understood my friend wouldn't harm me—it was unreasonable to expect my Valahant to abandon me in any situation that carried the smallest risk of harm.

I sighed, letting my exhaustion and shame pull me down as I rested my forehead on my knees. Hollow inside, this drain depleted all reserves, both physical and mental. The burden of it all made me hesitate to retreat to my room for sleep, afraid the guilt would return with even greater force upon waking. My friends needed me more than food and rest.

"We shouldn't have come," Ethyan whispered.

I held my breath, waiting for him to lash out, to curse. When nothing more came, I peeked over at his shadowed form. "I shouldn't have left."

His arm, the one he used for throwing, hung limp and swollen at his side. I couldn't shake the thought of how long it had been broken, questioning if he'd ever regain his uncanny accuracy. His relaxed posture belied his discomfort, head tilted back, eyes locked on the dark ceiling. Slowly, he lowered his legs, spreading them out in front of him.

"I don't blame you, El," he murmured. "I blame your *Valahant*. The inane idiot that pulled us all into this mess."

"He didn't–"

"Don't fight his battles." Ethyan's gaze locked on Sainte, the moonlight catching the fire in his glare. "He's big enough that he can handle it. Unlike Lyana."

Sainte's jaw clenched as he took a slow breath. He knew my friends wouldn't relent with him present. Their hurt was too fresh, their anger too raw.

"Please," I begged, "just a few moments."

"I'll be in the hall," he paused, giving me a long stare, "and the door will stay open."

I nodded, grateful for his understanding, though he shook his head, features etched in disbelief as he slipped out. He left the way ajar to storm in if needed.

And rescue me from my friends—my family.

Ethyan's shoulders sagged, then a guttural cry escaped him, his face contorting in agony. I rushed to his side, and he neither flinched nor glared. At that moment, I was his El, not the Princess of Wynterborne.

"Gods above and below, Ethyan," I cursed, tearing his tunic's sleeve to inspect his arm.

In the dim moonlight, the darkness of his skin worried me—bruises, I hoped, not old blood pooling. He didn't yell or push me away, a sign of his acceptance. I brushed the hair around his head, checking for swelling or knots on his skull.

"How long has it been like this?" I hissed.

"A few days—I don't know. Gods, El. It hurts."

"You need a healer."

"No!" His gaze snapped to mine, fear flickering in his eyes.

"Lyana needs care. How will we convince her to accept help if you're too scared to let anyone near you?"

"I'm not afraid," he hissed through clenched teeth. "You weren't here."

"And you were sleeping. We all messed up. Now play the hand you've been dealt and I'll fetch Gilead."

"No, I can handle it!"

"Perhaps." I rocked back on my heels, throwing my hands up. "Maybe you'll lose an arm! You might not *die*, but do you think Niena will grant Lyana the same luck? Have you *seen* her? She's not going to make it." Fresh tears welled and spilled over. "Her body is broken. Her spirit is crushed. She won't fight unless we force her."

Ethyan crumbled, his anger collapsing into a sob—his mask shattered. I moved to his uninjured side and wrapped my arms around him. We held each other, tears mingling, the weight of our shared grief pressing on us. We couldn't undo what happened—and it would change us all forever.

CHAPTER 22

I sent for Gilead that night, the only one I trusted near my friends. She entered, her voice a soft murmur as she dimmed the lantern, casting a warm, flickering glow around the room. The scent of herbs clung to her robes, and she gave Ethyan plenty of space until he calmed.

The darkness along his arm I'd been concerned about revealed deep bruising, but no internal bleeding. When asked if he would regain full range of movement and control, Gilead pressed her lips together, and told us it depended on the gods.

With her assistants kept at the door, I helped set his arm. The sharp tang of antiseptic stung my nose as we cleaned him and bandaged his wounds. Once he was mended, we started on Lyana.

Her refusal of anyone's touch tore my heart. We couldn't honor her wish. She lay in bed for days, too traumatized to rise and relieve herself. The sight of her, pale and trembling, made it impossible for me to leave her like that.

Ethyan understood the need. Tears streaked his face, mingling with sweat as he grimaced in pain, helping me tend to his sister. The metallic reek of blood and bodily fluids was hard to stomach. Gilead kept her distance, only stepping forward to examine the cuts on her sides and inner thighs.

Ethyan threw up twice, adding the stench of bile as we struggled to care for her. She fought and kicked, her screams piercing the air, teeth bared as she bit at our fingers.

Sainte stayed near the door, arms crossed, hands away from his daggers, gaze fixed on the wall. Now and then, his eyes met mine, sharing in my misery.

I pushed the horrors of that night to the back of my mind, ignoring the sight of her deep cuts, the dark bruises, the burns tarnishing her legs. The acrid stench of her state lingered in my senses, even now. I buried those memories, letting them resurface in quiet moments, when silence echoed with her faint haunting cries.

When I departed for the council meeting, Ethyan stayed with his sister under Urien's watchful eye. He made no apology for stabbing the Wynterian, but accepted his presence. Apparently, when Lyana left to meet my brother, Urien faced ten guards to intercede. When more arrived, she begged him to let her go, and he released her to them. I didn't hold him any more accountable for what happened than I did Sainte.

I scanned the table, my face a rigid mask, examining the council members' expressions. They allowed this to happen within their walls, hiding behind the pretense of her willingness, claiming no laws were broken. How many of them watched her torture, choosing silence over intervention?

Anderz withheld the names of the few witnesses he knew, but their power was evident—no one would question their word.

What sickness lurked within this castle that men would stand by, witnessing such horrors, only to speak of them later? What kind of fiendish ruler did they follow, someone capable of such heinous acts who strolled freely, as if untouchable by vengeance?

Leihim lounged in his chair, his gaze locked on me with a subtle intensity. His proposal still hung between us, a delicate thread connecting our ambitions. His backing in exchange for information regarding the Dire Wolf. Yet, my path to the throne stretched far beyond passing the next Rite, an event ordained by divine whims. I needed to garner support from the nobles. Though the common peoples' superstitions would sway many to my cause, if I would end my brother's life, I required a widespread alliance. And Leihim Hinyte held the key to persuading the majority.

As the high court droned on about trade routes, my finger tapped against my temple. Anderz's advice lingered in my thoughts—he urged me to stay attentive, to make a spectacle of interest even when my mind wandered. The charade of caring was crucial—but the only thing I cared about was removing my brother's head from his shoulders.

"And what of the merchants traveling through Gladiers?" someone asked.

"They're moving with confidence," Leihim said. His gaze slid along the counselors until he found who spoke. "There's tension, and the Glades are wary, but Wynterians are traveling without hesitation. It appears our princess has not only taught King Reid a lesson, but our citizens as well."

"You have won the faith of the people, Your Highness," said Aliea, the slender noblewoman to my left. "When are the God Stones to arrive?"

"Careful, Counselor," Reuthland warned.

Her rigid posture mirrored the hard lines of her dark, malicious stare. Her gaze roamed the table before settling on me, my demeanor deliberately nonchalant. She posed no threat to me—a pawn of Adastrus—one I would banish when given the opportunity.

"The people have faith in the gods, not only in the princess," Aliea retorted, her chin lifted in defiance as she spoke. "We should be ready for the coronation that will follow the next Rite."

Despite my victories in two Rites and the widespread acknowledgement of my status as the Gods' Chosen, everyone played along with Adastrus' game. The staff, the servants, even the high court, all deferred to the Rite of Favor, as if my brother stood a chance.

"We *should*." Reuthland's lips twisted into a slow, unsettling smile, hinting at knowledge beyond my grasp. "Preparations are underway."

"We should send invitations to our allies and neighboring kingdoms—a symbol of goodwill."

"Dignitaries are already arriving," Hinyte supplied. "The lull in the Howl means the stones should be arriving soon."

Aliea nodded along. "The entire world will witness the gods' favor bestowed upon their chosen."

I shut my eyes, clenching my teeth as the council continued their deliberations. The divine were absent throughout my entire existence. When my brother sought my demise as a child, did they intervene? No. I lived in the slums, unwanted and unloved. Did they care? No. Sainte forced me back into this world of politics and intrigue unprepared. Did the gods dare rouse themselves when my loved ones, those who *actually* believed in them, were hurt and abused?

No.

I didn't believe in the gods any more than I believed I would sprout wings and fly. My success in the previous Rites stemmed from a mix of sheer luck and an unstable mind. The upcoming Rite of Favor boiled down to a mere coin toss—a fifty-fifty chance they'd glow when I formed my question. Failure would pave the way for Adastrus to wield Grimm against me.

When I stood, I nudged the chair back with my knees, drawing the attention of those who paused their conversations, expressions perplexed by my interruption.

"My apologies, but I wish to retire to my chambers," I stated, lips pressed into a thin line. I had no energy left to indulge in their political maneuvers.

"You must be weary from your travels to Gladier," Anderz provided.

Or, I was weary of pretending everything was fine while my friends suffered halfway across the castle, and my brother, a tyrant in his own right, reigned as regent.

"Yes, rest. When the God Stones arrive, you will be tested," Aliea added. "We must prepare, regardless of the outcome."

I suppressed the urge to roll my eyes and offered a demure nod instead. Sainte pulled my chair aside, clearing a path for me to navigate around the table.

When I left the hall, I slipped down a side corridor, rubbing the bridge of my nose. To be honest, I dreaded visiting my friends. Lyana's glare of animosity softened over the past few days, replaced by a defeated resignation whenever we approached her to wash up. She finally mustered the strength to attend to her basic needs, though eating still required persistent encouragement.

Whenever I entered that room, a tidal wave of guilt engulfed me, drowning me in self-disgust. For a few breaths, a few fleeting moments, I didn't want to feel like a rotten excuse for a human.

Sainte snagged my arm, then shoved me into a cramped closet. I let out a startled yelp as he squeezed in after me, easing the door shut with a soft click that plunged us into darkness. The whiff of oil from the stored lanterns cut into my senses, mingling with the musty reek of aged wood.

"What are you–"

His large hand slapped over my mouth, muffling my words as he pressed in close, crushing his body against mine.

"Shh!"

I squeaked and bit his finger, eliciting a hiss as he tightened his grip, silencing me. My head jerked back, slamming into a low shelf. The impact sent a jolt of pain through my skull, but before I could reprimand him, voices snared my notice.

My brother.

"—set to arrive within the week?"

I trembled, blood boiling as my rage returned like a flood during a monsoon. Sainte cradled my face against his rough cheek in an attempt to still my temper.

"That is our prediction, Your Highness," someone replied.

My fingers traced the contours of his sides until they reached the hilt of his dagger. I gripped it tight.

His hand left the back of my head, sliding down my arm to cover mine, squeezing it in silent warning.

"The Priests of Fiera are prepared?" Adastrus' voice resonated just beyond the closet door.

Lost in thought, I hadn't noticed anyone coming down the corridor. I kept my promise—I hadn't sought him out. And now here he was, mere paces away.

Ready to end him, I gripped the dagger, tugging it free of the sheath, prepared to strike—when Sainte's teeth sank into my ear. Pain lanced through me, and I jerked my head to the side.

He bit me!

Fury ignited, and I snapped forward, biting down on the first thing I found. His sharp intake of breath confirmed I latched onto the curve of his neck, and

I held firm, not letting go as the voices faded down the hall. My fleeting chance passed me by.

Sainte growled low in his throat and wedged his fingers between my teeth and his skin. At the same moment, I yanked the dagger free.

"Togamar's light, Ellie! He's gone!" he hissed, his breath teasing my hair.

I muttered a slew of foul curses and snared a fistful of his tunic. I wanted to hit something—*hurt* something. Preferably my brother, but I could settle for Sainte.

"Come," he urged, then guided my hand to return the dagger to its place.

A frustrated growl crawled past my lips. Rage and helplessness churned within me, that angry, vengeful creature gnawing at my insides.

He pressed against the door, giving me much-needed space. He glanced down the corridor before yanking me out, placing my hand firmly on his forearm. Without a word, he moved with quick strides, dragging me along. At first, I thought he was taking me to Lyana's room, but relief washed over me when we passed it. He opened the door to my chambers, startling the maids inside.

"Oh! We'll be heading out–"

"You, stay," Sainte commanded a girl covered in soot from the hearth.

Her jaw dropped, not just from shock at his order, but because he singled her out to remain behind. Her fellow servants cast worried glances her way before bowing and darting out the door.

He latched it after them and turned to the girl, her soot-streaked hands clasped nervously in front of her dress. Her wide eyes pleaded with me for salvation or, perhaps, feared damnation. I almost laughed at her silent anguish. Sainte wouldn't harm a dock cat without cause, but she didn't know that.

"Strip."

I spun on him, shock evident on my face. "You order my servants about now?" I asked, voice pitched high. What was he playing at?

He waved me off. "You as well. She's about your size. Trade dresses."

Providing no further explanation, he headed to my sleeping chambers. I turned my frown on the maid, who watched him with her jaw still hanging open. She was thinner than me. Royal food added some cushion to my frame, something I would have appreciated in the slums. Now, staring at her dress and imagining myself squeezing into it, I grimaced.

"I'd be happy to fetch you a dress!" the maid offered, her voice urgent.

"The one you're wearing!" Sainte called from the other room.

A small thrill ran through me, and a smile tugged at my lips. "Best we do as he says," I said with a shrug.

My Valahant was promising an adventure.

Soot covered me from head to toe.

Not just my clothes, but every inch of my skin. Sainte gathered fistfuls of ashes and rubbed them into my hair, dulling its blue sheen. He smeared it across my face with rough strokes and made my hands look filthier than the maid's.

We left the poor girl in my rooms, with strict orders to bar the door and not leave until our return. Practically in tears, she sat draped in my pale green silk dress.

Sainte wore an aged and tattered tunic, paired with brown trousers. His armor and ax remained behind, replaced by a single, wicked-looking sword at his hip. Draping a dark cloak over my shoulders, he led me through the halls to the servants' quarters. There he pilfered a servant's cloak with a flawless skill that sparked my jealousy.

We hurried out of the castle, hoods low and heads down. My peridot green eyes, an unmistakable mark of my lineage, were a constant risk of exposure, so Sainte insisted my hood stayed up to avoid unwanted attention. I followed him across the bridge and into the city proper. After an hour of walking, we reached a quiet tavern.

The inhabitants of Wynterborne worked by daylight, and so in the winter months, when twilight fell sooner, villagers sought refuge in the warmth of the taverns. The sun lingered high in the sky, covered by clouds, offering enough light for laborers to continue their tasks.

Sainte shoved the heavy door open, letting it swing shut just in time for me to catch it before it collided with my face. The air within, while warm, was stale, tinged with the lingering scent of ale and old hearth smoke. The faint crackle of embers added a subdued calm to the space. I kept my stare fixed on his broad back, squinting against the feeble light filtering through the windows.

I stuck close to his heels as he nodded a greeting at the barkeep. His weathered face betrayed a hint of suspicion as he observed us with a cautious gaze. We chose a secluded table, far removed from the only other patrons. The young men were armed to the teeth with an arsenal of unfamiliar blades and weaponry. They sipped at their mugs, dipping their chins to show they noticed my stare.

I pulled my hood lower, concealing my features, then leaned closer to Sainte.

"Oi, well there! First to the cup is first to the fun!" a buxom tavern wench called, her laughter echoing through the space as she sauntered our way. A confident grin lifted her cheeks as she propped her large hip against our table. "What will it be, then? A meal for weary travelers? An ale to start the party?"

"Bane's Tonic."

"Oh, you mean our Baneberry Tonic? Few ask for that. Cost ye a pretty coin, it will."

"Wolfsbane."

"'Tis the same, so it is." She placed her clean hands on the table's worn wooden surface. "I'll have to pop in back to see if we have any, though. Might not be in yet."

"Check. We'll be here," Sainte rumbled, sliding a gold coin her way.

My lips pressed tight. That was more wealth than I could've hoped to steal over a year's time in Landing's End.

She raised an eyebrow, her gaze shifting between us and the coin. "We don't just give that out to stranger folk," she remarked, her tone cautious yet curious. "'Tis a secret recipe. The master keeps a close eye on who be partakin' of it. Give me yer names and I'll be passin' them along to him."

"Nytestorm," Sainte said.

"And yer friend? Suppose they want the tonic too?"

"Aye."

"Well, who are ye? Speak up, now."

She leaned forward, attempting to peer beneath my hood, but Sainte intervened, wrapping his arm around me, pressing my body against his side. I curled into his embrace, burying my face into his shoulder.

"She's my lass," he said, "under my protection. That's all your master needs to know."

"Hmm. Well, we'll see. I'll check if we have it in stock. Just wait here a minute." With that, she walked off.

Sainte released his grip, and I glanced around the table, realizing the wench had taken the coin.

"Are we meeting–"

"Shh." He quieted me with a finger to his lips, his arm settling at my waist.

I cleared my throat and adjusted my hood, pulling it back slightly to get a better view of the room. The tavern, with its narrow windows, allowed glimpses of the dusky evening outside, where the overcast sky bloomed with soft hues of lavender and gray. Inside, the space carried the scent of aged wood and faint traces of herbs from the kitchen, mingling with the murmured conversation of the two patrons.

The wench leaned over the counter, speaking to the barkeep, who turned our way with a skeptical squint. He shook his head and said something, jerking his chin. At that, she slipped into the back room, shutting it behind her.

Sainte shifted, dropping his hand across his body to rest on the hilt of his sword. He nudged his thigh against mine as we waited, and I smiled to myself at the warm contact. I wondered if 'lass' meant I was playing as his daughter or something more exciting.

Moments later, the wench returned, leaning against our table. "We'll have a delivery soon, if ye don't mind waitin'. The master says he's heard 'bout ye 'round these parts. Ye'r trustworthy enough. Not goin' to steal his recipe."

"We will wait," Sainte agreed.

"Would ye like a bite? Midday meal came and went—by the looks of ye, doubt ye had anythin' where ye came from."

Her judgemental words hardly fazed me. My years on the streets thickened my skin to such assumptions.

"Bread, if you have it."

"Coming up!" she said, then sauntered off.

When she was a safe distance away, I gave Sainte a nervous glance. He arched a brow, amused, but kept his features void of expression. I wasn't a fan of being left in the dark, but if her comment didn't bother him, maybe I could relax. Learning to rule meant learning to trust—a lesson I still struggled with.

She brought over steaming bread and a small pat of butter. The aroma had my mouth watering in seconds. It wasn't castle fare, but it reminded me of my childhood. Simple fresh loaves were as fancy as the meals at Landing's End got. It was my comfort food. When Sainte and I reached for the last portion, I realized I'd eaten more than my share.

A small smile quirked the corner of his lip, and he shook his head, placing the slice in my hand. Never one to pass up an opportunity, I grinned and shoved the bread into my mouth, savoring the warmth and taste.

The wench returned some time later, collecting the plate. "The master says the delivery came, but he asks that ye take yer tonic in the next room. Worried 'bout others seein' it, I'd wager."

We stood, and I tugged my hood lower. He kept his hand on the small of my back, guiding me along. The woman knocked on the same door she disappeared through earlier, then stepped aside, allowing Sainte to open it and usher me inside.

The space, lit by a single lantern, remained cloaked in shadows. I craned my neck, trying to see the figure at the table. The door shut behind us with a click, and a jolt of panic surged, hearing the lock latch in place.

"Wolf," he ground out. His tone held steady, his hand on my back a calm anchor. He stood firm, unfazed by the eerie room or the fact that we were locked inside.

"The only Nytestorm I know of has completed the velebond to none other than our Lost Princess, Elspeth the Second Born." A low, feminine chuckle filled the eerie space. "Come, come, Princess. You have words for me, I imagine."

My body tensed, caught in a moment of indecision. Trapped within these walls, facing off against an uncertain foe, awareness pricked my skin. The truth of my identity lingered like an unspoken secret. Sainte's touch grounded me, a firm presence at my back. His thumb traced soothing patterns against my spine, a silent reassurance amid the tension.

"You're the Dire Wolf," I said, voice raspy with intrigue.

"Ah, someone's been telling you stories," she mused. "Come into the light so I can see these fabled eyes everyone speaks of."

I inhaled a slow breath, composing myself before I stepped away from Sainte's reassuring presence. My cloak fell back as I moved, and I struggled to conceal the rush of revulsion that swept through me upon seeing the figure seated at the table.

Underneath a deep hood, a wolf's skull grinned. Her posture relaxed with her fist propping up her chin, as if awaiting a game of cards. Bleached by the sun, the bone gleamed bright and pristine, evidence of meticulous care in its upkeep.

Cloaked in black, the woman behind the mask remained shrouded, her form obscured by the folds of her attire. The lantern's glow danced in her irises, reflecting off their golden hue—reminiscent of a wolf's gaze. As I drew nearer to the table, those eyes seemed to hunger, adding a layer of anticipation to the already charged atmosphere.

"Marked by the gods." She gestured toward the lone chair opposite her. "I heard tales of a goddess' touch upon your skin, yet it seems some blessings fade with time."

"I returned from the second Rite with handprints on my face, be they Togamar's or not, I don't know."

"One who doubts the gods?" Her tone carried a hint of mockery as she sat straighter, feigning surprise. "You are in good company, then! I, too, doubt the things I've seen."

Her words hung between us, shrouded with uncertainty. She leaned back, her eyes narrowing as she studied me. "A princess, believed dead, emerges on the very day of her brother's coronation. The people hail you as the Gods' Chosen, yet your disdain for them is palpable."

The room seemed to shrink with the sharp edge of her words, the tension thickening. I shifted uncomfortably under her scrutiny, feeling the weight of expectations press down on me.

"I've heard the whispers of your deeds," she continued, her voice measured. "Riding to confront the Glades, seeking retribution for your own. Yet, I find myself asking, why? Why return unprepared to stake a claim to a throne you know nothing about? Why provoke conflict with Gladier if not for war? What drives a free spirit to embrace the chains of politics and morality?"

Her questions echoed in the silence, each one a dagger aimed at the heart of my resolve.

"You assume I had a choice." I spoke without emotion, my expression a challenge in itself.

The room grew still as she scrutinized me, a flicker of uncertainty crossing her features.

Then she laughed.

She threw herself back, howling at the ceiling as she clutched her belly. The sound was wild, untamed, like the call of a distant wolf. As she composed herself, she tilted her head in a very canine way.

"So, who brought you? Who's the puppet master pulling your strings? I would say Adastrus, who I've heard recently puppeted your friend about–"

I snarled, slapping my hands on the table. "Don't speak of things you know nothing about."

"Oh, is that what you think?" A haughty smirk crept beneath her mask. "That my information is false? That I wasn't there?"

"You couldn't–"

"He called for witnesses. Do you believe he cared who saw your friend splayed out like a–"

Rage erupted within. I snapped, shrieking as I flung the table. It was heavier than I expected, and the lantern went flying. She lashed out, catching it before it hit the ground.

"Don't you *dare* speak of–"

She lunged, cutting my threat short as she crashed into me. Breath rushed from my lungs as I collided with the hard floor, pinned by her weight. The Wolf's skull mask leered down at me, its hollow sockets mocking my struggle. I strained against her, desperate to free myself.

"Oh, you weren't there," she growled. "You have no clue what happened."

"You're sick!"

"No—your brother is," she said, voice cold and calculating. "Now, I want to know how he plans to use this to manipulate you—pull your strings."

Beneath her weight, I froze, teeth gritted in fury, but also pondering her words. What drove him to such cruelty beyond mere spite? What end did it serve?

"Ah, there it is. Now she's thinking like a player, not a pawn," she crooned. "Adastrus acts with madness, but he's guided by many *sane* minds."

"You use his name—not his title?"

"He is no regent of mine," she grumbled, displeasure evident. "Nytestorm, your princess is in no danger. Remove your sword from my neck, if you please."

His shadowed silhouette moved behind her, and she pushed herself upright, straddling my hips. Her hood slipped back, revealing a cascade of light brown hair falling over her shoulder.

"I'm pleased you sought me out, Princess. It's good to know madness doesn't poison you both."

"I came to discuss your attacks on the merchant convoys, not to argue my sanity," I snapped.

"Hinyte's caravans?" She smirked, as if proud of herself.

I shoved at her until she moved off my lap. "You're stealing from hardworking families."

When she stood, she offered her hand. I stared at her with unveiled skepticism, then glanced at Sainte, who blended into the shadows, sheathing his sword.

"Negotiations belong at a table, conducted by civilized individuals," she said.

I scoffed, accepting the gesture. "Says the woman in a wolf mask."

She chuckled, hauling me upright. "Tip for the future," she mused as we settled in our places, "only throw a lantern when fire is acceptable collateral damage."

"At the time, it seemed acceptable."

She barked a laugh and crossed her arms, slumping into her seat. "So, you're in Hinyte's pocket, then?"

"No, of course not. We–"

"Hard to believe, Princess. You need allies, and he would be a fine one."

I shook my head in disbelief. "You say that, but you raid his caravans."

"Only the ones that benefit Adastrus."

"So my brother is the target, not Hinyte."

"Sharp as a tack, you are!" she jeered, amusement flickering in her gaze.

"He doesn't feel the pinch," I said. "He's unaffected."

"Are you certain?" she asked. "Leihim came to you... but who's pulling his strings?"

Was she insinuating that my brother directed Hinyte to manipulate me? It made sense. He could exploit my influence to draw out the Wolf, positioning himself to strike against the bandit that plagued his working class.

"Ah, there it is." Something glittered in her eyes. "It's all coming together, isn't it?"

I drew in a short breath.

Ruling involved knowing when to trust—but also when not to.

"I'm not here for Hinyte."

"No?" She reclined, head tilted in curiosity.

"I'd like to negotiate on my behalf," I said, a mischievous smirk playing on my lips.

"Oh, do tell."

That afternoon I stepped out of the tavern, inhaling the crisp winter air. It stung my lungs and nipped at my flushed cheeks. I welcomed its bite with a smile.

I may not have been raised in this world of rulers and noble deceit, but I was adapting.

With a grin plastered to my lips, I linked my arm through Sainte's. This had been just the push I needed to get through the day.

Yes, my friends suffered, and my heart throbbed with pain and conflict. But my brother would pay. Alliances were falling into place, allies joining my cause.

As Sainte said, I had no power yet...

Yet.

CHAPTER 23

I was in good spirits upon my return, right until I saw Counselor Reuthland waiting outside Lyana's door.

No one entered her room without my express permission.

Regent's pawn or no.

We narrowly missed being caught by the woman, sneaking into my room not a moment too late. The servant girl was in tears, trying to hold herself together. When I asked what was wrong she wailed, claiming if anyone found her in my clothes, she'd be kicked onto the streets, her reputation as a maid ruined. Sainte gave her a silver coin for her troubles and sent her on her way with a long, warning look.

"You trust her?" I asked.

"Servants are the worst gossipers," he said, changing into his regular attire, "but the best secret keepers."

With that, we stepped into the corridor, off to check on my friends.

Dark, hooded eyes turned toward me as Reuthland lifted her chin. My teeth clenched at the arrogance in her glare. Beside her, a servant kept his face down, clutching a teapot, and a healer stood at her back. The braids piled atop her head had me wondering how heavy all that hair was.

"Reuthland," I called, pulling myself up to my full height to meet her gaze.

"*Princess,*" she sneered.

The door to Lyana's room was open, but Urien blocked the way, his hip propped against the doorframe, arms crossed tight, with a weary glare darkening his features.

"I would have you know—you are not allowed to post personal guards in the castle," she said, "not to mention, he's a common soldier–"

"Actually, *Counselor*," I shot back, mirroring her condescending tone. "General Jorgeson assigned Urien to my personal guard. As a member of the high court, I'm sure you're aware that within this wing, I am permitted to post my guards as I see fit."

"While that may be true, the prince regent has final say over his guests," she arched a dark slash of eyebrow, "and he has ordered that Lady Lyana take the bitter waters."

I knew of moon tea, used to bring on a woman's cycle, but bitter waters? Never heard of it.

"Urien, send for Gilead," I said, pushing inside.

Sainte followed, plowing into Reuthland, eliciting a shocked gasp. Urien rushed off, and I turned to flash a smile at the counselor.

Then slammed the door in her face.

I frowned, pinching the bridge of my nose to ward off the beginnings of a headache. "What are bitter waters?"

"Gilead would probably know. I have my guesses, but nothing certain," Sainte answered.

After a stiff sigh, I offered Ethyan a small smile. He sat beside his sister, his arm splinted and secured with a sling. I couldn't help but notice how his uninjured hand stayed close to the hilt of his throwing blade. His accuracy wouldn't be as great with his left, but he could still inflict some pain if needed.

Lyana, sitting up, lacked her usual cheery demeanor, but her gaze showed awareness. Our efforts to keep her clean and prevent infection improved her mental state. She fought us the first few days, draining her strength, but it only ignited the fire she needed.

Ethyan sent a nervous glance Sainte's way before nodding toward the door. "Is that bastard trying to kill her now?"

"He already had the chance," Lyana murmured.

Guilt consumed me with her soft voice. Where was the fierce girl I roamed the streets with? The one who would've faced a battalion of Wynterian soldiers for my sake? Where was my best friend and her spitfire attitude?

Oh, right. My brother crushed her spirit with unknown torment.

"I doubt he would," I said, approaching the bed on slow, cautious steps. "You're still of use to him."

When her ocean eyes filled with fear, I grasped her hand in mine.

"I won't let him near you," I assured her. "The threat of causing you harm is his way of controlling me, and he knows that. What he did—"

She shuddered, biting her lip.

"—He's sick. Demented and disgusting. But intelligent. He wouldn't kill you when he can still use you against me."

"We shouldn't be here," Lyana breathed, tears filling her eyes.

"This isn't your fault." I rubbed her cold hand, drawing her distant gaze to mine. "He is ruthless and will exploit anything and anyone to win the crown."

She fell silent, unwilling to speak. The bruises around her neck looked worse, though severe injuries often did before they improved. The gash at her temple and a few along her thighs required stitches. Her sunken black eyes worried me the most. She wasn't sleeping well, if at all. She wouldn't allow me or Ethyan in the bed with her at night.

That loss of closeness stung the most.

This was my fault. *My* brother did this to her, and now—she couldn't even stomach my comfort anymore.

A soft knock pulled me from my thoughts, and Urien slid inside. Gilead lingered in the hall, her quiet voice carrying a hint of concern as she spoke to that other healer. She took the teapot from him, her movements stiff and deliberate. When her eyes met mine, jaw clenched, Urien let her in and shut the door behind her.

"The Priests of Togamar know nothing of this," she said sharply, then set the pot on a small table, eyeing it as if expecting it to transform into a serpent and strike.

A terrible preface for whatever else she had to say.

"What are bitter waters, Gilead?" I asked.

She took a deep breath, closing her eyes to regain composure. "A tea brewed from wyrmwood. It has certain... properties that cleanse a woman's womb."

"He's worried about a bastard," I spat.

Lyana withdrew her hand from mine, tucking it beneath her blankets, her gaze distant. She was shutting us out, distancing herself.

Curse my brother a thousand times over.

"So it would seem." Gilead perched on the edge of the bed, studying Lyana. "There are other methods, all I would choose, but the prince regent denied them."

"Why?"

She understood my question, and our eyes met, confirming the truth. There was something ominous, dangerous about the tea, a side effect that would harm her. Another string for him to pull to hurt me.

Gilead's lips pursed tight. "It only takes a single dose."

Confusion clouded my thoughts. The tonics, teas, and tinctures I heard of to avoid unwanted pregnancy were used daily as a preventative. There were potent options as well, taken up to ten days after intimacy—never in one cup.

"He doesn't want her dead," I said, testing my theory, gauging the healer's reaction.

"It won't kill her." She dipped her chin, speaking to Lyana, "But it will be... very unpleasant."

Tears streaked my dear friend's cheeks. "I don't want it."

"It works quickly, only taking a few days to run its course," Gilead assured.

Lyana's gaze widened with panic, and she snatched my hand, clutching it tight. I struggled to decipher the message she was trying to relay, but couldn't grasp it. Was she afraid of more pain? Did she doubt the healer, fearing poison?

"Pour it," I hissed.

Gilead took a sharp breath at my order and rose from the bed.

"El..." Ethyan's warning was slow, his gaze guarded and dangerous as she poured the tea.

I silently begged him to trust me.

"Here, you must drink the whole cup."

The healer held it out, and I shifted to reach for it, but Lyana gripped me tighter.

"Please, don't make me," she whimpered, voice a strained whisper.

Ethyan straightened, glare hard. "Elspeth!"

At the edge in his tone, Sainte came closer, tension crackling in the cramped space. Even Urien shifted near the door, sensing the unease.

I tugged my hands free of Lyana's hold, offering her a sad but earnest smile. "Trust me."

I took the cup. The tea, having cooled during the long wait, gave off a potent herbal stench. Bitter was a fair name for it. I arched a brow at Gilead. "Can I assume her rooms will be searched?"

"For the next few days, yes." She cast an apologetic grimace toward Lyana. "This was not a request. I am bound by Nothar, but the prince regent's orders hold sway over us mortals. We must obey his demands."

My teeth ground together. Would she *obey* his orders and poison a guest simply because she was *bound* by his commands?

Lyana gripped the blanket's hem, her knuckles white. "He's not my regent."

"I don't obey him." I raised the cup to my lips and tossed back the foul drink in two swift gulps.

Chaos erupted.

Urien cursed, Sainte stormed toward me, and Ethyan spun to face him, blade in hand.

"What have you done!?" Gilead shrieked, features twisted in horror.

After swiping my sleeve across my wet lips, I pushed to my feet and tossed the empty cup onto the bed. "I've cut my strings."

A flicker of a smile twitched on Lyana's cheeks—the first one I'd seen since this all started.

That was worth everything.

"It appears I'll be out for a while. Make sure our sheets are exchanged before your *healers* check on her. If my brother asks, tell him I've taken ill from the elements." I looked up, catching Sainte's stormy gaze.

"You will regret this," he growled.

That night, the cramps set in.

Did I regret my actions? No. Could I have done it differently? I wished. I experienced cramping with my cycles. They were manageable—something women lived with. In the slums, I didn't have the luxury of lying about while I bled. This surpassed anything I ever felt. Women screamed in childbirth, and as I trembled on my bed, curled tight, I battled the urge with teeth bared. Surely, this pain rivaled birth.

Only Gilead and Sainte entered my rooms. The healer used one of my provided excuses to keep me isolated. Nobody would risk a contagious plague escaping, so we stayed quarantined. Winter's Bite, the illness that claimed my father, could sweep through the castle within a week, infecting everyone and halving the staff in one blow.

Sainte avoided holding me, choosing his cot instead while Gilead tended to my misery. She offered tea to help me sleep through the worst, while I endured the waking hours with gritted teeth and groans. She draped blankets warmed by the fire over my abdomen and whisked away bloodied towels. Only once had I questioned if they were being smuggled to Lyana's room. Sainte's assurance that Urien handled the ferrying allowed me to rest.

After three days, the cramps eased, but the blood persisted. Gilead's worried expression darkened as she took another blood-soaked towel away.

"What is it?" I asked when she returned to my bedside.

She pressed her lips into a line, folding her hands in her lap. Her eyes, shadowed by dark circles, flicked to Sainte, who leaned against the wall, legs crossed at the ankles, arms folded. He had done nothing but glare at me and seethe in anger.

"This was reckless," she said.

I scoffed, flopping my head back onto the pillow. Their judgment was the last thing I cared about. I refused to let my friend be pressured into taking that awful tea. I couldn't save her from my brother, but I could endure this torment, sacrifice a few days to offer her relief. This chipped away at the boulder of guilt in my stomach.

Gilead took a long slow breath, as if regaining her composure. "You compromised your womb. Lady Lyana would jeopardize her ability to bear children, but you risk the very heirs to the kingdom."

"As if–"

"Nothar has favored you." Her firm voice cut through my response. Anger glittered in her eyes, brows drawn down. "You bore Togamar's mark and embraced Nellium's touch. You are the Gods' Chosen. Yet, you defy your heritage, your lineage, to spare your friend some discomfort."

"Careful," my glare sharpened, "what you say borders on treason."

"The lies I've told shattered my vows to the prince regent, and now you accuse me of treason? No. There's no falsehood in the claim that you've been chosen. You would throw it away for some false sense of loyalty?"

I turned, looking to Sainte for help. His accusing glare told me he would not be rescuing me.

His refusal only heightened my rage. "She's here because of me! What happened to her–"

"Happened because she was willing."

"Stop!" My arms trembled as I shoved myself upright. "Adastrus–"

"Lied—and she fell for the bait."

"You've never been in love, have you?" I sneered, refusing to look at Sainte even as her eyes darted his way. "You have no idea what it's like to lie with someone, feel secure in their embrace, invincible to the rest of the world simply because they're there."

My throat tightened. I paused, waiting for the sensation to ease so my voice wouldn't shake. "You have never loved someone so much that seeing them in pain breaks you in two—all logic and reason vanishes. You've never tasted the high that comes with passion! Or the contentment after it subsides. Don't speak of love like you know anything about it."

She sat back, lips pressed together, jaw clenched, fighting not to snap at me. The anger that stirred in her glare confirmed my words. She had no right to talk about Lyana that way.

Gilead rose, brushing out her white dress. She nodded to Sainte, then crossed the room on soft steps. The door clicked shut behind her.

I heaved a sigh and fell back on the bed with a curse. "You think I was foolish as well," I muttered to the bright ceiling. "Stupid and reckless."

"Yes." The word, harsh and blunt, echoed from Sainte's place against the far wall.

I snorted at his predictable response.

The mattress dipped beside me, and I turned my head, watching as Sainte eased himself onto the edge. The bedframe creaked under his weight.

"Though, I too know the feeling of having to act out of guilt." He reached over his shoulder and pulled his tunic loose from his trousers, exposing the small of his back. The scars from his recent flogging stood out, raw and jagged. "Every time I returned without you, failing to find a way to remove your brother and put you on the throne."

Unable to stop myself, I let my fingers trace the raised welts—a mass of mutilated flesh.

"I had to leave you behind," he said, "and I took the punishment. The floggings only relieved my guilt. They didn't provide solutions. Do you feel better knowing I endured these for you?"

"No." I jerked my hand away.

"Do you believe your possible infertility would ease Lady Lyana's suffering?"

I frowned, then tugged the blankets to my chin. "You think I should have let her drink it."

"I think you should have sought advice."

I huffed in irritation and closed my eyes. Why did I always make the wrong choices, the ones others believed could be avoided? I didn't care if I bore children later. To be honest, I'd never given it thought. Perhaps with the right man. I never considered the bitter waters might risk that. I never weighed the consequences.

To not act rashly was a lesson I still needed to grasp.

It proved challenging when Adastrus' goons were breathing down my friend's neck, pressuring her to drink something so horrible.

"A wise ruler seeks counsel."

"I'm no ruler."

"Not yet."

I opened my eyes to find him standing, adjusting his tunic. His gaze softened as he watched me, his angry storm subsiding.

If I'd have my brother's head, I needed to ascend the throne—and even then, it wouldn't be a fleeting affair. My entire future would intertwine with that accursed seat, and an entire realm would hinge on my choices. Acting out of haste and without thought would not only harm me, but inflict suffering on my people—countless Wynterians reliant on my judgment.

Vulnerability washed over me, a feeling I'd grown accustomed to with my history of mistakes and poor decisions. While I hadn't ascended to rulership yet, I knew I hadn't inspired confidence in those who might follow my lead. Beneath my shelter of blankets, I gathered my courage, posing my question.

"Would you have me as your queen, Sainte?"

He watched me, face void of expression. Silence slipped by, snaring my nerves, wreaking havoc on the scraps of resolve I had left.

"I would only have you as my queen," he said.

My heart swelled, threatening to burst with joy. Concealing my smile beneath the covers, a wave of gratitude warmed my spirit as he offered a small bow, then retreated to the wall. With closed eyes, I let myself rest, comforted by the knowledge that at least one person believed in me.

"Come in," I called, smoothing the fabric of my dress.

As Leihim stepped into the room, I acknowledged the servant beside him with a nod. The counselor's attire spoke of opulence. The luxurious green fabric of his overcoat and trousers hinted at softness even from a distance, a detail not lost on me.

"Counselor Hinyte," I greeted, dipping my head but maintaining direct eye contact.

His piercing eyes locked onto mine as he smiled and executed a formal bow. "Princess." He cataloged the space with a swift glance, his gaze catching on my Valahant. Undeterred, his smile remained fixed as he stepped further into my receiving room. "I see you're feeling better, recovered from a minor plague, was it?"

I settled into my seat, allowing Sainte to guide my chair in. With my hands folded atop the table, I maintained a composed posture, chin raised.

I had to play this right.

"Yes, something I picked up among the Glades. Isolated, I assure you, else the whole of the castle would have had it by now," I said with a guarded smile.

As of yet, no rumors surfaced that Adastrus suspected I drank the tea in Lyana's place. Anderz kept a diligent ear for any gossip regarding it, but thus far, no nobles pieced it together. It might have crossed the minds of a few, but if they understood the potential side effects, they knew it would've been foolish of me to consume it. Any sane person wouldn't have taken that risk.

Perhaps I wasn't as sane as they assumed.

"You caused quite a scare," he noted, resting a gloved hand on the back of a chair. "Some worried you might not be fit for the final Rite."

"Oh, I am fit enough," I replied with a coy smile. "Please, sit. We have much to discuss."

He nodded and obliged, appearing at ease in my company.

"I hear your merchant guild is doing well."

"It is, actually," he said. "We've experienced fewer attacks as of late. Have you considered my request?"

I stared at my hands, letting silence lapse between us before I met his stare with hooded eyes. "It's a pity the only caravans targeted have been those that carry my brother's goods."

Recognition flickered in his gaze, but he kept his face a mask of politeness.

I continued, "But I'm pleased no one's been killed... as of late."

"Your sources are impeccable, Your Highness." He formed his words with care, his smile faltering.

"It's unfortunate the fabrics my brother ordered for his coronation have gone missing."

He didn't speak, but I could see his mind racing behind that cold blue gaze.

"Although," I remarked, "I believe a shade of green would have complimented his eyes better, given his current efforts to gain favor with the gods. Dark blue wouldn't suit him."

What I left unsaid hung between us, a subtle message to Leihim. The Dire Wolf was under my influence—a negotiation to target only Adastrus' wagons and report anything of significance to me.

"I suggest you choose your words carefully, Your Highness," he warned, his grin replaced by an emotionless mask. "Some might deem this information treacherous."

"Ah, mere rumors and hearsay." I laughed, leaning back with an easy smirk. "But if you happen to see him, do remind him of your need for assistance with the Dire Wolf."

A dangerous glint humored his expression as he mirrored my posture, feigning his ease. "So, you've been swayed by him."

"Only as much as you've been swayed by Adastrus," I replied smoothly. "They have no control over me, and I'd like to think as a self-made man, my brother has no authority over you."

"Treasonous words if I dare utter them, Princess."

"Yes, but true all the same. Your loyalty lies with coin. You're a merchant at your core, are you not?"

"It puts food on the table and keeps the hearth burning, Your Highness."

"It also ensures your comfort." I dipped my chin, lifting a brow. "I simply want you to know that your coin is safe... as long as I am safe."

"Do you threaten me, Princess?" He leaned forward once again, his eyes gleaming.

Sainte shifted, resting his hand on the back of my chair. My smile grew as Leihim glanced up at him, then sat back with a calculating look.

"Not a threat—it's fact, Hinyte," I said. "I will protect your merchants to the best of my ability. All I ask is for your support. It seems like a fair exchange."

"And if you make a decision I disagree with?" he shot back. "You would blackmail me into submission, use a common bandit to sway my vote? You're no different from your brother."

"Do not compare us," I said, voice clipped and flat. I was nothing like him. I relied on wits and the advice given to me—not cruelty or manipulation based on spite or amusement. "It is not your blind support I seek. I ask for a chance to discuss decisions in private if you find them unfavorable."

"You have the high court for that, Your Highness."

"Not everyone aligns with my goals," I replied, sweetening my tone.

"Ah…" He tilted his head, studying me as he processed my request. "So you propose limiting attacks on my caravans to specific wagons in exchange for public support and private counsel."

"I knew you were wise beyond your years when I first met you," I mused.

"Well enough. However, do you not think the prince regent will notice the isolated attacks?"

I raised a brow in challenge. "Who knows the mind of a *common bandit?* Their motives are as unpredictable as the wind. It's not as if anyone in power can control them."

"Indeed."

I chuckled and ordered tea, using the pretext of catching up on the council meetings. After the side effects passed, Anderz had filled me in on essential details while sparing me the intricacies of trade and politics.

Leihim, however, delved into commerce with enthusiasm. For an hour, he rambled and elaborated on the oil trade between Wynterborne and Tilamuik. Apparently, our oil wealth complemented Tilamuik's reliance on sea resources, making the exchange mutually profitable.

I strained to maintain a smile, and despite his occasional apologies for droning, he kept diving back into his monologue. He exuded sharpness, wisdom, and cunning. His passion for his guild was evident in every word.

His loyalty might be bought, but I would take advantage of it while I had it.

CHAPTER 24

I woke to a loud thud and muttered curse.

I jerked upright, scanning the shadow-filled room through my sleep-hazed vision. A surge of alarm shot through me as I realized Sainte was missing from his cot. My gaze darted to the entrance, where a figure loomed near the doorway.

Sainte stood flush against the wall, a knife gripped in his fist. Positioned out of sight of the intruder, he waited in utter silence, poised to strike anyone who entered.

His chest was bare.

The dips and curves of his muscled torso caught the moons' dim light, his trousers undone, hanging low on his hips.

My throat tightened, and I must have emitted a choked sound, because his head swiveled toward me. I forced a grin, pretending I wasn't appraising him like a piece of meat. He nodded, his expression solemn as his attention returned to the door. Whether he was unaware of my plight or simply focused on what lay beyond, I couldn't tell. I strained to make out anything, wondering if it had been his curse that woke me.

A smile played on my lips as I allowed my gaze to wander down his powerful frame, imagining him asleep with a knife in hand, ready to spring into action against intruders. The thought of his protective presence filled me with reassurance... and the sight of his physique sent strange flutters through my stomach.

Sainte's body showcased a divine blessing, his muscles defined without excess bulk. The firelight from the hearth cast shadows, highlighting the tautness of his frame. Each sinew stood out, even the smallest of muscles.

The door to my sleeping chambers creaked open, snapping my focus to the present. Lyana's head peeked through, her sunken features illuminated in the faint auburn glow. Tear streaks glistened on her cheeks as her gaze found mine.

I threw the blankets aside, and she burst into the room, not waiting for me to meet her. She flung herself onto the bed, crashing into me, and I wrapped around her, trying to steady us both.

"Shh, it's all right," I murmured into her hair, glancing at the doorway.

A shadow moved, and I caught Sainte's eyes. He spun, knife in hand, but the figure hissed something that caused him to pause.

Lyana sobbed, her weight pressing me into the mattress. Sainte spoke in hushed tones, then ducked inside, retrieving his tunic. With a frown drawing his features, he gave me a long look, then shook his head before slipping into the shadows, closing the door behind him.

"Hush, hush now," I murmured, guiding her closer.

I held her, feeling every tremor of her sobs. They echoed in the quiet room, each on a release of pain and fear. She curled into my embrace; her face pressed to my chest. I whispered reassurances in the darkness, hoping my words brought some comfort.

When her cries faded, I wiped her cheeks with the blanket and offered a pillowcase for her to wipe her nose.

"What good is royal bedding if you can't use it to wipe your snot?" I asked.

She wadded the silky fabric, then flopped onto the bed. When she rolled to her side, offering her back, my heart ached. I scooted in, pressing close. Her body shook with a shuddering breath. I embraced her, listening to the hearth crackle in the darkness, staring at the dark orange light flickering on the wall. I smoothed her frizzed hair, snuggled in, and nestled my chin on her head.

"El?" Her voice, tight and raw, broke the silence.

"Hmm?"

"Do you think he'll ever forgive me?" Another sob hitched her words, and she trembled, on the verge of tears again.

My embrace tightened. If she could just *feel* me holding her, everything would be all right. "Who?"

"Grimm."

Her body went rigid, wetness trickling down her cheeks as she opened her mouth in a silent sob. A gasp broke the silence as she shook against me, trying to stifle her cries.

"He loves you. Of course he will forgive you."

Thrice-curse Adastrus and may he rot beyond the Veil, endlessly devoured by Nothar's wolves.

"He didn't know." She sobbed. "He *didn't know!*"

She jerked the blanket over her head and screamed. I held her close, murmuring as she struggled to calm herself. Heart shattered, I waited, smoothing the hair from her face until her breathing steadied.

"What didn't he know?"

"That I—I did it for him." Her voice rasped and cracked, her nose too stuffy to make a sound when she tried to blow it on the blanket.

"Of course he did, Lyana. Why else would... would that happen?" I treaded carefully, not wanting to accuse her.

No one ever taught me how to handle someone with trauma like this. I feared triggering her into another fit of sobs.

"He—gods, El! He thought I wanted it!"

I frowned, staring at the wall, confused. If Anderz discovered Adastrus' lies to trap Lyana, and if she met with him the night before, Grimm would have known. A Valahant wouldn't have left my brother's side. He would have known she did it for his sake.

"Adast—your... the prince re–"

"Call him what he is, Lyana. Sir Pig."

She adjusted her head on the pillows, pulling the damp blankets from her face with a sad laugh. "He... he sent a missive first. Said he had a way out for Grimm if I talked with him."

I should have told her. Over and over, the notion hammered in my mind. If she learned it from me, she wouldn't have fed into his lies.

"I waited, El. Three days, I resisted his summons." Her words trembled, exhausted from tears. "Each day, I watched Grimm deteriorate. He refused to *look* at me. If only you saw him on the way here—if you'd seen his smile–" Her voice pitched higher until it shattered. "He is broken. That... that *pig* fractured something in his mind. He's not the same."

I believed her. I witnessed my brother's cruelty firsthand. He had a knack for breaking people, twisting their minds.

"I left to meet him. Urien tried to come... but it was like he *knew.* Soldiers were waiting, ready to escort me to his chambers..." She trailed off, lost in memory before continuing, "Niena, have mercy. Have you seen his rooms, El?"

"I haven't." Thankfully.

She shivered at the memory. "When I got there, Grimm had the faintest flicker of hope in his eyes." She laughed, a bitter, sad sound. "I really thought I could do something. I believed sacrificing my body might free him."

"Oh, Lyana–"

"Then he sent him away."

"What?"

"He told Grimm to piss outside like the good dog he was. So he left."

Oh, no.

No, that meant...

"He is sick... revolting. But he promised to release him if I gave him just *one* night." She swallowed hard and pulled the blankets close. "I feared he would rape me then, without warning."

"He couldn't," I whispered. "He would lose the high court's favor."

"Yeah, well, your girl from the slums here didn't know that," she scoffed. "I figured if I could make it through one night... I've faked it before. It's not hard."

I grimaced, imagining the act of pretending to enjoy lying with anyone.

"I almost didn't go," she said. "That guy, Urien... he's a decent man. He would have stolen me away if I let him."

I nodded my agreement, recalling the moment we met. He joked about not being one of the good guys, yet here he was, trying to save my friend from herself.

"But I went. I... I assumed it would just be the two of us."

I bit my cheek to stop from interrupting her. Adastrus needed witnesses to avoid my accusations.

"There were people—a *lot*, El."

"I'm going to need their descriptions later."

"So you can kill them?"

"Or worse," I snarled.

She let out a small, bitter laugh and snuggled closer. "Grimm wasn't there, and I figured it was a sick kink—that I could suffer through it." She paused, taking a deep breath. "I told myself we could run away. He hails from the Great Iceland. We could return to his homeland."

"My beach-loving, Lothar-worshipping, Lyana? In a cold, dark wasteland?!" I snickered.

"Love makes you do stupid things."

I cut my laugh short, pressing my lips together, regretting my mirth.

"He... I... he took me to the bed, and started... you know–"

I stayed quiet, unsure if I wanted the details, but if talking helped her through this, I'd listen a thousand times over.

"Then he called him in," she whispered.

"Grimm?"

There was another pause. "Yes," she choked.

I clenched my eyes shut against my pain for her. Had this been reversed and involved Sainte instead, I would have died.

"The look he gave me when he saw... he would have killed him, El."

And all of us would have been better for it.

"I had to lie to him." She sniffed as more tears came, but she was so exhausted she had no more energy left to sob. "I told him I wanted it... and he... your..."

"The pig", I provided again.

"Yeah, well, he... it was like he fed on it. He made him watch."

I gripped her tighter, disgusted by the one living person who shared my blood. What demented man would do that? What purpose did it serve? To make Grimm a mindless monster? To hurt me, influence my choice to challenge him? If anything, it fueled my rage. It made this fight my choice, not an obligation.

This mistake would cost him dearly.

"Grimm thinks I wanted this," she whispered, voice trembling.

"Those marks... the abuse... no man would believe you chose that. He had to realize there was some other reason."

"Your—the pig—is sharp with words. He twists them, makes awful things sound good. It really seemed as if he'd release him. He told me he never bedded a Muik—it was so simple. Who knows what lies he's been spewing to Grimm? He hates me."

"No, Lyana. He loves you. He would've taken on everyone in that room. It must be tearing him apart that he wasn't able to save you."

"I made everything worse."

I cringed, grateful my face was out of her line of sight.

"It's fine, El," she said. "I did. Don't lie to me."

"To be honest, things couldn't have gotten worse. We're stuck in this mess."

"I just wish he knew."

"We will send word," I assured her. It was the least we could do.

"No. Maybe it's good he doesn't. This way, he won't notice I failed."

"He'd realize you tried."

"No. I don't want him to know I was so... naïve."

I pressed my lips together to keep from contradicting her. She knew Grimm better than I did, but if he was anything like Sainte, he would prefer to understand. Curse it all—I would demand the truth if I were in his boots. But this was about her trauma, her healing. I had to let her go at her own pace.

"Well, if you change your mind, I can tell him myself. Or send word through a sneaky spy."

"You have spies?" She laughed, stealing a glance from the corner of her eye.

"Maybe not yet, but I will soon."

"Ha! Acting like a queen already."

I smiled, curling against her, my heart humming with pleasure as she sought my comfort.

One day, when I was queen, I would have my brother's head.

Anderz clasped his hands atop the table. "The God Stones have arrived."

"Thank Nothar," Aliea said, features settling into a relieved grin, "another Howl is echoing across the plains."

Leihim leaned back in his chair, sharp blue eyes on me, anticipating a comment as the high court convened. "Do we have a date for the third Rite?"

"Prince Regent Adastrus has not announced it," Reuthland snipped.

I didn't bother gracing her with a glance as she spoke.

"We can assume sometime within the next few days. We should not delay–"

"What you mean, Counselor Greer, is we shouldn't keep the God Stones longer than required." Reuthland straightened her shoulders, lifting her chin. "The date will be settled and announced tomorrow morn."

I shifted in my seat, leaning toward Anderz, who subtly turned his ear my way. "Why don't we want to keep them?" I asked.

If they provided answers from the *gods,* why not use them? Perhaps people were afraid of what they'd say? Nobles might lose their status—laws practiced for generations could change.

He cleared his throat, then whispered, "Legend has it they hold up the world."

Ah, more myths and fables.

"Funny how we're still standing," I murmured.

Anderz's golden eyes met mine, a silent warning in their depths. He rested his fingertips against his lips, and I smiled, reclining in my seat. Doubt gnawed at me—this test seemed more like pure chance. So far, the odds were in my favor during the Rites. I had to imagine that trend would continue. If any god watched over me, it would be Niena of Luck.

"'Tis more of an analogy, Princess," Lady Aliea said softly to my left.

I glanced at her before leaning to her side so she could speak to me in low tones.

"The world balances on the word of the divine," she explained. "One wrong move, and we risk their displeasure, plunging everything into darkness."

Adastrus hadn't yet incurred their wrath? What kind of gods allowed him to rule without restraint?

"Then why not keep them here?" I whispered.

Leihim watched me from across the table with hooded eyes, his mouth a flat line.

"We trust that those favored by the divine will make the best choices for us," Aliea said. "We reserve direct intervention for... specific occasions."

"In other words, we don't draw attention until absolutely necessary?"

She faced me with a sly smile, her gaze sparkling with mischief. So far, she proved to be a valuable ally, explaining the nuances, while Anderz preferred me to remain silent and listen.

"We shouldn't give the gods more reason to forsake us," she breathed, leaning close as her stare flickered to a counselor further down the table.

"Surely the divine have abandoned someone already," I muttered.

"Not all have renounced your brother." Aliea's smile never faltered, but her eyes snapped back to mine with a silent warning. "Some that would see him ascend."

"Then why hasn't he won a trial?"

"Not all the Rites have been completed," she warned, her bright grin incongruous, as if discussing the weather.

Anderz's thin, wrinkled hand rested on the back of my chair. "Princess, the road to the North is vital to the Priests of Nothar."

I cleared my throat and offered Aliea a smile of my own, then returned my awareness to the topic of discussion. The council debated providing draft horses for the priests' winter travel. Adastrus neglected their requests for years, delaying the delivery of the Stones.

In Tilamuik, the common folk supplied goods for the temples. Their offerings kept their places of worship well-maintained. Perhaps things worked differently here?

"The priests are being tended to in the Temple of Togamar," Lady Aliea supplied. "They are in poor shape—donations being sparse."

Ah, there was my answer.

"Faith means little when you have no coin to fill your belly." Leihim's voice rang out clear, drawing the room's attention.

"Choose your remarks carefully, Master Hinyte."

"I'm stating a fact, Counselor Feyre," he replied, his gaze fixed on me. "Perhaps if our ruler prioritized the gods, the people would as well."

"The prince regent reveres the divine, Master Hinyte." Reuthland's words snapped like a whip at a rebellious servant. "The people provide for the temples, and the gods provide for the people."

In that case, one might question the necessity of a ruler.

"Tradition dictates the prince regent hear the priests' request," someone called further down the table.

"He *will* hear it." Reuthland's hand curled into a fist.

It was obvious, since I returned to Wynterborne, that she received more pushback than ever before concerning my brother. His standing with his court was slipping.

"As you all well know," she hissed, "he has more pressing matters to attend to."

"Like seeking the gods' favor?" I scoffed before I thought better of it.

The room fell silent, every gaze turning on me. Anderz's hand slid from my chair to his thigh, tapping a restless beat.

"He prepares for the Rite, *Your Highness*," Reuthland said, her tone clipped, promising violence. "As you would do well to consider."

I took a deep breath, sitting straighter. It was time to employ some of the political tactics I'd learned. "Counselor Reuthland, tell me... doesn't the second in line to the throne receive a yearly allowance from the treasury?"

She clenched her jaw, her glare dark enough to stifle the sun. "If only they were here to claim it."

What she meant was, if only I stayed away.

"Incorrect, Counselor," Lady Aliea interjected. "Tradition dictates that they are provided for as long as they live, by the ruling heir."

I owed that woman a pastry—a dress, a necklace—whatever it was that noblewoman liked.

Reuthland's lip curled in a snarl. "As we were unaware of her survival–"

"That my brother was unaware of my survival is irrelevant. Does anyone know how much of my allowance has accumulated?"

Murmurs hummed around the table as nobles pondered my next move.

"Counselor Hinyte, would it suffice to purchase a few top-quality draft horses for the Priests of Nothar?" I turned to Leihim, catching the corner of his mouth quirk into an amused smirk.

"Yes, I do believe you can afford a few beasts," he replied smoothly.

My vicious grin fixed on Reuthland. "You see, Counselor, I *am* preparing for the Rite of Favor. If I expect the gods to hear me, I can safely assume they'd expect me to care for their priests and temples."

I might not be religious, but I could play into the people's faith.

"Send word to the priests at Togamar's temple," I called to the messengers lined by the door. "Princess Elspeth has heard their request, and answered it. They will be provided for."

When I returned my attention to the high court, Leihim had his chin propped in his hand, an amused grin brightening his features, while Reuthland's glower promised my demise.

I simply smiled at her in response.

CHAPTER 25

The next evening, I felt Adastrus' wrath.

"I'm not going."

I ground my teeth, pacing the polished floors of my receiving room. Two maids stood by the door, shrinking to make themselves as small as possible to hide from my anger.

Anderz rubbed the crease in his brow with a heavy sigh. "You don't have a choice."

"She's not going," I snapped.

"Lady Lyana has no choice, either."

I bit out a curse, curling my fingers into fists. "This is about the last council meeting, isn't it?"

"Quite possibly." He tipped his head toward the maids, a reminder not to speak out of turn.

"Tell me there's a way out," I pleaded, resting my palms on the table. "She can beg sick?"

He leaned back, dipping his chin. "I'd have told you if there was."

"Pig dung!" I slammed my fist. "A pox on his–"

"Princess?" Anderz cut in, raising a brow.

I huffed, tugging at my short hair. This wasn't right. I could handle my brother. I had a goal in place—his head on a pike.

Lyana wasn't ready. She just started healing. Her body was as sound as it would ever be, but her mind was only now beginning to regain trust. She bared her soul to me and was finally coming out of her shell. I doubted she would ever fully recover, but this was a start. All her progress might be undone just by her being in the room with Grimm.

"I won't make her go. I'll sneak her out—"

"She is already being dressed—"

"No!" I spat, storming toward the door. They wouldn't force this. "I won't allow it."

"—under her own strength."

I froze in my tracks, facing him with a frown. "She's willing to go?"

"At this rate, she will be presentable long before you are."

I recoiled as if struck. She was getting ready? On her own? Was she truly prepared to face her tormentor and Grimm? It had only been a few weeks since the incident. It felt too soon.

"We wouldn't want her to enter the dining hall before her benefactor," Anderz said carefully—a veiled warning.

I needed to be there when she arrived.

"Counselor Dyre, I beg your leave. I have a dinner to prepare for." I stormed off to my dressing room, my heart pounding in my chest.

The maids worked quickly, summoning a seamstress to alter the dress. They let it out a bit so I could breathe. The gown, a soft gold and green, evoked a warm summer day. These colors adorned most of my formal attire, a reminder of Togamar, or perhaps the imaginary woman from my hallucination.

They braided the long section of my hair, tucking it under the rest, to create the illusion of length pinned tightly to my head. The scent of lavender oil and fresh linen only churned my nervous stomach. They gave me warm gold slippers embroidered with gems, though no one would see them under the floor-length skirts. Then they slipped a belt around my hips, adorned with peridots and sunstones, tying the dress together.

Sainte vanished only briefly to ready himself. He returned wearing a fine dark tunic decorated with tiny metallic snowflakes that caught the gentle light. His fresh black boots shone with a mirror-like finish. As he strapped on his black leather chest piece, I smirked at the exaggerated muscles formed into the armor. It was but a tease of the true strength beneath.

"Breathe, Your Highness," a servant urged.

My stare snapped away from my Valahant as he looked up from buckling the clasps. I bit my lip to keep from laughing as the seamstress finished up her task.

He observed me in the reflection of the polished mirror, my gaze purposefully avoiding his. When his focus returned to the buckle he struggled with, I found myself watching him once more.

The man embodied everything a woman could want. His trousers, loose for movement yet snug to reveal the strength in his legs, accentuated his physique. As he moved, his tunic stretched taut over his broad shoulders, seams straining. Large hands fumbled with the smaller buckles of his formal armor.

Impatience gnawed at me as the seamstress tied off the final thread. Without waiting for her approval, I stepped off the fitting stool and strode to Sainte. He glanced up, hesitating when he caught my gaze. I flashed a sly grin and strode close, smacking his hands away from the buckles. As I fiddled with the clasps, I ignored him as he lifted his head to stare down the maids and seamstress.

"That is all." I jerked my chin in dismissal without taking my eyes off my task.

"Yes, Your Highness," they muttered and scurried out.

The seamstress lingered, moving at a snail's pace. I arched a brow at her, challenging her audacity. She cleared her throat and quickened her strides, closing the door behind her.

Sainte grunted as I secured the tiny straps. "I can manage."

"Maybe I want to help." I peered at him from beneath my lashes. "You wouldn't deny a girl wanting to lend a hand, would you?"

His jaw tightened, looking terribly unnerved.

I couldn't resist. My fingers were *there*, and he was so serious, almost fearful of my proximity—I had to. There was no other option.

I tickled him.

He flinched, a surprised grunt escaping his lips as my touch danced over the leather, feeling the warmth of his skin beneath, the slight shiver of his reaction. The light filtering through the window caught the snowflakes on his tunic, making them shimmer as he spun out of reach.

A smirk lifted my lip. "I didn't know you were ticklish."

"I'm not," he huffed, tugging at the clasps on the other side of his armor.

"Liar."

That got his attention. He straightened, eyes gleaming with dangerous intent.

"Don't you dare," I warned.

He took a menacing step closer. "Are you ticklish, *Princess?*"

"No. I'm not." I choked out, then darted off as quickly as my gown would allow, the skirts swishing around my ankles.

"Coward," he muttered, returning to his buckles.

My smile hurt my cheeks as I neared the hearth. The warmth of the fire danced across the dress, making the gold hues shimmer. It was odd how easily I'd taken to wearing such clothes. I remembered Kelsie attempting to make me wear dresses as a girl, but at some point, I stole the older boys' trousers and claimed them as my own. They gave me strength, made me an equal among the boys. Kelsie tried to keep me in skirts, but my rebellion, coupled with her busy brood, won out.

I spun, the fabric catching the firelight, feeling both capable and feminine. The luxurious gown felt like armor, a different kind of strength, one that enchanted and empowered me.

Perfect for seducing a certain Valahant.

I turned at the jangle of metal and watched Sainte belt on his sword. His ease and familiarity chipped away at any insecurity I had.

He looked up and caught my gaze, taking a deep breath as if preparing for battle. I crossed the room and placed my warm hand on his cheek. His careful blue eyes watched me, and he swallowed hard.

"You look quite dashing."

That was the truth. The formal attire made his irises stand out against his tan skin.

He ran his fingers through his hair and cleared his throat. "That's not my intent."

"No?" I murmured, my thumb brushing toward his lips, my eyes trailing down his face.

"I'm naught but an accent to your beauty. A shadow to your flame."

His heating gaze met mine, and my smile grew.

"A modern poet, you are!" I whispered, stepping closer to close the small gap between our bodies.

He sidestepped, narrowly avoiding me. My heart twisted with rejection, though I laughed at the same time. He was attracted to me. I knew it. His lingering glances, how he held me in bed, tightly yet always rolling away in the night. I hadn't misjudged him. I felt it in my bones... but he was a man of principle, and for some reason, I was off limits.

A smile tugged on my lip, unbothered, as I made my way to the corridor where he waited. He offered his arm, and I took a slow breath before leaving the relative safety of my rooms.

It didn't take long before the evening descended into chaos.

We sat at an elongated table on a raised platform at the back of the room, positioned for all eyes to fixate on us. The space below was a medley of tables, a diverse gathering representing regions near and far, engaged in quiet conversations while stealing glances at our elevated setting.

The regent, exploiting my birthright, dragged me and my *guest* to the head of the table. Lyana, with her gaze downcast, avoided my brother and Grimm, who loomed a few paces away, Sainte beside him.

Before the first course arrived, Adastrus leaned in close, his breath hot in my ear. "I hear you've taken pity on the priests."

My teeth ground together. Not now. I would have his head—but not yet.

"Someone should look after them," I said, giving him a pointed leer.

He raised a brow, smirking as he swept back his hair with a lazy hand. "That's the gods' responsibility, wouldn't you agree?"

"And whom did the divine entrust with leadership?" I snipped, lip curing with disgust.

"Me?" He feigned innocence, placing a palm over his heart in an air of melodramatics.

"Clearly, you haven't garnered their favor thus far." I flashed a menacing smile. "I trust the gods will choose who will best care for their people... priests included."

"Ah, such cunning! You've come so far from the little rat you once were."

My glare sharpened. "I had a remarkable teacher."

"I've done my best, but I suspect you will still fall short of the gods' expectations." He snickered a haughty laugh as servants approached with the wine.

Among the spectators, my attention lingered on a woman at a nearby table. Her attire was unsuitable for our climate, a thin dress that hinted at her origins from warmer lands. What truly caught my eye were her ears—elongated and elegantly curled, unlike any I encountered before. Her presence emphasized my limited knowledge of the realms beyond, a reminder of the gaps in my understanding.

Adastrus smiled around his wineglass. "I believe your friend would say I've taught her a few things as–"

With a swift motion, I snatched my knife from the table and drove it down, the tip landing far too close to his hand. Grimm shifted, a silent reminder of his watchful presence.

"Careful, *brother*," I hissed, "I might just forego subtlety and opt for a more direct approach."

"Oh, please do. That would promise an entertaining evening."

I snarled and yanked my knife from the wooden surface, retreating into my chair with a snarl.

Patience. It was a virtue, one I needed to exercise until the opportune moment arrived. I had to bide my time.

"I'm sure my Valahant would appreciate some action. After all, he was left wanting when Lady Lyana graced my chambers."

I could do this. As a princess, I had to maintain composure. I could handle my brother's attempts to provoke me with grace.

"Have the Priests of Togamar voiced their approval of your treatment of him, particularly your disregard for half the ritual?" I clucked my tongue. "Favor of the Gods indeed."

"The latter part is for lovers."

My heart faltered.

He took another long drink, then smacked his lips. "The Ritual of Balance requests divine permission to bed your Valahant." He leaned low to scrutinize my reaction, seeing the sting of my blush. "You still haven't bedded him?" He turned in his seat, smirking at Sainte. "Gods, man. I know she's ugly, but have pity on the poor creature!"

And so the evening went.

I pushed my food around the plates, the texture of each dish like sandpaper against my senses, my stomach churning with every word my brother uttered. He shifted his focus away from me, directing his lies and venom toward dignitaries seated at our table. Their expressions ranged from forced smiles to grimaces, enduring his vitriol as I did.

I glanced at the ambassadors and visitors from distant lands, empathizing with their plight. They, like me, were ensnared in this gathering, compelled by duty to endure the regent and his venomous words.

"Is it true that the trade of one's body is forbidden in your realm?" Adastrus inquired, his tone dripping with disdain as he probed the ambassador from a southwestern kingdom about their stance on prostitution.

I averted my gaze to the bowl of soup before me, its aroma mixing with the sour taste of bile in my mouth.

"It is, Your Highness," the ambassador responded, his demeanor exuding patience as he clasped his hands over his substantial midsection. "We have abolished the practice of debasing oneself to such depths."

Adastrus sipped his wine, his words dripping with contempt. "Pity. It's the final recourse for a woman in society. I say let them spread their legs and take a coin. Right, Lady Lyana?"

That's it.

A surge of anger swept through me like wildfire, burning away any semblance of restraint. I began to rise from my seat, my hands clenched into fists, ready to confront him.

"Where's my coin?" Lyana's voice, barely audible, was sharp as a dagger.

The room fell silent, tension palpable.

My heart plummeted as her words sank in. I stood frozen, hovering above my chair, the weight of the situation pressing down on me like a heavy cloak. The carrots in my soup blurred before my eyes, a futile distraction from the harsh reality unfolding before me. I couldn't protect her here, not in this den of vipers. Any action I took risked setting off a chain reaction of consequences, each more dire than the last. And by the end of it all, I would be thrown into the dungeons to rot.

Or I would be killed.

"Your coin?" Adastrus' voice remained eerily composed. "Lady, you were a willing participant. Half the castle saw you lie there and enjoy–"

"Where is my coin, *Prince Regent?*" Her face lifted in defiance, anger and resentment brewing in her eyes like a storm at sea. "You made me a promise, one you failed to uphold. Are the rulers of Wynterborne not bound by their oaths?"

"Be sure to get it in writing next time."

A primal urge to slap him thrummed through my veins. Tradition be damned. Still, I froze when a shadow darkened behind him. Grimm—not focused on me or Sainte, but on Lyana.

"You promised to set him free," she said.

No. This was not the place.

I rose, ready to intervene for her sake, but she stood firm, meeting my brother's gaze with unwavering defiance.

"A man's words in private hold little weight," he sneered. "Don't take it too seriously—It's nothing personal."

A vicious snarl rumbled from behind, prompting me to turn just as Adastrus' chair scraped against the dais. On instinct, I stepped away, finding Sainte at my side, his presence a shield.

Grimm, gripping the back of my brother's seat, brandished his sword, bringing it down in a forceful swing. Adastrus, being no fool, deflected the attack with a deft movement of his dinner knife.

The rest of the world slowed to a crawl, the chaos fading into a distant hum.

Grimm's strike fell short, lodging into the wooden tabletop. Blood stained my brother's hand, his face an emotionless mask as he stared up at his Valahant, the one soul that was sworn to protect him. Grimm's features, once pinched with rage, softened as he staggered, his fingers wrapping around the knife embedded in his gut. He turned to Lyana and gave her a weak smile.

Then he fell.

The abrupt thud echoed through the hall, jolting me to the present. Castle guards rushed to their regent as my gaze shifted to Lyana. Shock and horror plastered her expression, lips parted and eyes wide.

I grabbed her, shattering her horrified daze. She screamed and struggled against me until Sainte intervened. He snared her arm as she clawed and kicked, twisting against his hold, gaze fixed on Grimm's lifeless body.

Without a word, I stormed out of the hall with Sainte dragging her behind. Her wailing screams echoed in my wake.

Lyana was escorted to her rooms, still reeling from the night's traumatic events. Once there, she retreated into herself, motionless. I arranged for a calming brew to induce sleep, and after I watched her drink the entire thing, she succumbed to rest.

I sat in my receiving room, my head buried in my hands. Sainte hadn't budged from his spot in my chambers since we arrived. Though visibly shaken, he managed to mask his turmoil better than Lyana. I couldn't fathom how long he'd known Grimm, but their bond was evident enough for him to entrust the task of returning me to Wynterborne.

A knock interrupted the heavy silence. Neither of us made a move to answer. When it sounded again, faint and polite, I groaned into my palms.

"Who is it?" My tone carried the weight of my exhaustion and disbelief, a reflection of the chaos that ensued.

"Counselor Dyre."

"Come in."

Anderz slowly pushed open the door as Sainte rose from his seat, moving toward the entrance to stand guard. The door clicked shut, leaving an eerie stillness within the castle walls.

"He's dead?" I forced the question out, needing closure. I had to confront this reality.

"Yes."

A wave of grief slammed into me, a visceral punch to the gut that doubled me over. He would have never been free, forever bound to my brother's tyranny. Death, in a twisted sense, was a release—a mercy from the perpetual torment of his existence. But for Lyana, who fought so fiercely to save him, it was a cruel blow—a heartbreaking end to her efforts.

"His body will pass through the fire," Anderz said, his tone cautious.

Sainte's reaction was immediate and fierce, snapping me out of my sorrow. Rage radiated from him, his usually calm blue eyes ablaze with fury. "Did the priests sanction this?" he snapped, every word edged with anger.

"They… did not." Anderz placed a small parchment on the table. "It was the prince regent's command."

A growl rumbled in Sainte's throat, as if the words physically pained him. His hand clenched the hilt of his sword as his nostrils flared—a visible sign he struggled to contain his wrath.

"What does that mean?" I leaned forward, a nagging suspicion that there was a crucial detail I was missing.

"The people of Tilamuik bury their dead, do they not?" Anderz settled into a chair with a sigh.

"They do. Or they're given a burial at sea."

"Here, it's different. The dead are offered to the wolves. An honorable death means the body is left exposed as a tribute to Nothar. A way for the flesh that once housed life to continue serving, even in death. Once the soul has crossed the Veil, the body holds no more purpose. Burial isn't an option in grounds that are frozen year-round."

"And burning?" I pressed, swiping at my wet cheeks. "What does that mean?"

Anderz's gaze held a stoic intensity as he traced the lines of the parchment before him, his golden eyes reflecting the gravity of the situation. "When a body's burned, it's a disgrace—a curse, if you will. The soul is seen as so worthless, so tainted, that people fear its wickedness might somehow infect the wolves that feed upon it. The body is wasted."

I threw my hands up. "That's a bunch of pig's dung!"

"Wynterians are a religious folk, Princess," he said, gaze fixed on the parchment.

"What options do we have? Can the Priests of Nothar intervene? Or Togamar? She named the first Valahant, didn't she?"

"That is where the conundrum lies. It is believed the prince regent moved against his Valahant because their bond was incomplete. The blame for his death would lie squarely on the regent's shoulders. However, it was Grimm who struck first. They cannot advocate for an honorable funeral when he broke the velebond himself," he explained, meeting my gaze. "But this could work in your favor. The people will be outraged, the priests unsettled. The temples will echo with–"

"I don't want to hear it," I spat, fingers clutching and tugging the hair near my scalp. "This isn't all some political game! He was my friend! Sainte's friend! There has to be something we can do! What of his family? Does he have a family?!" I demanded, scanning the two of them for answers.

Sainte shook his head, lips pressed tight. "He was an only son, and his parents perished in a Howl."

"Then we will advocate for him. I'll speak on his behalf." My desperate gaze turned on Anderz. "The high court must have a say in this!"

"He was the prince's Valahant. He has the authority to decide his final rites."

I cursed and buried my head again. Lyana might not understand, but this was unjust. While I didn't hold much faith in the gods, if this weighed so heavily on Sainte, it mattered.

"He chose to become the prince's Valahant to protect Lady Lyana," Anderz murmured under his breath. "He gave his life when he realized his sacrifice was for naught. Lady Lyana gave her body to save him, yet in the end, she could not. One would wonder how her story ends..."

Frustration boiled inside as I tugged at my hair, feeling the strands between my fingers. I despised this sense of helplessness, unable to act while my friends suffered. I'd been told to wait, to be patient. And I was sick of it.

"I want his heart."

"Hmm?" Anderz startled, head jerking back in subtle disarray.

"I don't care how you get it, or whose hands get dirty. Gods, I'll cut it out myself if I have to!" I met his wide-eyed stare. "I want his heart."

The old man studied me, his mind working to comprehend my request and its implications. After a moment of consideration, he nodded his agreement.

"It shall be delivered by morning."

I heaved a sigh, the weight on my chest easing up just the slightest. Lyana was devout in her beliefs. She might not grasp Wynterian traditions, but she would value this gesture.

Anderz interrupted my thoughts, holding up the parchment with his slender fingers. He tested its weight before speaking, his gilded eyes burned with warning.

"This came for you," he said, his tone somber. "I intended to wait, but there's news. The third rite will commence tomorrow."

CHAPTER 26

At dawn, a servant delivered a dark wooden box. In the privacy of my chambers, Sainte watched me open it. As I lifted the red and black silk inside, the scent of iron and flesh hit my nose. A large, bloody organ lay within, its surface slick and glistening in the dim light. I stared at it, fingers trembling. Heavy, damp air clung to my skin, and a metallic tang settled on my tongue.

Was this really what a human heart looked like?

I sought Sainte for assurance, and he clenched his jaw, giving a stiff nod. After a deep breath, I eased the lid shut. My fingers traced the carved swords and shield etched along the woodgrain, and a prayer for Grimm beyond the Veil escaped my lips.

I might not believe in the gods, but it just felt right.

Morning blurred by as seamstresses stitched a dress onto me. Sainte, ever modest, faced the door during the most revealing moments. Only when the dark green fabric fully concealed me did he turn.

The kiss of silk caressed my skin, cool and smooth. The thin material offered no warmth. Thick wool trousers layered beneath stopped at my knees, providing a semblance of heat, but I still shivered, my torso covered only by the evergreen fabric.

Gold-embroidered snowflakes began at the waist, condensing as they drifted to the hem. The full skirt demanded to be hiked up as I walked. As if the lack of layering on the top wasn't enough, the seamstresses pulled the silk off my shoulders, gathering it over my arms to expose my collarbone. I frowned at the amount of skin exposed to the chill, but the women just tsked and worked around me.

They supplied a necklace with a large Tiger's Eye gemstone at its center, with smaller sunstones embedded into the thin gilded chain. The gold ring placed on my finger depicted a rearing griffon with emerald eyes framed by snowflakes and sunrays.

My signet, a gift from my father at birth.

I clenched my fist, and the sunstones set into the band caught the morning light.

I was ready.

After weaving golden leaves and polished citrine into my braid, they wrapped it around my head into a crown. The final touch, a soft fleece shawl with gold threads woven into the fibers. The maids laid it atop the table before they drifted out, giving me a moment before Anderz collected me.

Nerves twisted in my gut. I returned to my sleeping chambers, reaching under my pillow for the parchment he had given me. Unfolding it, I read the words once more.

Little Kitten,

A shipment snuck past. Something important.

Beware of the favor, all may not be as it seems.

Wolf

Frowning, I tucked the note into my dress and returned to my receiving room, where the dark ornate box held Grimm's heart. Pain twisted in my chest, breaking over last night's events. Nothing could change—we had to face the consequences of our actions.

There was nothing else I could do to help Lyana.

Helplessness and anger swelled within as I clenched my fist atop the box, eyes shut tight.

Sainte draped the shawl over my shoulders, his warmth seeping into me as he stood close. I leaned back, drawing strength from his presence. His arms wrapped around me, tucking me against his chest.

"Thank you," he whispered, lips brushing my ear.

"I will give it to Lyana," I said, turning to search his face. "Is that all right?"

A sad smile graced his features, and he shook his head a fraction before resting his rough cheek against mine. "She had his heart from the moment he laid eyes on her," he murmured. "If she wishes, Urien will guide her to the western wolves."

A sigh pushed past my lips. "I wish I could go."

Instead, I had to seek the approval of a couple rocks.

"Some things are better done alone."

"No one should have to be alone when they say goodbye."

I shook my head, stepping forward. He let his arms fall, and I immediately missed his warmth, but I had to get moving.

He blocked me, then lifted my chin with his calloused fingers. "You will do well today."

My eyes narrowed. "Because the gods favor me."

It was all about them.

"Because you are a queen in the making."

With that, he leaned forward, pressing a kiss to my forehead.

It was chaste and unexpected—his warm lips on my skin. I didn't move, taken aback by the gesture. He pulled away with a mischievous smile as a light knock sounded. I jumped at the sound, causing him to chuckle and step aside.

"And here, I thought you were saving your kisses for your wife," I huffed, a blush heating my cheeks.

I started for the door, ignoring his amused grunt. When I reached it, I allowed Sainte to answer. As always, he preferred to be in the line of fire in case anyone made another attempt on my life.

My brother was much too interested in torturing me now—killing me would be too easy.

Anderz stood beyond the threshold, his thick gray hair neatly combed, clad in his regular black and viridian robes. His gold eyes lit up as they fell on me.

"Your Highness," he greeted with a bow, his gaze trailing down my dress, snagging on my signet ring. "Shall we proceed?"

He guided me down the hall as I balanced the box in one hand and gathered my skirts in the other. Behind me, the hem dragged along the floor, a beautiful yet impractical display that made me cautious of each step.

"I need to visit Lyana's room."

"Of course."

My gentle knock brought Urien to the door, his haggard expression softening when he saw me. Without a word, he ushered us in. Lyana stood near the window, her gaze fixed outside through the bubbled glass. Ethyan lounged on her bed, legs crossed at the ankles. I exchanged a questioning glance with him as I entered, noticing his sister's reluctance to acknowledge our presence.

At least she was up.

With a subtle shake of his head, Ethyan returned his gaze to the ceiling.

"Lyana?" I called softly, not wanting to startle her.

When she faced me, she seemed surprisingly composed. Her eyes were clear, not the bloodshot red I anticipated. A faint smile touched her lips, a fragile thing that spoke volumes. She glanced at the box, a solemn reminder of our loss. On slow steps, I approached, offering it to her.

"His heart was only ever yours," I murmured, guiding her hands to grasp it. "Do as you please with it."

Her eyes pressed shut, a silent gesture of her pain, before she cradled the box against her chest. When she looked at me again, her tears brimmed, threatening to spill over.

"Thank you, El."

A remorseful smile wavered on my lips. "I wish there was more I could do."

"I..." Her attention drifted back to the window, "I think I want to go home."

A pang shot through me at her words, like an arrow striking true.

I should've been grateful for the time she spent here, especially considering she only suffered since her arrival. Still, knowing the two people I loved more than anyone wanted to leave—hurt more than I thought possible.

"I understand." My voice remained steady. Perhaps my royal blood was finally asserting itself, allowing me to keep my emotions in check. "I will have preparations made."

"We'll be back."

Ethyan's reassurance barely registered through the haze clouding my heart. Her desire to leave, to return to what she knew as home, cut deeper than I dared admit. My composure became a shield, masking the raw hurt.

"Of course." I forced a smile, though it felt brittle as a tear slipped down my cheek. "When you return, the castle will be ready to welcome you back."

The weight of those words was heavier than the box in her arms. The journey from Landing's End to Wynterborne was grueling, and the chances of them ever making that trip again were slim to none.

I hurried my goodbyes and fled the room. As the door shut behind me, enveloping me in the quiet safety of the corridor, I closed my eyes and drew in a deep, steadying breath. After I swiped the tear from my cheek, I forced a grin at Anderz, but it felt hollow.

I would have to rule without my friends.

Sainte stepped closer, his arm brushing against my shoulder, and I startled, meeting his gaze. Understanding swirled in those blue depths, and he offered a reassuring nod.

I could do this.

Sniffling, I inclined my head to Anderz, who studied me with attentive eyes.

"Lead on, Counselor."

I thought the throne room was glamorous, but the Chamber of the Gods put it to shame.

My ancestors spared no expense in crafting this vast and magnificent space. The ceiling stretched above, our footsteps echoing along the stone floor. Veins of gold ran through dark walls, connecting them to the luminous white marble beneath our feet. Far above, chandeliers bedecked with crystalline mirrors scattered light with every gentle sway. Sculptures and shrines adorned each surface, evidence of meticulous craftsmanship. Designed by skilled hands, the natural cave gleamed under numerous glittering lamps.

High above the bustling crowd were statues depicting the gods. Among them, a white marble statue of a little girl caught my eye. Frozen mid-spin on one dainty toe, face bright with perpetual laughter, an intricate marvel of sculpted joy.

Nellie would have adored it.

At the opposite end of the chamber, a colossal sculpture dominated the space. Nothar, perched atop a majestic stag, towered over all others. The gilded antlers spanned wide, far beyond any ordinary deer's. It matched the stag from the second rite perfectly. The god sat tall and regal, a crown of ice adorning his head. His long hair billowed in a chilly breeze, adding an ethereal touch to the scene.

But his eyes—they stopped me dead in my tracks.

Their haunting, green glow seemed to watch me as I lingered at the room's edge. I swallowed, intrigued by their eerie luminescence. What kind of stone produced such a mesmerizing effect?

Perhaps it was merely a play of light.

"Your Highness?"

Anderz's calm voice jolted me from my reverie. I forced another smile, tilting my head, urging him to continue.

Onlookers lined the chamber's walls, their presence obscuring the smaller statues and alcoves filled with shrines. Never had I seen so many gathered in one place.

Anderz guided me along an aisle covered in soft golden fabric, providing a stark contrast to the chilly marble beneath our feet. Sainte followed close behind, a welcome presence as I glanced up at Adastrus, positioned on a raised platform underneath Nothar's imposing figure.

Clad in white and blue, he stood out against the room's earthy tones. His hair, often unruly, was combed back, save for a rebellious strand that lay against his forehead. The freshly shaved sides of his head accentuated the dark hue, emphasizing his presence amidst the ceremonial setting. When I spotted his boots, my nose wrinkled at the pristine white leather. Such luxury was foreign to me. How many times would they require polishing to maintain their impeccable appearance? Surely he had servants on standby to attend to them at his every whim.

On determined strides, I approached, disregarding the smirk playing on his lips. Confidence radiated from him, but I countered with a vicious grin, reminding myself of my two victories, solidifying my position. This was merely a formality, a spectacle to affirm the gods' favor toward me.

The note tucked close to my heart felt like a brand, a reminder of the Dire Wolf's message. As I reached the stairs, the gaze of Nothar's eyes, that eerie green, still bore into me.

What a trick!

A deep breath filled my lungs as Anderz stepped aside, granting me a solitary ascent to the dais. Sainte knelt at the top of the stairs, one palm resting on his dagger, the other on the cool marble, his gaze sweeping over the crowd.

Adastrus strode forward, offering his hand. The gesture of assistance twisted my stomach, but I accepted it for the sake of appearances. His grip was tight, unnervingly damp, and as soon as I reached the dais, I withdrew from his touch. With a sick grin and airy chuckle, he wiped his palms on his trousers as if he were actually nervous.

Several priests lined the back end, each representing different gods. Some donned colors and symbols hinting at their deity affiliations—light blue for Nellium, vibrant green and gold for Togamar. White and viridian marked the Priests of Nothar, their collars fashioned from polished antlers. One stood out among the rest, who held a dark cape with formidable metal pauldrons, each adorned with intricately carved sockets. A second priest took up the space behind him, holding a pillow with two stones resting on its cushion.

The first, pure white, the other black as onyx—the God Stones. They didn't look like anything special.

"Ready, little sister?"

Something about his tone unnerved me. And as I took my place beside him, facing the crowd, a thrum of uncertainty chilled the blood in my veins.

I passed the other rites—I'd pass this one.

Faith in the gods, right?

I glanced at Sainte, seeking reassurance, but he was preoccupied, observing the line of priests.

Adastrus shifted his attention to the hushed, eager crowd, then raised his arms in cordial reception. "Citizens of Wynterborne! Friends from afar! I welcome you to the Rite of Favor!" He beamed at their applause.

Various emotions played across their faces, from nervous smiles to pure joy. Anderz, at the front, clapped, his observant stare taking in everything.

"Since Nothar's seed first spread among men, this sacred tradition has upheld the natural order of succession and confronted those who seek to disrupt it." Adastrus motioned toward me with a good-natured smile, even as his eyes demanded my death. "My sister, our long-lost princess, has returned to our great kingdom and presented me with the Gods' Rites. With Nothar's favor, I embraced this challenge! After all, it's only fitting that the divine determine your leadership!"

Murmurs of agreement rippled through the crowd.

"We have seen, in the past two trials, indications of the Gods' Chosen."

I narrowed my eyes at the back of my brother's head. Was he acknowledging they singled me out, that they granted their mark?

"However, those indications are just that—hazy and ambiguous. Distorted by the expectations of the people, and perhaps a few malcontent nobles. There is no definite victor from the previous trials. For that reason, the Rite of Favor is last! Finally, we will receive a clear answer, a solution to mine and my sister's supplication. The God Stones have never failed, and they will not do so now!"

He turned to me again, a wicked smile on his face. "Today, we shall see who the gods truly want in power!"

My teeth ground together, a sinking feeling growing in my gut. Something was off.

"After much reflection, I won't keep you waiting. You've heard the rumors and seen the signs. All of you wonder if Elspeth is their chosen. You shall have your answer!" He motioned to the Priests of Nothar, then to me. "Make your plea, sister."

His voice dropped low, his next words only for me. "*Beg* the gods."

I took a sharp breath and strode forward as my brother stepped back. A strange buzzing filled my ears as I scanned hundreds of eager faces. My heart pounded, fingers trembling as my shawl was removed, exposing my shoulders to the chilled air.

With my chin held high, I locked eyes with the distant statue of Togamar. Her wavy hair caught in a breeze, her scarf draped over head, wrapping around her.

A heavy cape settled on my back, the pauldrons pressing down with unexpected weight. I braced myself against their burden.

The goddess held my gaze, as if challenging me.

I was chosen—marked. This would work.

The stones slid into their sockets, white on my right shoulder, black on my left.

I trembled, anxiety knotting in my chest. After clearing my throat, I crossed my arms, palms resting on the cold stones, their smooth surface chilling my skin. "I, Elspeth of Wynterborne, Second Born of Veiled King Vardis seek the Favor of the Gods.

"Today, I ask the gods to proclaim me as their chosen, mark me as a true victor among my rivals. I seek to rule their people with a strong but gentle hand." My eyes drifted shut, as an unspoken plea formed within my thoughts—begging, as my brother instructed.

Nellie's words echoed in my head, *'You've got my papa in you, chicken!'*

"Will my father, Nothar, give me his blessing?"

Tense silence gripped the chamber. No sound, no breath, no movement. Every soul awaited a sign, an answer to my plea.

Then gasps rippled through the crowd.

I opened my eyes, fear striking a note in my heart. Hands covered mouths in horror, expressions wide with shock, heads shaking in disappointment.

I jerked my touch away from my shoulders and looked to the right. The white stone maintained its form. No change.

A sick sensation thrashed in my stomach as I peered to my left. The black stone glowed blue, that same eerie hue as the pool in the Temple of Togamar.

"Dear sister, it seems the gods have answered your plea."

His tone, that haughty smug arrogance, sent a chill through me as the priests removed the stones, then the cape.

The Wolf's note itched against my chest, a constant, irritating reminder of my position. Sainte's mouth pressed into an angry line, his frustration evident. Anderz's eyes darted over the priests behind me, searching their faces as if they held the answers to our plight. They returned the shawl over my shoulders, and I stepped back.

Numb.

The cape draped over him, and the stones settled into their sockets. His words drowned in the roaring in my ears as he reached toward the ceiling, making his plea. He crossed his arms, hands resting over the stones.

Heavy silence fell, broken only by my pounding heart and the rush of blood in my veins.

The white stone lit—a bright blue glow spread under Adastrus' hand, and the crowd erupted into cheers and applause.

The gods had spoken. And I was not their chosen.

CHAPTER 27

I rushed back to my rooms with Sainte and Counselor Dyre trailing behind, using the excuse of needing to prepare for the celebratory feast. It was meant to mark my victory, the third win affirming my status as the Gods' Chosen.

Instead, it would become a gathering for gossip, centered on Adastrus' clear favor. There would be endless questions about what I'd done to earn the divines' ire, and doubts voiced about the legitimacy of the *indications* I received during the first two rites.

Once in the safety of my rooms, anger, frustration, and confusion brewed like a chaotic storm within me. This was meant to be a divine message, but what did it signify? If the gods were involved, why lead me on only to drown me at the end as if it were all some cosmic joke?

"What was that?" I asked, striving to keep the accusation from my tone.

This situation wasn't of my choosing. They forced this path on me. They paraded me in front of the people, instilling hope that Adastrus might not be their destined leader, only for it all to come crashing down, leaving their faith shattered while I struggled to stay afloat.

Anderz held up his hands in a placating gesture. "You have won two rites–"

A knock sounded, stopping the curt response on the edge of my tongue. I pivoted toward the door as Sainte opened it.

"Counselor Hinyte," I bit out with a smile that was all teeth.

"Princess," his eyes flicked between Anderz and me, "I hope I'm not interrupting."

"Not at all," I snipped, though my expression proved otherwise.

"May I have a word?"

"Now is not the best time," I said. "I'll gladly answer the onslaught of questions at the feast. Save it." My fists curled tight, knuckles turning white with the strain.

"I saw the... *gods* move as clearly as anyone in that room. I only wanted to suggest that a trip to the Temple of Togamar might *enlighten* you on your future path." The smile he offered didn't reach his eyes, but he dipped his chin in a show of dismissal. "I'll see you at the feast, Your Highness." With that, he took his leave, departing as if his words hadn't been cryptic.

A deep frown carved a wrinkle between Sainte's brows. I looked to Anderz for clarification. If anyone could decipher his meaning, it would be him.

He gave a slow shake of his head, a silent answer to my question. "I would advise you to visit the temple tomorrow, Princess. Perhaps seek Togamar's forgiveness for any offense."

He meant it as an excuse for me to go, but it only fueled my frustration.

"Is there a way for me to challenge this?"

"Because of today's outcome, he remains in power as regent. He cannot ascend the throne unless you pass beyond the Veil. The witnesses saw him marked as favored. With so many observing the outcome, you cannot contest the result, as much as he cannot rise because of your victory in two rites."

"What about the Rite of Combat?"

"You think you stand a chance against him?" Sainte snapped.

"It's better than–"

"Than what, my petulant princess?" Anderz interjected, tone soft, using that infuriating nickname. "Is risking your immediate demise worth your challenge? The prince regent will surely plot against you, but for now, you can seek the gods' favor and perhaps sway the high court with any evidence you gather. You still hold influence there."

With a long, deep breath, I attempted to rein in my emotions. Lashing out served no purpose. This was the hand I'd been dealt, and I needed to strategize accordingly. I had to uncover how my brother manipulated the God Stones. There was no logical explanation for the gods choosing him... assuming they even existed, which I was counting on now.

I would have his head, one way or another.

He would pay.

After taking a few moments to compose myself and allowing the maids to change me into more appropriate attire, I entered the Hall of Feasts. The dress that should have celebrated my victories in all three rites now brought a bitter taste to my mouth.

Chin held high, I met every questioning glance with defiance. I refused to be subdued. There was a reason my brother emerged victorious. Whether through manipulation or divine intervention, I was determined to find out.

In the meantime, I would carry myself as the princess I was—the victor of two rites.

I strode to the raised table at the back of the hall, sensing my brother's eyes tracking me as he laughed at something Reuthland said.

"To my sister!" he called, lifting his wineglass. "And to her exploits that led to her loss of favor!"

Poor taste, brother. Poor taste.

I maintained a smile as the room tensed, people reluctantly raising their drinks to their lips. Adastrus winked at me over the rim, and I took my seat, waiting as a servant filled my glass to the brim with wine.

"To you, brother," I called, lifting it with care, "and your sudden, *unexpected* Favor of the Gods."

His features brightened with mirth as my Valahant pulled the drink from my hand and sipped. I focused on Adastrus, my smile not reaching my eyes as he drank from his cup. Sainte returned mine, and I brought it to my lips.

There was a first time for everything—and after the reactive toast, this seemed like the perfect opportunity to start.

I took a small sip, the sour and fruity scent warning of its bitterness. As the liquid scalded a trail down my throat, my eye twitched in distaste.

Adastrus grinned, noting my reaction. "Drink up, little sister. It's a time for celebration."

My jaw clenched as a servant set warm soup beside me. Sainte sampled it first, and I gripped handfuls of my skirt, nails digging into my thighs. I anticipated a long night of questions and accusations, so it surprised me when everyone at Adastrus' table ignored me. Even the regent himself seemed more focused on gloating.

Just when I thought the evening would glide by without incident, my brother rose from his seat. The cruel gleam in his eye did not bode well for me.

"Good ladies, and fine sirs!" His voice echoed through the hall, silencing all chatter as nobles, ambassadors, and dignitaries directed their attention. "I realize you've traveled far, endured our harsh winter, expecting a coronation. Until today, there were premature rumors of my sister's ascension. Those were misguided hopes. The gods have chosen me as their favored." He paused, his smile growing as he gave Counselor Dyre and Lady Aliea a pointed leer.

"I wouldn't have you leave without news," he continued. "Take with you, back to your homes, your castles, your kingdoms, a message worthy of celebration! I would like to announce that the coronation of the new King of Wynterborne will proceed as planned in a fortnight!"

Cheers mixed with confused murmurs, and I frowned as my brother's gaze narrowed on me. Madness sparked in his bright eyes as he sipped from his glass, letting uncertainty ripple through the crowd. The fact that he couldn't take the throne while I lived clashed with the fear that he might have me killed in my sleep. If he persisted, the high court would have to assume he intended to eliminate me before ascending. That would be grounds to delay the coronation.

"You can't–"

"Oh, but I can, little sister."

"Not while I–"

"I, Prince Adastrus, *First Born* of King Vardis," he declared over the crowd, commanding their attention once more, "Regent of Wynterborne, challenge Elspeth, Second Born, to the Rite of Combat."

My breath caught in my chest. I held his stare, avoiding guidance from Sainte or Anderz. Was refusing an option? Would I, if I could? Teeth grinding, I stood and offered a small bow. When I met his gaze, I lifted a brow in challenge.

"I accept, brother."

"I trust you'll keep this between us? For the people's sake?" Mocking placation tinged his tone. "Your Valahant need not fight in your stead as I am without one. We would give the good folk a fair fight?"

I glared, remaining silent.

His grin widened, and he raised his wineglass, eyes trained on me. "To the death, little sister. To the death."

The walk to my rooms felt like I was in someone else's body, as if I navigated through thick fog. Memory, rather than conscious thought, guided my steps through the castle. Sainte's presence remained steady, a silent shadow.

Once inside my chambers, the maids dressed me in my nightclothes, then I dismissed them. With a blanket draped over my shoulders, I stood by the fire, its flames flickering across the room while I pondered the gravity of the situation.

My brother essentially ordered my public execution. I never engaged in a formal duel before. Gods, I wasn't even handy with a sword. While I knew how to fight with a dagger in a dark alley, such tactics were neither proper nor sanctioned. No, I'd be given a sword with the order to defend myself, miss the first strike, then Adastrus would remove my head from my body.

My expectations were grim, and Sainte's silence echoed my apprehension.

"There's no escape now, is there?" I murmured, watching the flames flare, then subside, consuming the wood with vigor.

"No."

His validation tightened my jaw.

A bitter laugh escaped my lips, heart twisting, as I pulled the fur blanket tighter over my shoulders. "I've come this far only to face beheading." Disbelief tinged my words.

How could I have stayed so long, endured so much only for it to culminate in death?

I sniffed, then faced him. "We need to get Lyana and Ethyan out of here."

He leaned against the table, his arms crossed over his chest, a hint of agitation rippling beneath his calm exterior. A furrow formed between his brows, and a strand of dark brown hair cascaded down to his temple. I started toward him on slow, careful steps. His nostrils flared with restrained rage, and I reached up to caress his cheek, offering what solace I could muster.

"How long do I have?"

"Until the coronation," he replied through gritted teeth. "As the challenged party, you have the privilege of setting the time. It's expected within the week." His eyes pressed shut, and when he met my gaze, it filled with resolve. His warm palms grasped my face, gentle and sincere. "I will do my best to prepare you."

"Don't get your hopes up." I whispered, leaning into his touch.

"You couldn't disappoint me."

I let out a breathless laugh. "Oh, I'm sure I could manage."

"I mean it, Ellie," he rumbled, his thumb caressing my cheek. "You've exceeded expectations. I won't abandon you."

"Such fine words," I murmured. I turned, pressing my lips against his palm. Our eyes locked as I moved, his gaze sharpening where our skin met.

"We should visit the temple."

He made no move to pull away, and neither did I.

"Relying on Leihim's guidance?"

"If there's a chance that we might find answers, we need to try."

"And if there are none?"

"We'll confront that path as it unfolds."

I nipped his palm, and he withdrew, thumb brushing my lips. Hunger blazed in his eyes, and I closed the distance, his hands settling on my hips, neither drawing me closer nor pushing me away.

I took hope in this revelation.

My voice trembled with nerves, heart racing. "What if tonight was our last?"

A rejection now would shatter the facade I maintained into a thousand pieces.

My hands slid to his sides, tugging at the buckles of his formal attire. His eyes ignited with desire, throat moving as he swallowed. It was empowering to see this fearless man, unflinching in any punishment my brother could mete out, now tremble at my touch.

"I would serve you," he said, tone husky and raw.

His fingers curled at the small of my back, drawing me closer. Blood rushed in my ears as I pressed against his armor, the barrier suddenly unbearable, and I tugged at the buckles with heightened urgency.

"Serve me how?" I breathed, tipping my head.

He cleared his throat, eyes dropping to my lips. His hold on me tightened, relaying his apprehension. "With my life."

"With your body?" My teeth sank into my lip to contain my grin.

"If you asked it of me."

"What if I didn't?" I abandoned the buckles in my impatience, lacing my fingers around the nape of his neck. The gesture pushed my frame flush against his, and I tugged his face closer to mine.

"I wouldn't act without your consent." His voice was rough, and he searched my expression as if seeking affirmation.

"And if I *did* want your advances?" I murmured, threading my fingers into his short hair, tugging him close. "What if I dreamed of you, craved you?"

His breath hitched, and he closed his eyes, collecting himself. I was his undoing. Power thrummed through my veins, watching my Valahant, my champion, my steadfast Sainte attempt to compose himself against this flame burning between us. When his gaze returned to mine, fierce desire bloomed in those swirling depths.

"Do you dream of me?" I asked.

"We are connected through the velebond," he said. "I am bound to you. You will always lead."

He dropped low, gripping my thighs, then lifted me against him. I gasped and, on instinct, wrapped my legs around his waist as he spun, settling me on the table. My heart pounded without mercy as I stared into his eyes—I was so sure he could hear it.

"If I were but a man," he leaned close, lips pausing but a breath from mine, "or a noble worthy of a queen–"

"You–"

He darted forward, cutting my words short as he pressed his mouth on that tender place just below my ear. Heat exploded within me, a delicious flush that sent flutters low in my belly.

"I would have you," he whispered, his breath tickling my skin. "Every night I lay with you, I would have you. I would have you on this table, on the bed, before the hearth. You test me, rile me. You're an itch I can't scratch. Elspeth, you're a fire in my chest that cannot be tamed."

My arms tightened their hold, pinning him against me.

"Of course I dream of you," he said, teeth grazing my ear.

It felt as if my soul left my body and passed beyond the Veil, and I clung to him for all I was worth. Heat surged through me, and I arched against him, craving more.

"Now," he jerked out of my embrace, the motion abrupt and swift, putting plenty of space between us, "sleep."

Disbelief washed over me, cold and consuming. He regarded me with strange uncertainty. It was as though the man standing before me, shy and hesitant, hadn't been pressed against me in a moment of passion just seconds ago. Had I done something wrong? Reacted in a way he didn't like?

I had time.

Not much, but enough.

I hopped off the table, bridging the gap between us. My fingers curled around the back of his head, drawing him closer until our breaths mingled, a mere heartbeat apart. His breath was ragged as his hand instinctively cradled my waist.

"Tonight, I will dream of you."

I planted a swift, innocent kiss on his lips. His exhale was sharp, as if he'd taken a punch to the gut. His expression had me torn between pushing for more and falling to the floor in a fit of laughter.

The man was clearly out of his element.

Wide-eyed, his breath hitched in controlled bursts. I winked, a playful spark in my eyes, and turned away, giving him his space.

For all of Sainte's knowledge and expertise, women seemed to be an uncharted territory for him.

"For that reason, Princess," he called, clearing his throat. "I will sleep on my cot. Fully dressed."

I threw my head back and laughed. With a glance over my shoulder, I started for my sleeping quarters. "Not in my dreams, you won't."

CHAPTER 28

The cold of the next morning seeped into my bones as soon as I stepped outside. Wrapped in furs, hood pulled low, the wind still slapped my face with a breathtaking ferocity. Streets lay quiet under dawn's glow, people sheltering indoors as a Howl brewed. Sunlight struggled to break through the thick cloud cover, casting a dreary gray over the snow-covered ground. I clutched Sainte's arm as another gust slammed into us. My cloak snapped behind me, exposing me to the frigid elements. The weather seemed intent on thwarting our journey.

That, or the gods.

Sainte forged ahead, head bent low. Thick flakes spilled from the dark clouds, swirling in the fierce wind. We could have taken a carriage to the temple district, but I wanted to avoid drawing attention. The last thing I needed was Adastrus appearing and goading me into our duel. Though now, with my fingers numb and body aching, regret gnawed at my resolve.

My thoughts drifted to the note from the Dire Wolf. Did she know anything about the Rite of Favor? It was a warning... Could she prove my brother cheated somehow? Perhaps there was something to Leihim's cryptic words. I had to at least *try* to figure it out.

I braved Winter's Bite for this—it had to be worth it.

My knees buckled, and Sainte caught me before I collapsed. I gripped him tight, shielding my eyes from the blinding flurry. Heavy snowfall obscured my view, structures vanishing from sight. Even the distinct statues in front of each temple were indistinguishable.

Still, he led me with unwavering confidence, his firm grip guiding me through the accumulating drifts. He never faltered, never stumbled. Eventually, we passed through an iron gate. Snowflakes clung to my lashes as I strained to see

Togamar's statue in the courtyard, but the world dissolved into a swirling white haze.

As Sainte tugged me up snow-smothered steps, eerie silence enveloped us, the snow's relentless howl drowning out all life. When we reached the immense entrance, I heaved a sigh of relief at the sight of Togamar's portrait. At least we arrived at the correct temple.

He pounded on the door with his left hand, as I still clutched his right arm, fearing I'd blow away at any moment. It had nothing whatsoever to do with how I enjoyed the sensation of his muscles flexing beneath my hold.

The door creaked open, revealing a young girl's face. Her eyes widened in surprise before the wind yanked the handle from her grasp. She shrieked as it slammed against the wall, echoing through the temple. The priests inside scrambled, breaking out in chaos.

"Oi, shut the–"

"We have patrons!"

"Get them out of the cold!"

"Is that Princess Elspeth?"

Sainte dragged me into the warm sanctuary, a stark contrast to the biting chill outside. The transition from freezing winds to the stifling heat inside was like stepping from winter's grasp into a cozy hearth. Priests scurried around us, their movements a blur in the rush. Two of them hurried to shut the door, the icy draft vanishing as it closed with a thud.

The sudden warmth pricked my skin, thawing the chill that had seeped into my bones. As I stood there, my breath steaming in the heated air, two priests approached, removing my cloak with practiced hands.

Amidst the flurry of activity, a hunched figure caught my eye. She limped toward us, her steps heavy with the weight of years, her cane tapping out a steady rhythm on the stone floor.

"Princess."

My jaw trembled with my shiver as I dipped my chin in greeting. "Priestess Edne."

Sainte discarded his cloak, handing it to a priest before shaking his head like a dog, scattering water and snow. A chuckle escaped me as I watched the droplets fly, and I raked my fingers through my own damp, freezing hair.

A twinkle sparked in her eyes. "She told me you would come, though I did not expect you to brave a Howl."

"I'm pressed for time." I offered a casual shrug. My red, aching hands burned with cold, and I cupped them over my mouth, seeking warmth from my breath.

"A fortnight is enough time to wait out a Howl, dear." She smirked with a shake of her head. "Come, she has told me what to do."

I glanced at Sainte, uneasy with her belief in prophetic dreams. These people placed immense faith in intangible, unproven things. But then, my reasons for being here were unclear. Perhaps Leihim sent word?

That was a plausible explanation.

My Valahant arched a brow at my doubtful expression and motioned for me to follow Edne. She hobbled off, and a young girl left the comfort of the roaring hearth, where our cloaks dried, to assist her. It relieved me to see she had support this time.

Conversations buzzed through the space as people resumed their tasks, barely casting us a second glance. We trailed Edne down the stairs. The girl clutched her arm with a worried frown, underscoring the strain of navigating the steep, dark stairwell. When we reached level ground, the breath I held in my chest finally loosed. If the old priestess fell now, at least the risk would be minimal.

The cavern felt desolate, with only our small group breaking the stillness. Priests didn't gather here, nor did children scurry about. Silence hung in the air, the muted noises from the upper level barely audible.

The girl hastened to retrieve white clothes from a shelf. I stifled a groan in my throat as Edne hobbled off to grab a capped bottle and cup, then rushed to her side to steady her, preventing her cane from slipping.

She smiled up at me, eyes twinkling as she uncorked the top. "You seek answers."

"I seek solutions," I corrected.

She chuckled, clearly amused by my response. "The gods do not always act on our behalf."

"And the God Stones do?"

"They are but an answer..." she murmured, her focus intent as her trembling hands lifted the bottle to the cup, tipping it with care.

Dread filled me as a luminescent blue liquid spilled out. When it reached the brim, Edne secured the cork and flashed me a wide, toothless grin.

"Tell me that's for you," I whined, lip curled.

"Oh no, dear."

"My insides will light up like the northern sky."

"You are not ready to seek the divine without help. This prepares your mind and body."

I squinted at the old woman, recalling the hallucinogenic mushrooms sold in the slums.

Sure, I would see the gods.

With a glance at Sainte for assurance, I watched as he removed his armor, handing it to the little girl, who placed it in a neat stack on the shelf. He tugged his tunic loose and drew it over his head, revealing his scars.

After an airy sigh, I peered into the glowing cup, then at Edne's expectant grin, and tossed the liquid back, downing it in one long gulp. My features pulled into a grimace. It had no flavor, but the thick consistency made my mind balk as it slid down my throat. It was just wrong.

Edne looked me over, leaning heavily on her cane. "Change. You wouldn't want to ruin your fine clothes."

I squinted as a light, airy sensation flitted through my head. "Couldn't I sit against the wall or something?" I asked, gesturing vaguely around the cavern, my wrist drooping weakly. "Anywhere?"

"Into the pool, Princess."

I hummed my reluctant agreement, swaying as I fumbled with the laces. Everything felt thick and fuzzy, a sense of wrongness I couldn't quite grasp. It took too much effort.

When I tugged my dress off, I stumbled, warm balmy air kissing my skin. My eyes pressed shut in a long blink as I staggered to the side, and when they opened again, I found the girl standing before me, offering a thin white gown, her smile bright. I tried to return the grin, but I swayed again on unsteady feet. Whatever was in that drink surpassed anything from the slums.

After shrugging into the shift, I tugged at the neckline riding high against my throat, wondering why the back dipped so low.

"She put it on backwards. Should I fix it, Priestess?"

The little girl's words reached my ears as I turned and staggered toward Sainte.

"No, child," Edne's raspy voice replied. "Valahant!"

He faced me and, as he did, my knees buckled.

He was so handsome.

Clad in naught but thin white trousers, his chest bore a light dusting of hair that thickened as it trailed downward. A flush tickled across my skin as my stomach melted. He hurried over, lifting me from the ground. I gaped up at him, lashes fluttering as I gave him my dreamiest smile.

He chuckled, his smirk crooked, then hoisted me against his chest, heading toward the pool. My head lulled back, catching Edne's grin upside-down. Her expression beamed with pride and mirth, as if I were her favorite child.

When he stepped into the glowing water, its eerie glow brightened with each stride.

"I hate this," I whined, features set into a stern pout.

"You've faced tougher situations," he murmured.

He loosened his hold, and my body floated, legs drifting away from him as he cradled my head, hands supporting me beneath my shoulder blades. Water soaked into my bones like a warm embrace. It wasn't unpleasant—the novelty of the strange hue just took some getting used to.

He glanced down at me, and I met his gaze, careful not to strain my neck as he snorted a laugh. I smiled, content, and wriggled, causing small waves to lap against the stone.

"Close your eyes, Princess."

I sighed and did as he said. "You're supposed to... call me Ellie..." I mumbled, fading into sleep, my mind disconnecting from my body.

"Drift, Ellie," Sainte's voice beckoned me. "Drift."

A gentle, feminine hum tugged me toward consciousness. I resisted, shifting in my cozy bed to find a better position.

I tumbled into a pond, warm water flooding my senses. Arms flailing, I struggled to stay afloat. My eyes squeezed shut against the rush of liquid, hands groping in the dark for a branch, a tree, anything to grab onto.

A strong grip seized my arm, and I clutched onto it for dear life. When I broke the surface, I gasped and sputtered, fingers clenching into warm flesh.

"Put your feet under you!"

I kicked, thrashing, as I struggled for breath.

"Stand, girl!"

I thrust my legs downward until I found solid ground. With a determined push, I raised my chest above the waterline and released my hold on the arm. My lungs burned as I coughed, sputtering as I swept my hair aside and wiped the fluid from my eyes.

A light laugh drew my attention to the woman before me.

She *glowed*.

"There was something in that blue stuff..." I breathed.

Her luminance rivaled a candle's flame, emanating from every pore in a subtle yet discernible glow. Golden strands cascaded like warm sunshine on a summer afternoon, framing eyes that shimmered in a green hue reminiscent of evergreens, simultaneously deep and vibrant—akin to new spring growth. Her complexion was fair, adorned with a rosy blush on her cheeks. A smile graced her lips, adding radiance to her features.

"I did not know you feared water," she teased with a playful tilt of her head.

The cavern lay empty, devoid of shelves or people. Sainte's absence only affirmed it was a dream.

I huffed, dragging myself from the pool to perch on its dark ledge. "I can't swim."

"You don't need to swim in but a few paces of water."

"Great. Even the gods poke fun at me." I sniffed, pinching my nose against the water's sting.

With a laugh, she nestled beside me, her fingers dancing over the surface, sending droplets flying into the pool. I observed as they landed, each splash creating delicate ripples of azure waves.

"Why do you seek me, child?" she asked

I shuddered. Even her teeth glowed.

"You were expecting me." My head tilted with curiosity. "Edne mentioned you told her to prepare for my visit."

"I might have anticipated your arrival," she remarked, her emerald eyes lighting up as her smile brightened. "Yet, I would still have you ask. I don't dispense knowledge you do not seek."

Her words heightened my frustration. If I forgot to mention something crucial, would she withhold that information?

I drew in a deep breath, reminding myself that this was a dream. Trust was essential. "Did my brother cheat?"

She laughed with a raised brow. "No one can *cheat* the gods."

My hopes shattered, and I glared at the rippling pool.

"Deception is impossible with the divine," she affirmed, extending her hand towards me, just a whisper away from my cheek. "Should one seek our favor, we shall provide an answer."

"He asked. You answered."

Togamar withdrew her touch, the warmth of her smile fading from her gentle face. Her patchwork gown might have appeared worn on someone else, but on her, it resembled miniature fields of green under a sunlit sky. She extended her bare foot to dangle in the water, her eyes fixed into the distance.

"We hear him as we would hear all our children." Her features softened with contemplation. "Some we acknowledge, while others are so distant, beyond our reach." Her gaze met mine, anger flaring in her vibrant green depths. "We did not answer his call."

"The God Stones, they glowed in response to our prayers. Did you answer me?"

A sad smile crossed her lips as she shook her head. "You sought favor from your father, Nothar. I would not respond to a prayer for him."

Exasperation coursed through me, and I tilted my face toward the ceiling, frustrated. I came to the wrong place.

Her palm settled against my thigh. The heat of her touch seeped through the thin, soaked fabric of my shift—almost uncomfortably warm.

"I can offer you this," she said. "Your answer resides within my temple, but with Nothar."

"Then why did Edne make me drink that foul concoction?" I asked, my irritation palpable.

"Because I told her to." Togamar snickered another laugh, ignoring my scowl. "Nellie divulged many details about you. She mentioned you were to bring syrup the next time you visit her?"

My teeth clenched tight. My dream gods spoke to each other now?

"It has been too long since the rulers of men sought us out," she sighed. "Having a queen who worships us would be a refreshing change."

"You're a figment of my imagination."

Her head whipped my way, all traces of good humor gone from her features. She wrenched my arm, and I hissed as her too-warm fingers encircled my wrist.

"Am I?" Her glare sharpened. "Your lack of faith is troubling. We listen to your prayers, answer where we can, and yet you mock us. One would wonder why we bother."

With a cry, I tugged at my arm, but her grip remained unyielding, like iron.

"I would favor you over Adastrus, but we gods are not in agreement. You are weak, needing our aid every other day. You are careless with your words and tone, forgetting you speak to the divine themselves. Not all are as forgiving as I."

She spoke with a sternness that cut through me, her accusations like sharp icicles in a winter storm. I winced as her grip tightened, feeling the searing heat against my skin as I struggled to free myself, my wrist throbbing with each heartbeat.

The pain felt too real for a mere dream.

"You've never given me reason to believe you're anything more than a myth," I spat. "Where were you when I was a child? When my brother tried to kill me in my own home?"

"It was Nothar who sent Sainte to your aid," she countered, voice laced with authority as she released my hand. "It was he who intervened when you were in peril. I ask you this: when have you last sought our guidance?"

"The Rite of Favor."

"And before then? You blame the divine for your lack of faith, but when have you ever pursued us? You simply doubt our existence. It is your blood that saves you now, offering you a tangible link when a mortal would not be offered one."

Her words cut through the air, sharp and direct, leaving a trail of icy realization in their wake. I lowered my gaze to the pool, cradling my wrist where her grip seared my skin. Did I dare believe in the gods now? Was this encounter more than a dream or mere coincidence?

"You are weak because of your disbelief," she continued, tone gentle but firm. Her eyes shifted back to that soft, ethereal spring hue. "Yet, I have blessed you with a Valahant whose faith is unwavering."

I frowned, teeth clenched, not liking how she pulled Sainte into this mix. Would she demand something of him, too? Would she punish him for my incredulity?

"Do you not realize you are one?" Her features lit with mischief. "He is yours as much as you are his. Perhaps it is time to observe his lead. Tell him to seek your father, Nothar."

"Another temple?" I barely held back a groan.

My vision blurred, and my head felt light as the room swayed.

"You fade, child," she said with a sigh. "Follow your Valahant's lead. Keep him close. Cherish him. It is not often we bless them so freely."

My arms flung out to steady myself, trying to focus on her face one last time. Her expression, both mournful and angry, settled along the pool's rippling surface.

"To cast him aside will not be taken lightly."

CHAPTER 29

I jolted awake, my body floating. Panic swelled as I flailed and thrashed.

"Easy."

Sainte's thick arms pulled me close, and I clung to him, wrapping my arms around his neck. His warmth steadied me as my toes found the soft, glowing sediment at the bottom of the pool. My heart raced, breaths quick and shallow. Blinking, I peered over his shoulder at the cavern—empty, save for Edne and the girl. No goddess with a patchwork dress of green.

"This is madness," I gasped, trying to force my pulse to slow.

A flash of color along my skin snared my attention. I jerked back, fingers digging into his muscles. A wreath of ivy encircled my wrist, the red, angry outline of leaves and stems swollen and stinging in the cool air. I winced, turning my hand over. It formed a complete bracelet.

I shoved out of his embrace and held it up for him to see—the accusation hot on my tongue. "Did you do this?!"

I staggered, and he steadied me with firm hands on my hips, his head tilting as he studied the mark. A bead of water trailed from his temple to his chin, and I watched it fall.

"No." A hint of a smile tugged at his lips.

My eyes narrowed, and I threw my hand toward Edne and the young priestess. "You?!"

"Togamar has heard your request for faith." The old woman chuckled, showing what few teeth she had left. "She has answered you and given you a token to bear for the rest of your days."

I frowned, pulling my hand close to my chest. The heart-shaped leaves tapered into fine points, and the vine formed a perfect circle without a discernible beginning or end.

It stung.

When I met Sainte's patient gaze, I drew in a slow breath. His eyes searched, waiting for me to accept that the gods were real—that they heard the people's prayers, if not mine.

I didn't recall ever praying for faith.

"I need to see the priest from the north," I said. "And Nothar wants to speak with you."

His smile vanished, replaced by a furrowed brow. "We will go to his temple when you are ready."

I huffed, pulling away from him and slogging toward the pool's edge. The warm water stung the mark on my wrist, and I held it above the surface, hissing in pain.

"Be careful," I warned, struggling to pull myself out, the wet dress clinging to my skin. "I don't want to see what kind of damage he can do." I waved my hand for emphasis.

If these visions truly were the gods, Nothar didn't care for me. If the second rite was anything to go by, he would readily leave me in a snowdrift. And I was supposed to be his kin.

I couldn't think about what he would do to Sainte.

We dressed quickly, a fur between my damp hair and my dress, and followed Edne as she hobbled up the steps. She led us through well-lit corridors to a warm, cozy room.

Whitewashed walls reflected the hearth's light, candles adding a soft glow. The space felt inviting, but the frail figure on the bed seemed out of place amid its warmth. Swaddled in furs and blankets, his features appeared gaunt and discolored. Red and black splotches marred his skin, and open blisters on his ears oozed blood and fluid onto the white linen pillow. I swallowed nervously, taking in the unsettling sight.

Edne tsked, giving me a prod with her cane. "Go on now."

I took a hurried step forward, glancing back at her. She smiled, shook her head, and closed the door behind her hunched form. I peered at Sainte for help, but he leaned against the wall with his arms crossed. When he caught my gaze, he arched a brow, a silent challenge as if to say I got myself into this mess. Now I had to see it through.

I heaved a sigh and turned to the feeble man who looked to all the world as if he were sleeping. Sparse white hair revealed the extent of his injury. It wasn't just his face. Any exposed skin bore the ravages of Wynterborne's harsh kiss. I frowned. Locals knew to cover themselves against the elements. The cold bit deep here, and it wouldn't be forgiving to someone who braved its wrath unprepared.

This was a Priest of Nothar, and an aged one as well. He should have known how to prepare for the trek and withstand the Howls.

His wrinkled mouth thinned into a smile, his eyes, the color of snow-laden clouds, opened, seeking me out. I offered an unsteady grin as he tilted his head. A raspy sound escaped his dry lips, and I instinctively moved closer.

"Wat—er."

I glanced around, then grabbed the pitcher from the end table. After I filled the mug, I eased onto the bed's edge and chewed my lip. How could I help him drink while he lay flat?

Sainte stepped close, solving my conundrum by slipping his strong arms under the man's head, lifting him upright. I raised the mug to his lips, waiting as he drew in slow sips. His eyes fixed on my face as he drank, but I was too nervous I might drown him to divert my attention from his mouth for more than a second.

When he turned away from the drink with a soft sigh, Sainte lowered him to the pillow. I set the cup aside and offered a gentle smile now that he didn't look as pale.

"You must be the Lost Princess," he rasped.

The blankets slipped off his chest while he drank, and my grin faltered as I noticed the same sores along his torso, the black of dead skin and red, open blisters.

"Princess Elspeth, at your service," I said quietly, tugging the furs up to his chin.

"Thank you, child," he whispered. "You are sweet as honey—an answer to the people's prayers."

He lifted a weak hand from beneath the covers, and I fumbled to expose his weathered palm. I steeled myself and grasped the wound-covered limb.

"Ah, see," I grimaced with a soft shake of my head, "the gods didn't actually choose me."

He frowned, cloudy eyes searching my face. "What do you mean, child?"

"The Rite of Favor," I explained, "they chose Adastrus, not I. Though, don't ask me why I had to endure the other rites if the last one settled them all."

"Show me your hands."

I tilted my head in confusion at his request, but lifted them to his line of sight.

His eyes snagged on my wrist, still red and angry from Togamar's touch. "Your palms."

I obliged, wondering if he intended to read the lines like some witches did in Tilamuik. I never placed much faith in their ability to predict my future from wrinkles in my skin, but maybe the priest did.

"You did not seek favor," he said.

I flinched, retracting my hands to my lap, a frown pulling my features. "I did, during the final rite. We both used the cloak–"

"You touched them?"

"Aye." I sniffed, offended by his doubt. Perhaps he was too old, or his mind too brittle from the toll of his journey.

"You have not laid hands on the God Stones."

I glanced at Sainte, but he was no help, offering a shrug as he returned to his place against the wall.

"And how do you know this?" I asked.

"If you saw them, you would understand," he sighed, eyes fluttering shut.

His mouth pinched. Whether in pain or worry, I wasn't sure.

"The rites are not only to prove the gods' choice... but to strengthen the people's faith." He blinked at the ceiling, long and drawn out, unseeing. "They need to believe the divine will receive their prayers and answer them. The rites are as much for you as they are for the whole of the kingdom."

"You're saying the stones used were not the God Stones?" I asked carefully.

"Nain, the stone that answers 'no' is sharp, child. It is all jagged edges and vicious points. It would cut you if you but touched the surface with the tip of your finger. Yail is so cold that even holding it for a breath would burn your skin with its chill." His eyes darted to mine as he pressed his lips together. "I would offer my oath as a Priest of Nothar that you did not touch the God Stones."

I sat back, head spinning as his words resounded.

The gods hadn't denied me.

They hadn't chosen Adastrus.

This was simply another trick of his, another lie. The Wolf's warning made sense now. My brother stole the stones and switched them out for some other form of vile magic.

Against the Priests of Togamar's advice and Sainte's reluctance, we braved the walk to Nothar's temple. It was just a short distance across the lane, but the Howl descended in full force, shrouding everything in a frigid, snowy haze that limited visibility to mere arm's length.

I refused to let a storm stand in the way of my quest for answers. Time was not on my side, and staying in the district felt safer than trekking to the castle.

Clutching onto a green scarf tied around Sainte's waist, a precaution to prevent me from getting lost in the Howl, we plowed through the snow. With my head bowed against the biting wind, I placed my trust in my Valahant to guide us through the whiteout.

We trudged through the cold for what felt like an eternity before Sainte stopped and I pulled short, stumbling into his back. He turned, causing the piles of snow that clung to his shoulders fall to the ground, silent amid the howling wind.

"We've veered off course!"

His voice cut through the gale, and I raised my arm to shield my face from the stinging flakes, squinting to meet his gaze. Frost dusted his brows and lashes as he scanned the area above my head, searching for any landmark.

A knot of unease tightened in my gut. This was why no one ventured out of their house during a Howl.

It should have been a straightforward path, just across the lane. How had we managed to stray so far without encountering any sign of a temple?

Unless, as Togamar had cautioned, the gods were not aligned in favor of my ascension.

I was weak.

Unfit to rule.

Sainte closed the gap between us, enfolding me in his embrace, his gaze scanning the swirling snow as though seeking a hidden path through its white veil.

Togamar's words echoed in my mind, accusing me of weakness due to my lack of faith. She blessed me with a Valahant strong in belief, and according to her, Nothar protected me this far. If any god made an investment in me, it was him.

Seeking solace, I pressed my face into the warmth of Sainte's cloak, my cheeks burning with embarrassment of what I was about to do. With eyes scrunched tight, I sent a silent plea into the icy air for Nothar.

Hear my prayer. Lead us straight and true. Guide us to your temple.

A naïve sense of hope gnawed at my resolve. There was no going back after this. If he answered, I would know they were real.

I kept my face buried against Sainte's chest, his strong arm holding me tight as he waited for a clue as to the right direction.

Seconds passed, his grip grounding me in reality. Anger brewed within me, not aimed at the gods, but at myself for entertaining such fantastical notions. These dreams or visions were mere figments, not the fabric of my life's reality, which I alone shaped.

The wind slapped my face with such cold and brutal force that I staggered. Sainte caught me, and I pulled my cloak tighter, struggling to pull in a breath of icy air.

Behind him, outlined against the snowy backdrop, stood a wolf.

Its fur blended with the drifts, but the gray eyes framed by dark skin sought my soul, its nose a black blot against the white landscape. It observed me, head lowered and ears pricked forward—alert but not aggressive.

I should have been afraid.

And I was, but not in the face of this predator come to rend me from limb to limb and consume my organs like delicacies. My fear stemmed from a different source. Nothar answered my prayer.

A shiver ran up my spine that had nothing to do with the cold.

Sainte spun, following my wide-eyed stare, then his grip on me tightened.

"Nothar sent him!" I shouted over the wind's roar.

The beast's gaze held an eerie intelligence, a hunger lurking behind its measured movements. It licked its chops as if it would rather eat us, but instead of pouncing, it turned and vanished into the swirling snow. Without hesitation, Sainte lurched after it, determined to track the fleeting glimpse of white amidst the flurry. We plowed onward, drifts deepening to our knees, rising as high as our hips, each step a battle against the tempest.

I cursed Nothar and his choice of creatures. Couldn't he choose something with darker fur? Always white, leaving us second-guessing if we followed the wolf's trail or merely chased phantoms in the snow.

The wolf halted, and its dark nose swiveled toward us. Its chest was buried, yet I hadn't seen it leap through the drifts, or leave any tracks.

"Here!"

Sainte tugged me along to an iron courtyard fence, and I peered over my shoulder one last time. Surely a ghost wolf could fend for itself in a Howl.

The scarf cinched around my waist, urging me forward as my Valahant carved a path toward the temple. When we reached the entrance, his breaths heaved as he rested his weight against the stone wall. I shot him a concerned look before I raised my fist to knock.

The door's surface was rough and unfinished, lacking a handle for me to tug it open. The only indication that it led to the Temple of Nothar was the vivid painting adorning it. It depicted a striking image of a man, a god, with piercing green eyes. A crown of antlers graced his brow, his expression stern. His features were distinctive, with a long face, prominent cheekbones, a sharp nose, and thin lips. He held a terrible, fierce beauty, not conventionally handsome or appealing. His skin was as pale as milk, and his sun-bleached hair hinted at a subtle golden hue.

I swallowed hard. It felt as though I was being judged by those eyes, as if they could cut through my disbelief and lack of faith in the divine.

A gust shoved me forward as the door swung open, and I yelped, staggering as the robed figure stepped aside, parting the way for me to fall flat on my face. Thankfully, the woven rug of blue and green cushioned the impact.

As voices clamored and a crowd gathered, I groaned and rolled onto my side with a weakened smile. Exhaustion pulled at my eyes, slowing my blinks.

"We seek sanctuary," Sainte called out, voice weak.

His slumped form showed his strain. He must have been more exhausted than me. Though, as I lay there on the floor, I had no desire to rouse myself, content to remain in a heap of cold, wet clothes.

At least he managed to stay upright.

"The Temple of Nothar receives you. We offer you hearth and home," someone answered.

"There's a wolf out there," I mumbled, shivering against the damp chill gnawing at my bones.

"A wolf?" another asked.

My fingers twitched as I tried to gather the strength to get up and move closer to the fire. "Aye. Big. White. Brought us here."

"Deitrus. He acts as Nothar's guide." A young man leaned over me, a playful grin tugging his lips as he took in my fatigue. "Perhaps you would do better in warm, dry clothes."

"Please," I whined. I'd have given my left thumb for such comforts.

He grinned, gesturing for the others to leave, then bent low, arms outstretched as if to lift me. But someone else beat him to it, raising me to a strong—very wet and cold—chest.

"I am Falon, head priest of this temple," he said, his features settling into an amused grin. A mischievous glint brightened his gaze when he looked my way. "And you must be the princess. I would ask why you were wandering through a Howl with naught but your Valahant, but since Deitrus led you here, I have to assume it is Nothar's will."

"We were told to seek out Nothar," I explained.

"Of course," he said with a bow. "First, dry clothes."

His teasing tone brought a feeble grin to my face, and he straightened, ignoring the lingering stares and watchful eyes of those still in the room.

This temple differed from Togamar's. Where hers was soft, bright and inviting, this was austere and imposing. Its rough-hewn walls were dark stone stacked like colossal bricks, giving the impression of a smaller, more foreboding space. The priests were all dressed in white and green, and as we made our way through the lantern-lit halls, I noted they were all male.

Why did no women serve Nothar?

Another striking difference was the display of gilded weapons adorning the walls instead of art or tapestries. Vivid shields were interspersed with daggers and swords, their jeweled hilts caught the sparse lantern light.

Falon led us to a modest chamber with roaring flames in its hearth. Though compact, it exuded warmth and coziness. The fire's amber glow painted shadows on the uneven walls, casting a comforting ambiance over the room furnished simply with a small table and four chairs.

I smirked at the ax that hung over the mantle.

Clearly, Nothar loved weapons.

The priest excused himself to find a robe that might fit me, and I shed my wet cloak. I draped it on a hook near the hearth, then held out my aching hands. Sainte did the same, only, with a long screech, slid another chair along the stone floor, then stepped back, allowing me to sink into it and pry off my boots.

"Why are there no priestesses?" I asked, grimacing as a glob of wet slush dripped out of my sock as I peeled them off.

Sainte sighed, easing into his seat with a groan. He took a moment, resting his elbow on his knee to prop up his head. His damp hair fell over his forehead, and he gripped it tight before smoothing it back.

Guilt tainted my thoughts. He braved that Howl because of me.

With shoulders sagged, he glanced my way before facing the fire. "Nothar does not choose women."

"I thought people chose which gods to serve."

"They may, but the god or goddess decide who serves in their temple."

Nothar had to be swallowing his pride then, to be backing me instead of my brother.

"These priests have to complete an initiation by combat," he added. "They must defeat a seasoned priest, and train with weaponry daily."

He rolled his head to look at me, and my heart did a little flip when a lock of hair fell loose and dangled against his brow.

"So a girl wouldn't have a chance?"

"To defeat a man whose sole purpose is to fight and serve his god? No."

"You're severely underestimating women as a whole," I huffed.

"You will find out soon enough."

He leaned back, stretching his arms overhead. His muscles tensed and he grimaced. A blush warmed my cheeks as I studied his form beneath his wet clothes which clung to him like a second skin. I knew I couldn't best Sainte, not because of my gender, rather his training. My skills with a dagger came from necessity, not from the rigorous discipline he endured. In a fight, he would overpower me without effort.

He lowered his arms and caught the tail-end of my stare. I shifted my gaze to the flames, but not before I spotted his raised eyebrow, hinting at his amusement.

"I will prepare you as best I can," he said.

"Hmm?" I forced myself back to the conversation, trying to avoid thoughts of Sainte's body.

Not the definition of his chest.

Not the lines of his abs.

I definitely didn't need to be thinking about the trail of hair that ran down his stomach, disappearing into his trousers.

"...why Togamar sent us."

My lips pressed tight, and I shook my head as if that would be enough to stifle the heat blooming low in my belly.

Look at his face, El.

His face!

He frowned, confusion creasing his brow. I swallowed past the lump in my throat and forced a bright smile, hoping it didn't betray my thoughts.

"What worries you?"

A strangled sound escaped as my grin faltered. "Togamar told us to come here for you, not me."

"... because I feel Nothar will show me how to best prepare you."

Oh, that's what he had said.

"Right," I nodded, turning my gaze back to the hearth.

A knock saved me from my thoughts straying once again. We rose as Falon entered, blue and white robes draped over his arms. His gray eyes flicked over me to my Valahant, lips lifting in a smile.

"Please change. You will be far more comfortable, then we can discuss the ritual."

I scrunched my nose in distaste. Hadn't I endured enough divine encounters already?

"She won't be participating," Sainte said as he secured his robe from Falon.

The priest dipped his chin, curious. "You seek Nothar, do you not, Princess? Your Valahant does not share your lineage. You may be one, but the blood calls to–"

Sainte cut him off. "I will suffer the Ritual of Blade and Blood."

Gods, that sounded terrifying.

Without waiting for Falon's response, he took the second robe, handing it over to me. His jaw clenched.

"He won't answer," Falon said, puzzled, as if unsure.

"Nothar wishes to speak with him," I tried, glancing between the two.

"And he told you this?" he asked, turning his questioning eyes to me.

I straightened, pulling myself up to my full height, still a head shorter than both of them, but it helped empower me, as if I had a right to use this tone with him. "Priest Falon, I am weary. Do not question my actions, or those of my Valahant. We will dress and expect the ritual to be ready as soon as possible." I lifted my chin, holding his mildly amused gaze, watching his smile grow.

"You have courage, Princess."

Something twinkled in his eye, and I couldn't place if it was admiration or irritation.

"Please, dress." He dipped into a small bow, eyes trained on me. "The ritual is ready when you are." With a parting, unreadable smile, he took his leave.

"*Blade and Blood?!*" I hissed.

"What? You worried?" he taunted, his shoulders dropping as we were once again left in the privacy of each other's company.

"If something happens to you–"

"Togamar said I should seek Nothar. That's what we're doing."

"Couldn't you just say a prayer? Light a candle? Thrice-curse it all—I would settle for an animal sacrifice at this point." I snatched a robe out of his hand and held it up, checking the size.

"Oh, she cares!" Sarcasm dripped from his tone.

"Ugh!" I hurled the garment at him, then snatched the smaller one.

"Truly, Elspeth," Sainte chuckled, "we are in Nothar's temple, the Father of Wynterborne, Highest of Godkind. Do you think if he meant us ill will, he would wait until a ritual?"

"I don't pretend to know the minds of the divine," I huffed, fumbling behind my back to loosen the laces of my dress. "What exactly does this entail?" I demanded, glaring.

"It's nothing, Ellie."

The laces snapped as I stepped forward, clutching my chest to keep the fabric in place. My fury reflected in his open smile of amusement.

"Don't you *Ellie* me!" I hissed. "You probably think the scars on your back, from years of flogging, mean nothing, too! Well, you are my Valahant now," I poked his shoulder, "and I have a say in what happens to you!"

He arched a brow, his head tilting in warning—or perhaps daring me to go on.

"You're *mine*, Sainte. You don't get to make choices concerning *this*," I gestured over his body, "without laying out all the details."

He caught my hand, careful to avoid the angry red mark of Togamar. He yanked me against him, my palm pressed to his chest, forcing me to clutch the fabric tighter.

"The vows go both ways, *Princess*." His tone took on a dangerous edge, his face a breath from mine. "I have a say in how to best protect you, even if it costs me."

My glare darkened. "And if I refuse?"

"You don't get to."

I slapped him.

My dress fell to my waist, and his head snapped to the side, the imprint of my fingers reddening his cheek. Angry breaths heaved from my bare chest, furious at his assumption that I had no say in what he did. This bond was meant to unite us, not force secret choices upon each other.

What good was being a princess if I couldn't protect the people closest to me?

He turned back to face me at an infuriatingly slow rate, his eyes burning with rage, nostrils flaring. I struggled to pull the dress up over my chest, tugging against his iron grip.

I failed.

He opened his mouth to speak, but a knock silenced him.

"Is all well, Princess? We heard shouting," a voice called out.

Sainte's barely contained fury met mine.

"Should I let them know you're about to kill me?" I hissed through clenched teeth.

He exhaled through his nose, his features a visual representation of controlled rage. His grip, however, spoke volumes. He was anything but calm.

"Tell them we'll be out shortly."

"Promise me you won't hurt yourself," I demanded, my whisper harsh.

"Elspeth." He groaned my name as if pleading with not only me but his own sanity.

"Princess?!" The voice grew more urgent.

"Promise me!"

"Gods, Ellie. It's a simple cut on the–"

The door burst open, and Sainte moved in an instant, spinning me to face the fire. His hand darted behind him, the hum of metal against wood ringing out. A twitch tightened his jaw as he closed his eyes. I craned my head, peeking past his arm as he pulled me close, my bare chest pressing against his damp tunic.

An apprentice in light blue robes stood frozen, the door ajar enough to reveal his shocked expression. A dagger quivered in the frame, mere inches from his face.

"We're fine," I said, flashing him a smile.

"I... I–"

"The Princess of Wynterborne answered you, boy," Sainte snapped.

I smiled at the underside of his chin as he glared at the wall above my head.

"Right then." The man swallowed nervously, then eased the door shut.

Sainte let me loose as if I burned him, then spun away. Guilt mingled with my anger. I shouldn't have lashed out, yet it felt justified. Why was I always powerless when I was meant to be a princess? People used my title for their own ends.

"They will cut my palm with a ceremonial dagger," he said, voice low.

My lips pressed together, and I hurried into the robe. Sainte did the same, not speaking or glancing my way to check if I respected his modesty... which

I did once he removed his tunic. Silence enveloped us. He secured his belt and retrieved his dagger from the frame, sliding it into his sheath.

"I'm coming," I stated, crossing my arms over my chest.

"I never doubted it."

We traversed the quiet, dim corridors, where hushed voices and scarce lighting created an atmosphere akin to a dungeon. As we delved deeper into the temple, the lanterns on the walls became more sparse, forcing me to squint in the darkness.

I followed Sainte's bulky figure as he strode behind the young priest. He was brooding and angry, and I didn't like it. I was accustomed to his unwavering support, even when he disagreed with me. Now, his frustration was palpable, leaving a bitter taste in my mouth.

Not without reason.

I did slap him.

I lowered my head to hide the smirk spreading across my lips. Perhaps I wasn't as remorseful as I pretended. Asserting my independence felt empowering, despite the consequences. Did I regret slapping him...

Minutely.

He bore physical pain on my behalf, suffering years of floggings and countless beatings, enduring my brother's wrath. He shielded me with his body. I reached my limit.

I cared for him.

Not that I would tell him that.

It pained me to see him suffer for my sake, even if it was his duty. I resolved to spare him every possible ounce of misery.

Falon claimed Nothar wouldn't respond to Sainte's blood...

I glanced up at his broad shoulders, a mischievous grin forming on my lips. As if catching onto my scheme, he peered over his shoulder. I masked my expression with an innocent smile, fluttering my lashes. His mouth curved downward in an endearing manner before his attention focused ahead.

The priest guided us into a vast chamber, its illumination as dim as the corridor we traversed. A fire at its heart cast shadows across the stone walls, adding to the room's rustic allure. I glanced upward, marveling at the sloped ceiling, wondering about the skilled hands that fashioned this space. The fiery burn of coals within the center outshone the four lanterns' feeble glow.

Falon stood on the opposite end, bearing a small dagger resting upon a white cushion, its silver blade catching what little light there was. His demeanor had shifted, his smile replaced by a solemn expression in respect for the ritual about to take place.

"Come, kneel, Sainte Nytestorm," he said.

I followed tight on his heels, and his shoulders tensed as he realized I trailed him, but he refrained from rebuking me in front of Nothar's priest.

Falon's gaze flicked toward me, signaling for Sainte to halt by the expansive fire pit. I responded with a slight nod as he lowered himself to his knees, facing the radiant embers. The coals stirred with his movement, their dance catching my attention as they seemed to pulse with an eerie life of their own.

Falon approached with small careful strides, and I stepped forward, holding my hand out. Sainte's cool stare practically burned into me as the priest dipped into a bow and offered the pillow.

Ignoring my Valahant's fury, I picked up the dagger. Its weight surprised me—solid steel adorned with an engraving that depicted wolves in pursuit of a stag. The gemstone eyes of the creatures glinted vividly, while red rubies trailed from the stag's wound, leaving a trail for the beasts to follow.

The blade's brutality was evident, its glint reflecting the ember's light. Despite its short length, about a hand and a half, its sharpness was unmistakable. I knew I had to be cautious to avoid cutting too deep.

Without hesitation, I jerked the naked blade across my left palm. Blood welled up, surprising me with the rush before any discomfort set in. As the pain intensified, I hissed, dropping the bloody dagger to the pillow and turning my attention to the fire and Sainte. He made no move to assist me, his expression a mask of indifference that overlaid the swirling irritation in his eyes.

"Spill your blood into the flames," Falon said, voice soft, yet commanding. "Let it consume your mortality, leaving only Nothar's divinity to shine through."

I approached, extending my fist over the embers, letting a flood of crimson spill out. The coals hissed and spat, before a sudden roar of flames burst out. I jerked back before the flare could scorch my skin.

"Stand behind your Valahant. Lean on him, as he is your support."

Nervous, I licked my lips and moved over Sainte's legs, positioning myself with my feet on either side of his calves, then placed my hands on his broad shoulders. I winced as my open wound protested against the fabric beneath my palm. Both my wrist, marked by Togamar, and now this cut by Nothar's dagger, stung with each movement.

At this rate, I feared I might run out of limbs before my duel with Adastrus even began

"Repeat after me," Falon commanded.

My gaze shifted from the top of Sainte's head to the flames, which greedily consumed my blood, its heat cracking and flickering in the pit.

"Nothar, the Most High, Father of Wynter and King of Godkind. I, Sainte Nytestorm, Valahant to Elspeth, Second Born of Veiled King Vardis, call you from the Hunt."

He echoed the words, his voice deep and resonant. With each breath, his shoulders rose and fell, and crimson stained the fabric beneath my touch.

"I seek the face of our father. I ask that the King of Gods receive the plea of his own blood across the Veil. Hear me. Answer me," Sainte concluded, his voice carrying a weight of determination.

The fire died.

The flames didn't just fade; they winked out of existence with a pop, leaving the embers black and cold. The sudden darkness and chill sent a shiver through me, and I looked to Falon, whose figure was now a silhouette against the lantern-lit wall.

"Don't move, Princess," he said.

Sainte stiffened, his shoulder muscles tensing like a rock beneath my touch. I heard his sharp intake of breath.

"If you remove your hands, you will sever his connection."

I tightened my grip, hoping he could feel my presence wherever he was.

Togamar told me Nothar *wanted* to see him.

Nothing would happen...

He grunted and pitched forward slightly, as if struck, and I held onto him tighter, ignoring the pain in my hand.

Surely the gods would not beat him as well.

"He is beyond the Veil, whether Nothar has answered him, or another. If you sever the connection, his body and soul will be torn in two."

He trembled beneath me, and doubts crept into my mind about the wisdom of this course of action.

"Togamar sent us here," I whispered.

His muscles were taut, and with a low groan, he fell forward, catching himself with his palms. I leaned with him, maintaining my hold.

"Why would Nothar...?" Concern choked my throat. "How do I pull him out?!"

"You cannot." The priest's face was shrouded in shadow. "He may only return when he is sent back."

I cursed, adjusting my position.

"*If* he is sent back."

I bared my teeth in a silent snarl. No one would take him from me. He suffered too much for my sake for anyone, even a god to deny me him.

"Nothar," I whispered. "Father, hear my voice. King of Godkind, Founder of the North, heed my call."

An unearthly wind swept through the room, extinguishing the lanterns' light and plunging us into darkness. Panic swelled within me as I gripped my Valahant so hard my hands ached.

"Protect him."

Sainte gasped as his breath returned, and I pressed against his shoulder, embracing him as he panted. Shivers wracked his body, and I clenched my jaw, anxious about what I couldn't see or hear.

We sat like that for what seemed an eternity, my own limbs starting to tremble and shake from holding the awkward position. Sainte eventually stilled, his breathing evened out, and his muscles relaxed. I focused on just keeping my hands from moving.

The room was cold and dark, and I didn't hear anyone move—not Falon or the young priest. No light illuminated the space from the hallway, indicating they were still with us.

Sainte sucked in a quick breath and grunted, drawing away a fraction. I gripped his robe, trying to stay with him.

"Elspeth."

Relief swept through me at the sound of his rough voice.

I shifted, moving in front of him, wrapping my trembling arms around him. He sat back, pulling me with him and settling me against his chest.

"Don't ever do that again," I ordered, pressing my forehead into the curve of his neck.

His chin dropped to rest on top of my head. "I would never leave you, Princess."

"Never?" I pressed.

"Never."

CHAPTER 30

T he next morning brought my friends' departure. Only a single tear tracked down my cheek. I hated goodbyes. I was lousy at them. It was far better to part ways with a wave than to force words to express feelings.

Lyana was a shell of her former self, but she was functioning under her brother's care. I ensured they had enough coin to settle in a real home and fill their bellies, then wished them Niena's luck in picking pockets.

I reserved my tears for when I retired to my rooms, in the privacy of my sleeping chambers. Sainte held me as I sobbed, abandoning the pretense of strength. He knew my weaknesses, and I needed him to accept me as I was.

Human. Flawed. Lonely.

Besides my Valahant, I felt truly alone in this castle. Anderz remained an enigma, his motives for wanting me on the throne unclear. Leihim pursued his own desires. Lyana and Ethyan were the only ones who loved me for myself. Everyone else had an agenda, some plot to either see me crowned or killed.

Which was still a possibility.

"Up."

I moaned, burrowing deeper into the blankets.

"Come," Sainte urged again, pushing off the bed.

I groaned in protest as he rummaged through a chest near his cot. My head felt fuzzy, and my nose throbbed. My eyes, swollen and burning from tears, didn't want to face any more pain. Wasn't saying goodbye to friends enough for one day?

He hadn't shared much about what happened to him during the ritual. He only mentioned that Nothar wasn't the god who welcomed him across the Veil, but assured me of his blessing. Then he clammed up, refusing to disclose more. I took it as a warning to be cautious when seeking the gods.

Even Togamar warned they were not all in agreement. If some were actively helping me, I had to assume that others worked against me. I hadn't considered that before I sent Sainte across the Veil, and guilt reared its ugly head for not going myself.

"Ellie, if you don't get out of bed…"

I propped myself on my elbows and arched a brow, daring him to finish.

He pointed a sheathed dagger at me, then when he took in my sullen expression, he let out a heavy sigh. "Come, I will teach you to fight."

Curious, I shoved myself upright, tilting my head. "You think I have a chance?"

"No," he said, tone flat. "But—while Anderz and the Wolf search for the God Stones, you should at least prepare for the worst. Up."

I doubted Sainte could teach me to defend myself against a man who practiced with a blade every day for years. Just my luck that my conceited brother didn't get lazy with his dueling skills.

With a scoff, I kicked the blankets off, then threw my legs over the edge. "You should have asked Nothar where they were," I grumbled, swaying as I stood.

Sainte grunted and handed me the dagger as I walked past him to my receiving room. It was the most spacious place in my chambers to spar, and we were trying to keep our heads down, avoid wandering about. There was less chance of Adastrus bothering himself to come to my rooms than if he happened upon me roaming the halls.

"A game," he said, moving chairs against the wall.

I rubbed at my puffy eyes. "Oh, I like games."

Not that I would win anything that involved blades. I wasn't terribly competitive, but I was always a willing participant.

"As I expected."

He grunted as he shoved the table to clear more space. His movements were stiff and sore from the past few days. This morning, he stretched in ways that made my mind wander to forbidden places, but each motion came with a grimace when he moved too quickly.

"Adastrus uses a blade. His is longer than this, but it's close enough." He unbuckled his belt and slid off a single long, thin dagger, still in its sheath.

I examined the one he'd given me and tried to remove it from the leather hide, but it snagged on some twine tied to secure it in place.

He smirked at my efforts, then retrieved another piece of twine from his pocket, tying it around the hilt. "I'd rather not shed any more blood, if you don't mind."

"For once, we agree," I huffed.

"You're familiar with a dagger?"

"I grew up with them."

I flipped the weapon in the air, catching it with ease. The sheath added an odd weight, but it was still more familiar than a sword or anything else they might shove into my fist.

As the challenged, I couldn't choose the weapons, but I could set the date. It would be held at the castle's armory, where there was a stage for duels. The room could hold a large group of witnesses and offered the benefit of being indoors. I'd have to ignore the bloodstains on the floor, grim reminders of my impending doom.

"I would rather have you in trousers–"

"Would you now?" I taunted, kicking my skirts to free some space around my legs.

His mouth snapped into a frown. "Aye, you're used to fighting in them."

"Alas, 'tis not appropriate for a lady of the court to wear men's clothing."

"No."

"Just as kicking him in the sack will probably be inappropriate as well."

"There are rules to the rite, Elspeth."

"And here I thought the most important one was: Don't die."

He sighed, then came closer, pointing his long dagger at me for emphasis. "That's your main priority," he agreed. "But remember, people will be watching—nobles, dignitaries, ambassadors. If you win by sleight of hand or by *cheating*, you'll have to bear that burden."

"Better that than death. Do you think Adastrus plays fair? He clearly hasn't thus far."

"In his mind, he's already won. Now he plays his political game. Let him," he said. "Enough. Ready yourself."

"Can I kick you in the sack?" I snorted, readying my stance as I braced my weapon.

His eyes flitted over my form with a frown. "If you try, you will regret it."

I laughed, and he lunged.

I yelped as he moved quicker than I expected for a sore warrior, and threw my arm out to block his attack. The sheath of his dagger smarted against my hand as I ducked under his blow.

He backed away, shaking his head. "Tell me why you cut yourself during the Ritual of Blade and Blood."

I jerked with subtle surprise. "Is that the game?"

That could make things interesting, though if I ever landed a strike, I doubted he'd grant me a chance to ask anything—and I had a great many questions for him.

"Aye. For every hit you land, I'll give you an answer." He wriggled his eyebrows in a rare, playful manner. "I would wager you have one or two."

My grin widened. I braced my feet once again, wagging my fingers to beckon him, then shrugged. "I didn't want you to hurt yourself anymore."

"Care for me a bit much?" he asked, stalking closer.

With a haughty smirk, I winked. "You'll have to land another blow for that answer."

He took a quick step forward, his strike obvious, and I danced aside, throwing out to parry. He moved with me, grabbing my weapon arm. I spun against him, slamming my head into his chest, then my heel down on his toes. He grunted, and I threw my elbow into his gut, then jerked free of his hold. With a fierce spin, I whipped around, slapping his face with my braid, and raised my dagger to his throat.

"Not bad," he wheezed.

My triumphant grin was bold and bright, but he smirked, and a soft tap pressed into my ribs.

"I landed first."

"I let you."

"Ha!"

I shuffled back a few steps, needing distance to form my question. He lowered his weapon and dropped his arms to his sides, rolling his shoulders as he waited.

"Have you ever loved anyone?"

His impish smirk faltered, as if hiding a flinch. "Loved?"

"Yes." I kept my playful mask in place, hoping he wouldn't notice how much his answer meant to me. "You know, love? That fluttery feeling in your heart?"

"There are many kinds," he drawled, arching an eyebrow in silent challenge.

He was making this far more awkward than it needed to be.

"You know what I mean," I huffed.

"Yes."

I blinked at his sudden, curt answer, my smile slipping. "A girl?"

He tsked his tongue against his teeth, then readied his stance. "That's not how the game works, Ellie."

"Well, then come at me, Sainte."

He shrugged, his shoulders flexing as he rolled them, muscles tightening beneath his tunic. I drew in a deep breath, focusing on his movements, aiming to immerse myself in the fight. Any previous scuffles I'd been in were frantic and confined, never paced with calm assessment.

My brow furrowed as he moved with deliberate intent. Sidestepping, I aimed a slash at his exposed midsection, but he retaliated with lightning speed. He deflected my attack and seized my arms, drawing me close. A sharp hiss escaped me as his dagger found its mark, grazing my side.

"Have you ever loved a boy?"

I gazed into his cool, inquisitive eyes and returned a smirk. "Boy?" I scoffed. "No."

He emitted a curious hum before releasing me. I spun away, needing a moment of space. With a shaky breath, I mustered a cocky grin before facing him again.

"Girl?" he asked.

My head flew back with a bark of laughter, then I wagged my dagger. "That's not how the game works," I mocked.

His lips pressed together with a nod of understanding. He would wait until the next–

He charged with a quiet grunt, and I gasped as he snatched my wrists, shoving me against the table, pinning my weapon to its top. His grin was wolfish and predatorial as he loomed over me, hips pressed hard against mine.

"I thought we were playing with daggers!" I snarled, struggling to free my hands.

He scoffed, a mirthful, throaty sound as he yanked my dagger from my fist and tossed it aside, then tapped his own against the hollow of my throat.

"So, girl?"

"No," I hissed.

"Never loved then, eh? Never gave your heart away to have someone mistreat it—leave it shattered in pieces?"

"Oh no, I didn't say that."

My lip curled in a snarl. He found this amusing. He got all the answers he wanted while I was left wanting.

"You want to know?" I asked.

Something flickered in his eyes, hungry and dangerous.

"I loved a man once—dreamed of him every long, lonely night. I lay on that cot, surrounded by kids who hated me, with a woman in the next room who saw me as a burden—and all I cared about, all I thought about, was him."

He blew out a breath, and a flicker of some strange emotion danced across his features. Was that jealousy?

"And you claimed to have only kissed a few boys."

"Oh, I did far more in my sleep."

A muscle ticked in his jaw. All playfulness melted from his expression, his teeth bared in a grimace.

"Do you want to know, Sainte?" My tone dropped to a raspy whisper, a wicked smirk lifting my cheek. "What we did in my dreams?"

"I'm sure you'll spare me."

My barked laugh was bitter. He started this conversation. I would not let him get me riled just to walk away from it. I was done with him playing with my feelings. In a few days, I would meet my end. I didn't have anything to lose.

"Oh, no—I wouldn't. I would tell you everything he did in great detail. Every touch, every *lick* that burned me with pleasure—"

His breath came fast and his hand tightened over mine. I snatched it away and shoved his chest, though he didn't back off.

"—everything I did to him."

"Who," he growled. Anger seeped from him like venom, slow and insidious, as he leaned close to intimidate me. "Name him."

"You."

He jerked as if slapped, his grimace melting into a frown.

"It was you, Sainte. I loved you. Always have. There's never been anyone else. Every boy I kissed, that I let *touch* me—I was looking for you."

He clenched his jaw as his eyes danced between mine, searching for a hint of deceit.

"No one ever lived up to the feeling you gave me when I dreamt of you."

He choked out a bitter laugh. My smile sweetened, my anger and hurt fading, giving way to something dangerous. He hadn't pulled away. Still pinned, his hips pressed to mine and I resisted the urge to move against him, to give in to that need burning low in my belly.

"Your turn, Valahant." My palm rested at the center of his chest, feeling his steady pulse beneath my touch. "Who has won your heart?"

He shuddered, then his guard snapped in place. Funny how when we talked about *me,* he was an open book of bright green jealousy, but when it came to *him*—he shut me out.

"She did not win it." He closed his eyes as if in pain—as if the words were being torn from his throat. "She didn't have to."

My heart raced.

Me.

Let it be me.

"What's the lucky girl's name?" I whispered, my touch trailing to his warm cheek.

His brows drew tight, and he groaned, turning to press his lips against my palm. He loosed a long sigh, then met my gaze, holding it as if it anchored him.

"Elspeth."

My breath caught, frigid and burning all at once, as my heart pounded a chaotic beat against my ribs. I could barely breathe, barely think. "Me?"

"Only you."

His hands slid to my hips, fingertips grazing my backside, searing me through my dress. His grip was a claim—I was his, and he was mine.

I wasn't wrong.

He wanted me—loved me.

My fingers threaded through the short hair at the nape of his neck, pulling his face close. His grip tightened, eyes flicking to my lips.

This was nothing like the boys I kissed.

This was Sainte. Strong, steady, loyal. With him, I had nothing to lose. He knew me at my worst and my best. And yet—because I loved him, cared for him, this was beyond nerve-wracking. I couldn't mess this up.

He halted a breath from my lips, tensing as his teeth ground tight. What he battled with, I didn't know. In my experience, every other man would gladly take a woman thrown at them...

But Sainte wasn't just any man.

"Kiss me."

Anxiety widened his gaze, despite his cocky grin. "And if I don't live up to your dreams?"

His breath brushed against my lips, and heat coiled and bloomed as butterflies took me by storm.

"You wouldn't have to try hard," I whispered.

"And if I was saving this for my wife?" He ducked close, speaking against the corner of my mouth.

I sucked in a sharp breath and dug my fingers into his neck, letting him feel my need. "Then marry me."

I doubted he would have frozen any faster if I had stabbed him in the heart. He pulled away, and a quiet ache settled deep at the loss.

"Don't say that." A rough edge, full of hunger, consumed his tone.

"There will never be anyone else." I tugged at him, desperate to pull him back to me.

He remained stiff and resolute, features set into a stern frown. "You're a princess." His voice cracked as he stepped away, hands falling to his sides as if he woke from a dream.

"I've always been one." I fought to keep my words steady as he freed me from the table in every way I didn't want. "Nothing has changed."

With a staggered breath, he turned, shaking his head. "Elspeth, you're a princess. You'll get betrothed to some heir or king out there, forging alliances."

"No, Sainte. My brother will kill me soon," I spat. "I'm not going to marry anyone! I have a few fleeting days to live out my pleasures and desires before I cross the Veil, never to know a husband, let alone a man."

He turned on his heel, his face set into a mask I didn't recognize. "And if you live? If you rise to the throne? I'm only your Valahant, Ellie."

He ran a hand through his dark hair, giving it a tug as if the minor pain would ground him.

"I would give you everything." He closed his eyes as if he couldn't believe his words. "Anything, but you don't know what you're asking."

My breathless laughter drew his gaze back to mine. My fists propped onto my hips, missing the heat of his touch there. "You think I could wed anyone else? You must be a fool. I'm full of dreams and delusions—such as marrying for love. I would *never* marry for an alliance, Sainte."

"You will be queen. Your marriage is a weapon, a shield." His voice pitched higher. "You want me. I would please you. But for gods' sake, Ellie, don't brandish marriage about like it's worthless."

A subtle, quiet realization whispered in my heart.

Sainte would never take this lightly. The notion was instilled and embedded so deep within him. Men typically didn't remain chaste until their wedding night, unlike women who had to out of necessity or else they might bear a bastard child.

But a man?

They could walk off with no remorse, no responsibility.

Men never waited—but he did. He offered his body to me after waiting for so long, promising himself to his future wife, holding himself to that standard. He was willing to throw it away for me—while in the same breath, berating me to raise my standards.

Sainte didn't think himself worthy of marrying me, and yet there was no one else. Not a soul in this world could measure up. He was the only person who *was* worthy.

He offered me his virtue in exchange for me not wasting a marriage of value.

As if his virtue had no value to anyone besides him.

I would show him, prove his worth.

And yet...

When I failed the Rite of Combat, I would die, and so would he. We would never share that passion with one another.

A heavy ache settled over my heart. I couldn't look at him, couldn't watch his face as I refused his offer.

"No," I growled, turning my back on him. "I won't accept you without marriage."

"Elspeth–"

"I make a wager," I snapped, braving his stare. "I am slated for death. If, by some divine miracle, I survive, I ask for your hand."

Slow shock slackened the anger on his features. "You're foolish," he breathed.

"So is everyone in love." A sad smile lifted my lips.

"You could command me."

"To lay with me? Wed me? To command you would be to rob those things of their meaning," I scoffed. "You talk of *my* marriage as if it is the only thing that bears significance. Well, that's a lie. Your choices have value, Sainte." I took two hurried steps to his chest and settled my palm on his cheek before he could pull away. "Choose me."

His eyes snapped shut, as if in protest of his internal struggle.

"If I survive the rite," I whispered, "choose me."

CHAPTER 31

I strode through the Hall of Feasts with my chin held high, eyes locked on my brother. Conversations fell silent as I wove between tables. He turned from speaking with a woman in red and black robes, his gaze snagging on me, a vicious smile spreading across his face.

"Dear sister!" he roared. "Finally shrugging off your shame to join those truly favored by the gods?"

My mouth quirked into a sly grin. He didn't know I had the Dire Wolf searching for the *real* God Stones, and if anyone in Wynterborne could find them, it was her.

"To dine with a pack of wolves in the Great Icelands would be preferable to your company," I mused, climbing the few steps to his table's raised platform. "I've decided on the date."

"It can't be soon enough." He spoke through his white-toothed grin, peridot eyes glinting with twisted amusement.

"Eager to be rid of me?"

"Eager to see Wynterborne with a crowned king. 'Tis long overdue, little sister."

"You do mean monarch, brother?"

I plucked a grape from his plate. His brows dipped, his glare tracking my movement. Unfazed by his attempt at intimidation, I leaned my hip against the table, blocking his view of the woman.

"Surely you wouldn't want to put words in the mouths of the divine." I lifted a single brow. "There's still a chance I could win."

Anderz advised me to keep him busy, his mind focused on the rite while the Dire Wolf conducted her search. So that's what I intended to do.

"You?" He scowled, shoving his plate away. "Tell me, while living in the arsecrack of the world, did you receive any formal training?"

The woman snickered, but I ignored her. She wasn't my target.

"And you've, what? Practiced with that fancy sword of yours?" I leaned in close to his sneer, lowering my tone. "I lived in the slums, Adastrus. That *arsecrack* taught me to fight for every scrap of bread, while your *formal trainers* praised your blows to a wooden post," I scoffed, then eased away, grateful for the distance.

Just being near him violated my soul. Evil rolled off him like a stench from a pig.

"You know nothing of the gods' plans," I mocked. "Perhaps I will emerge victorious, not you."

His blackened fingertips tapped against the tabletop with such force, I wondered if they'd crack—his calm, careless demeanor shattered.

"When?" he snapped.

I sighed as if explaining something to a child, then lifted my chin to address the quiet room. "In three days, the Rite of Combat commences! The gods shall reveal their favored, and the defeated pay with their life. Wynterborne will have her monarch, be it king or queen, and they are to rule without question!"

I turned back to Adastrus, lifting his wineglass in a toast. "To the death, big brother. To the death."

The next days passed in a blur of relentless training. From dawn until exhaustion claimed me, Sainte's grueling pace never let up. His frown deepened, and his mood darkened with each hour no news of the God Stones came.

They were my only hope of avoiding this fight. If we retrieved them from Adastrus' hiding place, I could prove my favor with the gods, and the rite would dissolve as if it were nothing more than a bad dream.

Yet that moment lingered out of reach.

My body ached from endless hours of sparring with Sainte, wrestling him with dagger against dagger. Each defeat ached like a personal failure. He taught me the simplest blocks, but I remained at a severe disadvantage. Adastrus, with his greater size and strength, wielded a shortsword that outmatched my reach. Despite my bravado in the dining hall, he was more skilled than I was. Anderz's advice to keep my brother focused on our fight worked, as he spent his days training as intensely as I did.

It wouldn't matter now. Without those stones, he'd kill me.

The morning of the rite dawned, and a sinking feeling settled in my gut. I rose to meet Anderz for breakfast, but the sight of food turned my stomach. He shook his head.

The God Stones remained lost.

I sat at my table, eyes closed, heart shattering into a thousand pieces. All this effort, wasted. Sainte hid me away for most of my life, and for what? I endured hunger, neglect, lived in squalor, only to face an early death.

At least my friends were well on their way back to Landing's End, beyond my brother's reach. He couldn't harm them there.

Fragments of conversations from the high court echoed in my mind. Adastrus was closing the borders, preparing for something ominous—it felt like war.

My friend's safety might be fleeting.

My gaze drifted across the room, finding Sainte against the wall, arms crossed. His eyes, darkened with shadows, stared into the distance, unseeing. He moved his jaw, teeth grinding, lost in his thoughts.

His life would be sacrificed.

As tradition dictated, when I died, he would take a blade to the heart, following me across the Veil... and I could do nothing to stop it.

Regret washed over me. I chose Sainte as my Valahant, binding him to a fate he didn't deserve. He shouldn't have to die for me. An overwhelming urge to tell him to run surged within, but I knew he wouldn't.

Taking a deep breath, I turned to Anderz and forced a smile. "Pardon me, Counselor Dyre, I have a rite to prepare for."

Anderz's golden gaze softened as he sighed, shaking his head before pushing from the table. "We've done all we can," he said, placing a warm hand on my shoulder. "You've surpassed every expectation."

I closed my eyes, his words feeling like a farewell.

"Wynterborne will remember you." He squeezed lightly, then stepped away.

I waited until his footsteps faded and the door whispered shut before glaring at the table, blinking back the threatening sting of tears. My heart shattered further with each beat. There were no more rites, no gods to invoke, no time to seek magical stones or plot a coup.

This marked the end of my story.

Historians would note the brief life of Wynterborne's Lost Princess, ending with her brother clutching her head in front of an adoring crowd. Adastrus, firstborn to Veiled King Vardis, would have many years recorded—years that would see the downfall of Wynterborne. I felt the truth of that deep within my bones.

How could Togamar and Nothar let this happen? Nellium? Was it my fault? Had my disbelief kept them at bay? Would they punish an entire people for one person's faulty faith?

"This is it, then?" I asked, voice cracking with emotion, a rogue tear slipping down my cheek.

"It has come to this," Sainte rumbled, his eyes closing in silent pain. He rose, pushing himself off the wall and walked over to me, resting his hand on my shoulder.

"No hope of running now?" I half-sobbed, half-laughed.

He ground his teeth, shook his head, and wiped away the tear with his thumb. "For what it is worth... I'm sorry."

"It's not your–"

He silenced me with a finger over my lips. "I brought you here. This is my doing, Ellie." His voice grew raspy, and he cleared his throat. "I am truly sorry."

My smile wavered, and I pulled away from his stare, focusing on the table. Sometimes words weren't needed. Assurances that didn't ease the pain only added weight. This was one of those times.

Sainte was dying inside, convinced he led me to my demise. I harbored no blame toward him. Until now, we had a chance. He fought to shield me and salvage a realm—a daunting task for a lone recruiter. My hand found his, resting atop it, a brief respite from the impending storm—one last moment in this sanctuary from prying eyes and intrusive whispers. Ahead was only my death, a spectacle for the masses to witness.

A knock sounded, a disturbance I longed to disregard. Yet Sainte's hand squeezed my shoulder as I waited too long, the fleeting peace slipping through our fingers.

"Come in," I called, voice thick with reluctance.

The door creaked open, revealing two maidservants, the same who helped dress me day after day. Alongside them was Floria, the master seamstress who had made every one of my exquisite gowns. She offered a sympathetic smile, then dipped into a curtsy as she entered.

"Shall we prepare you, Your Highness?" she asked.

With a steadying breath, I pushed to my feet. Sainte's touch slipped away from my shoulder, leaving an ache in my chest that defied explanation. My heart urged me to turn back, to grasp his hand, to flee this fate and seek refuge anywhere but here. It demanded defiance, a refusal to accept what lay ahead—to forge my own path.

Yet, my mind countered with the inevitability of this moment. I was meant to confront my end, not evade it, only to be caught unaware later. No, I would face my fears head-on, embracing my fate like the princess I was.

"I'm ready."

The attire surpassed all expectations, a true masterpiece. Though classified as a dress, it defied convention. Black trousers hugged my legs, while the full skirt danced between them with every stride. Its length, reaching mid-calf, featured elongated points at the hem, enhancing its fluidity and grace with each sway.

The snug top embraced my form, wrapping around my torso and chest, secured by laces that ascended to the neckline. Despite the high collar, its thinness made it feel more like a second skin than a constriction.

The ensemble was entirely black, adorned with peridots along the bodice that accentuated the hue of my irises. They braided and pinned my hair, ensuring no strays would disrupt my vision.

Not that the fight would be a prolonged affair.

With every step, I held my chin high, matching the confident stride of my black boots as they echoed through the corridor toward the training chambers.

Around me, servants bustled, adorning the throne room with flowers and tapestries, a flurry of preparation for the impending coronation. Their curious gazes brushed past me, likely etching the sight of the Lost Princess walking toward her fate into their memories. This would be the talk of Wynterborne for generations to come. The very least I could do was muster every ounce of pride to carry me forward, even as I approached what seemed like my doom.

My dagger hung from the thick belt around my hip, a sleek ebony blade suspended in a silver sheath. Engraved on its hilt was a scene of a wild cat's hunt for a boar. It fit my palm perfectly, its weight and balance were everything I could wish for.

As we neared the guards' wing, our pace slowed, and a chill crept over my palms, damp with cold sweat.

This was it.

Sainte strode ahead, bracing his arms against the massive wooden doors, straining as he pushed them inward with a low groan, throwing them wide open.

The room teemed with people. A vast expanse of polished floorboards encircled by tier upon tier of seats ascending higher to ensure an unobstructed view for every spectator. Not a single seat remained unoccupied.

Dread hit me like a hammer to my chest as Sainte moved aside, unveiling Adastrus, awaiting my entrance.

My brother stood tall, clad in a sleek black overcoat and matching trousers adorned with sparkling garnets that shimmered under the soft overcast light seeping through the windows. I approached despite the trembling in my knees, knowing there was no escape now.

Adastrus sported a thin, menacing shortsword at his hip, its gleaming blade exposed and secured only by a strap of black leather tethered to his belt. It was a lethal weapon, poised to strike at the slightest provocation. His hair cascaded in its usual style, long down the center and closely shaved at the sides, framing his face like a wild stallion's mane, a blend of majesty and menace. His piercing eyes locked onto mine, a malevolent grin stretching across his cheeks, baring his white, predatory teeth.

Beside him stood a priest adorned in red and black robes, bearing a symbol of a dragon, one I didn't recognize. Was that the god who answered the regent? A deity who thought me weak and unworthy to rule?

I strode into the middle of the arena, my posture tall but unable to conceal the quivers that raced through me. His grin seemed to widen, fueled by my visible fear.

Sainte, my loyal Valahant, didn't follow. I gritted my teeth against the blow that landed on my battered heart.

"Sister," Adastrus called in a sing-song voice.

"Adastrus."

I refused to acknowledge him as my blood. Not anymore. He represented my death, and kin would never hurt each other. Lyana and Ethyan were my true family.

Sainte was my family.

Solitude stabbed like a knife, realizing none of them could stand with me at my end. With my Valahant lost in the throng, poised to journey past the Veil after me, I had to face this alone.

"I've challenged you to the Rite of Combat, and you have answered."

"I have."

"Any last words?" His sneer cut through the air. The distance offered some safety yet left me exposed, his glare sparking with malice.

"I only request that High God Nothar protect his people when I pass through the Veil."

He barked a mocking laugh, lifting his chin with wild fervor. "Not so cocky now?" he taunted, then addressed the crowd. "Elspeth, my sister, Second Born of my father, King Vardis, ran away from her home," he declared, voice carrying regal authority. "She fled from *you*, her own people, and hid! Why? No one knows." His gaze shifted to me, daring me to refute. "She abandoned you, left you to the cold of winter's grip. Yet, I stayed. I weathered your darkest years!"

Darkest only because he was the storm cloud.

"I was here for you when Winter's Bite ravaged our populace. I was here when the south threatened war. I was here when the men from the east came to try to claim our oil mines—I was here for you when she was basking in the sun at Tilamuik's ports.

"At the final minute of the last day, just as I was about to ascend to my rightful place, she shows up, demanding the Rites of the Gods. She ripped your king from your grasp, stringing you along with her royal privileges. People of Wynterborne, I offer you myself. I will rule for you, wield what is given to me, reclaim the throne, and make this kingdom a nation to be feared and respected once more!"

That sounded a lot like the speech of a warmonger.

"I will save Wynterborne from the delusions of a child." He whipped toward me, hair slapping against his face, giving him the look of a madman. "May the gods have mercy on your soul."

I lifted my chin, a silent snarl curling my lip. Drawing my dagger, a sudden calmness spread over me. Adastrus' grin widened as he unsheathed his blade. I eyed its length, longer than my arm, yet small and deadly in his grip. He spun it with an air of confidence, his dead fingers not hindering his movements. He savored each step, pacing with deliberate strides, extending his victory. His feet moved without thought, crossing as he sidled around me.

With my lips pressed tight, I clutched my dagger, readying myself.

I accepted my death, and I'd face it head-on.

He jerked, feigning a step, and I braced myself, flinching. He snickered, raising a mocking eyebrow.

Rage flared within. His taunts, the pain he caused my friends, this predicament I was in now—all stemmed from him. Sainte was bound to death the same as me. All because of Adastrus.

Ignoring Sainte's training, I lurched, throwing myself at him. He spun, but I grabbed his overcoat and yanked, pulling him off balance. With a grunt, he swung his sword, the hilt smashing into my face. I yelped, releasing my grip to create distance. My nose throbbed, trickling blood, and darkness edged my sight as I crouched, trying to locate him in the dim room.

My vision cleared, revealing Adastrus settled in a crouch a few paces away. He smirked as he stood, fingering the torn hole in his sleeve. I braced my left palm against the floor as he smiled and sheathed his weapon to remove his overcoat.

"Come, little sister. Playtime is over."

He charged. I leapt to my feet, trying to dance aside. His sword moved too fast, and the blade caught me under my ribs. I hissed, pain blooming and splintering. Still, I raised my dagger and spun to the side, throwing myself inside his guard. I limped as I went, my leg buckling beneath my weight, but I snared his arm and swung at his chest.

He evaded the blow with ease, jerking from my grasp. The motion sent me stumbling.

This wasn't a challenge, this was a mockery.

I panted, and clutched my stomach, frowning when my hand came away bright with blood. Each step brought an onslaught of agony, and though my breaths were shallow, the cut hadn't sliced deep enough to do permanent damage.

I pulled myself straight as he charged me once again, swinging his sword in a lazy arc, daring me to block it. I barely managed to lift my dagger in time to catch his blade, but the force sent a painful tremor through my arms, and my knees buckled beneath me.

He was unfairly strong.

My teeth ground together as my leg gave out, the sting in my side too great. Adastrus struck like lightning, his boot smashing into my face, crushing my nose.

I cried out, falling hard on my back, and my dagger skittered across the floorboards. Blood gathered in my throat, and I coughed, sputtering as I rolled onto my side. Pain radiated from every part of me. My vision blurred with unbidden tears, my breathing labored. Each movement brought a new wave of agony. The room's silence confirmed no one was coming to my rescue.

No one would save me.

His heavy boot pressed down on my chest, crushing the air from my lungs. I gasped, blood filling my throat, then gripped his ankle with desperate fingers. My nails dug into his flesh like talons. If I could've reached his leg, I would have bitten down in sheer desperation.

Adastrus leaned down, his face swimming in my blurry vision. His white teeth glinted in a smile as he whispered, "May your journey through the Veil be a miserable one."

He snapped up and my head slammed back against the wood. Panic froze me as he lifted his sword in a fluid movement, then swung it down–

"*Adastrus of Wynterborne!*" The clarion call rang out across the crowded room, joined by a stag's bugle that echoed through the room.

Any remaining breath fled my chest as he stilled, turning slowly to his left.

"Child of mine, the mists of madness beckon you."

Sainte walked toward the center—except it wasn't Sainte at all. The god might have borrowed my Valahant's body, but it was Nothar's eyes that stared our way. Those glowing green orbs held Adastrus in a trance as he dragged his foot off my chest, taking a stumbling step away.

"You're not a god," he whispered, horror in his tone.

The room rang with an unnatural, suffocating silence.

"Not your god, but you are my seed, and you will answer my call."

"I do not answer to you," Adastrus dared, raising his sword. "You have no right to my reign. You are but a trick of the light, a man with a spell… and I will remove it from you."

He lunged, quick as a whip, slashing at Sainte. I lifted my hand in warning, but the green eyes didn't look my way. His body moved with inhuman speed, leaving a verdant glow in his wake. He drew his long daggers, blocking the strike with ease.

"Heed my call, son of my blood."

Adastrus growled like a cornered animal and danced to the side, striking at Sainte's exposed flank. He parried with a slash to his chest, forcing him back.

"I answer to no god!"

Something happened as he uttered those words. A ripple of power, waves of raw energy, unseen and unheard, spread from him. His eyes flashed wildly, as if realizing he made a fatal mistake.

"You are a god unto yourself," Nothar said, his voice deep and rough like grinding stones. He turned, locking that eerie stare on me.

Adastrus seized the moment, attacking with renewed fury. Without looking, Sainte deflected his strike with ease.

"Heed me, daughter of my heart. Answer my call."

"I..." Blood choked my response, but I grasped onto that faint thread of hope. The gods finally decided to act. "I hear... and answer my father, Nothar." I coughed, rolling to my side, unable to sit upright.

"Only my seed may rule the land of Wynter."

A ghost of a smile rode Sainte's lips as he parried and blocked Adastrus' blows blindly.

Even from this distance, I saw the panic in my brother's stare. He denounced his relation to Nothar, calling his vessel a trick of light. He mocked the gods' power in front of hundreds. In a final, desperate move, Adastrus charged at me.

A jolt of terror surged through me before he let out a quiet gasp, his eyes widening in shock. He stumbled, catching himself on his sword as he doubled over. Sainte's blade protruded from his stomach. A green thread of unmistakable magic connected my Valahant's hand to the dagger. When he pulled, the weapon jerked free with a sickening, wet squelch.

With a seething glare of sick hatred, Adastrus crumpled, rolling onto his back with a wheeze.

Sainte stalked over, green eyes flaming. Each step grew in volume, sounding as if the very foundations of the earth were being shaken and shattered. Gritting my teeth, I looked up into his mask of fury, twisted by his own hatred and the disappointment of a god.

"The time has come to cull the weak from the herd," he rumbled in that eerie voice, then lowered himself to one knee.

His fingers brushed across my cheek. His touch was a chilly spring day with my face to the sun and my belly full—it felt like *home.*

"Child..." he said, *"heed my call, and I will heed yours."*

With unspoken understanding, his request settled deep within me. He urged me to ascend the throne, to wear the crown with resolve, and fulfill my duty as queen without hesitation or retreat.

"I... accept," I choked out, hot tears staining my cheeks.

"I have chosen," he declared, rising to his feet.

Dizziness twisted me as though I was falling, tumbling downward.

"I choose Sainte Nytestorm as my hand, and name Elspeth Wynterborne as my heir."

A resounding crack reverberated through the air, as if it split our very souls asunder.

In a blink, Sainte's eyes reverted to their cool blue hue. He shuddered as if shedding Nothar from his skin, then looked down at Adastrus. Features void of emotion, he flicked his wrist, spinning his dagger, then slashed down in a single decisive strike.

I yelped and rolled away from my brother's detached head, curling up on my side. Sharp pain drew a hiss, and I groaned, resting my temple against the cool, polished floor.

A warm touch pressed against my shoulder.

"Ellie."

Slowly, through clouded vision, I blinked up at Sainte crouched beside me.

"It's over," he said.

His face was the last thing I saw before I slipped into oblivion.

CHAPTER 32

After Sainte removed Adastrus' head from his body, a stunned silence fell before chaos erupted. Nothar used him as a vessel, but his actions in decapitating my brother appeared to be his own... or so it seemed.

We left the training chamber in a whirlwind of guards amid mixed cries of joy and rage. In Sainte's arms, each step he took jostled my body, wreaking havoc on my aching ribs. Every inhale was a struggle, shallow and rasped. My eyes would barely open, I assumed, because of severe swelling. Warm sticky blood streamed from my nose and a split in my lip, staining his tunic. Unable to do more than wince and hiss at each jab of pain, I focused on one breath at a time. I was alive.

Unlike my brother.

The high court called an emergency meeting, thankfully without me. Anderz advised that I stay in my quarters until summoned, a relief in my current state.

The door creaked open, and I squinted to see Sainte striding past four guards, his grip firm but careful as he carried me into my chambers.

"Fetch Master Healer Gilead," he bit out, his voice rough and cracking.

With a forceful kick, he shut the door behind him and stalked over to the table in my receiving room, laying me down. His face, usually so composed, now bore a deep frown, his brows knitted in frustration. He let out a heavy breath, reaching out to wipe away the blood that trickled down my cheek. I turned my head, attempting to avoid more of it sliding down my throat. I'd swallowed so much at this point that the coppery tang stained my mouth and churned my stomach.

"Did–"

"Shh." Sainte silenced me with a finger over my lips. "Save your words."

He offered me a sympathetic wince before he tore at the fabric of my bodice. Water pooled in my eyes, and I clamped them shut as a frigid coldness seeped into my bones, draining me, pulling me toward sleep. His sleeve brushed against my skin, wiping away blood to assess the wound along my ribs. I whimpered at the probing touch, longing for peace and quiet.

Time passed, marked by the creak of a chair as Sainte settled in.

At some point, Gilead entered, her voice a soothing murmur as she tended to my injuries. I bit down on a leather strap as she worked a needle through my flesh, stitching the gash shut. Once my wounds were clean and tended, Sainte moved me to the bed, his movements slow with care, as if I'd dissolve into dust in his arms. The tea Gilead gave me was bitter and foul. Its warmth barely touched the chill that ached through me.

And then there was nothing.

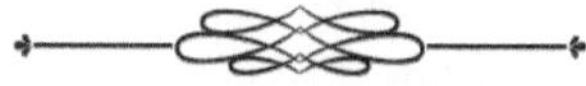

I glanced up from our card game as the door creaked open, admitting the handmaids and seamstress into my chambers at my call. Anderz entered alongside them, a familiar sight as of late. His updates, though cautious, kept me informed.

The past weeks were a whirlwind of events, yet progress seemed slow. Sainte faced a summons and endured a grueling interrogation by the entire court and their accompanying priests. They debated whether he had the authority to execute Adastrus. Nothar's clear influence over him complicated matters, rendering the law almost irrelevant in his case. He belonged to Nothar as much as I did.

Aside from the business with Sainte, the council convened with the priests, debating my right to rule. The Rite of Combat hung in the balance, its sanctity questioned in the wake of divine intervention. Counselor Dyre didn't hide his skepticism about the lack of support from Fiera's followers. Their vocal opposition to my claim cast a shadow over the proceedings. While others hesitated to challenge Nothar so openly, they stood firm in their stance. Sainte's bristling when Anderz discussed them spoke of something in his past, his lip curling in disdain at their mention.

Confined to my chambers, I awaited the high court's summons, forbidden from venturing outside until their call came. Though, seeing the trio of women, I had to assume that moment finally came.

"The God Stones have surfaced."

I snapped a card onto the table, startled by the revelation. Sainte pivoted in his seat, gaze locking on the newcomers as they rushed off to prepare my dressing room.

"The true God Stones?" I leaned forward, searching his features.

He responded with a pleased smile and slow nod. "Yes, my princess. They were concealed in Veiled Prince Adastrus' chambers," he said. "The high court requests a retrial of the Rite of Favor."

A knot formed in my stomach, a mixture of excitement and apprehension. The gods' decisions were never predictable. The last time I'd been in the presence of my people, I faltered. I failed them miserably, and the thought of disappointing them again drew a sour taste from my throat.

After a deep breath, steeling my nerves, I headed for my dressing room. Sainte trailed behind, and I took comfort in his silent presence. He was an anchor of reassurance amidst a storm. He offered his hand, helping me step onto the stool at the room's center. As the handmaids set about removing my sitting dress, I caught his reflection in the mirror. He kept his back to me, for modesty's sake, with a wary eye on the maids as they worked.

A bitter smile tugged at my lips as I took in the dark blotches marring my skin. Beneath my eyes, the fading bruises painted a sickly yellow-brown hue—a reminder of the recent violence I endured. My nose remained swollen and tender, a constant discomfort that woke me in the night whenever it brushed against my pillow. A thin, jagged line snaked from my side along the curve of my ribs down to my navel. The wound looked wicked, flat and warm to the touch, but Gilead's expert stitching kept it together.

I rotated my wrist, studying the healed ring of vines etched into my skin. Togamar's mark calmed from its angry red to a placid, healed pink. I suspected it would eventually scar to white, like any other wound.

I eased into the skirt the seamstress offered, lifting my gaze back to my reflection. Despite being battered and wounded, Sainte and I were still among the living, and there would be a price to pay for the breath that flowed through our lungs.

When I shoved my arms through the tight sleeves, Floria, the seamstress, called to Sainte. He turned, leaned against the wall, and let his eyes trail my figure, his stare taking in every inch, unhurried by the company.

The maids busied themselves with pulling the lacing snug at the back, pausing when I winced at the slight pain. The white dress shimmered with a sheen of bluish-green, like ice. Gems of matching hue cascaded down, clustering at the hem. It reminded me of the gown I'd worn during the previous Rite of Favor, with its bare shouldered, elegant design.

Sainte's gaze lingered on my exposed neck and I smiled as Anderz walked in with a hum of approval.

"You have outdone yourself, Floria." Anderz's laugh filled the room as he circled, observing the maids and the seamstress making their final adjustments.

"You are too kind, Counselor Dyre."

"I assume there will be a crowd?" I asked, easing off the stool to sit so they could start on my short hair.

"Yes, Your Highness. Just as before."

I sighed, bracing myself for the inevitable. I owed this to Nothar for his intervention. He was calling, and I would answer.

"This will relieve the high court's concerns?"

"Indeed. Though their approval isn't necessary if you are favored." He seated himself, surrounded by his usual calm essence. "If the godking speaking through his vessel wasn't confirmation enough, the Yail and Nain shall provide a clear response from the divine. Many will gather to bear witness—the more the better."

Sainte pushed off the wall and moved to his chest of clothes. He picked out items with deliberate care, oblivious to my gaze that lingered over his body.

"And if the gods give their favor?" I asked, smiling as he compared two daggers, setting the smaller one aside.

"You may choose the day of your coronation. No counselor can stand in your way."

That burden rested squarely on my shoulders.

I didn't know the first thing about leading a kingdom, but I had Anderz by my side. His motivations remained a mystery, but he proved himself worthy of my trust. Leihim's advice would guide economic decisions, albeit taken with a grain of salt. Sainte's wisdom would help with matters of gods and men. Then Counselor Aliea would assist with navigating the intricacies of state affairs. Nothar wanted me on the throne. With their backing, I would rule. Their support was essential.

Somehow, we survived this. Lyana and Ethyan were safe in Landing's End. I was alive and Sainte was well. It was more than I expected.

Sainte's eyes caught mine, and he raised a brow, likely questioning the expression painted across my face. I responded with a smirk and a soft shake of my head, earning a tsk from the maids as they finished pinning my hair in place.

"That's the best we can do, unfortunately," Floria said, wringing her hands.

I grinned, ignoring the tightness of my lips as the smile tugged at my scar, then dipped into a small bow. "You've worked a miracle."

Their eyes widened, and Floria flustered, returning the gesture before they hurried out the door. Anderz followed them out, his pace far more steady.

I eyed Sainte, trailing my gaze down his body as he looped his thumbs into his belt, waiting for me to leave and grant him his privacy. He dropped his chin, tilting his head with impatience. I snickered, then took my leave.

"With Nothar's blessing, we should plan your coronation with haste," Anderz said. "We must act quickly to prevent priests and counselors from casting doubt on your right to reign."

"If you think that's best."

I propped my hip against the table, hearing Sainte's sheath and daggers clatter to the floor. He changed with the door open, ready to intervene if anything dared happen to me. As if Anderz would lift a finger to harm me.

"The ambassadors remain, and most of the foreign royalty Adastrus invited are still here. We could hold the coronation within the week, unless you wish to invite anyone else?"

"King Reid of Gladier," I said. "If I don't extend an invitation, he'll stew in his bitter rage. If he's here, I can soothe his ruffled feathers."

Anderz studied me with his golden eyes, a smile spreading across his face as he placed a hand over his heart. "Look how far you've come, my petulant princess."

I scoffed, shaking my head as I waited for Sainte to finish.

After a few moments, Sainte stepped into the receiving room, buckling his belt. His black, fine-embroidered overcoat and trousers stood out against my white dress. A dagger hung at his right hip, a longsword at his left. His polished boots gleamed, and I smiled, knowing he spent the previous night shining them—a small, private secret of his that no one else knew.

I stepped closer, mindful of the stitches tugging at my side as I adjusted the chain around his neck. I pulled the center loop held by the wild cats' fangs to rest in the hollow of his collarbone. His eyes darkened, following my movements, his face a mask of calm.

With a small smile, I turned toward the door.

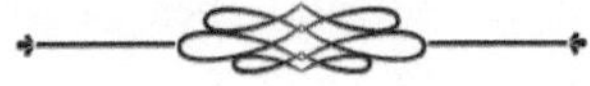

Once I saw the God Stones, I knew without a shadow of a doubt the previous set was nothing but simple rocks, a trick of witchcraft.

A weight of importance thickened the air, charged with tension and reverence absent the last time I was here. Perhaps the cause was my brother's death, combined with the weight of this moment. Yet when I saw those stones, I sensed it was far more profound. Just being in the same room with them was unnerving, as though the gods themselves scrutinized every soul present, probing our past actions and motives.

I schooled my face as I studied Yail. Placed atop a cushioned pillow, carried by a priest, its smooth white surface bore an icy frost. Despite the room's warmth, his fingers appeared pale and blue.

Nain, however, told a different story. I understood now why the Priest of Nothar asked to see my hands all those weeks ago. No bigger than my palm, it bristled with sharp spines, resembling creatures from the tide pools on the coast—except this was hard stone, not a soft fleshy beast.

Facing the crowd, I fixed my gaze on the far wall. Deep breaths steadied my nerves as the cloak settled on my shoulders and the stones found their sockets. I inhaled again, forcing my hands to remain steady as I crossed my arms and touched each stone.

Pain seared through my palms. Nain's spikes lanced into my skin, tearing with impossible ease. Despite my gentle pressure, it cut my flesh to ribbons. Yail's fierce cold burned beneath my hand, sending an ache through my fingers and up my arm.

With my chin raised high, my eyes closed, shutting out the crowd and the pain. I searched for the feeling of rightness, the sense of *home* I felt when Nothar touched me.

"I, Elspeth Wynterborne, Second Born of Veiled King Vardis, call on the Favor of Nothar. Heed my plea. Answer my call as I would answer yours."

My voice echoed through the chamber, resounding over the crowd that thrummed with tangible anticipation. Heart pounding, I paused for a breath, two breaths, waiting for something—anything. I opened my eyes and dared to peer over at Nain. It looked unchanged, save for the blood trickling down my wrist, over Togamar's mark, staining my dress.

A searing burn shot through my left palm. I gasped, whipping my head around. My hand, frozen solid to Yail, glowed with an eerie green light. Frost crept from the stone, crawling up my fingers, spreading across my skin in a fern-like pattern. I took shuddering breaths, struggling to maintain composure as the agony intensified.

Murmurs and whispers rippled through the crowded room as a pained whine escaped my throat. I couldn't stifle the sound or keep my hand from jerking free of the stone. Stumbling, I took shaking breaths and sought Sainte's reassurance. From his place crouched on the stairs, he dipped his head in a bow, and when he lifted his eyes, they were alight with joy.

With a breathless laugh, I straightened. The priests approached, removing the stones with care, then eased the cloak off my shoulders. The chill on my exposed skin paled in comparison to the deep ache throbbing through my left hand.

I raised my palms high for all to see.

"Wynterborne, your gods have spoken! I, Elspeth, am chosen of the godhead, marked by Togamar and Nothar!"

Cheers erupted, and my heart swelled with pleasure at the show of support, not only from the crowd, but nobles and ambassadors, as well. My grin hurt my cheeks as I scanned the throng, noting a few who didn't share in the excitement. This was just the beginning of my story.

As I lowered my hands, I turned to face Sainte, and gestured for him to join me. A slight smile curled the corner of his lips as he obliged. With purpose in his strides, he approached, his gaze never leaving mine, as if offering me one last chance to back out.

My grin grew, if that were possible, as I clasped his hand in mine. The crowd stirred, a wave of murmurs and hushed words spreading like a ripple through a pond. Cheers died out one by one as people craned their necks to witness the unfolding scene.

"Good folk of Wynterborne," I proclaimed, shoulders relaxing as Sainte's warm touch chased away the chill. "Our divine sovereign, the godking Nothar, has made his decree. He has chosen Sainte Nytestorm as his hand, and I, Elspeth, as his voice. Together, we shall guide your paths and steer our realm toward a bright future.

"Wynterians, I take this great moment in our history to announce my betrothal to Sainte Nytestorm, Nothar's appointed vessel. I present your future queen's consort!"

In one swift motion, I raised Sainte's hand alongside mine, lifting them high above, a gesture that triggered a blend of astonishment and delight among the onlookers, marked by stunned gasps and polite applause.

With a glance his way, I caught his composed blue gaze, a subtle gleam of satisfaction twinkling within, while my heart drummed a fierce, unwavering rhythm.

Yes... this was only the beginning of my story.

The End.

EPILOGUE

The morning's warmth kissed my cheeks, and a grin spread across my face as the cries of gulls echoed in the salty breeze. I rolled to my side, letting the sun bathe my bare back, and burrowed into sheets that still carried Sainte's earthy, familiar scent.

My husband.

The queen's consort.

The hand of Nothar.

My Valahant.

Mine.

My smile widened at the sound of children's joyous shrieks. I sat up, stretching leisurely, savoring this rare moment away from Wynterborne and its endless demands.

I threw off the blankets, swung my feet to the already warm floor, and stood. With my thin robe pulled over my body, I pushed my long black hair back and braided it loosely as I moved toward the balcony. A breeze lifted the curtains, carrying the ocean's scent and the chirps of great fish surfing the waves.

As I stepped into the daylight, joining the man who leaned against the sturdy wooden rail, his strong arm pulled me against his bare chest. I nestled close, tucking my head into the crook of his neck, watching Ethyan chase two small children down the beach.

I snickered when he tripped, face-planting into the sand before rolling onto his back with a loud wail. The boy, in well-made, play-torn clothes, and the girl, in a worn, battered dress, immediately turned, sprinting toward Ethyan's prone form.

They pounced, and he shouted as they landed, tickling them until their laughter echoed along the breeze. The girl bit his arm, and he yelped, shoving her off. Seizing the opportunity, the boy kicked at his unprotected nether regions.

"Kalen!" Sainte's voice thundered across the beach, silencing the gulls.

The boy's head snapped up, hand to his brow, shading his peridot eyes as he knelt in the sun-warmed sand.

I bumped my shoulder against him. "Serves him right," I muttered.

"There are unspoken rules to any fight."

"A code of honor?" I teased, trailing my fingers against his skin, pulling him to face me. With a raised brow, I tugged at his trousers, a playful smirk turning my lip. "No fighting dirty?"

"He has too much of his mother in him."

I batted my lashes, feigning innocence. "There's as much of me in him as you."

I laughed, glancing back at the children. Sainte's lips brushed my ear as Kalen flashed an innocent smile. Spared from a lecture, he offered his hand to the little girl sprawled on the ground. She giggled as he helped her to her feet. Her bright grin turned toward me, her blonde wind-swept curls a halo around her head.

"Auntie El is up!" she shrieked. "Kalen! Your mom is awake!"

Her green eyes, those of mine and my brother's, glimmered with pure joy.

She took off with the boy close on her heels, kicking up sand with every stride. Ethyan propped himself on his elbows, peering our way with a grateful smirk.

Lyana sat near the turquoise waves, the shade of palms shielding her from the morning's heat. She watched the children run, then looked our way with a small wave. I flashed her a bright grin in answer.

Yes, this marked the start of many new stories.

MORE COOL THINGS!

Scan the QR code for more details concerning merch, signed copies and even a top-secret, super-secret, not-so-secret club with bonus content!

The Codeword is: Pandemonium

M.A. FRICK

M.A. Frick is a mere peasant.

Once upon a time, she read to escape the world. Now she writes to create worlds.

Not only the mother of worlds, but the mother of three children—she is joined by her husband who supports every adventure, no matter how absurd it may be.

The Codeword is: Pandemonium

THANK-YOU!

"So you see, you can't do everything alone." – Rosemary Clooney

The Petulant Princess started out as all my stories do—a blank document and a decision to wing it. However, as "pantsers" often do, I would have quit if not for Jessie. Always my first alpha and my biggest cheerleader. Thank you.

As with the Fate Unraveled Trilogy, this would still be a manuscript if not for my husband who pushed me toward publishing. Thank you for always pushing me toward bigger things.

Special thanks to my editor, Erynn, who always goes above and beyond when editing and puts up with my constant "I don't know, let me figure it out." since, lets be honest—I AM making it up as I go! A huge thanks to Sirley who took on the proofreading! You're amazing!

Lastly, a huge thanks to *you*, my readers for actually taking the time to read my work! I would be nothing without you!